Jim and the Flims

Jim and the Flims
A Novel

Rudy Rucker

Night Shade Books
San Francisco

First Edition

ISBN: 978-1-59780-280-2

Night Shade Books
Please visit us on the web at
http://www.nightshadebooks.com

Contents

1: Four Mile Beach 1

2: A Sharper Tip 6

3: Val 14

4: The Portal 23

5: Brain Event 31

6: Weena Wesson 37

7: Yuel 46

8: The Boardwalk 54

9: The Whipped Vic Crew 61

10: Surf Party 69

11: The Jivas 77

12: The Tunnel 86

13: Meet the Flims 98

14: The Garden 109

15: Cruiser Couch 117

16: Under the Pit 127

17: Deeper 135

18: The Dark Gulf 145

19: Offer Cap 154

20: The Castle 164

21: Weena's Tale 172

22: Atum's Lotus 179

23: Lights Out 189

24: Yuelsville 197

25: Down to Earth 208

26: Missing Me 217

27: Pied Piper 227

28: The Goddess 235

29: On the Bluff 245

For Marc Laidlaw

1 : Four Mile Beach

'm Jim Oster. I grew up in Sunnyvale, a knot of freeways near San Jose, California. My father was an electrical engineer, and my mother sold online ads. Dad was what you might call piebald, with different colors in his hair. He stared off into the distance a lot, always thinking about his projects. Mom had warm eyes, and she'd smile and nod when she happened to look my way. But she spent most of her time staring down at her little phone's screen.

During my senior year in high school, I used to play hooky and go surfing in Santa Cruz—it was only a half hour's drive away. In the morning, I'd stuff my wetsuit into my backpack—instead of carrying books.

My parents didn't notice, and if they had they wouldn't have cared. They'd had their one child, me, and by now they'd turned to other concerns: their jobs and their investments. My grades weren't a big issue, as I'd already been accepted for admission at the University of California.

My favorite surf break was off a rocky point at Four Mile Beach, on Route 1 north of Cruz. My friend Chang would drive us over there. Chang wasn't into studying at all, he was planning to be a pro surfer, and he figured his day job could be dealing pot. He had a vintage blue Haut board with an epic feel. I was more of a short-boarder, working snappy moves up and down the tubes—when I wasn't wiped out and floundering in the foam.

Some the locals at Four Mile had taken to hassling us. A spaced-out raw-boned guy called Skeeves was on my case in particular. He was a little older than the rest of us. All he did was surf, and he lived in his van.

One particular afternoon, I did a drop-in on one of Skeeves's waves, forcing him away from the curl. When we got back to shore, he put his face really close to mine and started yelling curses at me, even throwing in some gibberish-type incantations that he'd learned. Skeeves had this idea that he was hooked into the magic of the pyramids—or some shit like that.

"Shit-beetle!" yelled Skeeves. "*Ankh salaam Amenhotep.*"

"Calm down," I told him. "It's just a wave."

"*Ruh nuh port mu hurra,*" Skeeves intoned, making weird gestures with his hands.

"Dude's having a fit," said Chang, standing at a safe distance. "His brain is slushed."

"It's a magic spell, fool," said Skeeves. "The chant is called 'leaving in the daytime.' I might send you two out of your bodies." He crouched and picked up a dense, sharp rock.

"Let's take a break, Chang," I said, briskly heading down the beach. "We'll get some beer," I called back to Skeeves. "You can have all my waves while I'm gone."

Skeeves's van was parked in the lot near Chang's pickup. Skeeves lived in this van, mostly, and he had tinted glass in the rear windows. He'd painted occult symbols all over the vehicle—ankh crosses with loops on top, scarab beetles, hovering eyes, hieroglyphs, and a long pair of wings flowing back from the front wheel wells. Peering in through the van's dusky rear window, we could make out a long gold box in the back of the van.

"Skeeves got into the Egyptian stuff when he started dealing dope to Julian Crocker in San Francisco," said Chang. "But, wow. Is that a casket?"

"Who's Crocker?"

"He's a screwball descendant of this rich old family. He lives in a mansion with all these wack antiquities. Skeeves is up there all the time. Last week he was putting together a deal to sell Crocker a bunch of ketamine."

I brooded about Skeeves on the short drive to the Quick Mart in

Davenport. And when we got back to the Four Mile Beach parking lot, I took a knife out Chang's glove compartment and slashed one of the front tires on Skeeves's van.

Chang and I carried the beer down to the beach and had a mellow hour or two on the waves. I even forgot about slashing Skeeves's tire—until we all went back up to the lot together.

Skeeves got all excited. Chang was laughing so hard that the weird old surfer quickly figured out it was me who'd done the deed. Skeeves said he was going to kill me—he fetched an axe with a green-painted handle from the van. I was scared. It was hard to tell what Skeeves might do. And it looked as if the axe blade already had blood on it.

Chang and I ran, leading Skeeves in a big circle. We got back to Chang's pickup first, then hopped in and drove away.

It was maybe the next day when we saw in the paper that Julian Crocker had been found dead in his home. The cops thought it might be a drug overdose. Crocker was found lying beside a fireplace filled with ashes. Apparently he'd suffocated from some smoke. And an ancient gold sarcophagus was said to be missing from the Crocker manse. But there were no actual signs of robbery. In any case, Crocker's surviving relatives weren't interested in trying to make a case. And the cops quickly lost interest.

Quite a few of the surf crowd must have suspected that Skeeves was involved—especially with that funky gold casket right in his van. A rumor was circulating among us that Skeeves was now fucking a mummy that he'd found in the gold box. Not that any of us was going public with this stuff.

Chang and I had switched to surfing Pleasure Point down near 41st Street in Cruz. There were some psychos there, too, and a few of them made a point of picking on us—especially when they found out that we were valley guys from near San Jose. Chang toughed it out and got in with the brahs—his steady supply of weed was a help. But I couldn't get past the hostility.

And then I was, like, fuck it—and I went back to skateboarding. I'd never been that good of a surfer anyway.

After high school I went to college at the Santa Cruz campus of the University of California. I decided to go for a bachelor's degree in bioengineering. Everyone said biotech was the coming thing, and the courses appealed to me. I'd always liked videogames, and I dug the idea of viewing the natural world as being a big program that we could mod and hack.

Of course there were people—especially around Cruz—who worried that biotech was going to bring on some filthy germs who'd kill us all. My professors said that wasn't a real problem because, if you looked into it a little, you could see that our whole entire ecology is made of plants, animals, and microorganisms who want to eat everything. All the species had been mutating and evolving for billions of years, each and every one of them striving for world domination. And no piddly-ass organism we were going to cook up in a lab had any chance of taking down the ancient, battle-scarred pros. To hear my profs tell it, home-brewed germs were like high-school grommets facing the gnarly surfers of Four Mile Beach.

Well, maybe they were right, and maybe not. Either way, I figured it would be good to have a rebellious, clear-minded guy like me on the inside of the biotech biz. I'd be ready to blow the whistle on the Earth-rapers, if it ever came down to that. Meanwhile I was hoping to discover some cool things, and to make a good living as well.

My old friend Chang was living down in Cruz by now, too, surfing his ass off. He won a few local contests, and during my junior year at UC Santa Cruz, he got invited to the annual Mavericks big wave contest a few miles up the coast. I went to watch him, that is, to watch the faint line on the horizon where the big waves were. On the TV monitors, we could see Chang carving sick curves into the wobbly mountains of glass. He placed in the top five and he picked up some sponsorship deals.

Chang came by my rented room a month after Mavericks and lent me a board so we could go riding at Four Mile like old times. Sure enough, our man Skeeves was still on the waves, indefatigable as a Terminator robot, still living in his Egyptian-themed van.

By now Chang was in some sense a friend of Skeeves, that is to say, Skeeves's over-tweaked synapses could successfully achieve a pattern-recognition of Chang's face. He walked over to us and Chang broke out a joint. Skeeves seemed to recognize me, but, so far as I could tell, he'd forgotten about the slashed tire.

I figured the joint was like a peace pipe. But after a few tokes, Chang, never one to let things stay calm, started ribbing the eccentric old surfer. "Getting much?" Chang asked him. "Still fucking the mummy?"

Even when Skeeves had his shades off, you couldn't really see his eyes, buried as they were in the creases of his weathered lids. He turned his head towards Chang, moving as slowly as a plant tracking the sun.

"Just the girl," allowed Skeeves in a low murmur, his tongue loosened by the pot. "Not the guy who's in the box with her. Julian Crocker and I smoked the third mummy, you know. Amenhotep. He was down under the other two, all crumbly like rotten wood. We burned Amenhotep in Crocker's marble fireplace, the two of us leaning into the fumes, very resinous, very tasty. What a rush. But then Crocker died, the fuckin' lightweight."

"Mummies?" I said numbly, feeling the layers of reality come peeling off.

"That mummy girl—she's softer than you'd think," came Skeeves's raspy whisper. "Good stuff. It's more like she's in a coma. Every now and then, in my head, she talks to me."

"Can we see them?" asked Chang. "They're in that gold sarcophagus in the back of your van, right? You're legendary, dude."

"I—I don't think Jim here could handle it," said Skeeves thoughtfully. "The spirit of Amenhotep destroys the weak."

"Did you say that you *smoked* Amenhotep's mummy?" I had to ask. "You and Crocker?"

Skeeves squinted at me for a long time.

"Remember the axe, Jim," he said, finally, and laid his bony finger over his lips.

I knew then that Skeeves hadn't forgotten about the slashed tire at all.

But, now that he'd shared his secret with me—or run me through a bizarre put-on—we were closer than before. From then on, when I crossed Skeeves's path around Cruz, I'd wave, and he'd favor me with a slow nod. Not that I spent that much time thinking about him or about the gunjy coma-chick who was supposed to be in his Egyptian sarcophagus.

2: A Sharper Tip

Though I didn't really like to admit it, I was in fact studying pretty hard at college. I sometimes dreamed of finding a new way to think about bioengineering. I imagined discovering some easy way to visualize how the low-level DNA base-pairs lead to the high-level morphogenesis that shapes animal embryos and plant sprouts. And then we'd no longer be groping in the dark, twiddling switches with no sense of what controlled what.

I didn't have much of a social life, or many relationships with women. I wasn't attracted to the grade-grubbing engineer women I worked with. And the alluring liberal-arts types always wanted to have that discussion about whether biotech was evil. When I wanted a break, I'd ride my skateboard downtown and thrash at the punk clubs.

Both my parents died the winter before I graduated. That was a really rough time. Dad had a stroke, and Mom, usually so quick and warm, sank into a depression that segued into brain cancer. It was hard to believe. I hadn't been all that close to my parents, but all those years I'd known they were there, in some sense standing between me and the Reaper. And now they were gone.

Only a few people showed up at my parents' funerals. Fellow workers: engineers and sales reps. No relatives. It sucked. My parents had never really connected with the larger world; they'd been eaten by their jobs. I promised myself I'd find a warm, loving woman and that we'd build a jolly close-knit family.

As it turned out, my parents didn't leave me any kind of inheritance at all. They'd fallen for some Houston company's wealth-management scam that involved getting a second mortgage and putting all of their cash into leveraged insurance-market securities which had totally tanked. I'd always thought Mom and Dad were smarter than that. The bank foreclosed on our house, and even the cars got sold.

Fortunately I had a student loan to cover my costs. I plugged along at school. In a way, that was easier than having a breakdown and dropping out. And, as a practical matter, I needed to finish up my senior project and get a job.

In the spring I got my Bachelor's degree in bioengineering and I started hitting the interviews. I didn't really want to stay in academia, even if I could have afforded it. My impression was that the real biotech scene wasn't at the universities—the big scores were at the industrial labs. Why be sitting out the action and getting a Master's degree or a doctorate?

I landed what seemed like a good job at a biotech startup called Wiggler Labs, right there in Santa Cruz.

Wiggler was about bioenergy. Some other companies had been designing new versions of our shit-eating friend, the *Escherichia coli* bacterium that populates our guts. The new, tweaked *E. coli* strains were brewing long-chain forms of alcohol that were just about as good as gasoline. But our bioenergy rivals still had to distill the alcohol from the germ slime, and burn the alcohol to get the energy—creating fresh pollution along the way.

My new employer's plan was to go straight from shit to electricity. That is, Wiggler Labs was designing germs that would eat whatever gross, random crud you fed them and they'd pump out power in return. The trick was to enhance our bacteria with some genes from a particular kind of electric eel, the *Electrophorus electricus*—a forty-pound, gray, slimy dude native to the stagnant backwaters of the Amazon River Basin. These eels can put out seven hundred volts a pop.

Wiggler had a giant tank with about a half dozen of the big electric eels in the lab's reception area, along with the shrimps and frogs that the eels liked to shock and eat. Not that we really needed to keep that many electric eels around, but the display impressed the investors who were coming by all the time. It was a professional-quality tank, with a muddy river bank along one side, and a mangrove tree with orchids and ferns.

We had pans full of eel-flesh tissue-cultures on the lab's work benches. Things were moving right along. We learned how to tweak the eel DNA, and how to splice eel genes into *E. coli* to make electric germs. And before long we had a couple of electric germ culture vats running—smelly tubs with tiny blue sparks crackling along their swampy surfaces. Brass collector knobs along the vats' edges drained off the energy and stored it in batteries.

But Wiggler wasn't anywhere near a commercial level of through-put. In those early months, if you'd you wanted to power your TV with a Wiggler vat, your bill might have run to fifty thousand dollars a month—what with all the tech support.

Week after week we tinkered with getting the genes right. We had to baby the eel-tissue cultures, and the electric germs were especially fragile. Our creations kept falling prey to wild molds and viruses that drifted in, looking for unsophisticated victims to trash. I was beginning to understand why the profs had been so skeptical about a biotech plague. Nature is a bitch—heartless, wily, and street wise.

But never mind the difficulties—Wiggler Labs had achieved a proof of concept. The venture capital came pouring in, and management was talking about having an IPO stock offering in about a year.

I was working insane hours and learning all kinds of stuff. But after nine months at the job, I started getting bored. As a low-level employee, I spent most of my time tending the eel-tissue cultures, or mapping genes with our scanning-tunneling microscope, or just mopping slop off the floors. Sometimes I felt like I worked at a slaughterhouse or at a sewage plant.

After the tenth or fifteenth time that our electric germs all died off, I began seriously doubting if our power vats would ever reach the market. I was getting a sense that the managers' plan was to pump up the stock price, and to dump their shares after the IPO. Sometimes I'd speculate about this with the other engineers, which created bad blood when the managers overheard me.

By way of running my mouth, I also enjoyed getting my co-workers to discuss the ethics of bioscience. To get a good argument going, I liked to play Devil's advocate, and to advocate various extreme scenarios. One day, in an antic mood, I started telling the guys in the lunch room that we should let the state of Texas secede. My concept was that, with Texas a foreign country, we'd be free to bomb the whole state with electric germs. And then we'd set up power collection plants around the state's barbed-wire borders and have endless free power flowing out!

I hadn't registered the fact that Wiggler's chief financial officer happened to be sitting at the table right behind me. He was—a Texan.

He led me into his office, showed me a photo of his family, and talked about collegiality, team spirit and public image. And the next day Human Resources gave me my thirty days' notice.

This left me just enough time to attend the company picnic.

Like a complete pinhead, I stole a couple of pans of mutant eel-flesh from the lab, doused them in tamari sauce, scattered on sesame seeds, and roasted them in the kitchen of the little cottage I'd rented in Santa Cruz. I sliced up the roasted electric eel meat, and laid it out on a big black lacquer tray like a fancy appetizer—to bring to the picnic. Chang happened to be at my house, delivering some pot, so I brought him to the company picnic too.

People were actually eating the gene-tweaked eel flesh, going, like, "Hmm, this is tasty." By the time the meat was about half gone I was drunk and stoned enough to announce what it was.

"We eat what we grow!" I whooped, and let out what I considered to be a Texas-style yodel.

Some of the engineers thought I was funny—but the execs and the staff were majorly pissed. Not that eating the tweaked eel would actually be bad for you. Your stomach acids break down all the DNA you eat—it doesn't go and crawl into your cell nuclei. But, still...

Nobody went public with the story of my misdeed, but word got around. From then on, I was pretty much blackballed from the biotech biz. I'd phone up for an interview, and I'd hear the receptionist fighting back a laugh.

I got a pretty good severance package from Wiggler. For awhile I had some hopes of striking out on my own—I still had my vague notion of finding a better mental model language for the process of genetic engineering. And if my theorizing didn't lead anywhere, maybe I could get into designing lab equipment. One of the few things I'd inherited from my Dad was a workshop's worth of tools.

The house I'd rented in Cruz was a granny cottage in the back yard of a biggish stucco home on Madrone Street. My house faced the alley. My landlords were a Dick and Diane Simly. Dick owned a high-end car dealership called Simly The Best. The lot was switching over to hybrids and electrics, so Dick and Diane drove a pair of gas-guzzler Jaguars that Dick hadn't been able to sell. Somehow Dick had made a profit by keeping these two cars—the guy always came out ahead.

Generally speaking, Dick and Diane left me alone. And when I adopted a puppy from the pound to keep me company, they didn't squawk. My dog's name was Droog—he was a collie-beagle mix. He liked to follow me around the house, watching everything I did. It was almost like I had an assistant.

Working on the screened-in side porch of my cottage, I built a scanning-tunneling microscope of my own—you call it an STM for short. I found the design on the web, and the parts only cost me about a thousand dollars. Why did I build an STM? Well, I still had some dreams of making a genomics breakthrough on my own—or of managing to patent a new wrinkle on the lab hardware.

Basically an STM works by bringing a tiny sharp tip close to a sample that's resting on a little sample sled. You run voltage into the tip and the sample, and you track the virtual current that seems to flow across the gap. A computer munges the data and turns it into a display that resembles a bumpy surface—with the bumps being individual atoms. Even better, you can use your scanning tip to manipulate the individual atoms.

Obviously it's important to have a very narrow scanning tip in your STM. For my home-built machine, I was using slivers of tungsten needles whose tips were only one or two atoms thick, just like we'd been doing at Wiggler Labs. I began wondering if there might be a way to find some better kind of scanning tip. If I could come up with that, maybe I'd have a way of getting better STM images, and that could lead to something marketable.

One afternoon, gnarly, funky Skeeves happened to come walking down the alley by my house. He didn't seem to be looking for me; I think he was just wandering around. I was feeling bored and lonely, so I called out to him, gave him a beer, and showed him some of the pictures I'd been making with the STM.

"This is a hair," I told Skeeves, flipping through the images on my computer. "This is a grain of pollen. And here's an ant's mandibles."

"Ant," said Skeeves, studying my computer screen. He reminded me of a dog trying to read. "Ants have hair? Can you see an atom?"

"Yeah, yeah. When I worked at the biotech lab, we were getting pictures of DNA. But those are pretty fuzzy."

"Which part makes it sharp?" asked Skeeves, running his long, shaky fingers over my scanning-tunneling microscope's boxes and wires.

"The scanning tip," I said, pointing out how it slid back and forth above the samples. I went on to tell Skeeves about my quest for the sharpest needle ever. Not that he seemed to be listening to me. As if paralyzed by boredom, he lolled back in his chair, staring up at the corner of the ceiling like someone else's voice was coming from up there. Soon thereafter, he'd finished his beer and left.

A week later, Chang showed up at my house.

"I've got something for you," he said, taking out a little matchbox.

"Dope?"

"Sure," said Chang. "But what's in this box is a weird little prong of exotic matter that Ira stole from the lab. A tip for your whatchamacallit. Your microscope thing."

"Ira?"

"You know him," said Chang. "Little guy? Gnarly surf punk? Gay? Has a crush on Skeeves? He works nights as a janitor in the UC Santa Cruz labs."

Chang handed me the box and I looked inside. The new tip was the shape of a toothpick, and at the sharp end, it cusped out into a point that was impossible to see.

"Ira gave you this for my STM?"

"Sold it to me," said Chang. "For a bag of pot. Which you'll have to pay for. Skeeves told Ira you needed a sharper tip. I guess he heard that from you?"

"Uh, yeah, I saw Skeeves not too long ago. But it didn't seem like he even understood what I was saying."

Chang laughed. "The way Skeeves works is that he remembers what he sees and hears and then he talks it over with the woman's voice he hears in his head. He's still living in his van with that casket with the mummies, you understand. And he talks to the spirit of the woman mummy that he fucks. He's let me see the sarcophagus up close—though he won't let me look inside. The box is all gold and covered with those wiggly Egyptian diagrams. Thousands of years old, according to our man."

"Why isn't Skeeves in jail? Or in the nut house?"

"He has this knack for falling between the cracks," said Chang, shaking his head. "Beneath notice. Beyond belief."

"And you're saying that Skeeves told Ira to find me a better tip for my STM?"

"What it is, brah. Skeeves's mummy woman's soul hipped him to your trip."

Again I had that feeling of reality being a laminate of layers—and that some of the layers were flaking off.

"Okay," I said. "I'll pay for Ira's pot."

I asked around a little, and found out that Ira's tip was a stiff whisker of metallic hydrogen. One of the UC physics profs had had found a way to keep the stuff stable at room temperature. And Ira had stolen a random scrap that just happened to have the shape I needed.

The tip's narrow end was, I initially thought, a single row of protons. But now, thinking back on where that tip led me, I'd say that it must have incorporated a unique quantum anomaly. I think it must have contained an infinitely thin cusp of warped space. Going a little further out on the edge, I'd go so far as to speculate that the soul of Skeeves's mummy woman had done some special tweaks on that tip.

But, to start with, all I knew was that Ira's scrap of metallic hydrogen was very sharp. And, so far as I could find out, the physics prof wasn't thinking at all about scanning-tunneling microscope tips. So for a couple of weeks I was hoping I might have lucked into a new and patentable technological process.

But, to my disappointment, my metallic hydrogen tip didn't work any better than the carbon nanotubes that the big labs were using. Although my new scans were cleaner than they'd been with the tungsten tip, they weren't any sharper than the carbon nanotube pictures that I could find online. And in any case, it didn't seem like a realistic business model to base a product on metallic hydrogen tips that a janitor friend of a friend was stealing from a lab.

So, okay, my STM was really just a hobby, a science toy. I wasn't going to find any patentable new process here. And I wasn't really going to be using my STM for any independent biotech research.

Truth be told, I'd come to think of bioengineering as slow, boring and, yes, potentially evil.

By now my severance pay had run out and I needed a job. Lacking any better ideas, I got a job as mailman working out of the Santa Cruz post office. In a way, I'd always wanted to be a mailman. It's a clear-cut social good. Nobody ever comes up and tells you that delivering mail is evil. And I liked going out to walk the streets every day. By now, my dog Droog was well-behaved enough that I could leave him home alone.

3: Val

I started noticing a certain woman my age on my mail route. She shared a house with a couple of other people, and most afternoons she'd be out in front reading, or tending to her cactus plants.

"Nice shorts," she said to me one day, commenting on my postal uniform. "And, hi, I'm Val."

"I'm Jim. I like your cactuses."

"Succulents. I've been collecting samples from other people's yards. I break off a couple of leaves, or a sprout, and I stick them into the dirt. They like to grow." Val smiled at me. She had nice eyes, green with flecks of brown. And shiny brown hair. "How did you end up being a mailman?"

"I got a degree in bioengineering at the UC," I said, setting down my mail bag. "And I had a job in a lab, but it didn't pan out. Not everyone gets my sense of humor. And recently I was doing a little research on my own. But now I'm delivering mail."

"You tweaked genes?" said Val. "Isn't that bad?"

"It might be," I said. "If we ever got good at it. At this point, it's like we're trying to program a computer by hitting it with a hammer. When I started, I thought I'd be helping people to decorate themselves with tentacles instead of tattoos. Or that I'd grow myself an extra dick."

"There's something wrong with your first one?" said Val pertly.

"Lately I haven't checked," I said, studying her. "I live alone with my dog."

Val was vivacious and cute, with a playful curve to her lips.

"What?" she said as I continued gazing at her.

I gathered my courage. "Would you want to go out tomorrow night? We could get some food and see a punk show."

"Not a regular punk show," said Val. "Zonked sweaty boys elbowing me. Maybe the women's roller derby? That's punk, too, a little bit. I know some of the women who skate."

"That'd be perfect," I said. "Just so I'm with you."

"Deliver the *mail*!" said Val, acknowledging the compliment.

"How come you're always at home?" I asked, wanting to keep the conversation going. "Are you a grad student?"

"I'm a kindergarten teacher," said Val, drawing herself up and giving me a stern stare.

"I'll sit on my mat. I'll eat my slice of apple."

"That's good, Jim." She went back to being a pretty girl in her yard. "I have a short work-day. It's nice."

We started seeing each other a lot. Val didn't seem like a teacher at all—she liked to dance, she joked about sex, and sometimes she'd smoke pot with me. Not that we partied all that much. I'd cleaned up somewhat after my Wiggler flame-out.

I loved talking with this woman. Even more than the things she said, I liked the music of her voice. Our conversations were like opera duets, where the rich, vibrant tones matter as much as the specific words. Val was naturally good-humored, always ready for fun. And my dog loved her.

Our romance took its course. Val moved in with me, and we got married.

Finally my life was on the right track. Val and I were, like, California-style salt of the earth: a kindergarten teacher who grew cactuses, and a mailman who dabbled in high-tech research. I liked how low-stress it was being a mailman.

Val and I spent a lot of time just hanging around our little pink cottage, being comfortable. Other times we'd go on road trips, camping near the sea, bringing Droog on the trips. We even started to talk about having a baby.

I became more and more removed from biotech. If I could enjoy life being happy with Val, that was enough. Even so, I was still playing with my scanning-tunneling microscope a little bit. It was cool to be able to see stuff all the way down at the atomic level.

"I have something to show you," I told Val one night after supper. "My favorite molecule."

It was February, with a fairly powerful rainstorm outside. Droog was asleep on his cushion by the heating vent. I'd worn a slicker and boots to deliver the mail that day, and had gotten wet just the same. Dear Val had greeted me with a nice pot of lentil soup.

"Where does your molecule live?" asked Val, her face warm in the candlelight. We liked having little romantic dinners, complete with candles and wine.

"The molecule's a she," I said. "I call her V. She's on the porch."

"Inside your junk pile?"

"That's it. Come on."

My STM was a small mound of random-looking tech equipment. I had a computer with a big-screen display, a binocular optical microscope for bringing the STM's tip close to the sample sled, a set of piezoceramic widgets for moving the tip, and an electrical transformer that smelled of ozone.

The rain was picking up, with water flowing down the window panes in wavy sheets. The dark palms were whipping back and forth, and thunder boomed across the sea.

"Lightning!" said Val, glancing out the window, her eyes soft and dark. "It's like you're the mad scientist in his laboratory."

"Just where I've always wanted to be," I said. "With a beautiful wife to care for me. I'm glad our roof doesn't leak."

"We wouldn't want your pet molecule, V, to get wet." She giggled and perched herself on the beat-up old armchair we kept out here.

I cranked up the scanning-tunneling microscope, and the transformer made just the kind of rising whine that you'd expect from a science-fiction lab. I checked the positioning of the sample, then threw the switch that engaged the piezoceramic manipulators. They made a nice clicking sound. I set them to sweeping Ira's metallic hydrogen tip back and forth across the sample surface. An image began developing on my computer screen, an archipelago of dots.

"What is this molecule?" asked Val.

"It's you! I took skin flakes from your hairbrush, extracted some DNA, and fixed one of the strands to a graphite plate. See how shapely you are?"

We could see a blurry double helix, coiled around like a kelp stalk on the beach.

"Oh, don't tell me you want to tweak my genes!" protested Val. "Ugh."

"Just admiring them for now," I said. "We'll use the old-school method for any tweaks."

"Tonight might be a good time to try," she said softly.

I went over to her and gave her a kiss. And then we were in bed, making love. It definitely added some spice to know we were doing it for real. Unprotected. Hoping to make a baby. I felt an odd tingle in my spine.

Just as we came, lightning struck a power pole across the street. It was a strange moment—for an instant I couldn't tell if the lightning was out in the world or inside my body. The lights in our house went out, and the scanning-tunneling microscope on the porch made a popping noise that was lost in the astonishing clap of thunder.

For a second or two, Val and I lay there stunned and half-deaf. Droog was whining in the kitchen. A siren sounded in the distance. In the velvety darkness, I seemed to see a glowing yellowish dot come zigzagging into our room. A tiny shape seemed to wriggle at the center of the dot.

Val cried out. The orb homed in on us and disappeared in the tangle of our bedding.

"Did something just now crawl inside me?" exclaimed Val, her voice rising. She sat up, throwing back the sheets. "I swear I felt a tingle down there—what's going on, Jim! Help!"

I fumbled for the matches on the nightstand and got a candle going. My hands were shaking.

Beautiful naked Val was next to me, her eyes big and wet. Seeing her made everything seem safe.

"It's okay," I told her, putting my arms around her.

"But I saw something flying towards us," insisted Val. "Like a bug."

"A lightning bug," I said, trying to joke. "It was just an afterimage. From the flash. Nothing crawled inside you. No way." I gave her belly a gentle pat. "Nothing in there but you and me."

Val peered down at herself and let out a shuddery sigh. She managed a little smile. "What a story for the baby. If this was the time."

A fire truck rumbled into our street with its radio going. The rain was still pouring down. We could see a charred utility pole and some sparking wires. We put on our robes, got some cookies from the kitchen, and stood by the window watching, with Droog at our feet. The firemen put up barriers around the live wires and left.

Before returning to bed, I looked in on my scanning-tunneling microscope—it had blown a heavy spark, charring the sample on its little sled. The metallic hydrogen tip had shattered into a little stub. I turned off all the power switches and set the sample sled on a corner of my desk.

The next day I figured out that the power surge had shorted out something in the STM—but I didn't get around to fixing it. The sample sled stayed there on my desk where I'd put it.

Winter turned to spring. Green sorrel sprouted all over the back yard. And one day Val had some news for me when I came home from work. As soon as I walked in, I could see it on her happy face.

"You saw the doctor?" I asked.

"We're expecting!" she sang. "It's gonna happen. Oh, wow, Jim, do we have to start being grown-ups?"

"Never," I said. "We'll be the cool kind of parents."

"How will we know what to do?"

"You've got a head start," I said. "From teaching kindergarten."

"I hope I'm not one of those mothers who's always *reasoning* with her baby," said Val. "Loudly so everyone around can hear. Because, because, if and then."

"The baby," I said, trying out the word.

"Baby, baby, baby," echoed Val. "That's such a funny word. It sounds chubby and cute."

"Mama Val. I like it."

It was a hard pregnancy. Val was hungry all the time, but she threw up a lot, too. She'd fill a plate with food, then stare at it in disgust. And she was having nightmares—but she didn't want to tell me what they were about.

One day in August I came home from work to find Val on the couch, sobbing into her hands. Droog was sitting on the rug, anxiously watching her.

"Oh, Val. What is it, dear?"

"That glowing dot, Jim—that's what's inside me."

"What do you mean?" I said, the hair rising on the back of my neck. I sat down next to her and put my arms around her. "Don't make yourself crazy, Val. Relax. It's just the pregnancy wearing you down."

"It's not a pregnancy!" she cried, pushing me away. Her voice was loud and harsh, and her face was blotchy from weeping. "That little spark flew inside me, Jim! From your horrible machine. It's not a baby, it isn't. I want it out!"

"It's...it's been six months, Val. Are you sure that—"

"Take me to the doctor," she sobbed. "Take me now!"

"Okay, fine. I can phone for an appointment. Or—"

"Now! I can't stand another minute!"

Our obstetrician was a calm, competent Vietnamese woman who had an office near the hospital. I phoned and told her that we were having a crisis, although I wasn't exactly sure what it was. Dr. Ngyuen told us to come straight to the emergency room.

The aides got Val into a gown and laid her one of those high hospital beds on wheels. A gurney. Ugly word. After a quick moment alone with Val, Dr. Ngyuen came over to me. Something was horribly wrong.

"We're going into surgery, Mr. Oster," said the doctor.

"What's wrong? Will Val be okay?"

Dr. Ngyuen reeled off some medical terminology. And then something about a tumor. My heart was pounding so hard I could hardly understand a word.

"I don't want to," Val was sobbing from her rolling bed. "I don't want to." An intern was injecting drugs into her arm.

"I love you," I told Val, my eyes stinging. I leaned over and kissed her. "You'll make it through this, darling. I'll be right here."

"It's all your fault," she said.

And then they wheeled her down the hall.

I sat in the waiting room. I'd look away from the clock for as long as I could stand it, and when I looked back, the minute hand wouldn't have moved at all. I prayed, wanting to connect to the one mind I've always imagined to be glowing behind the scenes. But what if Val and the baby died? I looked back at the clock. It still hadn't moved. Hundreds of people came and went, hundreds of names were called. And then, all at once, it was my turn.

Dr. Nguyen looked shaken, unsure. "I'm very sorry," she said. "Val's gone."

"But—"

Dr. Nguyen led me into a windowless office off the waiting room and got me to sit down.

"It was a very aggressive cancer," said the doctor, slowly rubbing her hands together—as if wanting to wash them. "A florid pathology."

"But where's Val? Can I see her? And what about the baby?"

"Incinerated," said Dr. Nguyen, pausing after the word. "As a biohazard measure. I'm very sorry, Mr. Oster. I know this is difficult for you."

"Incinerated? Like trash? Val and our baby?" I was on my feet. "My whole life? Incinerated?"

"Please, Mr. Oster. We'll get you a relaxant. You should call someone to help get you home."

I threw back my head and howled.

Three days later, I had a funeral for Val. Chang and Droog helped me dig a hole for Val's ashes in the sandy soil of a bluff above Four Mile Beach where she and I had camped. One of Val's friends was studying to be a rabbi, and she said some traditional words. I filled the hole and set a little pyramid-shaped rock on top. And then the mourners came to my cottage for a reception. My landlords, Dick and Diane Simly, stayed away, even though I'd invited them.

I served bread and lentil soup, the same as the meal I'd had with Val the night she'd gotten pregnant. And Val's friends brought some other stuff, like cold cuts and roast chicken. Funeral meats. I absolutely couldn't believe this was happening.

We sat in my back yard, drinking and smoking a little pot, with the guests chatting, and me not saying much. Whenever I tried to talk, my voice broke. To try and keep it together, I kept focusing on tiny visual details like a pebble or a twig, imagining that God and maybe Val were hiding inside.

And then Skeeves, of all people, showed up. With the barest of nods, he walked past me, got himself a beer in my kitchen, and started nosing around on the side porch where I kept my defunct scanning-tunneling microscope. I could dimly see him through the screen, touching things, picking things up. Skeeves rarely held still.

A minute later he was back outside, with his beer in one hand and his other hand in the pocket of his baggy shorts.

"What are you doing here?" I asked him in a low voice as he came near. "You didn't know Val."

"But I'm involved," said Skeeves. "I told Ira to get you that sharp tip. Chang told me about the sad outcome." He turned his head like a bird, fixing me with one of his oddly flat eyes. "Did you get a chance to see the thing that was growing inside her?"

"What the fuck kind of question is that?" I yelled. I didn't like being reminded that my half-assed experiments might have caused Val's death. I started up out of my chair, meaning to throttle Skeeves into silence.

"Jim!" Val's rabbi friend caught hold of my arm.

"Touchy guy," said Skeeves, and ambled back out to the street.

The guilt train was running in my head, and I couldn't make it stop. The doctors said the growth in Val was cancer—but I'd seen that glowing dot on the night the lightning had struck. My overamped STM machine had made some kind of hole in the fabric of reality—and an evil parasite had drifted through. Val's last words: *It's all your fault.* I'd ruined everything.

That evening I noticed the charred little sample sled was gone from my desk. Poor Val's zapped DNA. For all these months I'd left it on the corner where I'd put it right after the lightning bolt. Evidently Skeeves had stolen it at the reception, sinister creep that he was.

The next day I made an attempt to find Skeeves and ask him about that sample sled. But nobody around town seemed to know where he was. And Ira had disappeared as well. For whatever reason, they were lying low. Ira had always had a crush on Skeeves—perhaps the two men were together. Never mind, never mind, I needed to let go.

Crying while I worked, I dismantled the scanning-tunneling microscope. I smashed the parts with a hammer and put them all in the trash.

The wheel of the seasons rolled on. I missed Val's voice all the time, and the way she'd smile at me with her eyes. It was terrible to sleep in an empty bed. And always I had the guilt and remorse, right at my side, every hour of the day. Whether or not it made sense, I was sure that I'd killed Val with my stupid scanning-tunneling microscope.

That winter there was a nasty murder on Lover's Bluff. Two guys axe-murdered a couple and set one of the victims on fire. They'd burned that body right down to ashes. And the murderers had slipped away. It was one of those stories so sick and strange that even the newspapers didn't want to talk about it for long.

Actually, in the state I was in around then, I'd feel a twinge of envy whenever I heard about someone dying, no matter how. If you were dead you didn't need to keep it together anymore. You didn't need a career. You could rest. You'd be off the hook. Free at last. Gone to a better world. Merged. Not that I felt actively suicidal. I was numb, floating along like a jellyfish.

I could have moved away and looked for a new life. But I couldn't get it together to do anything that drastic. I had a feeling that—without Val—everywhere I went would feel just as blank and dull.

Around May, the Post Office put me on furlough, which was a sanitized way of saying they were busting me down to a three-day work-week. I didn't care. If I pinched my pennies, I could still buy pot and pay the rent.

As it turned out, it was good for me to be working less. I finally turned the corner on my grief and self-loathing. I got back into hiking along the bluffs, taking Droog along. I started reading again, and going out to clubs.

The dog had been sleeping on my bed with me ever since Val died, but now, as a real sign of change, I sent Droog back to his cushion in the kitchen. I was ready to stop being a depressed loner.

4: The Portal

One day that summer I decided to stroll downtown to eat a cup of ice cream. It was one of my numerous days off work. I hadn't gotten around to having lunch yet, and there wasn't much in my fridge. I like to think that ice cream is a complete food, what with the sugar, the fat, the milk proteins, and the bits of fruit flavoring.

Val and I could have had an enjoyable debate about this—and I was perfectly capable of imagining it, but I'd learned not to get into long mental conversations with her ghost. I was even starting to think about finding another woman.

Not that I had any good prospects. A big problem with Santa Cruz is that so many of the people who live there are stone cold crazy. They aren't bad off enough to be in the nuthouse, but they're crazy just the same.

Take my landlady Diane Simly. Diane liked to sit on her porch every afternoon, waiting to see if any of the high-school kids happened to throw a cigarette butt or a gum wrapper onto her front lawn. That was her idea of what to do with her time—and she was always sure that she was *right*.

On the crucial summer afternoon that I want to tell you about, I'd finished rummaging around my house for my sandals, my keys, my wallet, my cell phone, and Droog's leash. As I stepped onto my porch, I heard Diane yelling at a kid.

"Excuse me? Excuse me? I think you dropped something?"

I had a sudden mental image of cutting my landlady into tiny pieces with her electric hedge-clippers and feeding the pieces to the sea lions off the pier at three a.m. Okay, maybe I was a little crazy too—my grief had nearly pushed me over the edge. At least I still had a certain sense of irony. I knew to hold my toxic thoughts in quotes.

But never mind about Diane, I needed ice cream now, the good stuff from Mahalo Gelato on Pacific Avenue. I headed off down the alley. Droog trotted out from under my porch and dogged my steps. My faithful hound. I'd leash him later.

It was a perfect summer day, the first of July. The fog had burned off; the air was cool and salty. The faint roar of the surf floated in— along with the barking of the voracious sea lions beneath the pier.

To tell the truth, sea lions creep me out—I don't like the way their hind legs are flesh-bound within the blubber of their tapering rears. To me, they look they're in bondage, inching their ungainly way across a dock. It was easy to imagine that a sea lion would eat human flesh. Dogs eat their owners all the time—that is, they eat friendless owners who die alone with their pets in locked-up homes. Maybe that was in the cards for me.

A palm tree shuddered overhead, sending criss-cross shadows dancing across the alley like switchblades. Smiling at my not-quite-serious thoughts about Diane and the sea lions, I imagined a sound track of dissonant axe-murderer music. Sometimes I still thought of that murder I'd read about in the paper—and about the green-handled axe that Skeeves had shown me years ago. I put a sneaky crouch into my gait, bending my fingers like claws.

Droog sniffed one of my hands—just to see if I was holding food—and he glanced up at me with his alert, hazel-brown eyes.

"Never mind, Droogie," I told him. "I'm only playing."

And with that, I forgot about Diane and switched over to a different head game, to wit, the Infinite Paths project that I'd invented over the last few months. My discovery was that, with some thought, I could devise ever-new patterns for traversing familiar routes—without ever running out. It was a good way to stop thinking about Val.

My cottage on the alley behind Madrone Street lay some six blocks from Mahalo Gelato on Pacific Avenue—basically, I had to go three blocks south and three blocks west. I had a knack for planning routes in my head, and I'd worked out that there were twenty distinct ways to make this trip, assuming that I took an efficient route without any detours.

But who said that, as a semi-employed guy strolling to town, I had to be completely efficient? I could open up more possibilities by occasionally walking the wrong way. Suppose, for instance, that I allowed a block of retrograde motion to the east, and a compensatory block of extra motion to the west. According to my calculations, this gave me thirty-five times as many routes, yielding a glorious seven hundred possibilities. And if I added a jog to the north cancelled by an extra block to the south, I could find more than thirty-five thousand routes.

And there was nothing to stop me from detouring through three or even four blocks. Moreover, thanks to numerous alleys and footpaths, I had the option of splitting most Santa Cruz blocks in two, effectively doubling the size of my grid. So there were in fact millions of ways to get to the ice-cream parlor from my cottage—without going very far out of the way. With a certain amount of luck and industry, I planned never to use the same route twice.

Why? To some extent, my Infinite Paths project was just a distraction. But there was a deeper motive for what I was doing. I half-believed the world around me to be a kind of maze. I had a persistent fantasy that, if only I traveled along the right sequence of twists and turns, I might find my way out of my dull labyrinth of woe. Deep down, I thought I might still find Val.

Today, feeling energetic, I decided to try for a really odd-ball path. Like a mail-delivery bot with a program flaw, I trundled to and fro, backtracking some blocks and circling others, recrossing streets I'd already passed, and approaching familiar streets from unfamiliar directions.

Seemingly out of the blue, I hit upon the idea of visualizing my route in terms of synthesizing a molecule. Today's insight was that I could view the molecule's atoms as independent axes of variation. So a molecule was like a point in a higher-dimensional space, and synthesizing a molecule was like finding a path through this space. And—here came the punch line—projecting such a path onto the map of Santa Cruz could generate a fresh and never-thought-of route. I stopped walking and just stood there for a minute, letting the new idea sink in.

Perhaps I should have been suspicious of how easily the new insight had popped into my head. Perhaps I should have realized that, as of now, my thoughts were being warped by the will of a ruthless exploiter from a hidden world. But why would I start having sick, weird worries like that? For the first time in ages, I was having fun.

I found myself crafting a wonderfully unexpected route through Santa Cruz. The accumulating turns were wrapping the world in a welcome glow of strangeness. And then—triumph! Only a few blocks from my rental home of several years, I arrived at a street I could hardly recognize. My subconscious quest had reached fruition!

Logically, this *had* to be Yucca Street, but—there'd always been a vacant lot halfway down the block, and today that lot was filled with a dilapidated Victorian home that looked to have been there for eighty years, soft and dank as a decaying tooth. The Vic was dark green, with patches touched up in streaks of mauve and yellow. Gutters hung loose; some windows had missing panes. Junky overgrown eucalyptus trees crowded the free spaces of the yard. A primer-spotted van rested in driveway, perhaps abandoned. It looked as if someone had used the primer to cover up some earlier decorations on the vehicle.

Very strange. Even stranger, I seemed to be in some kind of spatial backwater. As I approached the dilapidated Victorian house, the other houses in the neighborhood became less clearly visible. I could only see bits and pieces of them, as if I were peering out from the center of a mirrored funhouse maze.

While I was still thinking this over, Droog took off down a narrow walkway beside the squalid Vic. As was his custom, he didn't look back at me for approval, lest I try to call him back. Nose to the ground, tail wagging, he made his move. And, god help me, I followed him, the litter from the eucalyptus trees crunching underfoot—leaves, twigs, fragrant sheets of bark, and tough seed-pods resembling oversized buttons.

Close up, the mysterious house seemed almost organic—like a fungus that puffs up overnight, or like a meaty jungle flower. The building was silent and, I hoped, deserted. Droog trotted forward uncowed. Intoxicated by my growing sense of wonder, I continued in his wake. I was telling myself that this passageway was a probably a public right of way—but now, as we passed the rear of the house, our path became a mere sandy track along one edge of the funky Victorian's back yard. A dozen paces ahead lay the haven of a crossways alley that warped off into vagueness where it led away from this ghostly house.

I paused and looked around, wanting to explore. The hind part of the house supported a deck of warped splintery material with a weathered gas-powered generator on one corner. All the windows were dark and dead. The euc trees rustled, and low branches knocked against the house.

I peered beneath the porch, wondering if there might be something interesting in the cellar. Instead of a regular basement door, the foundation wall had a recessed round opening, like the entrance to a tunnel. The hole was closed off by an odd circular door with a spiral pattern.

The sandy soil sloped invitingly towards this entrance. I took a few steps closer and touched the door. It was slick and iridescent, like something on a high-tech vehicle. A dark violet band spiraled in from the edge. Looking closer, I saw that the band was patterned in a frieze of raised glyphs. Perhaps my over-excited mind was fooling me, but I seemed to see a sloppy baboon, a flying turnip, a dancing mushroom, a plant with windows in its stems, and a naked woman amid rays of light.

Several yards behind me, Droog whined. I heard a thump from within the house. Someone was home! But I couldn't leave yet. For in the very center of the door, I'd just now spotted a depression in the precise shape of a human hand. I was filled by a sense that this door was meant for me. Quickly I set my right hand into the smooth cradle at its center—and, yes, my hand was a perfect fit. The door had been waiting for me.

The big disk shuddered, twisted from side to side—and abruptly flopped towards me, flattening me onto my back.

Fortunately the ground was soft, and the door didn't weigh all that much. Even so, I found it hard to push the disk off me. It was as if something behind the door were pressing it against me—as if I were a rat trapped by a janitor with a garbage can lid.

I heard a slithering sound, shortly followed by a clatter from within the basement. Droog began sounding the alarm—his barks low, hoarse and frightened. I heard a woman's clear, low voice, calmly soothing the dog. And then her footsteps hurried across the sandy back yard.

Finally the door's pressure upon me lightened, and I scooted back into the sun. The woman who'd run off was nowhere to be seen. Peering into the basement, I saw a gleaming golden sarcophagus against the side wall, unmistakably an Egyptian relic, its surface filigreed with hieroglyphs.

Instantly I thought of Skeeves, and the stories of his having stolen a casket from a rich wastrel's house in San Francisco. Was he hiding in this hard-to-find house?

The near end of the sarcophagus bore an idealized likeness of some pharaoh's face, with the figure's head-dress sweeping down the sides of the casket in tooled golden ridges. The basement also held a huge conical wad of gray-green material that fanned out from a pointed tip near the far wall. Perhaps it was a kind of plastic. A sheaf of the stuff was attached to the back of the door, highlighted all over with glints from the sun. The funky stuff tensed like a muscle, dragging the door back towards the wall—and closing it in my face. Very weird.

I heard a footstep on the porch above, and I looked up to see a well-built guy with sun-darkened skin and greenish blond hair. A surfer I'd seen around town a few times before. A jerk. His name was Header. His eyes were fixed on me, and his nose was bleeding bright red. Maybe Header was a coker. He raised a handkerchief to his face and made a noise.

In that very instant, a four-inch-long blue slug dropped down from the porch. The slug began worming around on the ground, eating dirt, growing with great speed. I had an odd, fleeting sensation then, as if an alien personality within the slug were rummaging through my mind. Was this how it felt to go mad?

The swollen blue slug kneaded its flesh against itself, growing lumps and taking on the shape of—a bull sea lion with large, golden eyes. Droog redoubled his barking, giving it everything he had.

Ignoring us, the odd sea lion wallowed out into the middle of the back yard and snuffled the air, perhaps tracking the woman who'd emerged before him.

Droog gave a despairing yelp, and was gone, off around the corner of the alley at the back of the yard.

"Hey!" yelled the guy on the deck above. "Old man!"

Two other grungy surf kids appeared from the house, a boy and a girl, these two a bit shadowy and hard to see. The boy was none other than the missing Ira—the surfer who'd stolen that scrap of metallic hydrogen from the physics lab. The girl was new to me.

"Who told you how to get here?" asked the girl, leaning over the railing of the porch to stare down at me. She had a halo of short-cropped dark hair, and her voice was a low purr. She was silhouetted against the sky.

"Do you know about Val?" I blurted, sensing some connection between this weird scene and my wife's death. "Is this magic? Can you bring her back?"

"Val's gone for good," said Ira. "I'm sorry that happened. We've all had some hard times around this weird scene."

The blue sea-lion-thing was back down on his belly, flopping towards me, his blubber shaking in waves. There was something odd and hypnotic about his golden eyes. Once again I had the feeling of something alien reaching into my mind.

"Tell your pet that I'm good people," I called to Ira.

"That thing's not our pet, asshole," said Header, the big guy with the muscles. "Did you just open our basement door?"

"Maybe," I jabbered. "I don't know what's going on. Did you bring that sea lion home from the ocean? And dye him blue?"

"Was Skeeves in the basement?" pressed Header. "Did he let you in?"

"I didn't see anything at all," I said, backing away from the blue sea lion. I didn't want the unearthly creature to touch me. "Come here, Droog!" I added, my voice breaking. "Protect me!"

The girl on the porch laughed musically, and then she imitated my cry, even putting a break into her voice—as if she was sampling my sound.

With an abrupt series of wriggles, the sculptured blue sea lion circled past me and disappeared along the littered pathway that I'd used to get back here in the first place. Perhaps he was making a break for the sea.

Thoroughly freaked, I took off across the back yard and down the alley like Droog had done. With every step I took, more of the alley became visible. I found Droog resting in a spot of sun on the sidewalk of Cedar Street. He gave me an innocent, unconcerned look. I stood there for a couple of minutes, catching my breath.

What had just happened? I'd opened some kind of giant plastic door beneath the house. A woman had run away, I'd seen a gold sarcophagus in the basement, and Header had had sneezed a blue sea lion out of his nose. None of it made sense.

Not to mention the fact that, as of yesterday, the whipped-to-shit green Victorian house hadn't been on Yucca Street at all. Nor had I ever seen this place during all the months that I'd been a mailman walking from door to door.

I paused on Cedar Street, thinking things over. Maybe, just maybe, that tunnel under the house could lead to Val. Ira hadn't exactly said no. Maybe I'd found a new level of reality beneath the workaday world. But maybe I was losing my mind. My heart was beating like a triphammer. I couldn't take any more just now.

Santa Cruz looked normal from where I was standing, and I knew where I was. That was good. I wanted things to stay still for a few minutes. I could find the ghost house again later. And keep on looking for Val.

But right now I wanted some slack.

5: Brain Event

Droog and I walked half a block along Cedar Street and cut down a side street to Pacific Avenue. And here was Mahalo Gelato, my favorite ice-cream parlor. A Hawaiian-themed place, managed by a plump woman who invariably wore overalls. Her name was Mercedes. I put the leash on the dog and tied him to a bicycle rack. I took some comfort from these ordinary things.

The parlor was an airy place with soft steel guitar music playing. They had fully forty flavors of gelato, made with fresh cream and fruit every day. An unfamiliar clerk stood behind the counter—a tan, medium-sized woman with a goofy smile and brunette hair in a messy, recently made ponytail. She was in the process of tying on her apron. Though her eyes were worldly-wise, she looked to be about thirty. Perfect for me.

"I'm here because of you," she said, looking right into my eyes, which felt way spacier than anything I was ready for. Sensing my unease, the woman giggled. "I began this employment one minute ago, following a two minute interview."

"You were right to sign on," I said, hoping to steer the conversation back towards normal. "I'm a regular here. Jim Oster."

"Weena Wesson," said the woman, miming a curtsy. "I'm tickled to be back."

"Back from where?" I had to ask.

"Let's not delve into that as yet." She wrinkled her nose in a smile—or maybe she was sniffing at me across the counter.

It had already crossed my mind that this Weena might be the unseen woman who'd run out from that tunnel under the green Victorian. But—had that scene been real? It didn't fit with any other part of my life. Better to focus on the now. On the ice cream.

"I'm here for a medium cup," I said. "With a scoop of pineapple and scoop of coconut."

"This treat will reconfigure your existence," said Weena assuredly.

"*Sell* it, Weena," interjected Mercedes the manager lady. "You go, girl." She thought Weena was cute too.

"And you're familiar with this man?" said Weena to Mercedes. "He's an upright citizen?" She had an odd, old-fashioned way of talking.

"You're wild," Mercedes told Weena with a laugh. She liked kidding around.

"For sure I need to be reconfigured," I remarked. "I'm in a deep rut. Deeper than the Grand Canyon." Gathering my courage, I decided to test Weena. "Just now I thought I saw a ghost house with a magic door and an Egyptian coffin and a big, creepy sea lion. Some woman I didn't see came through the door."

Weena twinkled at me, but didn't say anything. Moving with awkward grace, she dug out two exceedingly large scoops of ice cream. And then, with a quick gesture, she scattered sprinkles onto the scoops—twinkling, colorful specks. I didn't quite see where she got the sprinkles from.

Normally I'm a purist when it comes to ice cream—that is, I don't like chunks of candy junking it up, and I don't like glop on top.

"An amplified ice for Jim Oster," said Weena, handing my serving across the counter. She smiling so sweetly that I wasn't going to bitch about the sprinkles. And never mind that her eyes were calculating and hard.

I paid Mercedes, then ate my gelato rapidly and greedily at one of the sidewalk tables outside the store. The memories of the magic door and the blue sea lion were already fading.

The surf punks had just brought a sea lion home and dyed it for a goof. And Skeeves was living in their basement with his stolen gold sarcophagus. With a bunch of plastic. The sea lion was probably back in the ocean by now. Why get all bent out of shape? Why keep imagining I'd find a way back to Val?

The ice cream was great, and the sprinkles weren't bad either. They were very high quality, faceted like miniscule gems, and carrying the intense flavor accents of essential oils. I identified cinnamon, spearmint, clove, eucalyptus, violet, and bergamot. For a moment I almost thought the sprinkles were slowly crawling across my ice cream—but surely that was slippage from the melting. A remarkable treat.

I was filled with well-being, in tune with the world. I watched the Santa Cruzans go trucking on by. Bums, students, hipsters, bumpkins, and bossy bohemians—I felt as if I could empathize with each and every one them, as if I could hear bits of the ongoing thoughts in their minds. Or maybe the thoughts were coming from somewhere else. It was almost as if the sprinkles themselves had been full of voices.

I considered going inside to talk with Weena some more, but now she was busy with other customers. And there was, after all, no huge rush to get to know her better. I came to this ice cream parlor nearly every day. I could flirt more with Weena tomorrow. As if sensing my thoughts, she flashed a warm smile at me through the window-glass and tapped her wrist as if she were wearing a watch. She was miming that she'd see me later.

As I got to my feet, I thought once more of the blue slug that had taken on the form of a sea lion. Try as I might, I couldn't push that particular image away. I decided to try getting another look at the dark green Victorian house.

Droog and I found the same alley we'd followed from the back yard of the house to Cedar Street. But when we walked down this alley, I saw only a vacant lot where the surf punks' house had been. Wow.

We picked our way through the empty lot. It was scattered with cans and rags, and overgrown with dried brown weeds. The roots twined around little chunks of rubble from a house that had been bulldozed years before. Thick overgrown eucalyptus trees ringed the property. Had I only imagined the old Vic?

"What do you think, Droogie?" I asked, hunkering down beside him in the litter of narrow eucalyptus leaves. "Where'd they go?" I felt close empathy with my old pal. He wanted to lie down in the shade.

We took the most direct route back to my house and then I vegged out on my dusty Goodwill couch, reading a paperback fantasy novel.

It was a peaceful summer afternoon, with the sunlight lying across the roof and yard like heavy velvet.

After awhile I began having the feeling that I could read the pages of the book without actually looking at them. But I was having trouble making sense of what I read. Thinking I needed a nap, I laid down my book and curled up on my side. I dropped off to sleep.

The next thing I knew, I was lying on the living room floor, very confused. It was dark outside. I felt like I'd been—gone. I ached all over, in every muscle and joint. My tongue was bleeding. Something very bad was happening to me.

I crawled across the room to where my cell phone sat with my keys. I didn't trust myself to walk. It took all my concentration to dial 911. And then everything went black again.

I awoke in a hospital room. It was still night. A nurse was standing over me, a woman with a calm, sympathetic face. She had short dark hair, dyed blonde. Smallish breasts and nice wide hips. It's funny how, even on his death-bed, a man can still focus on women that way. We're incorrigible.

The nurse said I'd had two seizures. They weren't sure why. The doctors had scanned my brain and it looked normal. Maybe I'd be okay. They had me on an IV drip with painkillers and an anti-seizure drug. I needed to rest.

I slept fitfully. In the morning I was able to think a little. I could hardly believe I was in the hospital. Yesterday I'd been fine. And then I'd had that odd experience with the abandoned house. Maybe that's when my brain had started screwing up.

How disturbing to think that I'd been to death's door and back. I hadn't seen any white light or spiral tunnel or dead relatives while I'd been out—none of that cool, trippy stuff. Saddest of all—I hadn't seen Val. I'd been nowhere and I'd seen nothing. It just felt like I'd had a couple of time-sequences snipped out of my life. Discouraging.

There was something else disappointing me. No friends. Somehow I'd always imagined that if I had a major health crisis, some of the people I'd lost touch with would magically appear to comfort me. But that that wasn't panning out. Nobody at all was visiting me. I didn't have any relatives left. And my friends were hopeless flakes. As for Dick and Diane, my asshole landlords—surely they'd seen the ambulance taking me away. But they were probably hoping that I'd die or move into a nursing home. Then they could up the rent.

I was in the hospital for three days, having tests and being observed. When I wasn't thinking about death, I was obsessing about that strange scene at the crumbling green Victorian house, trying to figure out what it meant. Had it been a warning vision sent from beyond?

On the second day in the hospital, I asked my nice nurse with the big hips to wheel me to the ward's walled patio. She wore her skirt full-cut, it swayed enticingly as she walked. The tag on her shirt said her name was Alice.

I sat on the patio watching the clouds change shapes in the high summer sun. The leaves of a potted palm tree rocked chaotically in the gentle airs, with the fronds clearly outlined against the marbled heavens. It struck me, in a deep kind of way, that the world would keep right on running if I died. An obvious fact, yes, and I knew it in a theoretical way from seeing Val pass away. But, now that it was personal, it seemed horrible.

"I feel like death is stalking me," I told nurse Alice as she wheeled me back to my room. "My wife died last August. Her name was Val. We thought she was pregnant, but it was cancer."

"I remember that case," said Alice after a pause. "I was on duty that day."

"They incinerated Val and the baby," I said, my voice catching. "I never got to say good-bye."

"The hospital's public safety precautions can be a little zealous," said Alice in a calming tone. "But sometimes it's for the best."

"I don't know what to think anymore," I said, wanting to prolong our chat. "I feel like anything at all can fall apart. From one moment to the next."

"You're going to be okay, Jim," said Alice, patting my shoulder. "You're a strong man. You're recuperating very fast."

By the morning of the third day, they'd decided that my seizures could have been an isolated fluke. I wasn't very eager to be leave the hospital. I felt safe in there. But they said that I should go home that afternoon and taper off the antiseizure drugs on my own. And we'd see what happened next.

Lunch came and went as I lay there worrying. And then, just before it was time for me to check out, nurse Alice led a woman into my room.

"She says she's your new wife!" said Alice, her kind lips parting in an innocent smile. "I didn't know."

For a crazy instant I thought Alice was bringing the dead Val back to me. But, no, my guest was a tall, well-formed young woman with her curly brown hair in a ponytail. A woman with aged, knowing eyes. She looked familiar, but I couldn't quite—

"Weena Wesson?" said the woman. She mimed eating ice cream with a spoon. Of course. The new clerk from Mahalo Gelato. The woman who'd possibly come from the basement of that crumbling Victorian house.

"How did you know I was here?" I challenged Weena, suspicious and afraid.

"Pull yourself together, Mr. Oster," said nurse Alice reprovingly. "Be glad you have a partner who cares for you."

6: Weena Wesson

eena called a cab and rode with me to my house. I was reasonably glad to have her along. She was, after all, an attractive woman. But...

"Wife?" I said.

"I had to say that so they'd let me in," said Weena. "I'm quite the intriguer." She gave me a sly look. "Or perhaps you did marry me, but you forgot?"

I let this one slide. "It's weird to be outside again," I remarked, happy to be in the back seat next to her, our thighs touching, the two of us watching the world scroll by. "I was only in the hospital for those three days, but I feel like everything's changed. I never really understood deep down that I myself am going to die. Not even after losing my wife, Val."

"Did you glimpse the afterworld?" asked Weena. "During your apoplectic attack?"

"I didn't see jack shit. There isn't any afterworld."

"Oh yes indeed there is," said Weena, and I was glad to hear her contradict me. "I've lived there for many a year," she continued. "You people still on Earth full-time—you're less fanciful than we astral travelers."

Maybe Weena was saying she'd emerged from that slime-filled cellar that I'd seen under the green Victorian. Or maybe she was just being whimsical. Or maybe she was comparing men to women in some vaguely disparaging way. In any case, we'd reached my house. I noticed a small cardboard box on my porch.

"What's that?" I asked Weena, already guessing the answer.

"Some meager possessions that I've acquired this week," said Weena, in her curiously old-fashioned diction. "I don't have a proper place to stay. And I have special interest in you. So I've formed the plan of rooming here. Can you pay the driver? I have but little cash—I took the bus to the hospital. But never fear, I'll contribute to your rent next month. And I'll bring home masses of free ice cream. When it's a week old, they discard it."

The driver was mildly interested in all this—I could tell from the quiet, attentive way he was holding his head—although ostensibly he was gazing out through the windshield. Weena gave me a big grin—although, once again, her eyes seemed calculating and hard. Clearly this some kind of baroque scam, but she was putting on such a good front of being chirpy and sexy and quaint that I didn't really mind. Anyway, it's not like I had much to lose.

"Okay, fine," I said. "You can live with me for now, Weena. Welcome."

The cab drove off and we were on my porch, me and my pretend wife. Droog appeared, whining and jumping up on me. I hoped he'd been able to scavenge food from around the neighborhood. Dick and Diane Simly would never think of caring for a renter's dog.

Feeling a little dizzy, I filled Droog's water dish and poured out some kibble from the bag I kept in a cupboard on the porch wall. He set to work slurping and crunching.

"Good boy," I said. "Meet Weena. Weena, meet Droog."

"He and I became acquainted this morning," said Weena. "He tolerates me."

"What kind of name is Weena, anyway," I demanded, feeling suspicious again.

"It's from my grandmother," she said. "She hailed from the subcontinent, and her full name was Praweena. Unbar your door, please. I'm bursting."

"The bathroom's over there," I said as we stepped inside. "But I still don't get how you found me."

"I have secret channels," said Weena, tossing her head. She pecked a little kiss onto my cheek. "I'll return anon."

I sat on my couch, thinking things over. My house was calm and quiet, a shady shelter from the July sun. Would the house have noticed if I'd died? Did a house think? Would the Simlys have rented it out right away? What would have happened to my stuff? Would anyone have come to my funeral?

"Here I am, little husband," said Weena. She'd combed her hair and freshened up her lipstick. She was watching my every move.

"I want you to understand that I'm not completely slushed," I said sternly. "I'm happy if you live with me for awhile, but not if you continually bullshit me."

"How much truth can you handle?" Weena produced one of her giggles and held up her hands as if measuring the variable size of a fish. "A wee scrap? A vast lump?"

"Let's start with that crumbling Victorian house. You came from there, right?"

"Very well then, yes. You opened the portal from my world. And when we met face to face in Mahalo Gelato, I became quite sure that you're the man I seek. You'd already acted as my doorman, and I realized you could be my, my postman as well. So I—" She made a gesture of shaking on sprinkles.

I felt odd, as if my living room were stretching away from me, with Weena's face a pale disk at the other end.

"You—you drugged me?" This part hadn't occurred to me before. "You deliberately gave me those seizures?"

"I'd wager the sprinkles saved your life," said Weena. "They enriched your personality and gave you strength. You would have had the apoplectic fit in any case—this was your fate."

"What *are* the sprinkles?" I asked, more and more confused.

"Souls? Oh, never mind that. I'll just tell you that I harvested sprinkles on my way here from Flimsy. And that they served as a tonic to give you pep. And now you'll be able to host a jiva, and you'll be fit to battle that horrible yuel. The Graf must have smuggled the yuel over here. Do you know that right now the yuel is rutting under the Santa Cruz pier? The imbecilic sea lions believe him to be one of them! But soon the yuel will attack us and..."

Weena stopped, clapped her hand over her mouth and bulged her eyes at me. I couldn't tell whether it was a laugh or a scream that she was holding back. Obviously she liked being dramatic.

"Flimsy?" I echoed, groping for the right question. "Yuel?"

"I'm sure you take me for a madwoman," she said, lowering her hands. "I've chattered enough. Consider instead—the alabaster mounds of my breasts." Weena pulled her T-shirt over her head and unhooked her bra. "Alluring, yes? Caress me, Jim. We'll recline on your bed."

So we did that. The love-making was great, once I got up to speed. Weena was patient, and funny, and then hot. And that old-fashioned accent of hers made it the more exciting.

Afterwards, lying in bed next to her, I stared at the old frosted-glass light fixture on my low ceiling. I seemed to see the tint of the glass changing in slow waves, the faint pastel hues amping up and down, as if I were diddling the world's color balance sliders.

"I can teep what you see," murmured Weena.

"Teep—" I said. "Is that supposed to mean telepathy?" I kept having the uneasy feeling that Weena was a little crazy, or that she was totally putting me on. "If you can teep me, why can't I teep you?"

"You have no jiva as yet," said Weena. "This I will soon remedy. And then your mind will unfold like a spring jonquil. And you'll have the strength of three men. For now, the action of the sprinkles has already raised your vim. Swaying your inner vibrations is an occult technique for glimpsing the inner essence. Flimsy lies inside every electrical particle, you see. As you oscillate your vibrations, fix your attention on one particular object—perhaps that lamp on your dresser. And observe."

So I relaxed, and let the swaying begin again, and now I noticed that as the colors shifted, my lamp began to look like a cloud of bright dots. It was as if I were seeing the swarms of electrons around the lamp's atoms—as if my mind were a scanning-tunneling microscope. In my trance-like state, I perceived that each of the electrons was the same, and that each of them was somehow very vast. One single hidden form lurked within each. The mysterious Flimsy.

But—was I really forming these impressions myself? Or was Weena somehow putting them into my mind? Feeling myself under siege, I turned away from the lamp and glanced out the window. And now I seemed to see a demonic blue baboon, with his hairless skin rippling like the surface of a windblown—

"What!?!" I cried, sitting bolt upright. The world snapped back to being Santa Cruz on a mid-summer day. "Did you see that, that—monster?" My heart was pounding like it would jump out of my chest. "Is it real?"

"That's the self-image of the yuel I was talking about," said Weena. "He's teeping us, to some small extent."

"Is he coming here?"

"He's unlikely to attack unless cornered. For now he's occupied beneath the Santa Cruz pier. As you know, he's presently wearing the form of a bull sea lion. Yuels can change their bodies quite readily, you see. This particular yuel plucked the sea lion image from your mind behind the green house where I slumbered." She kissed me on the cheek. "Yes, yes, Jim, you're a crucial player in a cosmic drama. But before your special delivery mission, you need to recover from your indisposition. I'll unpack my box now. I brought some food to share. Lentils and rice. My grandmother Praweena taught me to cook."

In other words, the yuel was the blue slug that Header the surfer had dropped onto the ground. But I postponed discussing this any further. I was just happy to be living with a woman again. For his part, Droog tolerated Weena, without getting overly close.

For the next couple of days Weena and I stayed away from touchy conversation topics. In the mornings, she went in to work the day shift at Mahalo Gelato—she helped to make the ice cream as well as selling it in the afternoons. She got her pay every day, and she'd immediately spend it on clothes from the surf and skate shops downtown. She was fascinated by the Santa Cruz street fashions.

While she worked and shopped, I passed my time on my own. I stayed away from the pier and I didn't try swaying the colors again. I didn't want to face any yuels without Weena around.

I was finding it hard to settle down. Those sprinkles—or my seizures—had screwed up my ability to kill time. In the mornings I'd scan through my old SF paperbacks and pop science books, looking for something to read. And then I'd cruise the neighborhood.

Walking around with Droog, I'd look for people to chat with. Not that I was so good at chatting just now. Even with old friends, I'd freeze up after a few pleasantries, with the muscles of my cheeks bending my mouth into a fake smile. I wanted to talk about the inevitability of death and about whether Flimsy was real—but there was no way I could get those kinds of conversations going, especially with my friends wondering if my trip to the hospital meant that I'd lost my marbles.

On the second day that I was home, I tried to repeat the complicated path I'd taken to Yucca Street and the crumbling green house that day—but I didn't seem able to get all the turns right.

Home alone in my house, I noticed that smells had begun to seem overly intense—I'm talking about the odors of drains, garbage, or ordinary food. The meaty, oily scent of the skin fragments in the electric razor became so disgusting to me that I only shaved every few days. Most of the time I had a bum's dark stubble.

Weena didn't mind if I shaved. She seemed to have no preconceptions about how people should look or behave. In the evenings she'd wear her latest new clothes. We'd drink together, play the radio, and sometimes I'd tell her about what was going on inside my head.

"I feel like my mind is a giant warehouse where an earthquake knocked everything off the racks," I told her one evening as I fondled my soft stubble. "I have to reshelve things one by one. I'm like—oh, that's a shovel, that's a pot holder, that's a quartz crystal, that's my first day of nursery school."

"Shelves," mused Weena. She was wearing a black denim miniskirt with platform flip-flops and a long-sleeved red cotton jersey. "I often classify things by colors. Like ice-cream flavors. In my mind, I have all the cornflower blue things on one shelf, all the turmeric yellows on another, all the thistle greens on another, and so forth. I learned thousands of different color names at my job today. The manger let me explore with her computer. How far they've come. I memorized an online color dictionary from the National Bureau of Standards."

"You have that good a memory?"

"Thanks to my jiva. You unaugmented people hardly use your brains at all. Just wait until you acquire a jiva like me."

"I—I don't know about any of that," I said, wanting to steer the conversation back to something comprehensible. I pointed at a spot on my wood floor. "So, uh, what color is *this*?"

"Capucine buff," said Weena. "With shadings of mustard and barium yellow."

On the fourth day of Weena's residence, I went down to the beach for a long walk. It soothed me to stare at the waves and at the curves of the seaweed on the sand. When I came home in the late afternoon, Weena had someone else in our bedroom with her. I could hear that they were having sex. I went shaky all over, with my chest feeling hollow.

I threw a chair across the kitchen so they'd know I was home, and then I went out on our little front porch and started putting an edge my biggest carving knife, using a sharpening iron that made a sinister slithery sound.

A minute or two later I heard voices from the house, and then the sound of the bedroom window opening. Someone exited unseen and ran away. And now Weena appeared on the porch, wearing shorts and a T-shirt.

"Are you contemplating a psychotic rampage?" she asked, half smiling. Her eyes were watchful.

"I want you to know that I'm taking this very seriously." I set down the knife. "Don't you love me, Weena?"

"We've never spoken of love. Perhaps I thought you'd find it titillating if I bedded a stranger? In this manner presenting myself as a fallen woman of loose morals?" She gave me a mocking smile.

"Don't, Weena. I—I've grown very attached to you. Who was the guy?"

"Dick Simly. Your landlord." Weena put on a contrite expression and walked over to me. "Oh, Jim, I comprehend your chagrin. No more teasing. I bedded this Dick Simly for a simple and practical reason. I was implanting eggs in his flesh." She bucked her belly gently. "With my ovipositor. These are a very fast-growing kind of egg. Quite soon they'll hatch. Three of them."

"You're crazy," I said. But I sort of had to laugh. Weena was a step beyond spacy, that was for sure. But...ovipositor? Yuck. She was kidding, right?

I really didn't know what to think. And I didn't feel like talking it over with Weena. That night I slept on the sofa.

The next morning, after Weena left for work, Diane Simly came over from her house and struck up a conversation with me. It was the first time she'd spoken to me since I'd gone to the hospital.

"How are you feeling, Jim? I've been so busy lately. But truly we're concerned about you."

"They say I had a kind of electrical storm in my brain, and it scrambled some of my nerve connections. But I'm getting it back together."

"Was the attack, ah, brought on by, by—" She probably wanted to ask if I used meth.

"Just the luck of the draw," I said blandly. "I'm very clean-living.

Look at my stomach. Feel the muscle tone."

I opened my sports shirt, revealing my rather slack gut, and of course Diane Simly took a step back. "I understand that you've found a new friend to keep you company," she continued. "But I'm afraid that poses a problem in terms of your lease." I knew full well that the Simlys wanted to evict me so they could raise the rent. But renters had strong rights in Santa Cruz. At least that's what I'd thought.

"The woman's only a temporary guest," I said. "A friend."

"I gather that she's very friendly indeed," said Diane sourly. "I couldn't help but overhear what happened yesterday."

"Yes, she fucked your husband," I said. "And I asked her not to do it again. If you tell Dick the same thing, maybe we'll be okay. Until Weena's eggs hatch. You should be fucking Dick more yourself. Before the larvae turn him into hamburger." Really I had no idea what I was talking about—I just knew that, despite my jealousy, I wanted to stand up for Weena.

"You're completely insane," said Diane, fighting to control her voice. "And do you know what? I was ready to give you a break. But now you've gone far. I want you and that—that *whore* out of here within seventy-two hours. As soon as she moved in, you were in violation of the terms of your lease. Our lawyer is filing for a three-day eviction this afternoon." She turned and stalked off, her motions stiff and angular.

That night Weena and I sat on kitchen chairs in my driveway, sharing a few bottles of hard lemonade. It was balmy, with the surf audible down the alley.

"*Muuur*," said Weena cozily. A jokey mooing sound she liked to make.

"I love you, Weena," I said, and I meant it. I'd been thinking about our relationship all day. I was happy to have this young woman with the strange grammar here, no matter what she did.

"Dear Jim," she answered, running her hand along my arm. "I appreciate that you speak of love. And I'm flattered that you're jealous."

"But we might have to move," I said. And then I recounted my conversation with Diane Simly. "She says we have to move tomorrow," I concluded. "But I doubt if she can make that stick."

"And you told this woman of my three eggs?" asked Weena.

"I wanted to shake her up. She's always so smug. What are the eggs supposed to grow *into* anyway? New Weenas?"

"No, no," said Weena. "They're jiva eggs. What I jestingly call my ovipositor is in truth the tail of a jiva that's lodged within me. Her name is Awnee. She's my ally—she's been a part of me for many years." Weena lifted up her latest T-shirt, patterned in horizontal green and yellow stripes. "Fix your attention upon my navel." And now a tapering pink tendril slipped a short way out from Weena's belly button. The jiva tail—if that's what it was—bore a fuzz of tiny, luminous hairs. It had a tiny dark spot at its tip. An orifice.

"Oh put that away!" I cried miserably. I rose unsteadily to my feet.

"It's high time I told you the entire truth," continued Weena.

"Enough truth," I said, backing away from her. "To hell with truth."

"Tomorrow you will lead me back to that crumbling Victorian house where you first glimpsed the yuel," intoned Weena. "The house with the round door to Flimsy. You will open this portal again."

"Maybe," I said, starting to feel cornered. "How about some truth for you? It was that big surfer at that house who launched the yuel. Header. He had the yuel in his handkerchief or maybe in his nose."

Weena hardly looked surprised. "I might as well tell you that I had the Graf eliminated before I came. But his spirit seems to control one of those surfers. I'd already sensed some of this in your mind. Believe me, Jim, your eviction is but the smallest of our worries. When I join battle with this surfer and his blue sea lion of a yuel, we'll—"

"Oh, can't we stop talking crazy?" I implored. My emotions were spilling over. "You've never once said that you loved me, Weena. That's what matters. That's what I'm waiting for!"

"I *should* love you. You have an admirable forthrightness and vim. But—"

"Look," I said with a weary sigh. "I'm going to bed. Is it safe to sleep next to you?"

"Indeed."

"You won't implant jiva eggs?"

"Have no fears in this regard," said Weena cheerfully. "I'm quite finished with that task for now."

7: Yuel

That night I dreamed about sea lions barking.

"*Ork ork ork!*"

Weena woke me at dawn, bending over me, whispering my name. Her brown hair was tousled, her face calm. My dream of sea lions was real. Outside every window I could see whiskered snouts. The house shook as the beasts rubbed against the walls, the air rang with their hoarse cries. The sky was gray, filled with morning fog.

"The yuel's harem has accompanied him," chattered Weena. "He knows your fear of sea lions. He'd like to drive you away from me before I've prepared you for your mission. That unfaithful Graf took advantage of me, I told him about the secret tunnel. And then that stupid farmwife who's supposed to be guarding the tunnel took a bribe from the Graf. And somehow he smuggled through a yuel. It must have been hidden within his kessence body."

All of this was sheer gibberish to me. Droog was on the front porch, frantically scratching at the door. I opened the door to let him in. The blue sea lion was out there too, raised up on his flippers, glaring at me. An overexcited sea lion cow came wallowing around the corner of the house, her dark eyes fixed on the blue sea lion, whimpering her adoration, her body rippling with the effort of motion, her teeth prickly in her little mouth. God, sea lions were stupid. I slammed and locked the door. Outside, the creatures barked more furiously than before. An approaching siren wailed.

"Hurry and clothe yourself," said Weena. She was dancing around, pulling on layers of clothes, and cramming her extra shoes into a shopping bag. "We'll go to that green house and await further events," she said. "I can't readily kill a yuel with but one jiva. We have to wait for the others to hatch. You do recall our conversation of last night, no? Dress warmly. I believe you'll be sleeping in that basement for some days."

"I don't know if I can find the house," I said, pulling on jeans, a red T-shirt, and a checked flannel shirt. "I went looking for it a few days ago, and—"

"In one manner or another you will find it, Jim. You're the one who made the tunnel between the worlds."

"All I did was open that door in the basement for you," I said. "I didn't make the tunnel."

"Oh yes you did. With that strange tool of yours. You weakened an electrical particle so that my border snail could push through. The snail is the tunnel. And those filthy surf punks live in the rickety house that's the snail's shell."

Before I had any time to ponder this, the front door splintered and the blue bull sea lion came flopping in. Weena yelled sharply—and the creature's flesh flickered and folded, reknotting itself. And now the yuel was a muscular beast on all fours—a hairless baboon with sharp, red snaggle teeth and his skin that same shade of Krishna blue. He had a knob near the end of his tail. He made a noise at me—a snarl? Or was he trying to talk?

I rushed out the back door and Weena was with me, running down the block. Glancing back, I saw a cop car and an animal rescue van pulling up at my house. The yuel followed us, easily loping along.

"The baboon shape is the one preferred by the yuels," said Weena. "Although sometimes a number of them fuse together to make a shape like an elephant. I don't fully understand yuels."

"That baboon has sharp teeth."

"Remember that I have my jiva. I will assuredly inflict damage if the yuel engages us."

We cut down a side street, turned left, turned right, doubled back, and raced down an alley, Droog at our side. But now, just like on the other days when I'd tried to find the green Vic, I didn't know what came next. I leaned against the trunk of a palm tree, catching my breath. Tenuous strands of fog drifted past.

"I wasn't really paying attention when I found the way to the green Vic that day," I confessed. "I was just playing around. The path kind of popped into my head. And now it's hard to concentrate with that thing—" I craned to see down the street to see if the yuel was still following.

"Never fear," said Weena. She was bulky from all the clothes she'd pulled on—a pair of orange pencil-leg jeans protruded from beneath a pair of skirts. "I well know that the path struck you as a sudden inspiration. That's because I put it into your head. I reached out to you from the other side." She pulled a glassine envelope of sparkling powder from the pocket of a little red jeans jacket she was wearing, and dipped into it with the moistened tip of her finger. "Allow me to inspire you again."

"Are those things moving?" I asked, peering closer. "The sprinkles are alive?"

"Oh yes," said Weena. "Life is the essence of their virtue. I'm eating some to engage my higher powers. I have a robust supply. Ordinarily, a sprinkle hops straight over to Flimsy. But these sprinkles are well-fattened. They have enough psychic inertia to linger here on Earth for a time. Prime yourself with some of them, Jim."

"No way. You nearly killed me with sprinkles last week."

"I still maintain that they saved your life," said Weena. She licked the twitching little gems off her finger and let out a sigh of pleasure. "I enjoy how the sprinkles talk in my head. Do try some! We'll wander the streets, babbling at random. It's no longer possible for me to see the clear path, now that I'm reincarnated in your mundane world. I've lost my teep contact with the border snail—the creature in the basement of what those punks call the Whipped Vic. She's the one who generates the spacewarp camouflage, you know. They like to hide, the border snails, so that the flims and the living humans don't take advantage, using the snails as tunnels between the worlds."

I had trouble making sense of this. "The Whipped Vic is hiding from us?"

"You could say that. But I'll surely notice if we're getting near. Perhaps the route still lurks in your deeper mind. Perhaps Snaily hasn't changed it all that much."

"There's millions of routes through these blocks," I complained. "More. Do the math."

"Ah yes, he fancies himself a scientist, too." Weena let out a peal of mocking laughter. "Small man, big dreams, tiny job."

The glowing baboon appeared at the end of the block, trotting towards us on all fours, his bulb-tipped tail waving high in the air. I started running again, leading Weena in intricate loops, and eventually we arrived at Yucca Street.

But, shit, it wasn't the *special* Yucca Street. That stupid old vacant lot gaped where the green Vic should have been. Just an empty lot with ratty eucalyptus trees. I stood there, stymied. Droog sat by our feet, waiting to see what came next. The yuel kept his distance, still watching us. And, for the moment, Weena was too stoned from her sprinkles to be much help at all.

As the mist thinned, the sun was gaining in force. I unbuttoned my flannel shirt, thinking. If we couldn't rush off to Flimsy, we needed another plan.

"Do you know much about those surfers who live in the house?" I asked Weena.

"I know what you've told me," she said. "And what I see in your memories. And what I've garnered via surreptitious teep. And I know a bit more regarding the fourth one who lurks within that house. He and Header killed the Graf."

"You're talking about Skeeves!" I exclaimed. Light dawned in my muddled mind. "You're the mummy woman that he's been fucking all these years! He's been hearing your voice in his head. You've been telling him what to do. And—and you're the one who made sure that I got that special tip for the scanning-tunneling microscope. The tip that killed my wife."

"Calm yourself, Jim. Things are not as you may imagine. Look at me, dear. I'm no mummy. Yes, I've had some unwholesome interactions with Skeeves. The man is unspeakably vile. I'm only trying to help you people. And that's why I stopped the Graf."

"Maybe I'm saying that you killed my wife." I didn't totally believe the accusation. It was more that I wanted to hear Weena deny it. I wanted to be reassured.

"I didn't, Jim," said Weena right away. "Not at all. Poor Val had cancer. It had nothing to do with me." She took my face in both her hands and stared into my eyes as if hypnotizing me. "Help me. And if you play along—well, maybe I shouldn't promise this..."

"What?" I said, a crazy burst of hope blossoming in my chest.

"Maybe there could be a way to bring back Val. I had nothing to do with her death, no, but I might know of a way to resurrect her."

"Oh, Weena. Don't play with me."

"Trust me, Jim. But first of all we have to find that house. And Header. The Graf may be back in Flimsy by now, but I think that before he left, he somehow took control of Header."

So now we were back to gibberish. "So who is the Graf?" I dutifully asked. I wasn't quite ready to ponder what it might be like to bring back Val.

"The Graf is a flim who lives in Flimsy," answered Weena. "Like me. He's a friend of the yuels. And—I may not have mentioned this before—he was my lover. Besotted as I was, I shared the secret of my tunnel, and he pushed through before me, bribing the keeper as well. He planned to invade your world with yuels. More fool he."

"I have an idea about finding that trashed Victorian house," I said, thinking things over. "Probably Header and Ira and the girl go surfing every day. Maybe we could follow them home if we could find them around town. Or I guess we could check all the surf breaks. Or—how about this—can you do a telepathic search?"

"I can't promiscuously teep the whole county," protested Weena. "The lower my profile, the better I can ambush my foes."

"I've got it!" I exclaimed. "I'll just ask Chang. I've known him since high school. He knows everything about the surf scene. He was riding the pro circuit for awhile—but this summer he's giving lessons down at Cowell Beach near the pier."

"Capital!" said Weena, smiling at me. Her first rush from her sprinkles was wearing off, and she was more like her usual self. "We'll interview your friend, pass the day in idleness, and tonight, after my new jivas hatch—we act!" Weena shaded her eyes, glaring down the street at the enemy yuel.

The yuel squatted on the pavement, watching us with his shiny golden eyes. His gray tongue lolled over his thin lips. He almost looked friendly.

"Sea-lion-fucker!" yelled Weena. She'd been learning the modern style of speech.

"Does he understand what you're saying?" I asked. "Can I talk to him?"

"Don't squander the energy for this," said Weena dismissively. "Yuels are scum. They can talk, in a low, grunting fashion. All verbs.

And they use a kind of teep as well, via a low, gross channel that I can barely perceive. They exchange images, washes of emotion, and the like."

"I'm really getting curious about Flimsy," I admitted. "And you're saying that Val is over there?"

"Yes, yes. Let's hurry and find Chang!"

The sky had turned a bright cerulean shade. I tied my over-shirt around my waist and Weena threw her red coat over her shoulder. We walked to the pier. It wasn't all that far. We took side streets so there wouldn't be a lot of people getting excited about the yuel—who continued following us.

By the time we reached the ocean, the morning fog bank had retreated a few hundred yards off shore. The sky was luminous, like a stretched membrane. The surf muttered, endlessly chewing the shore. Shrieks and music drifted from the Boardwalk amusement park on the south side of the pier. I noticed an animal rescue van nearby—some rangers were herding sea lion cows into the sea, probably bringing them back from my house. The yuel, attracted by the cows' sexy barking, reconfigured himself as a bull, and slithered into the water for fresh conquests.

With Droog on his leash, Weena and I took the stairs down to Cowell Beach, a sandy crescent nestled at the base of the cliffs on the north side of the pier. The waves here marched to shore in regular lines, each of them straight and well-formed, none of them very big. It was a perfect spot to learn surfing. And there, at the far end of the beach was a shed surrounded by surfboards sticking up from the sand, the shed bearing a red-on-yellow sign declaiming, "SURF HERE NOW."

I found Chang talking to a pale young couple who looked to be honeymooners from the heartland. Raptly they listened to him. Chang had grown into a handsome man: tall, with bleached hair, prominent cheekbones, Genghis Khan eyes, and a laid-back way of talking. While I was starting to look maybe a little middle-aged, Chang still resembled a twenty-year-old. It was like he'd been preserved by the sea and sun.

He was telling his clients to start by catching some waves while lying flat on their stomachs on the boards, and then to try it kneeling. He said he'd paddle out and help them when it was time for them to stand.

"We're all waves," he concluded, gesturing at the sea. "And these humpers are your friends."

The honeymooners lugged their long, soft beginner-boards into the water. Chang glanced over at me. "Hey, Jim."

"Hi, Chang. This is my friend Weena. It's nice to see the master teach."

Chang shrugged. "Tubes for goobs. Seems like I've gotten too freestyle to win any contests these days. So here I am, grubbin' it. You're still a mailman?"

"A little bit. I was in the hospital this week."

Chang shook his head. "On top of losing Val last year? Too harsh, man."

The sympathy put a lump in my throat. Weena took the opportunity to pipe up. "We're on a quest for three surfers."

Chang considered her as if noticing her for the first time. "Why?"

"Header, Ira and this new girl," I said, regaining my voice. "I want to talk to them. They live in a crumbling old Victorian house somewhere downtown. I think it's on Yucca Street. But—"

"The Whipped Vic crew!" said Chang. "Sure I know them. Header, Ira, Ginnie—and don't forget Skeeves. I hear they're having a party today." He chuckled. "Their house is curiously difficult to find."

"Please lead us there," said Weena.

"I don't see the Whipped Vic as your kind of scene," said Chang, not liking Weena's looks.

"I, uh, lost something at that house," I said. "I need to get it back."

"What's with you, Jim?" asked Chang. "Is your woman friend a cop?"

"I'm a fallen woman," said Weena in a low, throaty tone. "A vamp. Just ask Jim."

Chang gave me a worried look. "You're this hard up, man?"

"It's all very freaky," I told him, unable to keep holding everything back. "Weena here—she's the mummy that Skeeves is always fucking."

"No doubt!" said Chang, breaking into wild laughter. He totally didn't believe me. "Same old Jim. What the hell, I'll bring you guys to the Whipped Vic party, sure. It might piss off Header. But that'll make me glad."

"I appreciate this," I said.

"Bro!" said Chang. "Remember the time you took me to that Wiggler Labs picnic and you fed them all that gnarly eel?"

"Well, I already knew they were going to fire me," I said, a little embarrassed.

"You were so frikkin' ripped," mused Chang. "It was beautiful. And then you started hassling me for more pot in front of everyone."

"I've matured," I said.

"Me too," said Chang. "It sucks."

A wail from the water distracted him. His woman student had lost control of her board, which was bobbing to shore.

"I gotta do my thing," continued Chang. "Meet me at the Perg coffee shop around seven-thirty, and we'll catch the Whipped Vic crew there. They always hit the Perg after they ride. Ginnie's a serious coffee hound."

"Should I bring a salmon for the party?"

"Nah, don't bother, of course not. Bring a bottle of tequila. That'll help with Header. He'll be trippin' about me hooking him up with Jim and—*the mummy!*"

8: The Boardwalk

So that left Weena and me with a long afternoon to kill. Going back to my house didn't seem like a good idea, what with the excitement about the sea lions, and with Diane Simly wanting to evict us.

"What are those immense machines?" asked Weena, pointing at the bright structures of Boardwalk. "Is it a, a fish-cannery?"

"Oh, come on, Weena," I said. "It's an amusement park." She looked doubtful. "I'll tell you what," I continued. "I'll take you on some rides."

"Amusement park," echoed Weena, thinking this through. "Of course. I rode on a Ferris wheel as a girl. And I've frequented Funger Gardens in Flimsy. But this one—so very many machines." Another pause. "How clanking and inhumane our Earth has become."

"You say there's an amusement park in Flimsy too?" I asked, wanting to lighten things up. We were headed along the oceanfront, Droog still on his leash. I still didn't really understand what or where Flimsy was—or why Weena seemed so unfamiliar with the modern world.

"But in Flimsy there's no machines at all," she said. "No bustling assemblages of clamps and screws and wires and paint and rust. We use zickzack and kessence instead. Have I told you this?"

"You've hardly told me anything, Weena. What are kessence

and zickzack?"

"Kessence is like aether. A subtle substance, a higher energy. Zickzack is more complicated. The jivas construct things from it. Zickzack is akin to—to hyperdimensional origami. Zickzack is a piece of space that's been folded or stretched or glued." Her hands moved rapidly, molding a shape in the air. "For example—take a slab of space and attach the inside to the outside in a certain way. And then anything that tries to pass through the slab bumps into itself coming back out—and it has to stop. In this fashion one makes a zickzack wall."

"Hold on—I don't get how the jivas can just start bending and gluing space."

"The jivas and the yuels of Flimsy see the world as if it were a bolt of cloth. They think in higher dimensions. A jiva can reach into the mural that is our cosmos and reconnect the zones."

I mulled this over as we continued walking. "Those zickzack walls—they can be any shape at all?"

"You see to the heart of the matter, Jim. A wall can be a tube, a block, a strut. My skeleton is enhanced with zickzack braces, and my muscles are strengthened by zickzack bands. Many of the clothes in Flimsy are zickzack as well. By use of diffraction gratings, the jivas can make zickzack of any color. Folded space is a universal construction material."

"What—what about a lightbulb?" I blindly challenged. "Where do your lamps get their juice?"

"In Flimsy, a lightbulb is a ball with its outside connected to the inside of a ball that stays near a glowing local sun," said Weena, proud of her experience.

"All right," I said, pondering the image. But, as usual, I had to wonder if she was putting me on.

By now we were at the Boardwalk entrance. A sunburned woman and her husband were staring suspiciously at us, overhearing our odd conversation.

"How about if I buy us some tickets for the rides?" I asked Weena. "How many do you want to try?"

"All of them?" said Weena, with a smile. "We have considerable time. But I must confess that I brought no money. I expected we'd proceed directly to the Victorian house, and thence to Flimsy."

I hesitated, remembering the slim contents of my wallet. But, hey, if I was about to leave this world, there was no harm in running up my credit card. I got us all-day passes.

Dogs weren't really allowed around the rides, so I walked down the stairs from the midway to the beach and settled Droog in a shady spot with a paper cup of water. I attached his leash to the steps so no meddlers would assume he was a stray although, really, I could have left him unleashed and he would have waited perfectly well.

Weena and I started with a ride that appeared fairly tame—it was a plastic pirate ship that swung from a tower like a giant swing. I didn't remember ever having gone on this particular ride but, come to think of it, I hadn't been on any of the Boardwalk rides for fifteen years.

"Can you handle this?" I asked Weena.

"I'm an adventuress," she said as we walked up the gangplank together. "My lover Charles and I were on wilder rides at Funger Gardens in Flimsy. I recall a ride that turns people upside-down. That is, a chute loops around and dumps you into a pavilion whose space has been flipped over. The pavilion is open all around, and the sky is up and the dirt is down because of a space-gluing. So it appears as if you're falling towards the ceiling. And a hysterical voice warns that if you touch the ceiling, you'll explode."

"Whose voice?"

"It's the pavilion talking. Pretty much everything in Flimsy is a little bit alive. In fact Flimsy herself is a living organism."

"How big is Flimsy, anyway?"

"She's larger than the universe—and smaller than what you call an electron. That baffles you, no? The world is a mystery." We settled into our seats, and tight bars swung down over our laps.

The cool ocean breeze blew across us; the mist was drifting away. I was happy to be on a ride with a sexy, offbeat girlfriend. For now I'd stopped thinking about Val. Maybe everything Weena said was bullshit, but at least I was alive. "Is there more to the story about the upside-down ride?" I asked.

"Oh yes!" exclaimed Weena. "On my first time through it, an enormous fat man above me really *did* explode—his scraps scattered all over the pavilion. Of course then Charles told me that the exploding fat man was only a fake, grown by the yuels running Funger Gardens, similar to a soap bubble, and that the man explodes hundreds of times a day. So!"

The horizon tilted weirdly as the ship swept expansively to and fro. Belatedly it occurred to me that going on the Boardwalk rides might not be a great idea for someone who'd just been in the hospital with a brain problem. But with Weena laughing at my side, I set aside my cares.

We went on a few more rides, then we hit the snack bar. We ordered fried squid, fried artichoke hearts, a hot dog, and a couple of beers—and carried them down to the beach where Droog was waiting. We fed him the hot dog.

After our own meal, Weena and I lay there cuddling, staring at the wrinkled sea and the ultramarine sky. We even napped for an hour. I was facing more kinds of doom than I could keep track of, but somehow this afternoon I felt mellower than I had in a long time.

"Thanks for all this," I told Weena. We were awake now, watching the sinking sun and petting Droog.

"Would you like a demonstration of zickzack?" asked Weena.

"Sure. Make us some beach chairs. You know, low chairs with no legs."

"I can do that," said Weena.

She flexed her fingers and gestured in midair. Tendrils nearly too fine to see crept from her fingertips. The air shimmered and glinted as something took shape upon the sand. I saw mirrored tubes, connected by glittering panels like fabric. Weena squinted and muttered to herself. The panels took on colors, candy apple red and cadmium yellow.

And now our beach chairs were done.

Gingerly I touched the red chair. The material was smooth, with the soft feel of—a fingertip. It was as if my own hand were pressing back at me. My mind was thoroughly boggled.

"Sit!" said Weena, flopping down.

We sat together for a while, letting the time slide by. I was very comfortable. Soon it was nearly seven o'clock. We had a half hour till our meet with Chang.

The sun was still slanting across the waters, but the Boardwalk's colored lights were coming on. I had a sense of exhilaration, as at the beginning of a great adventure.

"Before you got here, I thought my life was over," I told Weena.

"You're exactly the right person to be our cosmic postman," she said warmly. "A hero who's ready to battle with complete abandon! And I won't forget your quest for your lady fair."

"Too bad that yuel scares the shit out of me."

"You are modest," said Weena. "That's heroic, as well." As always, her eyes were unreadable. "Is it time to meet the others?"

"We have time for one more ride," I said, pointing up towards the Boardwalk. "How about the Big Dipper?"

"That clickity-clack lattice of wooden beams and rusty rails?"

"The Boardwalk's fabled roller coaster, yes," I said.

I herded the doubtful Weena into the very first little car of the Big Dipper's little train. The cars rushed through a darkened arch, then up the wooden hill, higher and higher above the beach. The streaming air was damp and salty, the colors rich in the setting summer sun, the sounds a mesh of screams and rattles and carnival music and breaking waves. It was wonderful.

But now we inched around a U-turn and faced the drop, far steeper than I'd remembered. We shot down, then up, then down, then up and around another turn. Weena looked ill, she was clutching both hands against her stomach.

Two more bumps and she collapsed against me, retching into my lap. Amid the partly digested food was a gently glowing object shaped like a pitty-pat squash—a flattened orb with a ruffle around its girth. It was hard to imagine how something this big had squeezed out of Weena's mouth. The thing had alternating stripes, and a long tail trailed from its base.

"My jiva," moaned Weena. "She popped out. I shouldn't have eaten all that fried squid." She retched again. "What nasty food you people eat." Her face was pale and lined.

The jiva stirred in my lap, swelling a bit larger, taking on fresh colors as the sunlight played across her. She canted this way and that, as if examining her surroundings—not that she had any visible eyes. With a few gentle motions of her supple tail, the jiva vacuumed Weena's vomit off my legs. The tail was covered with fine hairs, like a radish root—and now I recalled that Weena had shown me the tip of it sticking from her navel yesterday. She'd called it an ovipositor.

"Don't let that thing put eggs in me!" I yelled, shoving the jiva into the Weena's lap.

"This is my dear Awnee," said Weena, feebly petting the jiva. Without the jiva, Weena looked shockingly old. "Don't hurt Awnee's feelings. She can be dangerous. You should have left my zickzack rejuvenation props in place, Awnee. Please come back inside." Weena leaned over the jiva, opening her wrinkled lips.

Stubbornly the jiva wrapped her tail around my leg. I felt a telepathic connection with the creature, and for a moment I saw as if through her mind. The amusement park was a foreshortened construct of planes, like a cardboard model. I could pick up a sense of Awnee's emotions as well. She didn't like our alien world. She felt miffed and peevish.

Right then we swung through a final neck-wrenching turn. The cars were clattering back towards the loading platform. As we coasted to a stop, the jiva unwound from my leg, twisted free of Weena's grasp and floated into the darkening sky like a child's escaped balloon.

Weena hobbled down the stairs and into the open space of the Boardwalk midway. Looking bereft, she stared after her lost jiva, who was drifting inland over Santa Cruz. "Oh, Jim," she quavered. "I'm crushed. I can't teep properly without Awnee. And—" She gestured at her wasted body. "Don't look at me. That spiteful Awnee. Jivas can be so cruel."

"Maybe—maybe Awnee is looking for her children," I said, trying to comfort Weena. "Didn't you say they'd hatch today?"

"Well, yes, that's a good possibility," said Weena, brightening a bit. "Of course. She'll return after I call forth the three new jivas. Dear, dear Awnee. She's never let me down. We've been together for about a century—ever since I found my way from Earth to Flimsy."

That gave me pause. All week I'd been gloating about my hot new girlfriend. And now—oh, this was impossible.

"What?" said Weena, seeing some of my feelings in my eyes.

"So how old are you, really?"

"Oh, I suppose one might call it a hundred and thirty or so. But it's impolite to ask a woman her age." A dry cackle.

"Um—are you still up to meeting the Whipped Vic crew?"

"Indeed," said Weena. "But I require your aid. I seem to have some rheumatism in my hips. Awnee had been padding my joints with zickzack." He voice took on an aggrieved, whining tone. "It would have been quite simple for Awnee to leave her patches in place. But she likes to teach me a lesson. It's insufferable. I'm very close to the Duke of Human Flimsy, you know, and my lover Charles is the court Wizard, and I'm helping Charles with his monumental Atum's Lotus project, and—"

I quieted her down, trying to carry on as before. It was so weird to have my new woman friend turn incredibly old. And a little pathetic to hear her bragging about her supposed status in some possibly imaginary world.

"Let's go buy that bottle of tequila for that surfer dude Header," I suggested as we inched our way out of the midway. "Before we meet them at the Perg."

"One request," quavered Weena. "Don't tell these young people any of our secret plans. Let my enemies puzzle about my next step. It's a game of nerves."

"Fine." Not that there was much I could tell. Weena's ever-changing stories were a confused jumble in my mind.

9: The Whipped Vic Crew

The Perg coffee shop was a warped old house with a worn wooden deck and thickets of coarse, overgrown plants. It was a hip, funky place, and I often came here. Chang and the Whipped Vic crew were sitting at a table, lit by the late-setting summer sun. Droog followed us onto the deck and settled under their table.

"Jim Oster!" drawled Chang. "And—it's Weena, right? Whoah, what happened to you?"

"I'll be fine in a bit," said Weena, collapsing into a chair. "We went on those boardwalk rides."

"These are my surf-rat friends," Chang told her. "Header, Ira, and Ginnie." Chang and Header were drinking pints of draft beer, the other two were just slouched in their chairs.

I stepped forward as if to shake Header's hand. He just glared at me, overgrown bully that he was. He had a little crust of blood inside one of his nostrils. "Here," I said, waggling the bottle of tequila. "Peace, dude. Sorry I was poking around your yard."

"Apology accepted!" intoned Ira in his thin, ironic voice. He was a skinny, weak-chinned surfer in pencil-thin black jeans and high-top black basketball shoes. He never seemed to age.

Wordlessly, Header uncapped the tequila and took a snort. The planes of his handsome face glowed in the slanting light. He wiped his mouth, shot a spiteful glance at the ancient Weena, and stashed

61

the bottle beneath the table. Ira fished out the bottle and sniffed at it, but didn't put it to his lips.

"I hope this shit isn't from Weena?" he asked. "Or it might be poison. We already know about Weena, and—"

"I'm the one who bought the tequila," I interrupted, wanting credit. "Me."

"Are you a big stoner?" the new, dark-haired girl asked me pleasantly. Ginnie. "Were you tripping when you found our house?" She had warm brown eyes, slightly tilted. The eyes and her strong cheekbones gave her a slightly exotic look. Maybe she was Latina.

"I've always seen Jim as a dungeon master," said Ira, temporarily dropping his attack on Weena. "The geekiest player on his level. He even opened up our cellar door. That door won't let just anyone open it. It's fickle. What did you see in there, Jim?"

"A golden casket sitting on one side. And leathery slime. As if your whole basement were full of gray-green Silly Putty. And then a strand pulled the door closed."

"What about the blue sea lion?" asked Ginnie. "Did he come out of there? I keep seeing that sea lion out at our surf-break this week. He's always swimming near Header."

"You should realize that it's not a sea lion," said Weena, her voice thin and crackly. "That thing came to Jim's house this morning and shaped itself into a blue baboon." She fell silent and studied Header's reaction especially. Weena had a hard, appraising look in her age-dimmed eyes.

"Do you know what's going on?" I asked Header point-blank.

"I know everything," said Header. "The others don't know shit."

"Header's voice is the empty squeal of a bagpipe," said Chang.

Ira let out a shrill *deedle-deedle* sound and rose from his plastic chair to dance a jig.

"Fools," said Header, grimly grasping the neck of the tequila bottle. "I'm empowered to save your world from Weena's parasitic jivas, and you—"

"Header likes to imagine he's a visiting alien," interrupted Ginnie. "But if you want to talk about knowing stuff, *I'm* the one who found the Whipped Vic. Credit where credit is due. It happened this March. A big rainstorm, with the air like water. I'd hitchhiked into town, massively ripped on shrooms. I splashed down all these alleys—it was like a maze. And then I started hearing a man's voice whispering in my head. He had a monster-movie accent. He said was my friend, he was going to help me, he was going to show me a free place to live. He kept telling me which way to go. And then *boom*, a flash of lightning, and I'm walking up the sidewalk to this big old haunted house."

"Tell us the part where you open the round door," said Ira. "I love that. It's so mysterioso."

"It was still pouring rain," said Ginnie, running her fingers through her short, dark hair. "I wanted to go into the house, but it was dark and spooky. And that horror-flick voice was still talking to me. It told me to go around back and there'd be a door in the basement with a handprint shape. And that's how it was. The door was waiting for me. As soon as I touched it, it opened. But it was too dark to see any of the gooey stuff. All I saw was a sly-looking white guy who came out. He looked rich, old-timey, in a velvet cape. He had that same accent. It was his voice I'd been hearing in my head. He called himself the Graf. He said Graf means Count. Like Count Dracula. Not that he was a vampire. Not exactly. He kissed me on the mouth and—"

"Look we don't have to go over this again and again," protested Header. "Nobody cares."

"I care," said Weena intensely. "I'm extremely interested. What happened next, Ginnie dear?"

"Well—" said Ginnie. "My memory for that night is pretty screwed up. It breaks into these intense frames and then it goes blank. Right away, I realized that the Graf wasn't made of normal flesh. He was smooth and cool to the touch. I didn't like him, but I was in his thrall. He stole a car and took me for a ride. He made the tip of his finger change shape to be the car key. We got to Lover's Bluff, and he was kissing me a whole lot, like we were going to fuck. His skin was so cold. Someone opened the car door. And that's where my mind goes blank."

"Ginnie and I hooked up the next day," said Header. "At the Pleasure Point break. I couldn't keep her away from me."

"Something about Header obsesses me," mused Ginnie thoughtfully. "I haven't been able to fully analyze it. It's like I have a mental block. One thing—Header is one of the few people who even notices me anymore."

"What, in your opinion, became of the Graf?" Weena asked Ginnie.

"Well, he turned up dead the day after our tryst," said Ginnie. "I saw it in the paper. Some kind of weird murder?"

"Oh god, I remember that now," I said. "They found the remains in a stolen car. On Lover's Bluff, yeah. One person's body had been burned down to ashes. And wasn't there a murdered woman, too?"

"I only read to where they found the Graf's ashes," said Ginnie firmly. "In the very car that he'd stolen for our love nest. That's creepy enough."

"But, wait," I continued. "The ashes were weird. Not flesh. Like Ginnie said. But the woman they found—the woman was real. And she'd been killed by an axe."

Ginnie squeezed her eyes shut and shook her head in silence.

"It's classic how she keeps repressing her knowledge of how her story ends," said Ira in a low tone.

"Mister Psycho Shrink here," said Ginnie, abruptly opening her eyes. "Shut your pie hole."

"It's much cooler to die in a surfing accident," said Ira. His hair was a long black mop, with the beak of his white nose sticking out. "I almost went to college," he continued. "But then I got all hung-up on Skeeves. I could have been a guy with a head full of symbols. Brains to spare."

"That's why I like sculpting sounds with you," said Ginnie, turning casual again. "Did I tell you that I spirited away some contact mikes from that motor-mouthed guy at the music store? He's such a freak that he actually notices me."

"Work your charm, Ginnie," said Ira. "So now we can sample your tide-pool sounds for the party mix?"

"*Exactamente.*"

"Let's go home now," said Header, showing his teeth.

"And—Jim and Weena are coming to the party too," said Chang, also standing. He looked to be Header's physical equal. "My man Jim needs a night out."

"For sure," said Ira. "Maybe Jim can open the magic door again. If Weena has her way, Jim might be going through there pretty soon."

"Yes, bring Jim and Weena," said Ginnie, her voice as soft as velvet. "It'll shake things up. It's time for the next level." She ran her hand up Header's arm and smiled, as if cajoling him.

"I'll be glad to have them," said Header quietly. Perhaps he knew who Weena was—and he welcomed the chance to have it out.

"So we're all set," I said, wondering what I was getting myself into. "You guys have room in your van?"

"In back with the boards," said Ira. "Where the sarcophagus used to be."

"This is Skeeves's old van?" I exclaimed.

"Yeah," said Ira. "He signed it over to Header when he went underground. He was worried about some murder charges. Right, Weena?"

"You will suffer if you continue harassing me," Weena told Ira in a low tone.

"The two goobs have to buy us pizza," announced Header.

"Not a problem," I said.

"Ginnie, phone in an order so we won't have to wait," ordered Header. "Ten pies. One of each flavor."

"Ten?" exclaimed Ginnie. "Ira and I don't even eat."

"It's okay," I said. "I'll charge it. I don't care." More than ever, I believed that Weena was going to escort me to another world.

We walked to the van, Weena leaning on my arm, Droog at our heels. Weena smiled at Ira like a doting great-great-grandmother, turning on her charm. "It really is very nice to see you face to face," she said. "And I am sorry for whatever inconveniences you've had. What course of study might you have pursued, had you attended a university?"

"Physics," said Ira. "I never had the money to apply, or a high-school diploma, and I used to be really busy with the surfing—but lately I've been drifting into some cosmology lectures up the hill at the university. There's all this stuff about dark energy—it's like an invisible kind of matter. But I know it's real."

"Of course you do," said Weena. "Where I come from, in Flimsy, we call it kessence, as you may already know. A soul is but a speck of information, but with luck and effort, it gathers unto itself a kessence form."

Ira ran his bony fingers down his arms. "That's what I am these days. A kessence shadow of my former self."

"Yes," said Weena in a low tone. "And Ginnie is the same."

"How about finding the path to the Whipped Vic," I interrupted, still not quite understanding what Weena and Ira were talking about. "How does that work?"

"The trail changes from day to day," said Ginnie, about to order the pizza. "The house—or the giant snail that lives in the basement—changes the trail every so often. She's shy. But she likes me, and

I can always vibe her out. It's like I can find her inside my head. She doesn't like to be totally alone. She likes having a few of us parasites in her shell. And when there's a party, Ira texts the latest directions to our friends. It's great—the cops can never find us."

"Soon your snail's destiny will be fulfilled," said Weena softly.

"I love these enigmatic scenarios," said Ira. "Like we're in an alternate reality game. We'll move on to the next level, and—will there be a castle?"

"An enormous castle," said Weena reassuringly. "It's shaped like a geranium plant. My friend Charles and I are crafting some remarkable patterns of sound and shape there."

Ira opened the back door of the primer-patched panel van. It was rank in there, with weird symbols painted on the inner panels. Hieroglyphs. Skeeves's van for sure.

Weena and I squeezed in among the boards and the damp wetsuits. Droog scrambled in, and wormed around to find a comfortable spot.

Ginnie phoned in the pizza order while Header drove. They were heading for this one particular pizza shop that the surfers liked, a place called Ratt's. On the way Header made a point of cruising very slowly though the seaside parking lot called Lover's Bluff.

"Why do you always go by here, Header?" Ginnie demanded. "This is such a depressing place for me. This is where the Graf got burned."

"I like to see who's humping who," said Header robotically. "I come here with my bro Skeeves. We're tracking the decline of our generation's purity. The Graf wasn't the only one due for a hard lesson."

"And Skeeves lives with you guys right now?" I asked. "In the Whipped Vic? With his golden sarcophagus in your basement?"

"The mysteries of Skeeves," said Ira, not directly answering my questions. "He hears voices in his head, and some of us pay a stiff price. Right, Weena?"

Ira lit up a joint and passed it around, which was fine with me, although it seemed unfamiliar to Weena. I'd never gotten around to offering her any while she'd been at my house.

"One inhales this smoke?" she asked me, studying the fuming spliff. She looked fully a hundred and thirty years old.

"Hush," I whispered. "Try to act cool."

Weena took a toke and had a spasmodic coughing fit that filled the others with glee.

"Can you buy us a keg of beer?" asked Header as he let us out of the van behind Ratt's. "As long as you're gonna be our guest. The corner market over there has import brands. We'll have to buy some cups, too." He was testing how hard he could push me.

"I'm easy," I said, letting Droog out of the van too. "Let's go over to the market and run my card. And then we'll get the pizza. Weena, why don't you just rest in the van."

For the first time, Header smiled at me. Night had fallen. We were standing in a trapezoidal puddle of light from the pizza shop's back door, the cooks in white hats visible within. Standing in the pizza glow, I felt that everything was going to be okay. I was a mythic hero, reckless in the face of danger, joyfully abandoned to my fate, and righteously buzzed.

We scored a keg of Czechvar beer—and Header picked up a little bag of powder from the grotty clerk too, some kind of hard drug. They charged it on my card as if it were a second keg of beer. I was past caring.

And then we got the pies, piled into the van and drove downtown, sharing another joint. Droog was excited about the pizza—he kept sniffing the boxes and giving me imploring looks.

When we hit Pacific Avenue, Ginnie began issuing instructions—which Ira dutifully keyed into his cell phone, compiling today's route for the expected party crowd.

"Left here," intoned Ginnie. "Down that alley to the right, a left here and..."

Now and then she'd pause, holding her lovely face still—as if basking in the light of a hidden sun. During one of these pauses, I heard a scratching on the van's windowless back door, and Droog stiffened, alert for a fight.

"The yuel," Weena breathed into my ear. "Be prepared when we exit. Don't allow him to seize me."

"...go two blocks and then do a U-turn," Ginnie was saying. "Back up through that alley in reverse. Yes, reverse. And now, okay, straighten out and drive towards town. One more left and—home sweet home."

"I'm messaging the directions right now," said Ira. The van pulled to a halt.

"Come back here and open our door, Header," I said. "The pizza's getting cold."

"You just want me to be the first out of the van," said Header looking back at us with a mirthless smile. "Because of the yuel." So far as I knew, nobody had directly mentioned that word to Header yet.

Actually, I didn't see the yuel until we were all out of the van. Header and Ira were trundling the keg up the walkway to the porch steps. Weena and I were behind them, me helping Weena with one arm and carrying half the pizzas with the other. Ginnie had run ahead with the other pizzas to make some light in the house. A faint noise made me glance back at the driveway.

Sure enough, the alien blue baboon was perched on the van's roof. The yuel. His golden eyes glowed in the gloom.

In that moment, I heard the yuel's voice in my head, a smooth and oily sound. "Nurture bloom grow," he said. "Kill wallow leech." Whatever that meant.

"Be gone!" said Weena out loud, trying to make her frail voice sound authoritative. The yuel ignored her. Droog put his paws up against the side of the van and began barking like crazy.

Baring his teeth, the yuel hopped off the van, capered down the driveway and scrambled up the trunk of a eucalyptus tree. I could hear him rustling up there. Ira and Header didn't seem to notice him—being absorbed in humping the keg up the stairs.

"I don't know about trying for Flimsy just yet," I murmured to Weena, propping the pizzas against my side. "You'd better get back your jiva before I try opening that door again. What with the yuel watching us."

"Quite right," whispered Weena. "In a few hours my baby jivas will be grown. I'll summon them and they'll handily eliminate this yuel. Meanwhile, let us savor the degenerate revel of the surf folk."

"Come on in, dorks," yelled Header from the porch. "We want the rest of those pies!" A geyser of foam shot from the keg as he and Ira tapped it.

Glancing around the neighborhood, I noticed that, once again, the nearby houses were but faintly visible—as if seen at a distance, or through a mirror maze of many turns. The sounds of the town were attenuated as well. I was on my own here.

10: Surf Party

I escorted Weena inside and set my pizza boxes on a plastic table in the front room. The very image of alertness, Droog stared raptly at the table. Ginnie had lit the place with candles. For a heartbeat, our eyes locked. In the candlelight, Ginnie's eyes seemed to glow. Quite enchanting.

"Our house doesn't have any wiring," said Ginnie, looking away. "But we do have running water. Very sweet and clear. And there's a gasoline-powered generator we'll start up pretty soon." She flipped open one of the boxes. "Oh, this is Ratt's veggie Hawaiian, with fresh pineapple, smoked tofu, locally made mozzarella, and coconut shreds on top!" She tore off a drippy slice and offered it to me.

"You eat some, Ginnie," I urged.

"Actually—I haven't been eating since I moved in here," she said, looking abashed. "Everything's so—never mind."

I had the slice, and then another. Great, great stuff, the hot, greasy flavors burrowing deep into the crevices of my tongue. Ira wasn't hungry either. I found a sausage pizza in the next box down, gave a slice to Droog, and had a slice of that myself. By now, Header and Weena were feeding too, washing it down with plastic cups of beer. Gut joy.

I looked around the room, littered with cans, bottles, and junkfood wrappers. The house's pipes seemed to leak, making slick moldy spots on the walls and floors. Some of the wall material had crumbled away. The smooth, dark ribs of the structure's frame looked more like mother-of-pearl than like bone—which jibed with Ira and Weena's hints that this house was in fact the shell of an alien snail.

Ira went out the back deck for a minute. With a cough and roar, the gasoline-powered generator sprang to life, ten times louder than I would have imagined possible. Orange extension cords ran from the generator to work-lights hanging here and there in the house.

"Come see my tide pool," said Ginnie, leading me and the decrepit Weena into the next room—which smelled like the beach, in a good way. She'd set a claw-foot bathtub by one wall, with water dripping into it through a flaky home-made salination system—an orange crate stuffed with beach sand wrapped in ragged clothes. The tub's steady overflow drained through a pucker-shaped hole in the floor.

Plants grew in the tub water, keeping it fresh. Fat, chunky sea anemones waved their purple-green tendrils. Tiny crabs scuttled, whelks poked along, and ripples criss-crossed the surface from unseen creatures darting among the plants.

"A tiny world," said Weena. "Clever indeed."

"I'm their god," said Ginnie. She picked up a carton of Friskees cat-food and scattered kibble into the tub. "Feast, my pretties!"

Abruptly the surface teemed with hungry translucent tubes sporting dark eyes and bursts of tentacles.

"Squid?" I asked.

"Yeah," said Ginnie. "Plain old calamari. Easy to raise. Supposedly they talk by changing the colors of their skin. Sometimes I can almost understand them."

"And now we'll hear their voices," said Ira, hunched over the tub. "*Eeek!*" He'd gotten hold of Ginnie's contact microphones, and he was busily affixing them to the slanting inner walls of the tub—all the while pretending that the squid were biting him.

He ran wires from the mikes to a sound-card jacked into a grungy old laptop sitting on a table by the tub. Tinkling runs of squid squeaks chimed from the room's large speakers, offset by oozing anemone burbles and the percussive clicks of the crabs. Ira swept his fingers across a digital drawing pad, creating guitar ostinatos that looped into aural eddies.

"Louder!" yelled Ginnie working the laptop's mouse and keys.

"Thicker!" And now she found the sweet spot, a resonant mode that made the room reverberate like the bones of a psycho punker frying in an electric chair.

"We gotta take this public," said Ira. "Our sound is so deeply sick."

"Maybe bring the generator to your concerts," I remarked. "That heavy roar."

"And we could get our bass line by sampling the wind," said Ginnie. "We'd be playing beach parties, I think."

Ira plucked a pair of live squid from Ginnie's tide-pool and popped them into his mouth, thrashing his head back and forth with the tentacles showing. The frightened squid voided their ink sacks, turning Ira's mouth and lips a goth black, a perfect accent to his grunge-fop look.

"I used to play the flute in band," I said. "When I was in junior high. I never got very good at it—but maybe I could play with you guys too."

"Screechy squeaks," said Ginnie. "Why not? The uglier the better."

Footsteps sounded on the porch. The guests were arriving, one freaky weirdo after the next, materializing from the warped space-maze that surrounded the lot. The guests were pale, awkward, shadowy, with a very few normal humans in the bunch. I knew a couple of them besides Chang. I talked to a very pretty little woman for a few minutes at the pizza table—I was greedily trying to sample a slice from each of the ten boxes. But soon Header swept the woman into his orbit.

The next couple of hours went by at an accelerating rate. Feeling somewhat shy and out of place, I drank rather more than usual. Not all of the guests were drinking beer—some of them had brought along a punchbowl filled with a fuming spicy fluid that seemed like a dense gas. Echoing a word that Weena had used, Ira said the stuff was called kessence. The wispier and less talkative guests clustered around the kessence punch bowl, dipping their hands and even their faces into it. I tried a little, but it didn't do much for me.

By now Chang had gone. Weena was out of sight, and Header was busy with some friends at the other end of the big the room snorting powder off the back of his hand. Ginnie and Ira were into their noise-music thing, off in the other room, and lot of the others were in with them.

A creepy guy came down the stairs, heading for the pizza. He was tall and lanky, with his head constantly in motion. His tufty hair looked like he'd trimmed it with nail scissors.

"Skeeves!" I exclaimed. "I saw your gold coffin in basement." I'd thought the other guests might be surprised to see Skeeves as well, but I guess everyone but me had already known he was living here.

The gnarled old surfer cocked his head, studying me. "Jim Oster. The man who made the hole."

"Tell me the whole story," I said.

"You scratched a leak into an electron with the tip that Ira gave you. The other world is inside the electron, you dig."

"An electron's a cloud," I objected. "A probability wave. Not a hollow ball. I already heard this line of bullshit from Weena."

Skeeves cracked a faint smile. "Ah yes, Weena. She's up in my room right now. She's hot, huh? Even though she's old."

"I've been living with her all week." I said shortly. It was disgusting to think I was sharing a woman with Skeeves.

"She's even better when she's not in a coma," said Skeeves. He showed his teeth in an crooked grin and recited a limerick. "*Skeeves was a surf-monster man / With a comatose chick in his van. / They said shrink his head, she's practically dead! / He said 'I just wish she was tan.'* That last line needs work, doesn't it? Maybe you can help me with it, Jim. You're supposed to be so smart and everything."

"How did Weena get back into her body?"

"She was manipulating me from the other side. I heard her like a voice in my head. She set up Ira's tip for you, and she sent me to your house to take the charred sample with the special electron that you'd poked. By then the electron had healed over a little bit, but it still had a weak spot. I put your sample right next to Weena's sarcophagus in my van, and her soul found this giant snail to push out through the electron that you'd nicked."

"It's not one *particular* electron?" I asked. "But Weena said—"

"The other world is inside *every* electron, yes," said Skeeves. "You go inside any electron, you're in the same place. Heaven is everywhere. It's a hall of mirrors." But over on this side, only the one electron has a nick. Thanks to you, fuckhead." He laid his bony finger along the side of his nose and winked. "I'm a sage."

"And what about the thing that came through to kill Val, asshole?"

"Go to hell," said Skeeves, pushing me aside. "I want pizza. And some of Header's vitamin dust. And I want to hang with my boy Ira." He grabbed a slice and went off to the other end the room.

Wondering about Weena, I went upstairs to poke around. In the first room, I found the messy mattress where Header and Ginnie slept—I could see Ginnie's underwear and an overblown poster for a Metallica videogame that had to belong to Header.

Next door was a smaller room that was Ira's, with some library physics books scattered around. He'd drawn a bunch of occult patterns on the wall with magic marker, poor guy. I glanced out the window overlooking the back yard. Droog was sleeping down there, staying out of trouble. Fine.

The weird thing about Ira's room was that it had a miniature staircase in the corner that only went about half a floor down. That is, instead of going down to the kitchen, these little stairs went to an in-between room with a ceiling about three feet high. And I could glimpse a door to still smaller room beyond that. Just like—the chambers of a snail shell.

"Hello?" I called, crouching by the little staircase. No answer.

I took one of the work lights on orange cords and wormed headfirst down the little stairs, trying to see down the sequence of rooms. Skeeves's hide-out would be in there. But I couldn't squeeze in far enough to see Weena. Maybe the border snail had a way of shrinking Skeeves and his companions when they wanted to work their way in. Why not? Snaily was able to surround herself with a maze of space warps. She could do all kinds of things.

My hand was shaking, and the lights and shadows swayed back and forth. I could see a third room down around the doll-house corridors, and maybe a fourth. Something tiny was moving down there, like an ant on two legs. A little woman. The figure lurched this way and that, hiding herself in bits of shadow. She grew recognizable as she approached. It was Weena.

"Spying on me?" she said, her voice small and cracked. "Make way."

I scooted back out of the little staircase leading down from Ira's room. Sighing and muttering with the effort, Weena hauled herself up the stairs.

"I can't believe you'd let Skeeves—" I began.

"He's useful," said Weena. She regarded me with something of the old sparkle in her bleary eyes. "You're jealous, aren't you? How sweet. Help me back down to the party, and I'll see that Skeeves gets thrown out for the night."

I should mention that the surfers' marijuana was really strong, and they'd been passing around hard drugs pretty freely as well. On our way downstairs, I began getting an unpleasant effect akin to what audio buffs call "clipping." That is my sensations and thoughts were so radically spiked away from the norm that my cautious reptilian brain stem was cutting off the tops of the peaks to leave featureless mesas.

Ira's and Ginnie's mix of aquatic sounds, music samples and synth raged on. Tottery though Weena was, she prevailed on me to dance with her for awhile. But by now I didn't really like touching her.

Soon Weena twisted away and got into sharing her wriggly colored sprinkles with Header and Skeeves. They went after the stuff as if it were premium coke. After Header had his second round, Weena abruptly cut Skeeves off.

"No more for you," she told Skeeves, choosing her words for maximum impact. "You're a demented pervert. I don't want you here. A live woman has no use for you. I'll spend the night with Jim. Or perhaps with Header."

Instantly the tall, tormented Skeeves was in Weena's face, and it was only moments till the argument expanded to include Header, who stepped forward to give Skeeves a rough shove.

"You're a zombie, Header!" hollered Skeeves, windmilling his arms to keep his balance. "You've got an alien slug instead of a brain! I never should have kept you on."

Header took a step forward and punched Skeeves in the stomach so hard that skinny freak collapsed.

"Give him his comeuppance, Header!" said Weena, like a rabid floozy at some old-style barroom fight. "Remove him from the premises!"

Ira was in the mix now too, shrilling insults at Header, trying to keep the beefy surfer away from Skeeves. Header brushed Ira aside and hoisted Skeeves onto his shoulders. He lumbered onto the porch, down the stairs, and out to the point where the street faded into a spatial maze. Humping his thick torso, Header tossed Skeeves into the invisible zone.

"Hurrah!" called spindly old Weena, watching from the porch.

"Good show."

"I'm bringing him back in here later on, you bitches!" yelled Ira. "Skeeves lives here too!"

Back in the house, Weena gave Header more sprinkles. He got into an intense low-voiced conversation with her, all the while keeping one arm around the petite Marcy. Judging from Header's body language, he wanted something more than drugs or sex from Weena. For her part, Weena seemed to be temporizing, leading him on, all the while plying him with her pixie dust.

My sense of time broke into streaks and patches. At some point, I found myself on the back deck, leaning over the railing, wondering if I was going to puke—and then not wondering, just doing it, as naturally as a dog.

Weena appeared at my side, still looking well over a century old. With my consciousness slowly coming back, I observed that all the guests were gone—and that the fuzzed borders of the space-maze were starting to glow. Dawn. I'd missed out on the last couple of hours.

"I have grave news," Weena told me.

"Careful where you step," I said. "There's vomit on the deck."

Weena waved off this information. "Now I must kill the Graf's agent," she whispered, leaning very close. "Header. This is a key aspect of my mission."

Something suddenly came clear to me. "When the Graf was murdered in that car—you sent Skeeves to do it, didn't you, Weena?"

"I did what was necessary," she said.

"But why mess with Header now?"

"There is a link," said Weena stubbornly. "How else could Header have unleashed a yuel? Header knows who I am. He was pleading for a pardon tonight, and tendering offers. But I'm not to be swayed."

Hearing a clunk on the deck floor beside me, I glanced down.

"You have an axe?" The appearance of this unlikely weapon set off a firestorm of images and emotions in my weary mind. The axe's handle was painted green.

"I found it in Header's closet," said spindly Weena. "Do you know how to use an axe?"

"*You* use the axe," I said. "This is your crazy idea. Not that killing Header is necessarily a bad thing to do." Saying this, I giggled. I was still fairly high. Yes, Weena was holding the green-handled axe that

Skeeves had threatened me with in high school. "Ask Skeeves to do it for you," I said. "Your old boyfriend."

"You know that Skeeves is gone," was all that Weena said. "And you're barely in any shape to help me at all. A fine state for my cosmic mailman."

"Is, uh, Header teeping this conversation?"

"No. Header is a weak fool. He reeled upstairs in a stupor. And now he slumbers."

"Ginnie must be upset," I said. Weird music was drifting from the house—Ira and Ginnie were still jamming.

"Oh, now you're after Ginnie instead of me?" said Weena with sudden spite. "And what about your wife? Never mind. The salient fact is that my deadly enemy's guard is down. I'll restore my strength, and I'll do what's necessary. And then, Jim, then you'll open that round cellar door so we can escape."

"What about that, that—" I gestured at the shaggy eucalyptus trees that beetled over the yard. In my wasted state, I'd forgotten what Weena called the blue baboon thing. But sure enough, I could glimpse the faint glint of his yellow eyes.

"Yes, yes, the yuel," said Weena. "We'll eliminate him first, and then Header. All the Graf's Earthly influences must be annihilated. The Graf is the enemy of the jivas and of the Duke. He took advantage of the confidences I shared with him. He sought to thwart our plan." She gave me a stern look. "I don't look kindly on faithless lovers."

"Whatever you say," I said, beginning to wonder how I could get out of here.

Weena stretched high her arms and whistled, far and wee.

11 : The Jivas

Cued by Weena's call, intense cries and yelps erupted a block or two away, the sounds muffled by the spatial labyrinths. I recognized, in particular, the agitated and angry tone of Diane Simly, her voice growing in a crescendo. I grinned, coldly imagining her husband's fate—then felt guilty. Sure, the Simlys were jerks, but—

Lights appeared in the sky, blurred and warped by multiple reflections. But they were feeling their way closer to us, and soon their forms became clear. They resembled illuminated flying turnips with dangling tails. And now they were hovering over the Whipped Vic's back yard, four of them, their luminous tendrils brushing the trees. The uncanny jivas were quite beautiful. Each of them had a particular pattern of spots and stripes, a bit like children's tops.

The biggest jiva—Weena's partner, Awnee—had refined her look since I'd last seen her. Awnee was now a warm shade of reddish-yellow with three embossed blue bands like necklaces around her tail. She bore a mauve zigzag stripe around her waist, with six pale blue gems set above that, each gem centered in a splashy burst of color. She'd added something like a hat on top—a flat green disk with a golden knob. Her two children were equally elaborate, each in a different way.

The yuel gibbered his defiance at the jivas, something like, "Sing, fight, die." He leapt heavily to the ground and his eyes locked onto

Weena. Showing his teeth, he charged across the lawn, and then leapt up to the deck's railing.

The rush of events had me off balance. I had no idea how to fight the yuel. Fortunately the jivas entered the fray. Their vine-like tails lashed through the air, and wrapped the yuel around his middle, squeezing him tight.

But the yuel had another card to play. He began singing an eerie little tune, a song of almost unbearable sweetness. It seemed to get into my head and vibrate my sinuses—the sensation was somehow unbearable. The jivas were even more affected by the ghostly sound—they dropped the yuel and backed away.

The yuel might have won the day, but now Weena stepped in. Straining her spindly old arms to the utmost, she raised high her green-handled axe and slammed the butt-end of it against the yuel's baboon head, stunning him into silence.

The three jivas seized the opportunity. Within moments, the fine hairs of their branched tails were sinking deep and deeper into the yuel's blue flesh, dissolving him with a burbling hiss and a smell like ammonia.

The yuel's tune was still echoing in my head, like a particularly viral advertising jingle. "What was that creepy song ?" I asked Weena.

"We call it a yuel lullaby," she answered. "It's the yuels' preferred defense against jivas. A certain type of song."

"Grim and grimmer," said Ira, now standing on the back porch. He and Gina had drifted out to join us.

"I just hope those fighting things aren't devils and angels," said Ginnie. "I never liked the religion trip."

"The four flying turnips are jivas," said old Weena. "They're a part of Flimsy—some people say they're Flimsy's brain cells. And the yuels—they're a part of Flimsy as well, playing an obscure but vital part in Flimsy's metabolism. Don't trust the yuels. The jivas are our protectors and our friends. Behold." She held out a gnarled hand and beckoned to the zigzag-banded one. "Come, Awnee! Come back aboard, my dear one. I need you. Forgive me if I ever made you feel unwelcome."

The gaudy turnip compressed her branching tail into a single strand. And now she shrank—from the size of an armchair to a pumpkin to a fist and down to the size of a robin's egg. Weena opened her mouth and Awnee wriggled inside, disappearing down the old woman's gullet. My former lover pursed her thin lips and drew in the pinkish-yellow tail like a wayward strand of spaghetti.

Almost immediately, Weena grew young again. Her skin was smooth, her stance lissome, her lips plump. "You should do this as well, Jim," she said, her eyes sparkling with nervous energy.

"Why do jivas want to live inside people?" I asked, temporizing. "What's in it for them?"

"They're nosy," said Weena. "They like to learn personal secrets and to become involved with people's lives. Not intending any insult to Awnee, one might say that jivas have a dull emotional life when left on their own. So—are you ready, Jim?"

An awkward silence fell. Running on automatic now, Ira and Ginnie's ghostly sound-mix was echoing through the empty house. And upstairs, sodden Header slept on.

"I'd feel weird about eating a flying jellyfish," said Ginnie. "And what's with the green axe, Weena?"

Weena didn't answer that one. "Open that round portal door in the cellar, Jim," she told me, clutching the axe in her now-vigorous hands. "The border snail wants you to. Meanwhile, I'll proceed upstairs to serve justice."

"Stop her, Ira! " exclaimed Ginnie, suddenly getting the picture. "Sure, Header's majorly obnox, and right now he's cheating on me, but—"

"Hear me, Ginnie!" interrupted Weena. "This Header person is the tool for the fop whom you released from the tunnel. The Graf from Flimsy. The Graf took control of Header's mind. Now stand aside."

Not waiting for an answer, Weena brushed past Ginnie and Ira, carrying the axe across her chest like a firefighter. Just to make the scene crazier, two of the new-born jivas crowded into the house in her wake, bouncing along the ceiling like balloons on New Year's Eve.

Ginnie followed as far as the doorway and stopped there—shocked, scared, unsure, adorable. Ira put his hand loosely on her shoulder. The fourth jiva draped her tail over my arm. I could pick up a little teep from her. She was talking to me by stringing together nouns.

"Friend Jim partner life me Mijjy."

Lately I'd been Weena's pawn, reacting to events as they arose. It was time to do something for myself—or so I thought. "Come on in, Mijjy," I said, and opened wide. I wanted teep and the ability to make zickzack. I was ready to be a superman. Fool that I am, it didn't cross my mind that I'd be making myself into a slave.

The jiva shrank to the size of a radish and floated forward. I hardly felt her going down my throat. What I felt, rather, was a body-wide tingle as Mijjy linked her root hairs into my nervous system. Immediately I felt less drunk and stoned than before.

And there was a physical effect as well. The jiva was souping up my body. My belly grew firm and my features tautened—thanks to a web of tendrils beneath my skin. More than that, the jiva thickened my tendons, cushioned my joints, and bulked my muscles. I flexed my supple fingers, savoring my new strength.

Ginnie was staring at me, fascinated. I was as fit as a pro surfer.

But all this paled beside the jiva's mental effects. It was as if the world around me were made of glass. I could see microbes, I could see all of Santa Cruz. And I could pick up the vibes of the others' minds—especially Weena's. Our jivas seemed to be in a subtle connection with each other.

Looking through Weena's eyes, I could see her marching up to Header's room, her axe at the ready, the two other newborn jivas bouncing along behind her. Weena wakened Header with a rough shove and began talking to him in a low, even tone. She was reciting a death sentence. Header began to bellow. His voice sounded different than before. Less human.

"Oh this is horrible," said Ginnie, holding her ears.

"So okay, I'm going down to open the cellar door," I said quickly. "Do you two want to watch?"

I led the way down the deck's stairs—everything was pink and yellow from the dawning light. The round door was still in the cellar wall, with the hand-shaped depression awaiting my touch. My dog Droog appeared, yawning and shaking his ears. He'd been lying low. I took a quick peek into his mind, as simple and comfortable as a cartoon. Food?

Just then the screaming upstairs peaked, and we heard the nightmarish thud of that green-handled axe hitting home. I closed off my images of what Weena was doing. Shrieks and gurgles sounded in the air. Ginnie bust into sobs. More thuds, staggering footsteps, and—an upstairs window burst outwards in a shower of fragments. Header tumbled through, landing on the lawn with a sodden thump. He was wearing a blood-soaked terry bathrobe. The two extra jivas drifted in his wake, watching.

Header had a gory wound in his chest, and another blow of the axe had split the top of his skull. Surely he was dead. For two long seconds we silently stared at his remains.

But now—how horrid and strange—something moved. The halves of his skull. They were pulsing, quivering, spreading apart like a clamshell. Droog howled and ran into the house. Ginnie covered her face and groaned.

I saw a blue slug lurking within Header's ruined skull. Impossible. But this was real. The blue shape oozed forth from the skull's crack, growing protuberances and taking on a rounded form—it was another yuel, a four-legged baboon-thing, just as powerful as the one before. I was able to pick up on this one's name. Rickben.

"Save love buzz slosh," he teeped.

The two airborne jivas began flailing at the new yuel, but right away he started up with a sweet and creepy song like the other yuel had used. A yuel lullaby. Unable to bear the insistent vibrations, the jivas drew back a few dozen yards. And, given that I had a jiva inside me now, the music was even more excruciating for me than before—it disturbed me at a deeply visceral level. Rickben the yuel was crawling towards Ginnie, who seemed paralyzed with fear. The yuel had stretched out a slimy pseudopod, a slender vine that was already wrapping around Ginnie's foot.

To drown out the lullaby, I began braying out the first song that came to mind, some random classic of punk rock. Coached by Weena's teep, I held out my hands and willed my jiva to send tendrils from my fingertips. The tendrils appeared, glowing a faint red.

I sank my tendrils into the yuel and my resident jiva began siphoning off his energy. The doomed Rickben sent a pseudopod my way, but I dodged him. And then, aha, I'd drained him down to a lump, to a slug, to a last left-over noodle lying across Ginnie's foot.

Ginnie picked up the blue noodle and—ate it.

"What are you thinking!" I scolded. "It might be poisonous."

"Hell, you ate the rest of it," said Ginnie. "Yuels are full of—what's that word Weena used? Kessence. With the condition I'm in, I'm never hungry for regular food."

Ginnie was interrupted by Weena's cheers from the second floor. "Jim conquers the father yuel—the vile Rickben! You're a wonderful assistant, Jim! Glory shall be thine!" She was still holding the axe, its steel head drenched in gore. The two free-floating jivas were sweeping their tendrils across the lawn, sniffing out any last any yuel fragments that remained.

"Heavy," said Ira. "So who's going through that tunnel in the cellar now?"

"Jim and I!" intoned Weena from on high. "I'll take Jim to the Duke to prepare his great mission. This is urgent, the yuels are more aggressive than we'd foreseen. I find it interesting that the Graf would smuggle the yuel Rickben within his body's mass. The Graf was liquidated, yes, but the yuel escaped the Graf's body and entered Header's skull, undoubtedly to eat his brain. And Header slimed out a yuel-bud when Jim arrived. A Rickben Junior."

"Header," echoed Ginnie softly. "You're saying he was a zombie when I met him at the surf break. A dead body controlled by an alien yuel in his head. I guess that's why—"

"Quick now, it's time for Flimsy!" interrupted Weena, cutting off the conversation. She ran down through the house and joined us in the yard, all the while wiping blood off her hands and arms with one of Header's T-shirts.

"I'm not going anywhere with Weena," said Ira. "I don't trust her at all."

"Nobody's asking your opinion," said Weena tartly. "I only want Jim."

"I'd like it better if Ginnie would come," I said. I turned to the dark, punky waif. "Would you be up for it?"

"Well...maybe," said Ginnie, giving me a weak smile. Her short hair framed her pert face like feathers. "I've pretty well run all the changes I can on Earth. And I'm really upset about—" She gestured at Header's maimed corpse.

"Would you youngsters drag those remains onto the steps?" ordered Weena, ignoring our conversation. "The house and the porch and the steps are dimensionally obscured, but whatever we leave on the ground will be visible in the empty lot that the commoners see. No need to stir up trouble before you return with your delivery, Jim. Step lively and move that thing!"

Ira alone took hold of the corpse's legs and ineffectually tugged. Ginnie turned away and stared at the glowing haze. I blocked out Weena and stood beside Ginnie, putting my arm around her. How soft and insubstantial she felt.

With theatrical sighs and grumbles, Weena helped Ira schlep the corpse halfway up the steps to the deck, and tied it in place with the belt of the bathrobe.

"That's sufficient," she said impatiently. "And why are you canoodling, Jim? Open the goddamn fucking magic door!" She broke off and forced a smile. "I regret that I'm beginning to speak as coarsely as you."

"What about Ginnie?"

"Very well then, it's fine if Ginnie comes. You see how I cosset you, Jim? Ginnie, you should swallow one of those two jivas. She'll help you on the trip."

One of the two jivas got small and drifted over to Ginnie's face. She resembled a rosy grape with a curly tail.

"Tell me again what she's going to do to me?" said Ginnie.

"The jivas tune you towards optimal fitness," said Weena. "And you'll have telepathy. And you'll be able to make zickzack objects from of empty space. Oh wait, Ginnie, you'd do well to take a dose of my tonic first. Jim had already taken some last week."

Weena dug out her depleted stash of sprinkles and offered it. The jewel-like capsules were crawling over each other like ants in a colony. Weena drizzled a little kessence onto them, squeezing the aethereal substance from her fingertips.

"They're pretty," said Ginnie, leaning over the little bag.

"Like wonderful candy, my dear," urged Weena. "They'll put new voices into your head and make you jiva-ready. Go go go."

"My dose of sprinkles put me in the hospital," I told Ginnie. "Just so you know."

"I insist that was only a coincidence," cried Weena, flying into a passion. "You weakling. You whiner. You sensualist."

"At least I'm not a hundred and thirty," I yelled. "Killer. Schemer. Bitch."

"And wasn't it the sprinkles that put Header in a coma tonight?" interrupted Ginnie before we could continue.

"Oh, no, no, no," said Weena, calming herself by main force. "I rather suspect Header's slumber was from the opiates he sniffed." She gave me a cold look. "And, Jim, before you start accusing me of being a killer, do keep in mind that it wasn't really Header whom I axed. A yuel was controlling his body. Let's not muddle our discussion by flinging unwarranted epithets. Do eat the sprinkles now, Ginnie, dear."

"What the hey," said Ginnie, dipping into Weena's stash and taking a pinch of the plump, writhing sprinkles. "Something to pick me up. I'm so bummed from all this blood."

Having tasted the sprinkles, Ginnie leaned towards the little pink jiva and opened her mouth. The cherry-sized jiva floated in. Absorbing the new sensations, Ginnie gave a slow shudder and smiled.

"So don't offer *me* anything, Weena," said Ira venomously.

The single remaining jiva was hovering high overhead. She was a green turnip the size of a cow, with a vivid yellow zigzag stripe around her waist and a purple cap on top.

"That jiva's not for you," said Weena. "She's going to stay here and maintain a presence." She smiled up at the floating jiva. "Right, Sukie? You can go ahead and lay some eggs here when you're ready."

"So fine," said Ira shortly. "Skeeves and I will keep an eye on things here. I'm not ready to leave anyway."

Now that Ginnie had a jiva, I could feel a teep contact with her. Our invisibly fine jiva tendrils were woven together. Ginnie and I began swapping emotions and thoughts—although not without a certain reserve. There was some kind of mystery about Ginnie, something crashingly obvious that I couldn't quite get. Seeing more information, I turned my attention back to Weena.

"What about that guy who hatched out the jivas?" I asked her, looking for another piece to the puzzle. "Dick Simly. Did it kill him?"

"You're try my patience with your inquisition," said Weena. "Who cares about every petty detail!"

"I care," I said. I was liking her less all the time. "If you keep it up, I might not be going to Flimsy with you at all."

"It's possible that Dick Simly is as hale and randy as before," said Weena, trying again for a cajoling tone. "But why worry ourselves? He was your enemy." She threw her blood-smeared arms around my waist and tried to kiss me. "Really, the best thing about all this is that I've met you, dear Jim."

I twisted away from her.

"Think what you like about me," said Weena in a long-suffering tone. "But I promise you'll be welcomed by the Duke and Duchess of Human Flimsy! They'll commission you to make a wonderful improvement to your world. And, don't forget, you'll have the opportunity to find your dead wife Val. Perhaps Ginnie can be your mistress over there as well. Who knows? We're very liberal about these matters in Flimsy."

Clearly Weena was untrustworthy. But I was eager for more adventure. And certainly the journey was worth any price if I might bring back Val.

I went and put my hand on the cellar door.

As before, the door reacted to my touch. This time I'd meant to side-step it when it fell outwards. But I stumbled and, once again, I was pinned beneath the round panel.

12: The Tunnel

Working in harmony, Ginnie and Weena helped me out from under the door, with Droog digging at the sandy soil as well. Ira stood off to one side, sullenly watching.

"If you can't learn to open that door without getting crushed, you should just let me do it," Ginnie remarked to me.

"You can open it too?" I said. Now that I knew about the border snail, I realized the door was a disk of mollusk shell.

"Sure," said Ginnie. "Remember? I let the Graf come through. Snaily likes me. She even lets me find her house."

A direct ray from the rising sun filtered in through the space-maze and landed squarely on the hole of the cellar entrance—as if this were Stonehenge at the summer solstice. Weena emitted a throbbing chirp.

A greenish-brown mass pushed forth from the cellar door, a slimy surface of puckers and bumps, gradually taking on detailed form. A pointy tip protruded, then two flexible tentacles, and a pair of stalks with glistening black balls on the ends—

"See, Jim!" said Ginnie. "It's Snaily! With feelers and eyes. She grew us this house."

The snail swelled up her bulk and made a chittering creak in response—not with her mouth, but by shaking the Whipped Vic above her, lifting the place ever so slightly off the ground.

"Here we go, Jim," said Weena, once again assuming her kind and cozy mode. "This house is a snail shell, yes. There's plenty of these border snails, I think, but they're hard to find. Snaily sought me out because I knew of the weak spot in the wall that you made."

"With my special tip," said Ira, perking up. "But I still don't understand how anyone can walk *through* the snail."

"We go into her mouth," said Weena in the artificially bright tone one uses with a querulous child. "And her other end is in Flimsy. The land of the flims."

"That's not a real tunnel," I protested, not liking the way things were playing out.

"It's a tunnel through the border snail's body," said Weena. "In through mouth, gullet, stomach, and then out through her other gullet and mouth. She has two heads, you see, one in each world. She doesn't eat with her heads, she eats directly with her stomach—which she positions among the teeming sprinkles of the living water."

"What's the living water?" demanded Ira. "I never heard anything about that."

"The living water forms a shell around the Flimsy world," said Weena. "It's a womb, a hull, a rind. The surface of what you call an electron. Just now, this surface happens to intersect the center of Snaily's gut. She likes it that way."

I didn't have the heart to start an argument about Weena's odd image of an electron. Whether or not her notions made quantum-mechanical sense, they seemed in some way to match the bizarre levels of reality that I'd blundered into.

The giant snail raised her flattened tip, revealing a floppy, toothless mouth the size of a car door. The house groaned again, and Header's corpse shifted on the steps.

"I'm not sure I can handle this," said Ginnie.

"It'll be quite comfortable," said Weena. "I'm going to prop Snaily's mouth open with my tendrils. But there's something that Jim and I have to do in the basement first. I'll go get that part ready. I'll call you in a minute, Jim." She squeezed past the flank of the snail and into the dank basement—where I'd seen Skeeves's golden sarcophagus before.

"I'm glad I'm not going yet," said Ira. "It might be a one-way trip. And, like I said, I'm not ready to leave Skeeves, romantic fool that I am. Imagine me on the waves, guys. A ruffle of ripples, a flash of sun, a yesteryear memory."

"Oh, Ira," said Ginnie. "It's all too sad."

"Why do you say it could be a one-way trip?" I asked, wondering if there were some big snag that I hadn't heard about yet.

"You still haven't figured it out?" said Ira, his voice faint and mocking. "Surfing accidents? Woman's body in a car?"

Even now, I didn't want to understand what he was getting at. I turned away from Ira and took Ginnie's hand. Weena was still out of sight, clattering around in the basement.

Ginnie raised our joined hands, studying the pair like a cryptic glyph. "What do you really think is going to happen between us, Jim? You don't know anything about me at all."

But—thanks to our telepathic link—I did. Peering into Ginnie's memories, I saw her as an awkward lonely girl from a broken home in Sacramento, her father gone to Alaska, and her mother working as an administrative assistant at a megachurch. Ginnie got into the skater scene in high school, then spent a year as a student at Sacramento State, graffiti-bombing the government buildings and running the soundboard for a punk club.

Ginnie had a drummer boyfriend named Goon, not that Goon used actual drums—he had input gloves that amplified the taps and rustles of his fingertips. Ginnie left school and her kind-of job to go to San Francisco with Goon. On the strength of her avant-garde chops, she landed a job as the sound tech at a Mission dance club.

Goon found work at a surf shop on Ocean Beach, and he'd get Ginnie free rental gear on weekdays. She began exploring the slopes of the ragged Pacific waves. It was all good for awhile, but then Goon moved in with a woman lawyer whose flat tire he'd changed near the beach. Ginnie couldn't cover her rent alone. Looking for a mellower vibe, she hitchhiked down to Cruz...

At this point my access to Ginnie's memories broke off.

"So it all leads up to this," I said sententiously. "The fact that you've been able to find the Whipped Vic every night—that means something. And that Weena singled me out to help her—that's significant, too. It's destiny, Ginnie. We'll be big celebs. Especially if I resurrect my dead wife." I smiled, wanting Ginnie as well as Val.

"It's pretty weird to imagine running off with you," said Ginnie, letting go of my hand. "I mean—you've been living with that skanky Weena? And your wife died last year?"

"I can't hide my past," I said. "And I can't hide that I see you as, as—"

I hesitated, fighting back the phrase that had popped into my head.

"*A punky furburger?*" exclaimed Ginnie, reading my mind. "That's what you think of me? Of all the rudeness."

"I'm sorry, that's how my thoughts run, I play with words. But of course I'm not absolutely assuming that you and I will, uh—" Again my thoughts were getting out of control.

"Not assuming, but hoping?" said Ginnie, her voice shooting up high on the final word. She broke into a laugh. "Not that I'm sure it's even possible anymore. At least the jiva buffed you up. It's hard to believe I actually swallowed one of those things, too. Do I look different?"

"Like a gritty saint," I said, faintly perceiving a halo of jiva tendrils around Ginnie's head. "Our Lady of the Soundboard."

"There you go," she said. "*That's* the way to talk to a girl."

"Very touching," said Ira, watching us. "You move fast, Ginnie."

"Why are you men so interesting in monitoring women's sex lives?" said Ginnie sharply. "You're like bellowing elk. Lower than that. Like computer viruses. And, Ira, you aren't even interested in me that way. You're gay for Skeeves, for God's sake."

"So?" yelled Ira, his face dark with anger. "I think it's time we told your moon calf that we're dead. Duh, Jim! Don't you notice anything but the twitches of your dick?"

It took me a full minute to find my voice. The woman's body in the Graf's car—that had been Ginnie. And Ira—

"Skeeves drowned me," he said. "He says a voice in his head made him do it. And, dig this, the voice was Weena. You didn't know that either, did you, Jim? Weena's been orchestrating this whole freakshow."

"Why—why would Weena and Skeeves kill you?" I stuttered.

"They didn't want me walking around alive and knowing the secret of the tunnel. If I'm just a ghost, then most people can't see me or hear me. I will say that Skeeves wasn't a complete jerk about the hit. He brought along a big hunk of kessence from the border snail. And my sprinkle went straight from my flesh and into the kessence. And now I'm a wavy, groovy boy." Ira wriggled his arms.

"It's not like Skeeves *had* to listen to some crazy voice in his head," put in Ginnie. "That's no defense at all. You shouldn't give him a free pass, Ira. Hearing voices is one thing. Killing people is something else. As far as I'm concerned, Skeeves and Weena both bear the guilt for killing you. And someday we'll make them pay."

I felt numb, unsteady on my feet. I was hanging around with ghosts?

"Am I dead too?" I asked. "Has everything since the hospital been a dream?"

"You're still alive," said Ira, giving me a rough poke. "All meat and full of shit."

"You're alive, but you're very unusual," added Ginnie in a kinder tone. "You found your way to this house on the border. And you're able to see Ira and me. Mostly it's just stoners and crazy people who notice us."

"The people at the party last night?" I asked.

"A mix," said Ira. "Some live, some dead. As for the rest of it—well, we're as confused as you. Playing it by ear. Nothing left to lose."

Weena reappeared just now, smiling out at us from around the bulge of the snail. "I'm ready for you now, Jim. Come here in the basement and lie down."

"You're going to kill me!" I cried. "Just like you killed Ira and Header."

"No, no," said Weena. "I want you to visit Flimsy and bring something back to us. If you were dead, the mission wouldn't work. It's all very simple."

"So—so you want me to get in Skeeves's gold casket?" I asked.

"It's the Pharaoh Amenhotep's sarcophagus," said Weena. "He was in it for three and a half thousand years. My friend Charles and I have been at rest within it, too, of late—but only for a century. I was just now checking on dear Charles. I've taken off the lid. It's a roomy box, Jim, especially since Skeeves and his San Francisco addict friend recklessly burned the remains of Amenhotep in a fireplace. The casket will readily hold you along with Charles and me."

"I won't be dead?"

"Your body will remain in suspended animation here. And your spirit will visit Flimsy. Your nice new jiva will travel with you and give you a fine solid body. And, as it happens, I have a cache of kessence by the sarcophagus as well. You'll be an astral traveler like me."

"You're sure I can come back?"

"You know this is feasible, Jim. When you opened the snail's door, my soul came back here and I reincorporated."

"But your body was aging the whole time you were gone. Without your jiva, you look—"

"It's very rude to discuss a lady's age," said Weena, starting to lose her patience again. "You'll be back in a week. Your loyal dog can lie atop the casket's lid to guard his master."

"Skeeves will dipping his wick in the casket," said Ira, wanting to stir up trouble. "I'll bring him back into the house as soon as you guys leave. I like to know where my dreamboat is. Like—in the basement humping Weena's tender remains."

"Your coarseness reflects only upon you," said Weena haughtily. "Skeeves's ministrations act as a preservative massage."

"Go ahead and park your body now," Ginnie told me. She was wearing a feral grin. "It's the only way to *really* get it on with a ghost like me. You can help me through the tunnel to the other side. I'm sick of it here. And—Jim—maybe you can help me settle some scores."

Well—like I said, it had been a long, crazy night. I was hyped up from the sprinkles, and I had my jiva inside me. And my life was pointless. And I had my crazy hope of finding Val over there. What the fuck. I squeezed past the slimy bulk of the snail and into the basement. Droog came along.

The early morning glow was filtering through the cobwebbed and barred cellar windows. As before, I noticed that the rear part of the snail's body tapered off very dramatically—dwindling down to a point. Which made sense, I supposed, if the snail's other end was inside an electron. Whatever that meant.

The floor in here was really old concrete, cracked and rough. It smelled like mold and sewage. Over at the far end of the basement was a twisted little staircase that I hadn't noticed before. But the main thing to see was the magnificent golden sarcophagus of Amenhotep, resting by the wall with the lid leaning against it.

The numinous shape carried an aura of magic. Untarnished by the centuries, the casket's bulbous surfaces were alive with reflections. The sarcophagus almost seemed to glow from within. Bands of hieroglyphics ran around its base, and the exquisitely wrought face upon the lid resembled a dreaming god.

"We lie down in here and enter a trance," said Weena, leading me to the oversized casket. "Originally there must have been some inner coffins as well, like a set of Russian dolls, but those went missing before the sarcophagus came into our hands."

Hesitantly I peered within. A heavily bearded man was in there, his flesh waxy and pale, quite alone, ever so faintly breathing. There was indeed enough room for three.

"I just wonder if this is necessary," I said, playing for time.

"The magic is likelier to work if you're immersed in the aura," insisted Weena. "You need to be inside. I don't know if you can see it, but there's a nice big slug of kessence at the foot end. That's the body I was wearing when I came through the tunnel. I'll share this kessence with you. Here." She made some odd motions with her hands. "Still can't see it? I've divided into two portions—half for you and half for me. Lie down in the casket."

"How did you end up in the sarcophagus in the first place?" I asked, stalling for time.

Weena's voice took on a soothing, reasonable tone. "There was a secret excavation in 1895, and a Frenchmen named Lanier found the tomb of Amenhotep I in Egypt. A Parisian nobleman acquired the golden casket, and the son of a California railroad tycoon bought it around 1910. Randolph Crocker. He wanted to add some tone to his ornate mansion in San Francisco."

"Now we're getting somewhere," I said. "Go on."

"Randolph Crocker engaged Charles Howard to write a monograph on the casket and the mummy." Weena leaned forward to pat the inert body in the sarcophagus. "Charles was a disgraced expatriate British Egyptologist. A womanizer. He'd taught for a few years at Berkeley's fledgling University of California before being fired there was well. He was having an affair with an assistant, that assistant being me. Is that enough?"

"Tell me just a little more," I begged.

"Charles was a dabbler in the occult. He discovered what he considered to be a spell, embossed as a pattern of hieroglyphs in a frieze on the outside of Amenhotep's casket. The spell allows the petitioner to leave his or her body without having to die. Charles and I wanted to run away together—and so we decided to flee to the higher plane. And that's enough details for now."

Raising her legs high, Weena stepped into the golden sarcophagus, being careful not to tread on the comatose Charles. She lay back upon him and folded her hands on her chest, posing like an effigy on a royal tomb. "Stop staring at me like you're utterly demented," said Weena. "Come here now and lie on me like a good boy."

"Lie down and die," I said bitterly.

"You'll be back in a week," insisted Weena, her voice still more honeyed than before. "I'm sorry that we quarreled. I'll make it up to you, Jim."

"Hurry up!" yelled Ginnie from outside.

I felt a sudden wave of bone-weariness. All this was so weird and so hard. I needed some slack. Maybe I'd find it in Flimsy.

I stretched out on top of Weena—well, more like next to her, really, as the sarcophagus was so big. Droog put his paws up on the edge of the casket and poked down his snout, sniffing me.

"Good dog," I told him. "Wait for me if you can."

"The lid," said Weena. "Pull on the lid."

"God help me," I said. "I'm fucking doomed."

I sat up and dragged the wood-lined golden lid onto us, shutting Droog out.

In the intimate darkness, Weena began crooning a petition. I shut my eyes and let her words filter in.

> Time, jivas, space and goo
> Yuels, zickzack, kessence too
> Flimsy goddess old and new
> My blank future calls to you.

She sang it over and over—at some point I began singing along, first mumbling the words, then chanting them quite loud. Our two voices overlaid each other, making dissonant beats.

A slight amount of light leaked in through the crack where the lid rested on the casket. Mostly the light was yellow, but as we chanted, I began seeing the hue change, slowly sliding down into red and up into blue, over and over, in synch with our chant. It was like the time when I'd been staring at the ceiling lamp in my bedroom. Not only were the colors swaying, I was beginning to see tiny bright dots—perhaps these were the electrons in the atoms of the air.

Suddenly I heard a scratch and a clatter, as if from very far away. That was Droog outside the casket, scrambling onto the lid. Weena and I sang on, bathed in the sea of electrons. Weena's voice was very beautiful—sweet and thin and filigreed.

I don't know how much time passed, but at some point I felt fully rested. I stopped chanting and drifted out of my body. I was like a speck of dust. The casket seemed enormous. My point of view was sweeping around violently as the air currents moved me. I couldn't stay here like this. I felt an intense desire to make a wild leap out of this world into—what? Into the afterworld.

Just as I was on the point of jumping, something cool and pleasant flowed up around me. It was some of the kessence that Weena had stored in the casket. A ghostly body took form around the agitated dot that was my liberated soul.

I sat up. By rights, I should have bumped against the lid and spilled Droog to the floor. But I didn't. I was in a kessence body now. I passed right through the lid.

I was sticking up from Amenhotep's casket, with my kessence legs still nestled within my flesh body. I swung my kessence legs to one side, right through the casket walls, and now I was standing on the floor.

Perhaps surprisingly, Droog was able to see me. He made as if to hop down from the casket, but I gestured to him that he should stay.

I felt light on my feet, lively and strong. My jiva had come with me. I could feel Mijjy's movements within me, as she firmed up a zickzack skeleton within the kessence form that I'd drawn from Weena's supply.

And now Weena's spirit stepped out of the casket as well. As a slender, jiva-enhanced ghost, Weena took on a truly idealized form—she looked like an Art Nouveau poster of a vibrant, sensual muse.

"You look very comely as well," said Weena, reading my mind. Glancing down, I saw that my body was tweaked to an inhuman perfection. Via telepathy, I could see my face from Weena's point of view. My jaw was more clear and chiseled than before, my hair a lush bob, my skin a flawless sheet of kessence covering the powerful zickzack bones and muscles beneath.

My teep powers allowed me to see inside the sarcophagus. Our three flesh bodies were at rest in there, on their own, alive. Atop the lid, Droog stared at us, his eyes flicking between me and Weena.

I followed the now-lovely Weena out of the cellar and into the yard, where Ira and Ginnie were resting on the ground near the giant snail. That one remaining jiva, Sukie, was hanging overhead, large and luminous, silently watching.

"Now Jim's a ghost too," said Ginnie. "What an epic night."

"Our last night on Earth," I said. I have this habit of cheering myself up by predicting the most depressing possible outcome—and then backing off from that. Really I was stoked about the coming trip, and I was hoping I'd make it back into my regular body at the end. But I didn't want to jinx things by saying so.

"On to Flimsy!" said Weena. "Observe how wide I can make our tunnel." She stretched out her hands in a sorcerer's gesture. Jiva tendrils branched from her fingers and funneled into the snail's maw. The fine hairs of the jiva fastened onto the space within, stretching it, widening the diameter.

Peering in, I saw a gently ribbed tunnel to—was it the afterworld? A twinkling, transparent wall rose in the middle of the tunnel, and through it I could glimpse faint sunlight at the other end. Due to some weird warping of space, the tunnel didn't seem to taper, it appeared to remain about the same width throughout.

The great snail bobbled her eyestalks, peering inside herself, assessing her internal state. A faint odor wafted from her digestive tract: a blend of urine, mold and violets.

"Come on, my hero," Weena urged me. "I'll tend the gate. And Ginnie, you can come too."

"You go first," I told Weena.

"If you prefer," she said. She stepped into the tube, walking in little mincing steps, swaying her round hips. Soon, skewed by the weird warpings and scalings of space, her figure took on the look of a snaky starfish. Ginnie and I followed after her. Weena had the creature's gut stretched so wide that we didn't even have to stoop.

Ira sang out a wistful farewell, the Whipped Vic rumbled, and Droog—sensing something amiss—howled from the basement.

Not letting myself think too deeply about what I was doing, or where I was bound, I continued down the tunnel with Ginnie at my side. In my ghostly jiva-enhanced form, I felt like a prancing giraffe.

The sparkling wall at the tunnel's midpoint was a thick block of water, like a ceiling-high aquarium, perhaps two meters thick. The walls of the snail's gut had a series of fans and tendrils that were continually seining this water for food.

"Living water," said Weena, who was waiting there for us. "Force yourself into the wall, push to the other side, and worm out. Only watch that you're not swept away."

Certainly the living water was no ordinary form of matter. It seemed to intersect the snail's intestinal walls without breaking them. It was as if the living water were a translucent overlay, a grease-penciled addition to this extraordinary reality.

I saw sour-colored polyhedral gems within the water—they resembled Weena's sprinkles, only these ones were more highly animated, attacking each other and sweeping through the aethereal fluid in nested loops. I noted that the sprinkles had a general tendency to rise upwards out of sight, with new ones flowing up from below.

And these sprinkles were the food that the snail was interested in. Her sticky, fern-like feelers were systematically catching sprinkles. When a frond became quite rich with sprinkles, the snail would stuff it in into a digestive slit beside the water-wall. And then the frond would re-emerge, licked clean of its sprinkles.

Weena stepped into the living water, or rather, she pushed her way in. The skin of the water was leathery, gelatinous, and she had to force open a crack to slide inside. The living water seemed to welcome Weena. Her entry spilled not a drop.

The bright particles within the water converged on Weena, and for a moment she herself became a blur. She seemed to be working fairly hard to avoid being swept up through the tunnel's ceiling—and to stay clear of the snail's feeder-fronds. A moment later, she'd kicked across the two meters to the other side, and had clawed her way through the skin over there.

She waved to us with one hand, solid once again. While inside the water, she'd used her other hand to seine herself a catch of those colored dots that she and the snail so greatly prized.

Ginnie and I felt hesitant. To test things out, Ginnie poked a hole in the jellied surface and stuck her arm in as far as the elbow. A school of sprinkles swirled around her fingertips, intent as hungry diatoms.

"Ow," exclaimed Ginnie, flinching back. "They nip. Surreal guppies."

"How bad can it be?" I said, faking bravado.

"Lead on, oh cosmic mailman."

If the outer layer of the wall was a springy gelatin, it was all liquid within. I wormed my way deep into the living center, holding my breath. An insistent current nudged me upwards, as if to force me through the ceiling of the snail's tunnel. One of the snail's feeder-tendrils latched onto my foot, but it was pretty easy to kick it free.

The darting sprinkles were landing in myriads upon my astral form. They seemed to be drawing off bits of my kessence, which didn't seem like a big deal. But now, as if in reaction to the sprinkles' onslaught, my ghostly form went abruptly to pieces, shattering into a solid jigsaw puzzle with each piece at a tiny remove from the next. And I hadn't even begun to swim.

The water between the worlds flowed through me, dusting my innards, and it was only my resident jiva's tendrils that were keeping me together at all. With an all-out effort, I pulled my body together and kicked my way across the two meters, fighting the current.

On the way, I inadvertently drew some of the living water into my lungs—but it didn't seem to matter. Evidently you had a lot of leeway if you were a ghost. Flailing wildly, and twisting away from the sprinkles and the feeder-fronds, I made it to the rubbery membrane at the other side. I pried a crack into it, and wriggled through.

And there I was, on the other side of strange. Coughing out the living water and drawing in air, I managed a whoop.

"All right!"

"You look divine," said Weena, waiting there.

Ginnie followed us through the narrow wall of water. Thanks to the assaults of the sprinkles, her ghostly body also unraveled and reassembled itself en route.

"Sweet," she enthused, standing beside me now, even more fetching than before. "It felt like—you know how a light ray tightens up when it goes through a lens? I feel like I've been focused. My new jiva body was feeling like scratchy dress-up clothes—but now it's just right. It's almost like I'm really alive again."

I touched Ginnie's face. She was cool and smooth. Maybe a little bit like a plastic mannequin. But, still...

"Come on," ordered Weena, standing by the exit. "Stop lollygagging." She was all business again.

I could see another pair of eyestalks silhouetted against the faint disk of light that lay ahead, and the green of a field. And now Ginnie and I stepped forth into the other world, out through the border snail's other mouth—

13: Meet the Flims

nd found ourselves in a fresh patch of meadow. The air was moist and sweet. In front of us, the meadow rolled off towards a jumble of confusing reflections, and behind us, the meadow was bounded by a vertical wall of living water, a wall that arched upwards towards a shimmering tangle that obscured the sky.

It seemed we were hidden by a space-maze on this side as well. The light which filtered through the maze had an amber quality—perhaps it was dusk here.

Tight up against the vertical wall was a family of five mauve domes interconnected by shiny tubes—we'd stepped out of a door in one of the domes. I surmised that the border snail had grown the domes just like she'd grown the Whipped Vic.

Orange flowers bloomed amid the nearby meadow grasses. A man with a tight felt cap was sowing seeds into the furrows of a plowed garden patch, scattering pink specks from his hand, and squirting some kind of fertilizer into the furrows with the seeds. The fertilizer was silvery stuff from a squeeze-tube. In the further reaches of the garden were half-grown and fully mature plants; they were lumpy things shaped like... people.

Meanwhile the snail had once again closed her door, using another of her shell disks. Just like in Santa Cruz, the round panel had a hand-shaped depression in the middle. I wondered if I'd be able to

open this door, too. But—it suddenly occurred to me—maybe I'd
want to stay in Flimsy for good. Start a new life in—was this heaven?
If I could find Val or, failing that, get Ginnie to stick with me—

"Easy there, big boy," said Ginnie. "We haven't even kissed yet."
This telepathy thing was going to take some getting used to.

Each dome seemed to be a single room, with round windows on
all except for the one that held the snail. I could see a few people
inside: a man dozing in a shiny chair, a woman dandling a baby, a
boy fiddling with what looked like a pair of ice skates.

The sower from the plowed field walked over to greet us. He
looked about twenty-five, with deep eyes and a sun-weathered face.
He gave off a vibe of peaceful welcome, and spoke to us in accented
English.

"Hello, Weena," said the man. "You made it back. And you brought
two Earth beings with you. They're..."

"I present Jim and Ginnie," said Weena. "And this is Monin, the
keeper of the tunnel on this side. I installed him on this farm."

"He's not a yuel, is he?" said Monin, peering closely at me. "He
looks different from a normal ghost."

"Jim is an astral traveler like me, said Weena. "He has a living
body back on Earth. And, on the subject of yuels, Monin, did you
realize that when the Graf bribed your wife with kessence to open
the tunnel door, he carried a yuel? Thanks to my interventions, the
Graf's kessence body on Earth was destroyed, yes, but I found that
the smuggled yuel had survived, a creature called Rickben. To make
things worse, the yuel had spawned a Rickben Junior. The two of
them attacked me."

"I'm sure you held your own," said Monin. "I know you, Weena.
And don't start yelling at us about the Graf again. This is our farm
now, and we do what we want."

"Yes, I prevailed," said Weena. "I only hope those yuels didn't pop
out any clouds of yuel spores. It will be well, when the time is ripe,
to bring many more jivas to Earth. Sukie on her own is not enough
for the long term. All would be lost if the yuels were to become
established on Earth."

"The yuels aren't all bad," said Monin with a shrug. "So what
happened to the Graf?"

"Oh, did I forget to tell you?" said Weena airily. "Yes, an—acolyte
of mine named Skeeves eliminated the Graf before I arrived. But the

Graf's yuel was living in the skull of a vulgar man named Header. I terminated Header as well as the yuels. Header left me no choice."

"You conked Header with an axe while he was too stoned on sprinkles and dope to escape," put in Ginnie. "Some choice."

"That sounds like Weena," said Monin, his craggy face cracking in a smile. "That's why she's the Duke's favorite agent. I want to hear more about the yuel getting inside Header."

"Elementary," said Weena with a toss of her head. She loved being the center of attention. "To make room for himself, the yuel ate Header's brain. A small meal."

"Those were tough yuels," I bragged. "The jivas were having a hard time with them. It was my jiva and I who finished off the big one—Rickben."

"I see," said Monin, not all that approvingly. "You should know that my son Durkle has a yuel-built body—he's pure kessence. Some of the jiva-hosts here look down on flims like that. Of course I'm a jiva man, myself."

"Monin even sells copies of his body to the jivas," remarked Weena. She gestured towards the plowed field. Indeed the older plants were shaped a bit like Monin. And round bumps like baby heads were showing in the soft dirt where Monin had been sowing the seeds.

"Never mind all that," said Monin, with a wave of his dirt-stained hand. "Enough work and worry. Come on inside for supper."

The snail's door was shut tight. We found another entrance to the assemblage of mauve domes. It made me just a little uneasy to have that wall of living water nearby. Who knew how high it rose beyond the obscuring folds of the space-maze? But once we were inside Monin's house, I stopped worrying about it.

The rooms were larger than they'd appeared from the outside— perhaps the flims had stretched the internal space. The first room we entered was a sitting room, with the man I'd seen sleeping in an easy-chair. A globe hanging near the ceiling shed a faint light—I recalled Weena's remark about Flimsy lamps being tunnels to nearby suns. The walls were festooned with gracefully draped vines, and a wooden shrine held a golden statue of a jiva with an earthenware oil lamp burning before it. Some kind of Jiva Bible sat beside the lamp. The floor was cushioned by a mat of what looked to be colored moss. And the chairs were elegant patterns of curved zickzack.

"This here is my father," said Monin, nudging the old man's chair with his foot. "Wake up, Grandpa! Dinnertime."

"Eh?" said the man, stirring himself. Like Monin, he looked youthful. But his youth was only a cosmetic effect. He'd been around for a long time. In fact Grandpa's mind had decayed beyond the point where his resident jiva could fully smooth things over. He stared at us with confused, truculent eyes, resenting the disturbance.

"I'm five hundred and twenty years old," said Monin, picking up on my thoughts. "But Grandpa's six hundred. Those eighty years make all the difference. And I live right, too. Some day soon we'll plow the old man into the garden, right Grandpa?"

"Bastard," hissed Monin's father with senile venom. He lurched to his feet. "Eat?"

"Eat," said Monin. "Right through this passageway, you newcomers. Just follow Weena. She knows the way."

In the kitchen we were greeted by a lively woman with a crying baby in a carrying sling. "Hi, I'm Yerba," she said over the infant's wails. "Can you hold the baby now, Monin?"

Monin took the button-eyed baby, blubbed his lips at her to make her laugh, and gave her a crust of kessence to wave and to slobber on. The baby's name was Nyoo.

"I'm the lady of this charnel house," added Yerba as she set out the meal. The oven was a striped tube of zickzack with bright light within. The table was a sort of wooden mushroom, and the plates resembled shells. "I've roasted a joint that we got from the garden this morning," continued Yerba. "Don't grab the whole thing with your hands, Grandpa, I'll cut you a slice."

"Your grew this thing in the ground?" said Ginnie, admiring the crisp brown roast. "So if I eat it, I'm still a vegetarian?" She smiled at me. "Hey, I have an appetite again!"

"It's not really a vegetable either," said Yerba. "It's plain old kessence with a touch of zickzack. Like you and me."

"Why do we even eat?" I asked. "If we're just globs of ether and folded pieces of space?"

"We do need to take in fresh kessence every so often," said Yerba. "And I, for one, like it to resemble proper food."

"Come in here, Durkle!" called Monin over his shoulder, dandling baby Nyoo and helping himself to the imitation meat and vegetables. The baby focused on a bit of kessence shaped like a string bean.

With a clatter and a whoop, a boy ran in and took a seat. We'd glimpsed him through the window earlier. The motions of his limbs were rubbery and fluid, as if he lacked a skeleton. He looked about fourteen years old. "You people came here from Earth just now?" he asked. "And you're ghosts?" He had a pinched, yearning face, and I felt an immediate sympathy for him.

"Hi," I responded. "I'm Jim and this is Ginnie. Sure we're ghosts, but in a way, I'm still alive, too."

"What's he mean, Dad?" asked Durkle, looking anxious.

"What's that smooth wall outside?" interrupted Ginnie.

"Flimsy is like a vast bubble," said Weena. "The bubble is a skin of living water, a hundred meters thick. And bottom of the bubble is awash with living water, too. Like a spheroid goldfish bowl: air above, water below. There's a fringe of land around the water's edge. And we're here where the land touches the bubble."

"But there's a hole in the wall right here?" said Ginnie. "For your tunnel?"

"Not a hole," said Weena. "A thin part. Two meters across. You saw how we had to push our way through. It's thin because of Jim's nicked electron. And Snaily's been keeping it thin ever since I brought her here."

"So, okay, Flimsy is a rim of land around a pool of water in a ball," I said, trying to get a coherent mental image. "What kind of sun do you have? A light in the center?"

"We have lots of suns," said little Durkle in a knowing tone. "All along the edge. They go straight up and down every day. In and out of their holes."

"What happens if you jump into a sun's hole?" asked Ginnie, giddily.

"That would be a stupid thing to do," said Monin with a shrug. "Maybe you'd end up in the underworld or the Dark Gulf and the hungry new ghosts would eat you. More roast?"

"You can't see the suns from Monin's house," put in Weena. "Because of the border snail's space-maze. The border snails conceal themselves for self-protection."

"But here's what the view should look like," said Monin, teeping an image my way. I saw miles of rolling green meadow, and a fat, pale orange sun sinking towards the horizon. There was something odd about the sun—it had a thin spike of light projecting from its bottom, seemingly reaching all the way to the ground. A solar flare?

I could make out some secondary suns in the distance, smaller and smaller—each of them resting upon a line of light.

"Our suns are huge jivas," put in Weena. "Powerful living beings. The vast atoll of Flimsy is like a roulette wheel with a septillion slots. Each slot holds the afterworld of some intelligent civilization. And each slot hosts its own jiva-sun."

"A septillion?" I numbly echoed, trying to absorb the image of the world she described.

"We rarely see the other beings," said Weena. "Although I have occasionally met some of our nearest neighbors. Grasping and aggressive races. But now's not the time to talk about them."

"But what's in the middle?" asked Ginnie.

"I haven't gone there," said Weena curtly. "And I don't want to."

"It's vast glassy ocean of living water," said Yerba. "The surface of the Dark Gulf. And the goddess of Flimsy is a beautiful glowing figure at the core. Unimaginably far away."

Weena gave a derisive snort. "I say the middle can be closer than you deem," she insisted. "Flimsy's space is warped in very odd ways."

"Are you some kind of mathematician?" I asked. I was remembering how smoothly this woman had compared zickzack to hyperdimensional origami, and her talk about gluing together bits of space.

"What if I am?" said Weena, cocking her head. "Is that another thing to hold against me?"

"Why didn't you tell me back in Santa Cruz? We could have talked about my genetics research."

"My aim was to seduce you, Jim, not to conduct a seminar. I discuss science with my regular lover Charles, perhaps more than I'd like. He's an Egyptologist turned linguist, and he expects me to help with his calculations. With you, Jim, I was after something more—how should I put it? Something hot and nasty." She smiled coyly, as lithe and charming as a fashion model.

"Don't talk sex in my kitchen," interrupted Yerba. "Let's keep a high tone." She traced a reverent circle in the air with her finger and mimed an extra squiggle for a jiva's tail. "We call our local sun the Earthmost Jiva," she told me, smiling like a church-school teacher. "We like to say she's the most important jiva of all."

"At least that's what we say if we know what's good for us," said Durkle sarcastically. "The jivas inside my parents eavesdrop on them, and every time we go outside the maze, their jivas blab to the Earthmost Jiva about whatever we've been doing. I don't have a jiva in me. I'm just plain kessence. I think the Earthmost Jiva is a disgusting leech."

An uncomfortable silence filled the room.

"Holy holy," said Grandpa and made an indecent gesture that was a parody of Yerba's. He was poking his forefinger in and out through a loop made with his other hand's finger and thumb.

"See that?" Yerba scolded Weena. "You got the old man started, talking smutty."

"That must be a hella big hole the Earthmost Jiva burrows in," said Ginnie.

"One has a fine view of the Earthmost Jiva's sacred burrow from atop the Duke's castle," put in Weena smoothly. "We'll be hopping to the castle after supper, Jim. The Duke and the Duchess are most eager to prepare you for your mission."

"Oh, do stay the night," said Monin hospitably. "We don't get enough visitors here."

"Isn't there a steady stream of humans and flims asking to go through your snail's tunnel?" I asked.

"We don't publicize our border snail," said Yerba. "And, even for those who know of her, we're hard to find—thanks to Snaily's maze."

"But you guys can always get in? Like—if you go for an outing, you can find your way home?"

"Snaily likes to see her friends," said Yerba. "And if she feels really special about you, she'll let you open her doors."

"Jim's special," said Weena. "Jim opened the Earth-side door for me twice."

"But why couldn't I find the Whipped Vic the second time?" I asked.

"Snaily has her moods," said Monin.

"I have to wonder who opened the door on Earth for the Graf," said Yerba, looking around the circle of faces.

"It was me," volunteered Ginnie gloomily. "The Graf's voice got into my head. And then it got worse. Two guys killed the Graf and me with a green-handled axe."

"Rough way to die," said Monin conversationally. "Me, I was hung on the gallows."

Ginnie stared across the room, lost in her memories. "And they set the Graf on fire. I'd been blanking it out for the longest time, but today it came back. The Graf and I were in a car and he was getting ready to do me—but I could tell it wasn't gonna be sex. I saw the tip of a blue slug peeking out of his mouth, swollen up like a seed pod. The car door flew open and it was Header and Skeeves—"

"I could still pick up that vibe on Header," I said. "The yuel in his head must have kept some of his personality."

"It was Skeeves who had the axe," said Ginnie slowly. "Skeeves who lit the match. But, yeah, Header was egging him on."

"And Weena," I said. "She was in Skeeves's head."

"They were so surprised when the yuel oozed out of the Graf's body and crawled up Header's nose," continued Ginnie. "They chopped up the Graf before they lit him. There were some pieces they didn't burn. And then Skeeves axed me. I became a tiny dot—one of those sprinkles. And there just enough pieces of the Graf left over for me to make myself a kessence body. Somehow I knew how."

"I didn't tell Skeeves to kill you, Ginnie," said Weena very quickly. "That was his own inititive. All he was tasked to do was to eliminate the Graf."

"Why would I believe you now?" said Ginnie, glaring at her. "You've lied about so many things. Maybe one of these days I'll get a chance to kill you and Skeeves both."

"So—Ginnie's a brand new ghost with a jiva in her body?" said Durkle, skipping right past all the human drama.

"Putting it that way makes me think maybe Ginnie should leave now," said Yerba, suddenly uneasy. "And you go finish fixing up your plow shoes, Durkle. You've had enough excitement."

Durkle slid bonelessly under the table and lay there like a mound of dough, making moany-groany ghost noises. Grandpa leaned over to peer at him and fell out of his chair. Baby Nyoo started crying. Monin bent over to help his father off the floor.

I looked around, taking in my surroundings. It was dark outside now. The dome's walls had a faint glow on the inside, and little round lights glowed each of the rooms. I was starting to like the fanciful lines of the zickzack and the organic shapes of the bio-grown furnishings.

"We are grateful for dinner, Yerba and Monin," said Weena, rising to her feet. "Come outside with me, Jim and Ginnie. We've disturbed this kind family for long enough. Now I'll show you how your jiva can teleport you the fifty miles to the castle."

"Isn't anyone even listening to me?" said Ginnie, bursting into tears. "I'm having a crisis! I need to lie down."

I went and put my arms around her.

"Poor little thing," said Yerba, her kindly face softening. "I do feel sorry for you, Ginnie. But I have to think of my family. It's against protocol for a new ghost to get a jiva and a zickzack body right away. You're supposed to appear in the depths of the Dark Gulf and work your way up from there. If the Duke's guards were to find out about—"

"I say these two are welcome to stay," said Monin firmly. "We're hidden here in the snail's maze, Yerba. We don't have to be scared of those murderous, conniving nobles and—" Suddenly he put his hands to his throat, as if he were being choked. Perhaps the outer jivas couldn't see Monin, but he had one living inside of him as well. His family members seemed to take his anguish in stride—as if ectoplasmic choking were fairly routine in Flimsy. I was glad that, so far, I wasn't hearing much of anything from the jiva within me.

"I don't ever want to have a jiva in me at all," said Durkle, peering out from under the table.

"Of course you want a jiva," Weena told the boy, even as his father was gasping for breath. "Be a proper citizen. With a zickzack skeleton, you wouldn't be so floppy."

"Maybe you should bribe me with a dessert," replied Durkle slyly. "Did you catch some sprinkles inside the snail, Weena?"

"I have a supply," said Weena, gracing her symmetrical face with a perfect smile. "Pleasantly fresh. If your mother permits, I might dole some out before my hop to the castle."

By now Monin had recovered, not that he was saying anything more about the nobles. "Let's all have some sprinkles," he croaked, holding the baby against his shoulder and patting her on the back. "I could use a lift."

So Weena passed around her stash. Some of the sprinkles were considerably bigger than the others—maybe the bigger ones had managed to eat some of their fellows. Ginnie was still upset, but she took some sprinkles too. And then the sprinkles came to me.

The last time I'd eaten these things was when Weena had put them on my ice cream—and I'd ended up in the hospital. But I was out of my usual body now, and, hell, I didn't want to miss out.

So I had a few.

As before, the living gems were amazingly rich in flavor, like a whole case of tropical fruits. After my dose I was hearing fresh voices in my head, as if by eating the sprinkles I'd assimilated some strangers' minds. The voices were rapidly telling me their life stories. Probably it was just a hallucination, but what a rush. I felt calm and optimistic, enjoying my meds.

"I'm closely connected with the Duke of Human Flimsy," bragged Weena. "Given that Jim's on an important mission for the Duke, I can guarantee that there won't be any fuss about Ginnie gaining her body so easily. And it's acceptable to me if Jim and Ginnie stay here tonight." I glanced over at Weena, wondering if she had some secret ulterior motive. "In any case, the materials for Jim's parcel aren't quite ready," she continued. "You'll come straight to the castle tomorrow, correct, Jim?"

"If it's really allowable, I suppose that—" began Yerba.

"I'll watch them fuck!" interrupted Grandpa, clapping his hands.

"Time for bed," Monin told the old man. He poured two shots of clear living water from a finely patterned zickzack decanter. He tossed off one drink and handed the other to his father.

"Toot," said Grandpa, downing his nightcap.

"Toddle off to sleep now," Yerba told him.

"Toot, toot." Docilely, the geezer shuffled from the kitchen.

"My father's jiva will run his body for him now," explained Monin, taking a second drink. "The jiva will undress him, wash him and tuck him in."

"Otherwise I wouldn't let the old coot live here," said Yerba, shaking her head. "If the Duke's guards turn up here, we'll give them Grandpa first."

"Why does a jiva bother with a blown mind like that old man's?" I asked. "If that's not too rude a question."

"The less of a mind the host has, the more the jiva gets to do," said Monin with a shrug. "When jivas are breeding, or at war, they fly around on their own, but most of the time they like to be nestled into a ghost's body as a partner. They're bossy and gossipy. They like being involved with another being's mind."

"I'm putting the baby to bed now," said Yerba. "Monin can show you to the extra dome when you're ready. I'd rather not be involved."

"I'll be off too," said Weena in a polite tone. "Farewell and heartfelt thanks, Yerba. I'll see that you obtain some extra kessence. And Jim will be back soon. We're not done with our business on Earth. We have grand plans."

14: The Garden

Rather than going to bed right away, Ginnie and I followed Weena outside to watch her take off. Monin and Durkle came along as well, striding ahead of us across the meadow, leading us out of the maze.

We only had to walk about a hundred yards until we were free of the space warps that hid the farm. For the first time, I could begin to see the true size of Flimsy. The beauty of it made me catch my breath.

The wall of living water rose like a cliff, gradually arcing over towards the impossibly distant zenith of the Flimsy night sky. The towering dome was filled with rivers of faint pastel light, ever so slowly changing as I watched. The patterns were a bit like our Northern Lights—pinks, yellows and greens, branching and merging, streaming upwards and across the sky.

"Fabulous," breathed Ginnie.

"What causes it?" I asked Monin.

"It's all living water with sprinkles in it," said Monin with a cursory glance upwards along the wall. "I think we told you that Flimsy is inside a hollow shell of living water. The water is where the ghosts start out. If they do well, they make it into our underground caves, and then maybe up to the fields of Flimsy. If they don't do well, they're swept inward to the core and recycled."

"The colors are so wonderful," persisted Ginnie. "All veils and sheets..."

"Hungry ghosts looking for a main chance," said Monin dismissively. He was blandly accustomed to his night sky.

Weena was finally ready to leave. "When you want to teleport, just consult your jiva," she instructed me. "She'll know how to find the Duke of Human Flimsy."

"Could Ginnie and I just walk to the castle?" I ventured. "It'd be nice to have a look around." I gestured at the mad splendor of the wall and the sky. "We're still not used to any of this."

"In principle you can walk," said Weena carelessly. "It's a bit of a trek from here, but I'll be busy for a couple of days talking to the powers that be. And the Duke's castle is easy enough to find. You head for the nearest sun—the Earthmost Jiva. She hovers near the castle like a tethered blimp. Or if you walk at night, follow the direction of the sky's flow."

"What an adventure!" said Ginnie, whose sprits were beginning to rise.

"Don't stir up trouble with the locals," cautioned Weena. "There's much about Flimsy that you don't know. If you walked, you'd be in need of a—"

"Guide!" exclaimed Durkle. "Let me do it, Dad. I can find the castle, and I know all about the yuels and their elephants and the offer caps. I'll bring Jim and Ginnie to the Duke's castle, and then I'll come home on my own. I can teleport, too, you know. Even without a jiva. I can do yuel-style teleportation."

"Let's ask your mother in the morning," said Monin in a noncommittal tone. "Speaking of jivas, you'll notice a few jiva eggs out here, Jim. Wanting to come inside."

"There's one right now," said Durkle, pointing.

The free-floating jiva egg happened to drift fairly close to me. It was a glowing orange-yellow spot with a mauve tadpole shape at its center. It moved with a zigzag motion as if sniffing around for a good site to land. It reminded me of—oh, shit.

The jiva egg was the very image of the bright dot that had floated into our bedroom on the night of the lightning strike. In other words, a jiva egg had gotten inside of Val. And the loathsome tumor that the doctors had incinerated on sight—that had been an embryonic jiva.

I stood stock still, fighting for control, blanking out my mind. I had enemies on every side.

"Farewell for now," said Weena in a breezy tone. She didn't seem to notice what was I was thinking. "Don't tarry too long." She leaned over and kissed my cheek. "And remember, Jim, with your jiva inside you, I'll always know where you are. Hot and nasty." She emitted a giggle. I wanted to kill her.

A tangle of jiva tendrils wove a nest or cocoon around Weena. And then a sheaf of extra tendrils writhed from her chest to stretch out into the distance, feeling for her jump target. Moments later Weena made an odd virtual gesture with her mind—and the woman who'd ruthlessly toyed with me for weeks was gone. Thank God.

Following the teeped guidance of the border snail, Durkle and Monin led us back through the ever-altering maze that hid their home. A few of the jiva eggs followed us, settling into some of Monin's smaller garden plants. The father and son paused by the plot, pointing and talking. The largest of the lumpy shapes seemed to be throbbing.

"Give them a couple of squirts of ultragrow," Monin advised Durkle. "And a bucket of living water apiece. Tomorrow, I think seven of them will be ready to pop." Moving fluidly, Durkle got to work.

Monin led Ginnie and me to the spare dome, where we settled in. The bed was a soft blob of zickzack. Living flowers shed dim, colored splotches across the room. One of the flowers brimmed with water, another had a drain hole that served as a toilet. And on the wall was another little shrine to the Earthmost Jiva.

Ginnie and I laid down side by side on the bed. After a minute I put my arms around her.

"So now we're a pair of ghosts in kessence bodies," I said conversationally.

"I still can't believe I was murdered on Lover's Bluff," murmured Ginnie, nestling against me. "That's so loser, so tacky, so trite. "

"Poor Ginnie," I said.

"Well, at least these bodies aren't so bad," she said. "Do you like yours?"

Using my teep, I checked the vicinity for peeping Toms. "Grandpa's asleep. I don't suppose that—" I lost my courage, cleared my throat, started again. "Do you want to make love? Does that sound crass?"

"I don't know," said Ginnie. "Maybe crass, maybe polite. But, no. Just hold me. That's all I'm up for." She sighed. "I always thought that being dead would be more fun."

In the morning Durkle woke us by lugging in baby Nyoo and

dropping her onto our bed.

"I want to show you our garden," Durkle announced. "Seven of the Dad-fruits are ready to pop. The jivas put eggs into them a few months ago."

Thinking of Val's pregnancy and the horrible climax, I winced. Yet here I was trying to fuck Ginnie.

"Give us a minute, kid," I said. "We have to wake up. Is there a shower?"

"Use the bell-blossom over there." And with that, he trotted off, leaving the infant in our care.

The baby was in a cheerful mood, crawling around and cooing, two little teeth showing in her lower gum. It was nice to see her. I felt a pang, remembering my shattered dream of having children with Val. Was there really a chance that I'd find her ghost over here? I doubted if Weena would actually help me in the quest. And Flimsy seemed huge. But—maybe? The possibility provoked a mixture of longing and fear. What if Val's ordeals had warped her into something terrible?

"So it's been a year?" said Ginnie, reading my mind.

"And every day I've been saying goodbye," I said, playing this up a little to get some sympathy.

Ginnie got right on me. She rubbed her thumb against her forefinger. "Look! The world's smallest violin." She made a crackling noise. "Whoops! I stepped on it."

"Why do men have to pretend to be nice, when women don't even bother?" I snapped.

"Because we *are* nice in the first place," said Ginnie. "Most of us."

"I *am* going to look for Val."

"Fine," said Ginnie. "When you're not busy trying to fuck me. Is this supposed to be Heaven, do you think? I always hated that bullshit."

"I don't think our mass-market religions have any kind of handle on what we're seeing here. Maybe Val's already drifted to the center of Flimsy. But that might be a quadrillion miles away. Can you imagine taking a road trip that long? It could take, I don't know—a trillion years? With new scenery every single day."

"I don't think they don't have cars here," said Ginnie in a practical tone. "It's more like a network. People teleport. I say we go outside and start exploring."

"First we shower," I said.

After my night's rest, I was able to take in our room a little more clearly. It had an Art Nouveau look to it, with a braid-patterned wooden headboard behind the plump zickzack mattress. Blooming vines bedecked the walls, with a particularly large ultramarine flower across from the bed, a long narrow bell, hanging from the ceiling to the floor. I slipped inside it through the slit between two petals. The flower drizzled water onto me, and a mat of root hairs at my feet soaked up the drips.

A moment later, Ginnie joined me in the shower, cool and resilient. Her eyes were a rich brown, with soft flecks of gold. I held her naked body and now, for the first time, we kissed.

In a way this was like a dream of Eden. But the kisses didn't feel quite right. The insides of our two mouths were dry, and remained so. At least our bodies had genitals, although we didn't get into the details of that. For now, the kissing was enough.

On our way outside, we handed baby Nyoo off to Yerba who was sitting at the dining table, staring into space while absorbing information from her jiva. Although Yerba took the baby, she acted like she didn't see us. And farmer Monin was still asleep.

The sun—that is, the Earthmost Jiva—must have been high in the air by now, for a pleasant yellow light was making its way through the space warps that concealed Monin's farm.

The plants at the far end of Monin's garden resembled seven nude men, knee-deep in the dirt, with full-grown torsos and heads. I hadn't really gotten a good look at them the day before. Ever so slowly, they swayed their arms and twitched their fingers, as if they were asleep and dreaming. Their eyes were closed, their skins pale and nearly translucent. Their faces looked exactly like Monin's.

"See?" said Durkle, who was waiting in the yard, excited about our travel plans.

"Are these for eating?" I asked about the things in the garden. "Don't tell me that roast we had last night was a human leg!"

Durkle thought this was funny and, wriggly imp that he was, he bent double as if to bite me in the thigh.

"Look closer," he said when he straightened up. "Look under the Dad-fruits' skins."

The garden-grown globs of kessence had colored shapes in their swollen bellies, slowly writhing forms like fetuses—or like parasitic worms.

Pop.

One of the bodies burst open, and a newborn jiva wriggled out, glistening with slime. It shook out its tail, basking in the filtered rays of the Earthmost Jiva, hovering by the ruins of the body it had grown in.

"Life," it teeped. "Light."

More pops ensued—and now seven of the flying beets were hovering above the slaughter-ground of the garden. There was no blood—just pools of living water and scraps of kessence—but it was uncanny just the same. Ginnie backed away, taking shelter against the dome.

"I'm supposed to dig the leftovers into the ground," said Durkle. "To help the next crop grow. Some of the little guys got new eggs in them last night."

"Why do jivas have to reproduce in such a disgusting way?" asked Ginnie.

"They don't have enough kessence on their own," said Durkle. "The adult jivas are mostly zickzack. But an embryonic jiva needs a fair amount of kessence to nurture its growth. So the jivas need to plant their eggs somewhere juicy—like in my family's all-kessence Dad-fruits."

"Or in living human flesh," I added, thinking yet again of Val's fate, trying to fill in the ghastly details. One thing that puzzled me was why the eggs in Dick Simly had come to term so much faster than in Val. I asked the boy how long the eggs took to grow.

"The jivas are always changing things around," said Durkle. "It can be days or it can be months. The jivas are smart and sly. I'll tell you one thing, we don't let them stick their tails in here to implant the eggs directly, or they might make a rush for Snaily's tunnel. We make our deals outside the maze and we lead in the eggs ourselves."

Durkle fastened his translucent ice skates to his feet. The blades were long rectangles, with little levers at the rear ends. These were the things I'd seen him messing with when we'd arrived.

"How sharp are they?" I asked, just to keep talking, trying to bury my horror with words. "Can you actually push them through the dirt and—and the other stuff?" The garden was littered with twitching kessence models of human limbs. The expressionless Monin-heads were strewn about like goth soccer-balls.

"These are zickzack plow shoes," said Durkle, crouched over his special footwear. "Dad's jiva made them. The blades slice through whatever they touch. And the tops of the blade are space-linked to their bottoms. You use these levers in back to warp the shape so that the bottom's ahead of the top, and then the top keeps trying to catch up so—"

With a lurch and a wobble, Durkle slid into motion, skating smoothly through the dirt of the garden, his blades mincing up the remains of the Dad-fruits, with smooth curls of soil flopping out to either side. Back and forth he sailed, avoiding the younger plants, but taking particular delight in slicing the discarded limbs in two. His boneless motions were smooth and rubbery.

"What a brutal little boy that Durkle is," Ginnie murmured to me.

"He's a farmer," I said. "In touch with the wheel of life."

"Ugh."

The seven newborn jivas were drifting around, shaking out their tails, getting the feel of the air, talking things over. Via teep I could pick up the faint skritchy buzz of the their signals, a mix of nouns and of thought forms that I couldn't comprehend.

"And the jivas pay you guys for the use of the Dad-fruits?" I asked Durkle as he whizzed past. He was skating playful figure eights in the garden.

"Sure," answered the boy, "Dad gets a big wad of kessence for each egg that we hatch. Hey, did you ask Mom if I can be your guide? I'm hoping we can leave before Dad even wakes up. He's going to be crabby today. He drank that whole bottle of living water last night."

"Yerba didn't want to talk to us," I said. "She's tuned into some kind of teep."

"That's her court gossip channel," said Durkle disgustedly. "It's like everyone who lives in the Duke's castle is supposed to be so interesting that we country bumpkins are excited to find out who they're kissing and what they ate. Mom can zone into that stuff for hours. She walks out of the maze every day to let her jiva load up a supply of the latest news."

"What if we leave here without asking permission?" suggested Ginnie. "I mean—your father practically said okay last night. And we don't really need any supplies. With our jivas, Jim and I should be able to find all the food and drink we need."

"Yeah," I chimed in. "Let's skulk off."

Durkle grinned. "You two are great."

"I have another idea," I said. "It's quite a long walk to the castle, right?"

"Three or four days."

"Come here and let me look at your plow shoes."

Durkle skated out of the garden, hopping over a line of tiny, baby-sized Monin heads at the edge. He sliced through the meadow's turf and came to a stop at my side. Twirling his rubbery leg, and handed me a shoe. "Careful of that sharp edge."

I used my jiva tendrils to feel all over the device, teeping into its details. When I pulled back on the rear lever, the rectangular blade sheared into a lozenge shape. It took all my strength to keep the shoe from darting away, as the top edge tried to keep up with the bottom.

I was getting an idea for an invention.

Teeping into the house, I examined the design for Grandpa's chair, and I got my jiva to manufacture a zickzack copy that was three times as wide—like a sofa. It felt very elegant to work with the jiva, as if I had a zillion delicate tendrils issuing from my hands.

When the new couch was done, Ginnie flopped onto the iridescent cushions and made herself comfortable. But I still had more to do.

Mijjy and I put a support plate under the couch, a kind of sled. Using the plow shoes as a model, I constructed a pair of levers that could shear the shape of the sled, and implemented the subtle trick of linking the sled's top to its bottom. The topological moves were a little more complicated for this plate-like shape than for the narrow edges of the plow shoes, especially since the shear factor could be different along the plate's two sides. I was aided by my biotech experiences with folding long-chain molecules into proteins.

"What's all this about?" demanded Ginnie. "I thought we were ready to leave."

"I've invented a replacement for Flimsy's missing cars!" I crowed a moment later. "The cruiser couch. Hop aboard and we're on the road."

15: Cruiser Couch

We three settled onto my cruiser couch. I pulled back on the levers, balancing them so we'd go straight ahead. We chugged along, scraping a wide furrow into the ground. Pausing to think things over, I hit upon the idea of adding a second layer of tweaked space beneath the sled—a slab with its top glued to its bottom the wrong way round.

The new layer created an effect like antigravity. The couch jiggled above the ground as if on springs. We were really ready to travel now. We tooled onward across the rolling meadow that lay before Monin's dome house, making easily thirty miles per hour.

When we left the maze that concealed Monin's house, I finally saw the Earthmost Jiva, their local sun. Her light glittered on the great wall of living water which bounded the Flimsy world. Her dangling tail was clearly visible, a spike beneath the swollen sun, extending all the way down to the ground.

Durkle lolled at one end of the couch, grinning into the wind. Ginnie leaned against me at the other end. Our cruiser rode as smoothly as a vintage cream-puff Populuxe convertible.

"Awesome," said Durkle, wriggling with joy. "It's hard to believe that we flims never made a cruiser couch before."

"Well, who invented the plow shoe?" I asked.

"The jivas did. They showed Monin how to make it for our garden.

Mostly nobody in Flimsy invents things on their own."

"Jim's clever," said Ginnie, her kessence-strand hair tossing in the breeze. "Maybe he'll go beyond the plans of the jivas."

The seven new jivas had tagged along after us. Out in the open like this, they were able to pick up teep signals from the Earthmost Jiva—I sensed a redoubling of the skritchy buzzing.

"What are they talking about?" I asked the jiva within me.

"Earth Jiva Happy Face commandments babies destruction," said Mijjy, fleshing out her words with a flow of feelings and pictures, selecting the images from the library of my own mind. I saw the Earthmost Jiva wearing a smile, welcoming the newborns. She showed them how to cast a glittering net across the plains of Flimsy to fish for a flim to serve as a symbiotic partner.

The Earthmost Jiva also told the newcomers how to spawn. All the jivas were, in some sense, female—they could all lay free-floating eggs. And, given a particularly good target, they'd be able to implant the eggs directly into a host's flesh. I saw the new jivas' tails thickening with desire as they anticipated the day when they too would be parasitizing their victims.

The big jiva taught of war as well. She set the newcomers to dreaming of mighty battles against the yuels, with fleets of flying jivas darkening the skies and raining energy blasts upon the vile, shape-shifting enemies and their insufferable songs.

Before long, all but one of the newborn jivas had drifted away, each setting out on her own first mission—to find a flim she could partner with. Their egg-laying days were still a long way off.

The one jiva who lingered near us was a pushy little beet with orange zigzags around her waist and a silver onion-dome on top. She darted at Durkle on the couch a few times, making herself small in size, as if petitioning Durkle to swallow her up.

"I don't want a jiva," said Durkle through clenched teeth.

"Doll doll superman," teeped the jiva. Her words had a mocking, reckless vibe. She was taking pleasure in teasing the boy, and I feared she might do him harm.

I discussed the problem with my jiva, Mijjy. It was unpleasant to converse with her. Her jagged words were ungainly, and her thoughts had a snickering, sarcastic tone—as if she looked down on me. But finally Mijjy extruded a tendril from my hand, and we gave the hectoring new beet a whack, sending the zigzag-banded newcomer on her way.

And so we continued.

Given that long-distance travel in Flimsy was done via jiva jumps, we weren't seeing any real roads. Instead we were following footpaths, and cutting across meadows. For a time we skimmed the surface of a creek, our antigravity plate keeping us out of the water. We sailed along the stream's smooth curves, the scenery flowing past, lovely and hypnotic. Odd-looking trees hung down on either side. The stream water was so pure that I could see every detail of the bed.

Eventually the stream veered away from our intended route. I guided the couch up the bank, heading towards the unmistakable beacon of the Earthmost Jiva. Boulders and plinth-like outcrops dotted the plains here, and the land was sloping uphill. I maintained a good pace, bending our path around the rocks, the air always beating against our faces.

"This wind is getting to me," complained Ginnie. "And we need some music. Hold on—"

She got to work with her own jiva, and affixed a streamlined zickzack window to the front of our couch—a windshield. To sweeten the arrangement, she ran a jiva-tendril link between her own mind to the windshield's surface, setting it vibrating like a speaker. A familiar blues tune washed over us. And now the drum-track switched to hoarse grunts.

"I've got a pitch-perfect memory for songs," said Ginnie, tapping her head. "Thousands of files in here. And I can edit them in my head. It's so great to be doing this out loud." The singer's voice became a modulated version of an ocean's roar. "Do you like it?" asked Ginnie.

"I do," I said.

"Play it a little softer," said Durkle. "I'm not used to these kinds of sounds." It was like he'd never heard a musical instrument.

Up ahead, some houses were visible near the crest of the hill, no two of them the same. Some were largely biological, having the forms of plants or shells, while others were shimmering zickzack constructs, rich with arches and nooks.

"I've been to that place over there," said Durkle pointing to pair of giant, striped gourds. "That's where my cousin lives. Flam. His father is my father's brother. They grew Flam here, like me—he's a native flim. But Flam has a jiva."

"Let's not stop," I said. "I don't want to get hung up in your family scene."

"Fine," said Durkle, looking young and vulnerable. "I don't really like cousin Flam. He picks on me because he's older. And because my body was made by yuels. And because I won't get a stupid jiva."

"I don't really follow all these distinctions," said Ginnie. "It's like haute couture fashion or something."

"The jivas can make these spacewarp rods that we call zickzack, okay?" said Durkle. "And if you're a ghost with a jiva inside, like you two, you have a zickzack skeleton. A plain ghost is just a wispy cloud of kessence, or maybe just a sprinkle. And if you want a really nicely made kessence body, you have to get a yuel to make you one. They're very good at that stuff." The boy set his jaw. "I'm proud of my yuel-built body, no matter what the others say."

Passing these houses, I could see some local flims watching us, and I could teep the thoughts in their minds. They already knew who Ginnie and I were—the jiva-web had spread the news of our unconventional arrival from Earth. Like the farm wife Yerba, the flims of this village were leery of us, and not particularly eager for a visit. They knew we were on our way to the castle of the Duke of Human Flimsy.

Beyond the village we reached a bluff.

"Let's stop here to eat," said Durkle. "I came here once with Mom and Dad."

I pulled the cruiser couch to a halt. We got off the couch and stretched, admiring the view, a vast checkerboard of meadows and woods with abrupt towers of stone breaking the valley bed. Far away to the right was a glittering swamp, and to the left ran the hazy outline of a mountain range.

"So look way out there along the horizon," said Ginnie. "Is that an ocean?"

"The Dark Gulf," said Durkle without much interest. "Where the new ghosts appear." He was pacing back and forth, studying the ground.

"And to the left and right, those bright little dots?" continued Ginnie. "They must be the other suns. I don't see any end to them. What a weird world."

"Hey, I see a patch of pigpops over here," exclaimed Durkle. "We ate some when we came to this cliff before. Pigpops are good if you cook them."

"I'm ready for that," I said.

The pigpops looked like pink snouts projecting from the soil. Each snout had a ruff of triangular flaps like pig ears, and a plump round base that nestled into the dirt. Durkle yanked up a half dozen of them—they squealed as he snapped their curly roots.

"Ask your jiva to make us a zickzack oven," said Durkle to me. "Pigpops are too tough to eat raw."

"Let me make the oven," said Ginnie. "What do I do?"

"Get your jiva to assemble, I don't know, a square zickzack box with no top," I suggested. "And connect the inner walls to some squares of space that are up in the sky near the Earthmost Jiva."

Ginnie had a little trouble with this, but I reached into her mind and helped her. And then we had a box of sun blazing on the ground at our feet. Durkle tossed in the six pigpops. They wheenked and twisted for a minute, and then settled down to sizzling.

"Pluck 'em out when they're done all the way through," said Durkle, excitedly scampering off. "I'll pick some waffle cactuses."

I used one of my jiva tendrils to monitor the center of a pigpop, and by the time Durkle returned, the textured kessence flesh was nicely roasted. Durkle was carrying a dozen rounded pads, green and doughy. We took the pigpops out of the cook box and tossed in the waffles. And then, after a minute for toasting, Ginnie took the box apart.

I made us three self-filling mugs that linked to the clear stream we'd ridden along. We sat on the ground for our picnic. Thanks to some friendly subtlety of the kessence, the pigpops tasted much like pork tenderloin, and the waffle cactuses were like corn tortillas. A nice meal.

"I'm happy to be going somewhere new," said Durkle, surveying the view ahead. "This is about as far from home as I've ever been."

"Then how are you supposed to guide us to the castle?" demanded Ginnie.

"Heck, all we have to do is head towards the Earthmost Jiva," said Durkle, pointing ahead with his wobbly arm. He gave Ginnie an ingratiating smile. I had a feeling the boy had a crush on her.

Studying the Earthmost Jiva with Mijjy's help, I was able to make out more of this sun-like object's details. She was a brilliant pale yellow, with a darker yellow stripe around the middle. A small hump of orange was on the top, and a pale, flickering tail hung from the bottom, disappearing into the distant ground. I couldn't easily judge how big the jiva was—but I was thinking she might be less than a mile across.

"Is that the castle out there?" Ginnie asked Durkle. "The smudge of green under the big jiva?"

"I think so. I hear the castle is a giant green plant. But before we head there, I want to swing by some other spots. That swamp to the right? The swamp is crawling with offer caps. I'd like to have a try at outsmarting an offer cap. And in the middle of the swamp is Yuelsville. The yuels there run an amusement park called Funger Gardens. And right before the swamp, that big dusty patch? That's the *monster pit*."

Durkle said this last phrase as if he were talking about a world-famous monument. Seeing our blank faces, he elaborated. "The monster pit is a gigundo conical hole in the ground, all covered with slippery sand. My cousin Flam told me that he and his friends ride boards down the monster pit's slopes. I wanted him to take me there, but—"

"Flam and your parents said it was too dangerous for a kid like you," guessed Ginnie. "Fuddy-duddies. For sure we're swinging by the monster pit, Durkle. Before I got axed, I was hella good at riding boards."

"What did you ride the boards on, Ginnie?" asked Durkle, increasingly fascinated by her.

"Streets," said Ginnie. "And ocean waves." She crouched down and peered at the floaty region under the cruiser couch. "Hey, Jim, what happens if we drive your rig off the edge of this cliff? *That'd* be some kind of ride."

"I think maybe we'd crash and die." I pointed to the right, where a footpath ran along the bluff's crest. "We'll angle that way to get to the pit."

"Die?" mused Ginnie, running her hands down her shapely face. "But if this is the afterworld and everyone here is a ghost—"

"I'm not exactly a ghost," I interrupted, wanting to keep this straight. "I have a body waiting for me on Earth."

"I'm not a ghost either," said Durkle. "I never lived on Earth and I never died at all. I'm native-born flim, a tweaked glob of kessence.

And, like I say, my parents got my body from the yuels." He stretched out his arms and wriggled them like snakes. "It's better without a skeleton."

"Okay, but that's all beside the point," persisted Ginnie. "I'm trying to find out where I go if I die here."

"You turn into a puny sprinkle," said Durkle carelessly. "Didn't we already tell you that? And then you end up in living water of Flimsy, just like a newly arrived ghost. Maybe you make into the underworld and you work your way up. Or maybe you get swept across the sky. I hear the souls rain back down at the core."

Finally we were getting some decent information. "I can't quite believe that the sprinkles are souls," I said. "They're so small."

"They're folded-up," said Durkle with a shrug. "You hear their voices when you eat them. We don't worry about it, though. Sprinkles have no rights. There's a big pecking order, see, and too many flims anyhow. Don't forget, we've got a septillion intelligent races sending their ghosts in here, plus we've got the natives like me. The sprinkles are all trying to get a kessence body together so they can be respectable citizens, maybe with a jiva inside. If you push ahead in line—like you and Ginnie did—well, then some flims think it's their right to torture you to death."

"Sounds like home," said Ginnie, shaking her head in disgust. "A special welcome for the immigrants."

We cruised along the cliff's edge, with our windshield playing an miraculously long and detailed Charlie Parker solo—Ginnie had crafted it by sewing dozens of Bird's solos together into one.

The bluff descended in a series of swoops and humps, guiding us to the plain we'd seen from above. Rather than heading towards the glow of the Earthmost Jiva, we steered toward the haze of dust that betokened the location of the monster pit.

We cruised along for awhile until, upon rounding a grove of trees, I saw a break in the landscape and a distant cliff. It took me a moment to realize that the remote cliff was the far side of the monster pit. Soon we came upon the pit's near edge, which stretched for miles to either side, an abrupt drop where the meadows gave way to a sandy slope that slanted down at a fiercely steep pitch.

"The monster pit," said Durkle reverently. "At last."

The pit was maybe ten miles across, and probably even deeper, although it was hard to be sure. Its lower reaches were quite dim, with a single small glint from the very bottom.

Little slides of sand were continually rippling down the pit's sides, as if it were a gargantuan hourglass. Puffs of dust blew up the slope and got into my mouth, gritty against my teeth.

I heard a whoop. Feeling around with my teep, I located the bright minds of two kids riding the slopes. Now that I knew where to look, I could see the tiny figures a mile below us, wavering back and forth, throwing up rooster-tails of sand, carving short-lived curves.

Curious about the riders, I teeped a greeting—and a moment later, the two board-riders had jiva-jumped up to check us out. One was a snub-faced young woman with a shock of blonde hair, the other was a lanky guy with a beaky nose and a prominent Adam's apple. Each of them carried a zickzack board six or seven feet long.

"Durkle the turtle," said the lanky guy, surprised. "What are you doing here, floppy-boy?"

"Hi Flam. These are my new friends from Earth, Jim and Ginnie. New ghosts. But they didn't go to the underworld at all."

"Impressive," said Flam mildly. "Maybe I heard about this. They came through your family's big snail? Won't the guards be after Ginnie?"

"Not as long as she's with Jim," said Durkle. "Jim's important. I'm taking him to meet the Duke."

"But naturally you want to ride the pit on your way." said Flam. "Fine. I just wonder if you noobs can—"

"Hey!" said Ginnie. "Jim and I are from Surf City, my man. I'll make us three special boards with a levitation hack, and with a shear drive like we have under our cruiser couch."

"You rode here on that couch?" asked the calm blonde woman at Flam's side. "And hi, by the way. My name's Swoozie."

I had a fleeting urge to drop to my knees and nuzzle the sexy Swoozie's thighs like a dog. Seeing this in my mind, she favored me with a casual smile that said, "Thanks, but no way." If you were a telepath, you were accustomed to other people's extreme thoughts.

Meanwhile Flam watched Ginnie fashion us three long boards, each with a power plate on the bottom and a control lever in back. Ginnie was bright. She'd effortlessly picked the design details from my head. She decorated the boards with splashy pictures: jivas for me, pigpops for Durkle, and skulls with axes for herself.

"I'm a little worried about you, cousin Durkle," allowed Flam. "You can teleport, yeah, so maybe you can hop back to the top when you need to. But I know how stubborn you are. If you actually hit the bottom—" Flam threw his hands in the air.

"What's down there?" I asked. "A giant ant lion?" I pumped my hands like insect jaws, kidding around.

"A pool of hungry ghosts," said Flam, not smiling. "It's an underground lake that comes in from the Dark Gulf. The folks who go in there don't came back anytime soon. That's why it takes guts to ride the pit at all."

"And, no, I'm *not* going to teleport when it's time to bail," said Durkle, eager to show off. "That's for wimps. I'll use this lever to bomb uphill." He crouched on his new board, his snaky limbs wrapped into a knot, diddling the control. The board swung into motion, and Durkle carved circles around us.

"Whoo hoo," muttered Flam sarcastically. I could teep that he was little envious of our cool rigs.

"Ready to race?" yelled Durkle, heady with his board's power. "How about one of those chicken races, Flam?"

"What's that mean?" I asked.

"Oh, that's when you ride straight down and go faster and faster until someone falls off or bails," said Flam. "But—"

"Durkle shouldn't do that yet," put in Swoozie. "Not on his first ride."

"Should too!" shrilled Durkle, coming to a halt at our side. "I'm gonna be the pit master."

Swoozie glanced over Durkle's pigpop-patterned board. "That lever thing is radical."

"Flashy trash," said Flam. "Boards should be simple."

"You're weak, Flam," hollered Durkle. "You're lame!"

Flam's mouth tightened. With a practiced move, he flipped his long board through the air and balanced himself on the edge of the cliff. Wordlessly he scowled at his cousin.

"We'll ride full speed, and the first one in sight of the bottom wins," babbled Durkle. "Right? I've been dreaming about this all year. I'll be the new pit master, yeah. And if I beat you, Flam, you have to give me your board."

"Like that'll happen," said Flam cracking a smile. It was hard to withstand Durkle's gall. "And if I win—I get to keep Jim's cruiser couch. He can always make a new one, right?"

"No problem," I said. Flam wasn't really a bad guy.

Swoozie said she'd wait up here—she wasn't interested in little Durkle trying to prove himself. But Ginnie and I lined up next to the two boys. This seemed like too awesome an experience to miss.

"Remember that riding is supposed to be fun," Flam cautioned Durkle. "Please don't overdo it and get yourself killed. I don't want your mother coming after me."

"I'll watch over him," I said.

16: Under the Pit

And then the four of us were whizzing down the slope—Flam, Durkle, Ginnie and me. The sand rose behind us in plumes, the sky was a watery disk of blue, the Earthmost Jiva was watching.

Flam held the lead. He had a special way of crouching and rocking that set his board to bouncing. He arrowed down the slope like a skipping stone, moving his arms in rapid ideograms of grace.

Hell-bent on besting his cousin, Durkle lay down on his pigpop-decorated board, making his flexible body as flat as a fried egg. He pushed his lever all the way forward. Feeling a sense of responsibility for the excitable lad, I followed close behind, squinting against the flying sand.

Ginnie, to our rear, wasn't so interested in the race. She was getting a feel for the ride and the slope. She stood erect like a surfer, swooping back and forth in huge slalom loops, having fun.

For a little while, Durkle and I were gaining on Flam. I started to have some hopes of passing him. But then he glanced back at us, laughed, and began bouncing harder, redoubling the lengths of his hops down the slope. Our boards' power-drives didn't seem to make much difference in the face of Flam's skill at using the natural dynamics of the pit.

The miles flew by, and the pit grew steeper. In the process of our cat and mouse chase, we'd amped up to the speed of a Bonneville race car. I worried that if we wiped out and tumbled, we'd be sanded down to oozing scraps.

Up ahead, Flam rocketed into the shadowed zone near the cone's base. Seconds later, Durkle and I entered the gloom as well. Deep below, a wet patch twinkled. The cone was but a half-mile across here, and the walls were nearly vertical. The cavity murmured with the echoes of our headlong chase.

Something clunked and shattered against my board—shit, that was an abandoned zickzack skull! Flam continued accelerating down the tightening cone, continued increasing his lead. I was seeing damp spots and sparkles of color in the sands, and further down, the colors flowed into a sinister, glowing pool of living water. Flam had warned us about the bottom. Time to bail.

I hoped I could figure out how to teleport myself. Imitating what I'd seen Weena do, I wove an invisible cocoon of tendrils around myself. And then, reaching upward with some longer tendrils, I felt for a suitable a target zone at the cone's lip. Flam was still ahead. The race was done.

As if to confirm this, Flam disappeared. He'd jumped back to the top. And behind us, Ginnie had jumped too. But that crazy little Durkle was still racing straight ahead—what was he thinking? The pool below us flickered with pearlescent light.

Somehow I felt responsible for the boy. I decided to stay with him a little longer. I asked Mijjy if she'd delay the jump I'd just prepared. Mijjy gave me an answer of sorts, but not what I'd expected.

"Funnel puddle ecstasy death," she said, and showed me the image of a ghost-like Jim with his kessence smeared across an acre of gravel and his jiva wriggling free. The jiva in the image was giggling with titillation, savoring the sensations of the man's last spasm.

In plain words, my jiva was in this for kicks, and she didn't really care if I pulled out of my dive or not. Fine. For now I still had time to catch up with Durkle.

I pushed my board lever the last possible bit forward. With aching slowness, I drew even with the boy, coming up on his left. The converging walls of the dim pit were flying past in a blur, with more and more streaks of living water in the sand. Durkle grinned over at me, his eyes squinted to slits. He was loving his ride. Like kids everywhere, he imagined he was invulnerable.

I couldn't speak over the roar of our tobogganing, nor could I use jiva-teep to reach the boy. And so I fell back on gestures. I indicated that Flam was gone, and that the glowing, shifting walls were closing in on every side. I put my hands together as if in prayer, and bowed to Durkle, to show him that he was the true pit master. I pointed to the pool of melding pastels just below.

Finally Durkle relented. He pulled back on his lever and swung his board hard to the right, expecting to carve an upward path to the top of the pit. Too sharp a turn? For now it was okay—his board held steady. His right edge carved a deep furrow into the lambent sand. Durkle was going to make it.

I still wished he'd just hop himself out of here, using his yuel-style teleportation, however that worked. But for now I was stuck shadowing his moves. I steered to the right like Durkle had done. I was already imagining the ride to the top, the reunion with Ginnie, and the tongue-lashing I'd give my jiva. But just then—I screwed up.

I was tired, scared, over-excited. Eager as I was to escape from the bottom of the pit, I'd gunned it a little too hard—and my board scraped the side of Durkle's. We wobbled, bumped once more and—oh hell—rolled.

Mijjy hadn't entirely abandoned me. My tendril cocoon were still in place. I grabbed hold of Durkle, and my jiva firmed up my cocoon enough to keep our kessence intact as we bounced down the final meters of the pit's slope.

If I'd been fully accustomed to teleportation, I probably could have hopped the two of us up to the top. But, remember, I'd never actually teleported before. I wasn't quite sure how to pull the trigger. And Mijjy showed no inclination to coach me along. I think she was curious what might happen when we hit bottom.

The water at the bottom was flickering like the Flimsy night sky, or like the wall I'd passed through in the tunnel. I realized it was filled with sprinkles—hungry ghosts.

It was as if death had been stalking me across the worlds. It had already taken my wife, and it had nearly nailed me at the Santa Cruz Hospital. Perhaps to escape, I'd travelled out of my body for this great adventure. But now this. Too bad.

The shimmering waters splashed up around us and the sprinkles set upon us like tiny piranhas. As in the tunnel, the sprinkles' onslaught broke me into a flock of scraps—but once again my body pulled itself back together. Durkle and I drifted down through a few meters of living water, and emerged into air, dropping onto a floor.

Stunned by the sudden transition, we two remained silent for a time.

We were in a place that resembled—what a letdown—a ramshackle, cobbled-together shopping mall. A layer of living water floated above us like a ceiling, filled with sprinkles fighting their ceaseless battles. And here amid this collection of walls and corridors was a crowd of human-shaped ghosts—milling around, plucking at us.

The touches of their hands were feathery and insubstantial—these puny spirits had no jivas in them, and no zickzack bodies to their name. I flailed my arms and sent them tumbling like dry leaves. One of them, a man in green, hit his head on the floor. The other ghosts tore him apart, devouring the wispy scraps. The man's last remains shrank into a glittering emerald speck that arced up to enter the thick blanket of living water overhead.

The man's fate scared off our attackers. They lost interest in us for a time.

My jiva, Mijjy, was eagerly running exploratory tendrils into this reality. And Durkle was at my side. It occurred to me that Val might be somewhere down here. The thought was both alluring and creepy. There's a reason why we bury our dead. We can't bear to see our loved ones so terribly transformed.

Still silent, Durkle and I began to walk.

Narrow corridors veered off at crazy angles, holes pocked the floors. The ceiling was a continuation of that same sheet of living water. Durkle had called it an underground lake—presumably it was fed by the great Dark Gulf that filled the lower hemisphere of Flimsy.

Crooked store fronts lined the walls, none of them quite straight, nothing quite level. For some reason, the stores' signs were graphic icons: Chair, Fish, Vase—like that. This place felt less like a building than like an organically grown reef. The halls were evenly lit by a feeble, greenish glow, as if from the energies of decay.

To every side, the pastel ghosts darted in and out of nooks and passages, some nimble as insects in a colony, some streaming past us with hooded eyes, lost perhaps in memories, or intent upon power quests. The fainter figures were presumably the newer arrivals. Often the more experienced ghosts would set upon a newcomer, siphoning energy from their victim until he or she collapsed into a sprinkle that darted up to that sheet of living water overhead, perhaps to drift into the depths of the Dark Gulf.

Now and then a particularly vigorous sparkle in the living water overhead would eat so many of its fellows that it was able to blossom out and drift down in the form of a humanoid ghost.

All was in flux.

"The underworld of Flimsy," said Durkle softly. "I've never been here."

I touched his shoulder, gave him a pat, and then a hug. Although he was bendy and rubbery, he was good and solid. He had a lot of kessence.

"We'll be fine," I told him, hoping this was true. "We'll have a look around and then find our way out."

Despite the crash, I felt relatively fresh and healthy. I stretched my arms, savoring the supple strength of my kessence and my jiva-enhancements. My hand happened to block the ghost of a flat-faced woman wearing a shiny pink dress. She slid around me like a scarf of mist. A hip-looking man in a purple suit danced by, giving us a probing look.

"I hear that a lot of these ghosts never make it out of here," remarked Durkle. "If someone manages to eat your sprinkle, it's curtains. Or you can get stuck on a treadmill, bouncing back and forth between being a sprinkle and a newbie ghost. They say that eventually the global current might catch you, and sweep you into the sky. And it's hard to get down from there. Supposedly if you end up at the center of the sky, the goddess of Flimsy might recycle you. The sprinkles have it rough."

I thought back to the two times I'd eaten sprinkles. Those voices I'd heard while I was eating—they'd been real. Sprinkles were tiny souls. The ones that I'd eaten had merged into me, I supposed, melted into me like drops of ink in a glass of water.

"And how do they ever escape?" I asked.

"It's like we were telling you before," said Durkle. "They crawl up through the dirt of Flimsy. Or they get back into the Dark Gulf and follow one of the walls up into the sky. Either way, they make it to the surface of Flimsy, and have a shot at getting a zickzack body from the jivas or a kessence body from the yuels." He shook his head. "I wish we weren't down here."

"Your parents went through all this?" I asked, wondering what Val's odds were.

"Yeah. They died on Earth about five hundred years ago. They started out in the Dark Gulf like everyone does, and they worked their way up through the underworld. Once they were topside, they got some jivas and started a farm. And about a year ago, Weena got them to move into her border snail's maze."

"The stores down here are so weird," I said, looking around. "You notice how each place only stocks one kind of thing?"

We studied the Root shop beside us. Its racks, bins and shelves were filled with nothing but gnarly variations on the store's single theme: fat rutabagas, slim carrots, ferny flower rhizomes, tulip bulbs, tree stumps, and so on and on. It was hard to make out how far back into the wall the store went.

The next store was Ball, and it held floating balloons, metal ball-bearings, bouncy rubber kick balls, blown-glass ornaments, wooden croquet balls, and much more. I could see the hip purple-suited man in there making a deal with the clerk. The clerk was a mauve jiva the size of a woman. Her hide was decorated with embossed pink daisies.

The jiva used her tendrils to craft the man a copy of a reflective disco ball that hung from the shop's ceiling. The zickzack planes of the ball's facets were tweaked to reflect light.

"Gift return," the jiva told the man.

The man let her dig a tendril into him. Evidently the jiva extracted a design from the man's memories, for right away she crafted a zickzack version of a red and yellow soccer ball, using subtle zickzack diffraction gratings to produce the colors.

The flowered mauve clerk stood admiring her new creation, and the man exited the store, happy with his mirror ball. Thanks to Mijjy within me, I could make out the faint outline of the jiva clerk's extensible tendril, still attached to the shopper.

"Let's check that store up ahead," said Durkle, pointing out a place with a sign that showed the platonic ideal of a Sandwich. "I'm hungry again."

"In fairy tales it's bad luck to eat the things they offer you in the other world," I remarked. "Just saying."

"This isn't any fairy tale," said Durkle dismissively. "This is my actual life."

"You know more about it than I do. But I don't think we should stay down here for too long. We want to find the way out." Checking inwardly, I saw that Mijjy wasn't presently interested in helping us escape. She was excited about all the shopkeeper jivas in here—apparently they were extensions of the Earthmost Jiva herself.

Through a side-door in the hall, I saw a crooked little staircase leading down. It was lit by the ubiquitous glow, but I couldn't make out how far down it led. I shuddered at the thought of going any deeper into this Stygian mall.

Glancing up at the shimmering ceiling of living water, I realized that pushing upwards might not be so useful either, at least not precisely here. The way the hallways kept swaying and turning, I had no idea about how to get back to the spot where we'd entered this nightmarish zone. By now we might be beneath miles and miles of Flimsy's crust.

Some of the ghosts were watching us, probably waiting for a chance to move in. One hooded, peach-colored figure in particular was tracking my every move. Although I couldn't see her face, I sensed she was the ghost of a woman. What if I confronted her and asked her to leave me alone? As if sensing my willingness to go on the offensive, now she ducked into a store labeled with the image of an idealized Shoe.

"Come on and help me get my sandwich," said Durkle, nudging me out of my thoughts.

"Fine."

The Sandwich place had a pleasant smell, like an old-timey Italian deli that I liked in North Beach. Apparently the jivas had gone so far as to craft microscopic zickzack shapes that drifted through the air and locked into the simulated olfactory receptors of my nose.

Impeccable sandwiches rested on plates in glass cases, one of each kind: a turkey and bacon on a bun, a mortadella and provolone hoagie, a steak and pepper sub, a white-bread cucumber tartine with the crusts trimmed off, a baguette with red peppers and brie, a pastrami and sauerkraut on rye, a baked tofu on three-seed, a sesame muffuletta with olive salad and salami, an egg-salad with lettuce on whole wheat, and more.

The garbage-can-sized amber jiva behind this place's counter bobbed up even with us. She had a cute teal band of trim around her waist, and a shiny gold ball on top. Her tail was like an extension cord, winding off into the store's dark recesses. She wore a name tag that said, "May I Help You?"

"I want that one," announced Durkle, pointing to a triple-decker club sandwich. "How do I pay?"

"Sandwich dream food," said the clerk jiva. Extruding a tendril as delicate as a cucumber vine, she reached across the counter towards Durkle and—

"Get back!" I cried, shoving the boy to one side and getting Mijjy to dart out her own tendril to engage with the clerk's.

The clerk was disappointed not to invade Durkle's fresh young body. But she was willing to deal with me, as long as we had a tendril hook-up. It was the same kind of deal as in the Ball story. She wanted me to think of a sandwich that she didn't have in stock. She was working to enlarge the universality of her store, which was meant to become a repository of every variation upon the Sandwich form. You had to add a new exemplar in order to access one of the existing ones.

I explained all this to Durkle.

"Mutton plant on bread-flower petals?" he suggested. "Does she know about that?"

"Yesterday bread," said the jiva. With an insolent toss of her top-knot, she pointed a tendril to just such a sandwich, resting on a shelf in the next glass case.

"I bet you don't have red caviar on pumpernickel rounds with minced onion," I said to the clerk. But yes she did, that item was already tucked into a shelf on the wall behind us.

"Roast pigpop on toasted waffle cactus!" cried Durkle. "She won't know about that. My family made it up."

"Surprise food," said the yellow jiva clerk. She hung there motion-less, waiting for more information. I passed her the image via Mijjy. Thanks to our picnic on the bluff, I knew very well what this kind of sandwich looked like.

The jiva clerk created an archival pigpop sandwich for her display case, and crafted a club sandwich for Durkle. He snagged the offering with his long, flexible arm.

"It's all just zickzack," I told him. "Folded up scraps of space. Can't you get that through your head? You really shouldn't eat that thing. With no kessence in it, it's not going to nourish you at all."

"It's delicious," said the boy, biting in. "Those jivas can wrinkle up the zickzack so it tastes as good as kessence. Thanks."

The amber beet-shape bowed.

"I just hope that sandwich doesn't hatch inside you," I muttered to Durkle. "Like those eggs inside the Dad-fruits."

17 : Deeper

We drifted out to the hallway, with the boy stubbornly munching away. Almost right away I bumped into the hipster in the purple suit.

"Can you hear me?" I asked him aloud. I was hoping to learn a bit more about this place.

He looked me over, still clutching his disco ball. After a moment he nodded and showed his teeth in a smile. "It's a goof to see a fat ghost in here," he said. "Bursting with flavor-rich kessence! Give me a taste." He held out his hand.

I shook the ghost's hand, and as soon as we touched I felt him drawing off energy—although not enough to really affect me.

"Wiggy!" said the ghost, savoring the dab of energy that he'd extracted. "I'm guessing that you just died and came here from Earth. You must be a hell of a fighter to be so fat so soon. Why don't you and the kid fall by my pad?" He twirled his disco ball invitingly.

"Where is it?" I asked.

"On the bottom level, looming into the Dark Gulf. Ask any hipster about Bart's pad. Lots of the shades know me. I've been on this scene for fifty years."

"Maybe you could explain something to me," I said. "What are these stores all about? Why are the jivas accumulating all these examples of every possible form?"

135

"Jivas are the brain-cells of the Flimsy mind," said Bart. "They drone away at digging dirt and cataloguing facts. To fully understand, like, 'Cactus,' a jiva wants to see one of each. Every jive-ass cactus that there is."

"And they're willing to give you things just for telling them that kind of stuff?"

"Nothing's ever free from a jiva," said Bart. "You'll be digging that bye and bye. Me, I avoid the hoo-haw, hanging in my pad down on level three. Fall by, man. It's cool, don't worry. We won't cannibalize you. But, uh, could give me one more taste?"

"Okay. If you answer another question."

"Always ready to help a greenhorn," said Bart, drawing off another smidgen of my kessence.

"Have you met a lot of famous dead people here?" I asked him, thinking of some of the old-time SF writers I admired. "Like Robert Sheckley or Philip K. Dick? Or Philip José Farmer?"

"Never heard of them," said Bart shaking his head. "It takes a while to dig how big this place is. Like—the first time I went to L.A., I was sure I'd be jamming guitar with Tawny Krush, or eating Lureen Morales's snatch. But all I saw was crowds of goobs. It's the same here but more so. Here comes everybody. I gotta split now. Come see me."

Bart strutted down the hall, jazzed on the energy he'd leeched. And then he ducked into a staircase and was gone.

At this point my jiva, Mijjy, called for my attention. She'd been busy stretching tendrils to explore this sloppy maze of tacked-together rooms.

"Queen bed," she now told me, which meant very little to me. But by studying her teep imagery, I quickly learned that she'd found the lair where the Earthmost Jiva herself spent her nights.

"But—isn't her burrow by the Duke's castle?" I objected. "And that's supposed to be fifty miles from the monster pit."

Mijjy pulsed me a sound like a laugh. "Journey hop," she teeped. "Burrow hall corner."

Guided by Mijjy, Durkle and I continued on our way. The shops and side-corridors shifted in odd perspectives. We were passing stores of increasingly high-end categories—a Gem, a Violin, and an Orchid. The walls were encrusted with ornament, sporting bronze wreaths and panels of colored marble.

The hallway ended at a sloping lip that marked the edge of a vast, nest-like depression in the mall. And the living water overhead was arched in a static dome, its upper surface patterned with the agitated sprinkles.

The great round chamber was perhaps a mile across. A tassled crimson cushion covered half the floor, an absurdly large thing, mounded with what I initially took to be golden braid. But now, as the glowing tangles upon the cushion shifted, I realized they were the branchings of a monumental jiva tail, a thick tube that led up through the domed ceiling like a kelp stalk—presumably connecting to the Earthmost Jiva above.

Even as I grasped this, a vibration pulsed through the chamber. Everything got shorter, then taller, then shorter again. A wash of musical tones cascaded over us, and the space flickered with veils of color, shading ever higher into the bright. Amid a rising blare, the great jiva lowered herself into view. She passed through the living water ceiling as readily as an arm through a soap-film.

The Earthmost Jiva's enormous bristly bottom turned my vision dark with light. But rather than going blind, I went past white, past black, and into a new mode of sight. Call it a higher octave. I could still see the mall and the ghosts and the jiva—but everything had an ultramarine tinge to it, and seemed a bit translucent. Maybe it would be like this to see with X-rays.

"And, yea, when dusk falleth upon the world of flim, Her Serenity doth renew herself in the caverns of the underworld," intoned Durkle. "The Book of Jiva." Evidently he was quoting a scripture that he'd been forced to memorize.

Twenty times the length of a whale, the Earthmost Jiva was a brilliant pale shade that I may as well call yellow, with a marginally darker stripe around her middle and a reddish-tinged hump upon her top. She settled onto the vast crimson cushion, resting on the heaped tangles of her tail. She looked like a golden beet in a catcher's mitt. I noticed that one thick branch of her tail led down past the cushion and through the floor to the levels below.

Mijjy called out to the Earthmost Jiva, petitioning for attention, but for now the mammoth creature had other concerns. She was using her web of roots to feed—by leeching kessence from the local ghosts.

It worked like this. The Earthmost Jiva coiled and shortened some of the branches leading off her tail, drawing in hundreds of jiva clerks. Each of the shopkeepers in this district was but a nodule upon the Earthmost Jiva's tendrils. And the clerks themselves had secondary vines leading to their customers—who included most of the ghosts in this zone of the underworld, perhaps ten thousand of them.

A phrase beloved by spammers popped into my head: "We reserve the right to contact individuals with whom we have an existing business relationship." If you acquired things from the shops down here, the shopkeepers reserved the right to drag you into contact with the hungry bristles of the Earthmost Jiva.

I felt a tug as the clerk from the Sandwich store went lurching past. I realized that I was connected to her via an invisibly fine tendril that remained from our transaction. I might have been dragged down into the accumulating dogpile around the Earthmost Jiva, but fortunately I was strong enough to break my connection to the clerk.

Soon the Earthmost Jiva's nest was mounded with tendrils, jiva clerks and ghosts. The solar beet was draining kessence from the wretched spirits that she'd captured. They grew thinner and fainter as I watched. One by one they collapsed down to sprinkles. Many of the sprinkles were eaten as well, although a few rose like fretful gnats to the domed ceiling, returning to the living water estuary of the Dark Gulf. It was fortunate for the local ecosystem that new ghosts were continually arriving from Earth.

Among the Earthmost Jiva's captives was the peach-colored figure whom I'd noticed before. Taking pity on this womanly ghost, I had Mijjy send out a sharpened tendril that severed the Earthmost Jiva's links to her. Once freed, the pinkish-yellow specter flitted away, darting into one of the corridors.

I felt a curious attraction towards this ghost woman, and I might have gone after her—but at the same time she frightened me. Could she possibly be Val? But why then hadn't she greeted me? Did she still blame me for her death? I was jolted out of my reverie by the Earthmost Jiva.

"Greeting Jim Oster." The voice was huge and husky, like an echo in a cathedral. "Mission statement?"

"Hello," I said, groping for words. "Why I'm here? I fell through the monster pit. This kid Durkle and me. It's an honor to meet you, Earthmost Jiva. You're very large."

"Growth eternity," rasped the voice, filling the mile-wide chamber.

"Apocalypse plan Earth. Jim Weena mailman."

One of her tendrils lazily unfurled, unrolling towards me like the supple tentacle of a giant squid. Frozen in awe, Mijjy made no move to defend me. The glowing root wound around my waist, drawing me closer to the luminous beet, lifting me off the floor, hefting me.

"Don't—don't eat me," I stammered.

"Appetizer morsel," said the hoarse voice, as if considering the prospect. X-ray colors boiled in my brain. "Kessence lump treat."

"Earth mailman," teeped Mijjy from within me, as if to remind the greedy big jiva of my projected role. "Mijjy servant greeting joy."

"Hunger distraction," said the Earthmost Jiva. "Jim Oster meeting Duke urgency memory. Instructions Jim Oster. Jiva decrees. Hatred spies. Privacy jiva." As if still not fully decided, she wagged me from side to side.

"Teleportation castle directions," said Mijjy unctuously. "Confusion blindness layer water."

"Hold on!" I objected. "I want to go back to the monster pit first. I left my friend Ginnie there."

"Ghost girl," said the Earthmost Jiva, sweetening her tone operatically. "Jim Ginnie conjugation."

"I suppose I've thought of that," I replied. "Not that anything's likely to come of it. Mainly I want to be sure she's okay."

In silence the immense glowing figure used her tendrils to eat a few hundred more ghosts. And then with a negligent gesture she tossed me back to where Durkle stood. She wasn't going to bother helping me.

"Rabble boredom," boomed the Earthmost Jiva. "Castle tomorrow. Jim duty." Her appetite sated, and our audience over, she shook out her tendrils and settled onto her side. The shopkeeper nodules bustled to their stores. The great beet's light grew dim. She slumbered.

"What if she oversleeps?" I asked Durkle.

"It happens," he said with a shrug. "Our days start whenever the Earthmost Jiva gets up. Not that she's ever really and truly unconscious."

"We need to find a way out of here," I said.

"Did Mijjy say if she can jump us to the monster pit?" asked Durkle.

"You can't pick up on our teep at all?" I asked him.

"If someone's hip enough, I can do a kind of yuel teep with them," said Durkle. "It's like a dream-channel. But, no, I can't pick up the thoughts of jivas."

"My stupid jiva can't see past the living water," I reported. "She said 'confusion blindness.' So, no, she can't jump us out of here. I guess you can't do it either?"

"I have the same problem," said Durkle. "I can't see the way. That's cool. I want to see the rest of the stuff down here. Why don't we try going down some stairs? We'll head down to a lower level and see if we can get out from there." Without waiting for an answer, he took off down the hall, elbowing past the ghosts.

"Just a minute," I said catching up with him. "All this time you've been calling this underworld—but is there a part that's even more like hell? What if going downstairs makes things much, much, much worse?"

"I hear there's three layers to the underworld," said Durkle. "And under that is the Dark Gulf. You know. It's where the new arrivals show up. We'll go down two more levels, yeah."

"How is that going to help us?" I protested, trotting along beside him. "You're talking about *down*. We want *up*."

"We'll get to the Dark Gulf," said Durkle, not slowing down. "The Gulf's living water flows under Flimsy, up the walls into the sky, and it rains down at Flimsy's center. We'll ride the current into the sky and hop down when we see the monster pit."

"What's wrong with climbing inside the ceiling right here?" I said, coming to a stop and pointing up. "Flam said that it that connects to the Dark Gulf. We can climb into the ceiling's layer, and glide out from there."

"Don't be so uptight," said Durkle. "I'm curious about the lower levels, okay?"

As it happened, we'd come to a halt by another grotty flight of downward stairs. They were steep and narrow, like a companionway on a ship. By now a flock of ragged ghosts had gathered around us again. They were plucking at us and making creepy sounds.

"Don't worry about them," said Durkle, confidently. "We're thick and juicy with kessence. It would take a really big mob of these guys to seriously leech us down. Come on now, Jim. Follow me down the stairs."

The dimly glowing steps led even further down than I'd expected, perhaps two hundred feet. I was relieved when we reached open space again—but it was just another mall-like hallway. This second level had a solid, blank ceiling.

The stores on this level were in weirdly specialized categories. The nearby signs were for Fingernail Clipping, Shoelace, Hex Nut, and Burnt Match. Not quite believing the last one, Durkle and I peered inside the store and we saw, yes, shelf upon shelf of blackened matchsticks, some of paper and some of wood. The jiva shopkeeper beckoned to us with her tendrils, but we didn't go in.

A chattering mob of ghosts had tagged along after us. And now they were joined by some lower-level ghosts who seemed even hungrier. I swung my fists at the jabbering shades, but always they were moving closer, continually reaching out to pluck at me. I was beginning to feel faint.

"This is fucked," I told Durkle. "I say we go back up."

But by now the spirits had formed a solid cordon between us and the stairs we'd come down. And more of the hungry shades were appearing all the time—like hyenas closing in for a kill. We were trapped.

I saw a flash of pinkish yellow near the far side of the crowd. It was that hooded ghost whom I'd saved from the Earthmost Jiva. She was pointing past me, as if telling me to look at something behind me—

"Another staircase back there!" exclaimed Durkle, seeing the ghost's gesture as well.

The boy and I turned away from the mob and rushed to the low, mean door behind us. It was half the size of the stairwell door we'd entered before. The peach-colored ghost caught up with us and darted in ahead of us.

At this point I was too panicked to wonder about the helpful ghost's identity or to ponder her motives. The mob was pressing around us again. I squeezed through the little door and—

"These stairs lead further down," I cried in despair. "Not up."

"Perfect!" said Durkle, right behind me. "Remember my plan."

This staircase was even longer than the one before, and with several twists in it. Soon the peach-colored ghost was nowhere to be seen. As Durkle and I clattered down, I gathered my wits a bit. I thought to have Mijjy shoot a sheaf of tendrils towards the ghosts who were still following us.

Sure enough, the sting of my jiva's feelers halted our pursuers.

Pausing our own descent, I urged on Mijjy's attack. Soon she'd fully routed the mob, entirely driving them from the stairwell.

"All right!" I exclaimed to Durkle. "I should have thought of this before. I don't suppose you'd want to go back to the top level and try the ceiling now?"

"Boring," said Durkle.

"What the hell," I said. We went on down the stairs, waiting to see what we'd find below. Rather than leading out to the bottom level's floor, our staircase stopped abruptly at a hole in the bottom level's ceiling. Durkle and I paused there, sticking out our heads and peering around.

This third and lowest level of the underworld was a vast open space, a strange perspective dwindling into confusion. The great hall was filled with shifting, colored mists that took on ever-changing forms. A few actual ghosts were striding purposefully through the haze.

The floor was some fifty feet below the hole in the ceiling where we perched. I used my jiva's tendrils to lower Durkle and me the rest of the way down. And then the boy and I stood there for a moment, awestruck by the intricate combines of images that filled the air—like living collages or animated graffiti.

"I've heard that our dreams come from down here," remarked Durkle.

Dreams... As I stared into the luminous fog, the illusory shapes began to flow in synchronicity with the motions of my mind.

I seemed to see an earnest studious clown being shot from a cannon. He resembled me. The clown landed in a house in Santa Cruz. He was standing by the dining table, which was nicely set for two, with a vase of tulips. Soft reggae music was playing. The place looked great, all tidy and nicely decorated. The spicy smell of pork paprika stew drifted from the kitchen. Everything was calm, cozy, and just as it should be.

"Will you make the salad, Jim?" called a sweet voice. It was a vision of my dear wife Val, standing in the our kitchen door, her eyes full of love.

Sandbagged by the dream, I let out a sob.

Durkle shook my arm. "Someone's coming," he warned.

I rubbed my eyes, and looked around. A male ghost was walking briskly towards us, a dapper guy in a gold suit. I tried to step out of his way but, addled by my visions, I tripped over something and fell heavily to the floor.

Lying there, I could make out a projecting handle attached to a hatch. Before I could wonder about this very much, the gold-clad ghost had rapped a coded knock against the hatch. It swung open. I heard cheerful voices and interesting music. The ghost slipped into the opening and was gone. Durkle and I would have followed him, but the hatch slammed shut—and nobody answered our ensuing knocks.

Squinting through protean mist, I could now discern any number of hatches in the floor, each with a handle. Ghosts kept opening hatches and slipping into the hidden party rooms. Durkle and I began running back and forth, trying to get in somewhere, trying to ride on someone's tail. But we kept missing out.

"I wish we had a friend here," said Durkle, panting. "We have to get through a hatch to reach the Dark Gulf."

"How about that ghost I was talking to on the top level?" I suggested. "Bart in the purple suit. He invited us to a party down here."

A short red-bearded ghost came walking by. "Hey!" Durkle yelled to him. "Where's Bart's hatch?"

The ghost didn't answer. We asked three others, with no success—but then the hooded peachy-pink ghost appeared in front of us again, waggling back and forth, as if inviting us to follow her.

"What's with her?" wondered Durkle. "Why is she helping us?"

"I think she's the one I saved from the Earthmost Jiva," was all that I said. But by now I was seriously wondering if she might be Val. Perhaps she'd sent me that dream-vision I'd just had. Maybe she'd wanted to watch my reactions. Perhaps she was suspicious of me because I'd helped cause her death. Oh, Val.

Avoiding the hatch handles, we followed our guide through misty dream images—past tigers and locomotives, past redwoods and prawns. Everything kept interpenetrating and mutating.

Finally, our guide came to a stop; she was pointing downward with one of her trailing sleeves.

Durkle dropped to all fours and began tugging fruitlessly at the hatch's handle, warping his form into angular shapes. By my focus was on the peach-colored ghost. This was the first time I'd gotten close enough to touch her. Heart pounding, I reached out, wanting to push away her obscuring hood. She spun away. Something about the way she moved made me quite sure it was Val. She drew back, hovering out of reach.

"Help me with this door," Durkle was saying to me. "I can't get anywhere."

Distractedly I knocked upon the hatch, if only to shut Durkle up. The little door flew open, revealing Bart, merry in his purple suit. "Party time!" he cried. He surveyed Durkle, me, and the peach-colored ghost. "Welcome one and all."

"Come on, Jim," urged Durkle, already wriggling into the hatch. "Don't blow this."

"I'll catch up with you," I said.

The hatch closed—and I was face to face with ghost of my dead wife, Val.

18: The Dark Gulf

Although Val still had the hood pulled over her face, I sensed she was ready to talk.

"You were right," I said. "My machine scratched the side of an electron, and something evil came through. It infected you. It was my fault—in a way. But, Val, I had no idea. And these flims from over here—you've seen what they're like. They were gaming us. Manipulating me."

And now, finally, she spoke. "I don't like it here in Flimsy," she said in a barely audible tone.

"I've missed you so much," I said, stepping towards her. Again she backed away.

"You're dead too?" she asked. "What happened to you?"

"I'm not dead!" I exclaimed. "I used magic to leave my body. I'm going back to Earth pretty soon. And, Val, I think I might be able to bring you back too."

"Have you missed me?"

"Oh god. You have no idea. Can I see your face?"

"I'm sure I look horrible," she said.

"Please."

Val pushed her hood back a little ways. Her kessence body was a faint and wispy version of her real one. She had the same smart eyes, cute chin, soft cheeks and thoughtful lips. My Val.

I stretched out my arms and now, finally, she came to me, nestling against my chest. I began letting my kessence flow into her.

"That feels so good," she softly.

"What's mine is yours."

"It was hard getting out of that Dark Gulf," said Val, her voice gaining strength. "I was just a spark of light. Everyone was trying to eat each other. Dog eat dog. I fought hard and I grew. The current kept trying to sweep me away. I swam in through a crack in the rocks—and I ended up in this nightmare mall."

"It's crummy down here," I agreed. "It's a little nicer up top. They have green fields and a sky."

"That big fire-beet is always trying to eat us," said Val. "The Earthmost Jiva. She almost got me today." She seemed not to know that I'd been the one to save her. "I hate the jivas," she continued. "I think one of them was growing inside me when I died."

"We can start over when we get home," I said. By now I'd fed nearly half of my kessence into her. She felt nice and solid. I wasn't about to tell her I was currently hosting a jiva myself.

"What was that about using magic to get here?" Val asked now. "Does that mean you slept with someone else?" She didn't have teep, but she'd always had a keen sense for hidden meanings.

"With a flim named Weena," I admitted. "I think she's the one who caused all our trouble. I didn't realize that at first. She wanted me to come over here to do some kind of errand. But really I only came here to look for you."

"By now, maybe Weena means more to you than me," said Val ruefully. "I'm tired, Jim. I might let the Dark Gulf's current carry me away. They say it leads to heaven. Or to the goddess of Flimsy. She gives you a clean slate. That'd be better than grubbing around in this cheesy rats' nest with my horrible memories. I don't believe you could actually bring me back to Earth. Did you get that fantasy from that new woman, that Weena, the one who's making you her errand boy?"

"Stay with me," I said. "I hate Weena." I sought to change the subject. "It seems like a miracle that you and I met here."

"Not a miracle at all," said Val. "It's the way Flimsy works. I've been seeing it happen all around me. This place is set up so that people always find their mates."

"Like heaven," I said, trying for an upbeat tone.

"Or not," said Val gloomily.

I ran my fingers across her cheek. Just then the hatch in the floor popped up and Durkle stuck his head out.

"Join the party, Jim," he urged.

"This is Val," I told him. "My wife."

"The more the merrier."

"Want to give it a try?" I asked Val.

"Oh—okay."

Bart's place was the size of a ballroom, crowded with chattering ghosts. A combo was playing a jig on thighbone trumpets, catgut fiddles and skull drums. Rather than a keg of beer, the ghosts had a fuming kettle that smelled of cloves and cinnamon—I recalled the punchbowl at the Whipped Vic surf party.

"Tank up," said the convivial Bart, gesturing. "It's full of tweaked kessence. I scored it from some yuels. I'm high as a kite."

Sure enough, two pairs of blue baboons were tangoing across the floor, kicking their feet to the ethereal music. Crazy little Durkle had started dancing with a fifth yuel who was there as well. Durkle was excited to be hearing live music.

I was standing to one side with Bart and Val. "This guy knows a lot," I told Val after I introduced them to each other. "He's an old-timer here."

"I've never seen yuels before," said Val, regarding them warily. "Should I be scared?"

"Yuels are an organic part of Flimsy," said Bart. "They've been here from the start. The thing you have to dig about Flimsy is that it's a single organism. I was telling Jim here that the jivas are like Flimsy's neurons. And the yuels are like Flimsy's sap. I see Flimsy as a giant plant. This big hollow ball of air and living water is like a cosmic root, you dig."

"I've heard that Flimsy is inside every electron of our universe," I put in.

"And you had to go and make a hole in an electron," said Val, frowning.

"I feel horrible about that," I said. "But it wasn't like I had some evil plan. Weena set me up."

"Don't even talk about her to me," said Val, still angry but not entirely shutting me out. I was glad to be talking things over with her, to be getting into the familiar give and take.

"Flimsy's in the electrons, yeah," said Bart expansively. "But you can flip it around and upside down. Our good old universe is the foliage that Flimsy grows. We ghosts who travel to Flimsy are like the sweet sugar from the big plant's leaves. Flimsy grows our universe to feed herself. Really, everything is a part of Flimsy."

"Here come those yuels again," said Val. The blue baboons were twirling towards us. They'd let their arms flow out long to swirl like streamers.

"They're fully mellow unless—" Bart and suddenly broke off. "Oh hell, I just noticed that Jim has a jiva inside him. Why didn't I—"

"You do, Jim?" said Val, her face turning cold again.

"The jiva is helping me," I assured Val. "Like a partner. It's not at all like it was with—"

"You are really too much," said Val. She flipped her hood back over her head and stalked off to the other side of the room.

"Intense," said Bart, shaking his head as he watched her go. "Me, I've somehow managed to avoid my past wife. I just hope your jiva doesn't bring down the heat."

"My jiva can keep quiet," I assured him, hoping this was true. "Right, Mijjy?"

"Destruction devil yuel," said Mijjy inside my head. "Panic alert."

This didn't bode well at all. I sincerely hoped that the Earthmost Jiva was sound asleep—and that Mijjy wasn't going to rouse her.

Perhaps Bart should have started some evasive and defensive measures at this point. But he was too high to focus. He led Durkle and I to the kettle of punch and dipped in his whole head, soaking up the tweaked kessence. He grew another notch brighter, and more solid. And now, in his pleasure from the rush, Bart utterly forgot any worries about a raid. A woman ghost called out to him, and he left us on our own, executing a few flamenco-style maneuvers with the yuels on his way.

The punch-kettle was a smooth, shiny zickzack construct. Stinging from Val's rebuke, I scooped up a bit of the tweaked kessence in my cupped hand. The stuff was more like a heavy gas than like a liquid. It formed a pool of distortion in my palm. Before I could actually try tasting any, it had soaked into my skin.

Not that I felt any huge effects. A shot of kessence meant a lot more to a gauzy low-level ghost than it did to a kessence-filled jiva-enhanced winner like me. Or, wait...maybe this special kessence *was* doing something. I was seeing sparkles of colored light beneath my feet. Or had they been there all along?

The five blue yuels danced past me yet again, twirling and stamping their clawed feet. I could hear them talking to each other.

"Spin, slide, bump," said one.

"Aging, dying, being born," answered another.

"The floor is a jellied layer of living water!" hissed Durkle, standing at my side. "We're standing on the Dark Gulf!" He and I knelt, the better to peer through the floor. In the black waters below, a powerful current was sweeping a steady flow of colored sprinkles to the right.

"My plan's going to work," gloated Durkle. "We'll bust through this floor and ride the current out of here."

"Can I bring Val?" I glanced over at her. She was leaning against the far wall, pretending not to watch me.

"Sure. And remember that you can breathe living water. It's even better than—"

A splintering crash sounded from above, and a huge tentacle came rooting in through the smashed hatch in the ceiling. The angrily lashing tail sprouted a thicket of root hairs that wove throughout Bert's room, taking an instant census of everyone and everything here.

And now, via teep, I picked up the voice of the Earthmost Jiva. She was furious at Mijjy—who'd woken her for a mere five yuels.

"Mijjy noise ruination sleep," ranted the giant jiva. "Mijjy reportage yuel army."

Pop, pop, two of the yuels burst, sending vortices of kessence whirling through the room. The remaining three yuels took a stance against a wall and began singing yuel lullabies—those repellently sweet tunes that the jivas couldn't stand.

The room devolved into chaos. Although the Earthmost Jiva kept her distance from the singing yuels, her thick root lashed around the room, sweeping up ghosts and savagely draining them.

Some of the shades were trying to squeeze out the hatchway—a risky maneuver, as the big jiva's tentacle filled most of the hole. To brush against her was to risk being consumed. Other ghosts were caroming around the room like trapped birds. Inside my head, Mijjy was frantic—the overlapping sound of three distinct yuel lullabies was driving her mad. She would have crawled out of my body, but for the moment she didn't see a safe haven to flee to. Keeping my focus, I headed off across the room to get Val.

Just then the jiva's fat root smashed the floor out of Durkle's room. With extreme rapidity, it withdrew through the door in Bart's ceiling and slammed the hatch, leaving us to our fates.

The waters of Dark Gulf rushed in. Fierce currents tugged at us, sending us helter-skelter into the depths. Figures were tumbling every which way. I focused my attention on Val. She was quite some distance from me, and perhaps she was avoiding me. Be that as it may, I intended to catch up. Leaving Durkle to his own devices, I swam for her as hard as I could.

Before long I had a problem. Intellectually I knew that the living water was breathable—I'd already tried it while passing through the tunnel from Earth. But my body's reflexes where having none of it. And now, in my excitement, I ended up holding my breath until I was on the point of blacking out. I lost my coordination, my limbs spasmed to a halt, and only then did I finally draw in a tentative trickle of living water. It was chilly—but vivifying. In a way, living water was better than air. Quickly I began sucking in heady draughts and swimming as rapidly as before, following the peach-colored beacon of Val's receding light.

Thanks to the current, we were bowling along at considerable speed. It was as if we were within a chamber of some huge, pumping heart. Durkle had kept pace with me, he was right at my side. I might have caught up with Val quite soon—but now a swarm of sprinkles set upon me.

I was somewhat weakened, as I'd given Val half my kessence. There was a real possibility that the sprinkles might do me in. So I broke off my swim strokes once again—this time to focus on getting Mijjy to wrap a net of protective mesh of tendrils around me. I included Durkle within the shield as well. And now I resumed the chase.

But, to my dismay, I couldn't see Val anymore. Glowing like fireflies, the incalculable numbers of sprinkles were bunching themselves into great skeins and lacy swirls, hampering my vision. Perhaps some vagary of the currents had propelled Val further ahead than before. But I felt reasonably sure that I'd still find her.

As I swam steadily along, my emotional turmoil began fading away. Perhaps it was the effect of the living water, or perhaps it was the sinister grandeur of our surroundings. Below us was the sparkling abyss of the Dark Gulf, and above us were the odd, jagged shapes of the Flimsy underworld. Even if the underworld was akin to forever-under-construction immigration terminal, it's intricately fitted surfaces had the majesty of a great barrier reef.

Suddenly Durkle squeezed my hand and pointed into the depths. Far, far below we could glimpse the outlines of a leviathan, dark against the sprinkles' haze of light.

At first I thought I was seeing a sea serpent, a miles-long snake with a body some hundreds of meters diameter, with its head somehow out of view. And then I noticed the bulge of its main body, outlined as a shadowy form amid the flashing sprinkles. Could it be a long-necked swimming dinosaur? But the body's flank stretched much father than seemed at all plausible—the thing was the size of a small moon.

Peering again at the snaky part, I saw that the huge, slowly swaying tube had numerous branchings. Some of the branches were seining the waters around us, others of the branches penetrated into the ramshackle structures of the underworld above us.

This creature was the biggest jiva yet, a mega-monster that was surely linked into a few of the jiva suns, and, via the suns, into any number of lower level jivas as well. I wondered if there might be some roundabout chain of tendrils leading from this behemoth all the way to me. I sincerely hoped not.

And more than that, I hoped that its fans of tendrils hadn't captured Val.

Durkle's jerky gestures showed him to be as spooked as I was. Exchanging a frightened glance, we arched our backs and leaned into the current, bidding it sweep us faster. Slowly the titan of the deeps faded behind us.

Durkle tugged at my arm, bringing me back into the moment. Battlements of submerged cliffs were rushing past—we were drifting past the edge of Flimsy's land mass and closer to this world's bounding shell. Durkle's feet had fanned out into fins. We kicked hard, steering ourselves away from the sullen knots of stone.

And then the gulf thinned down to a shallow sea—or no, it was an encased wall of living water. Accompanied by untold numbers of sprinkles, we were drifting up inside the wall of living water that bounded the air bubble of Flimsy's atmosphere. The great wall was something like a hundred meters thick, with smooth rubbery surfaces on either side. The outward view was a jumbled haze, but peering inward, I could see the nighttime landscape of Flimsy, gently lit by the sprinkles' glow.

I strained my eyes, staring up ahead along our passage—but I saw no sign of Val. What if the leviathan jiva had eaten her? But, no, Val was smart and strong. Surely she'd made it this far. But perhaps she truly didn't want me to find her. Something thing she'd said popped into in my mind.

"*I might let the Dark Gulf's current carry me away. They say it leads to heaven. Or to the goddess of Flimsy. She gives you a clean slate.*"

So eventually maybe I'd go to the core of Flimsy too. But not yet. The thing was—with a jiva inside me, I didn't have free will. And at this point Mijjy wouldn't allow me to go to the core. I could sense that very clearly. If I thought too much about hurtling onward, I felt an unpleasant constriction in my throat.

The jivas had other plans for me. Mijjy, in particular, was obsessed with my promise to be at the Duke's castle by noon tomorrow.

And for now I was okay with that. My reunion with Val hadn't worked out at all like I'd hoped. Why not find out what Weena had in store with me? And, rebuffed as I felt, I liked the thought of spending more time with Ginnie. She had a sharp tongue, but at least she didn't hate me.

Durkle and I guided ourselves closer to the inner side of the wall and looked down at the landscape of Flimsy. In the middle distance, we could see a shaggy structure—perhaps the castle of the Duke of Human Flimsy. And beyond this was a hole in the ground, brightened by a subterranean glow—this would be the Earthmost Jiva's burrow.

I sensed the vibes of the monster beet. She was content with her attack on Bart's party room. And, even in her somnolent state, she knew exactly where I was and what I was doing.

Durkle gave me a sharp nudge. We were passing above the great conical monster pit where we'd begun this wild ride. It was time to break through the sky's skin.

Easier said than done. At the rate we were moving, there was no easy way to gain purchase upon the slippery inner wall. Fortunately I had Mijjy to help me. My jiva's tendrils sank into the rubbery border of the living water, and hung onto Durkle as well. With Mijjy holding on tight, we were anchored against the current's urgent flow. We bobbled back and forth like seaweed bladders.

Using our bare hands, Durkle and I pried open a long, jagged crack in the sky's skin. We slithered through the gelatinous stuff. The slit snapped shut behind us—and we went plummeting downward like rag-wrapped stones.

Mijjy was prepared to teleport me to the ground, and presumably Durkle could have teleported himself too. But, just for kicks, I had Mijjy fashion us two sets of zickzack hang-glider wings. Much more dramatic. Durkle and I got into the harnesses, and our tumble changed to an easy, spiraling ride. We were having fun again, perhaps a mile high.

Canting my hang glider to one side, I peered upwards at the sky's marbled dome. I felt oddly unconcerned about Val. We'd found each other once, and we'd find each other again. It was fate. For now I turned my attention downward.

Seeing by the sky's pastel glow, Durkle and I steered ourselves across the nocturnal landscape. Focusing on the monster pit below us, yes, I could see Ginnie, sitting on the ground near the edge. I sent her a teep signal. She spotted us and waved. We spiraled down to land at her side.

Ginnie kissed me, her mouth cool and dry. It felt good.

19: Offer Cap

"**W**e had an awesome trip," bragged Durkle. "We fell into some living water at the bottom of the pit. Then Jim and I fought our way to the bottom level of the underworld and escaped into the Dark Gulf—it's this cosmic sea of that fills the whole bottom half of Flimsy."

"We saw the Earthmost Jiva's nest," I added. "And a much bigger jiva in the Dark Gulf." I didn't mention anything about Val.

"You two were way down under Flimsy," said Ginnie, trying to put together the pieces. "So how'd you end up gliding down from the sky?"

"We were riding this totally savage current of the living water," said Durkle. "It runs from the Dark Gulf and all across the heavens—all the way to the goddess of Flimsy. She's in a glowing waterfall that drizzles from the sky at Flimsy's core."

"I don't like when people talk about gods and goddesses," said Ginnie. "It means they're about to rip me off. Let's stick to the facts."

Durkle gave her a sly, longing look. "Do I get a kiss for facts? Here's one—jivas are bulbous tubers that leech onto everything in sight."

My jiva, Mijjy, didn't like this kind of talk, and I'm sure Ginnie's jiva didn't enjoy it either. Meanwhile, Durkle had puckered up his mouth and was leaning close to Ginnie.

She gave the wriggling boy a perfunctory peck. "I'm a puff of kessence wrapped around some jiva-folded scraps of space," she said. "Big frikkin' deal."

"A Flimsy kind of girl," said Durkle, smacking his lips. "If only you'd lose your jiva."

"Then what?" said Ginnie in a flat tone.

"Do you know about flim sex?" said Durkle. "Conjugation? Maybe *you're* not right for me, Ginnie, but I'd like to tangle my crotch feelers with Swoozie, that's for sure. Flam's so lucky. Even though he's an idiot. Where did those two go anyway?"

"They ran off with our cruiser couch," answered Ginnie. "Flam said he'd won the couch fair and square."

"Well, that's true," I said. "Remember? Durkle here made a bet. Mr. Incoming Pit Master. But I can always make another couch."

"Garbage couch," teeped my jiva just then. "Hop Duke castle. Earthmost Jiva command."

"What's that supposed to mean?" asked Ginnie irritably. She'd picked up the jiva's teep as well.

"It means the Earthmost Jiva is impatient," I said. "As usual. Look, Mijjy, your boss said tomorrow would be fine. Right now, I'm weak and hungry. I lost a lot of my kessence down there."

"I'm hungry too," said Durkle, casting around for food. "Oh, look, here's another patch of pigpops."

We cooked them up and I ate until I was back to my previous size. And now I was tired. "Let's make up some beds," I suggested to Ginnie.

"My jiva and I already made us a bed," she said, gesturing towards a pale rectangle on the ground. "I figure we don't need a tent. It'll be fun to sleep under that wild light show in the sky. But, yeah, let's make a separate bunk for the kid. Not too close to ours. He's a horn-dog, talking about conjugation. Who even wants to know?"

So I made Durkle a bed that was a hundred feet away from us—and then Ginnie and I got between our sheets together, just like last night. Pinheaded male that I am, I insisted on trying to make love.

"Did you see Header's ghost down there?" Ginnie asked, pushing me away. "I'm scared he might bother me again."

"I didn't see him, no," I said. "There's more ghosts in Flimsy than you can imagine. And a lot of them get eaten by the others—or swept off to some glowing light at the core."

"How about your wife?" persisted Ginnie, teeping deeper into my mind. "You saw her, didn't you? Val."

"I did see Val, yes," I admitted. "There's, like, some kind of synchronicity that brings married couples together here."

"I'm worried Header might bother me again."

"I seriously doubt that we'll ever see him again. It's not like you two were really a loving couple or anything."

"No," admitted Ginnie. "But tell me more about Val."

"Val's mad at me. I think maybe now she's headed for that light at the core."

"Don't you want to go after her?"

"Kind of. Yeah. I mean, Val has a right to be upset. And she is the love of my life—and shit like that. But it's a moot point. My jiva won't let me to anything but go to the Duke's castle tomorrow. So, uh, we might as well fuck."

"How romantic. How suave." She paused a moment. "Oh, why not. It's not like anything matters. I'm dead."

Ginnie's limbs were chill as marble, and so were mine. Once I accepted this, her touch felt fine. In short order I had an erection. I was fondling the slit between her legs, and I was beginning to feel a slight ooze of kessence. The equipment worked, but—

"What's wrong with your dick?" Ginnie asked, feeling along the length of my penis.

My organ was taking on a strange form. Little feelers were branching out from the tip, like tentacles on a sea anemone. And the shaft was discouragingly flexible. Meanwhile the aethereal flow from Ginnie's crotch had increased, forming a low, glowing mound with its own set of anemone feelers.

Bizarre as this was, we were both quite excited. Sex is, after all, largely in the mind. We engaged our alien genitals. Rather than lying on top of Ginnie, I stayed on my side facing her. The branches of my penis entwined with the tendrils of her vulva. The surfaces smoothed over, and now we shared a pulsing, slightly gnarled tube which connected our crotches.

We bucked our hips, feeling exquisite tingles of sensation. The orgasm, when it arrived, was a powerful bright flow, deliciously oozing up my kessence spinal cord to flower within my zickzack skull.

"Oh yeah," said Ginnie as we lay there afterwards, calming down. Our crotches were slowly disentangling themselves.

"Conjugation," I said. "Like paramecia do. Durkle was right."

"I was worried we'd just be good friends," said Ginnie. "That's always the worst, isn't it?" She laughed comfortably. "Not that I'm looking for a heavy relationship with a flaky mailman whose body's in a coma in a basement back in Cruz."

"In real life, I'd never make it with a girl as hip as you," I said. "I'm thrilled."

"I appreciate that," said Ginnie. "It feeds the dark gulf of my self-esteem." She yawned. "Funny that ghosts get tired, too."

"It might be okay here," I said. "And we can stick together for awhile. I'll help you."

Ginnie nestled up against me. I held her till she dropped off.

Not ready to sleep myself, I lay on my back, staring up at the pale, flowing sky, thinking about Val. This stuff with Ginnie was just a diversion, and we both knew that. Not that my friendship with Ginnie was something I'd want to explain to Val. Whew. Val had really gotten worked up about Weena. But there, of course, she had a point. Basically it was Weena's fault that Val was dead.

I thought of a time when Val and I had been over at our friend Pete's house, and he'd been playing Pixies and Nirvana songs on the piano and we were all singing along, especially Val. She'd been standing in front of me, swaying to the music and occasionally turning, still singing, to grin at me, full of juice and life. Could I ever get us back there? Back to the old life? What was waiting at the center of Flimsy?

A scrabbling noise interrupted my thoughts. I sat up and stared into the darkness, sending Mijjy's tendrils out towards where I'd heard sound. But we couldn't pinpoint the source. Really I had no idea what kinds of creatures I should be worrying about here in this strange land.

I sat up for awhile longer, listening into the night. Overhead the glowing sky flowed on. It was hard to believe I was actually here, in the land of the dead. How had it all happened? I reviewed the sequence of events in my mind.

Weena sent a special sharp STM tip my way and I popped an electron—whatever that really meant. Something nasty came through and infected Val—probably it had been a jiva egg. Weena got hold of my thin-walled electron and sent through a border snail from Flimsy. And then she guided me to the magic door in basement of the Whipped Vic, and she came through. A yuel bud popped out of

Header's nose. Weena fed me sprinkles and I had my brain attack. Weena moved in with me, and showed me the jiva that lived inside her.

And then...the yuel came for us, and we went to that crazy party at the Whipped Vic. We killed the yuel with the help of some new-hatched jivas. Ginnie and I swallowed jivas of our own, and they buffed us up. Weena murdered Header with an axe. We found another yuel in Header's skull and we killed that one too. Weena talked me into leaving my body and traveling to Flimsy. Ginnie came too. And over here in Flimsy, I was supposed to deliver something for a Duke. But on the way to getting my orders, I'd made a trip through the lowest level of Flimsy and I'd found Val. And now Val had fled across Flimsy's living water sky.

My true mission was clear. I had to protect the Earth from whatever it was that Weena and her friends were planning to do. And I wanted to bring home Val—assuming this were possible. And assuming that Val wanted to come. I'd been taking that last one for granted. But maybe I was wrong. My backup strategy, if I couldn't get Val, would be to find a flesh-and-blood woman to live with. After I did cosmic battle to save the Earth, that is.

This scene was batshit. But, in a way, I was loving it. I yawned, feeling the fatigue. There were no more sounds from across the plain. I stretched out beside Ginnie and fell asleep.

In the morning, Durkle woke me with a nudge of his foot. I heard a babble of voices nearby. Sitting up and looking around, I saw something like a pale purple parasol projecting from the ground a short way off. It swayed gently on a stalk that was about the thickness of a man's leg.

"It's an offer cap," said Durkle. "Did I tell you about them? A mobile plant—see those snaky roots at its base? They can walk, a little bit. It must have teeped us here. Like I told you, they live in the swamp, a few miles off. Isn't the offer cap cool? I've heard you can get anything you want from them—if you're quick enough. Watch how I outsmart it."

All sorts of desirable objects were dancing beneath the offer cap's pinky-mauve umbrella. Evidently the offer cap could read my mind, for as I stared, it produced some items that I would have liked right about now: a cup of tea, fried eggs on rye, a map of Flimsy, a bag of pot with rolling papers, and a slice of cantaloupe.

Apparently this odd, alien plant had perfected a type of direct matter control. The objects on offer seemed quite solid, albeit made of kessence. Rocking from side to side, they marched in a giddy parade around and around the plant's flexible stalk.

It seemed obvious to me that I shouldn't try grabbing for the goodies, but Durkle either had a plan—or, more likely, he was even more naive than I'd thought. He began circling the offer cap, irregularly reversing his path and curiously flexing his rubbery limbs—as if he meant to bewilder the thing.

Alertly monitoring Durkle's movements, the plant's cap made continual slight adjustments in its position. And, as Durkle drew closer, the items on offer changed again. I noticed that the underside of the cap was spongy and damp, as on a toadstool. The thing's roots gripped the soil, as if preparing for a burst of speed.

Durkle seemed heedless of the risk—his eyes were fixed upon a dust-riding board identical to Flam's, a tasseled orange racing cap, a little chessboard, a short sword, and a pink glob that was forming itself into the shape of—a naked woman, but with rounded off arms and legs and a smooth bulb for a head.

"Stop right there, Durkle!" cried Ginnie, sitting up beside me.

"I know I can beat this stupid mushroom," said Durkle, glancing back at her. "You want me to get you something too, Ginnie? Offer her something, cap! I dare you."

Sensitive to our group's dynamics, the cap added two more offers to its jolly little parade around its base: a steaming mug of coffee and a very fashionable pair of sunglasses in wide tortoise-shell frames.

"Watch me now," said Durkle, crouching lower.

His erratic skipping motions had brought him near me. Fearing for the boy's life, I ran forward and seized him around the waist.

"Geeky loser!" he yelled, struggling against me, his limbs flailing like long feelers. "I'm gonna win. You're jealous that I'm so young and fast! Ginnie wants me, not you!"

Maybe I was a little older than Durkle, but I had a jiva inside me. Durkle wasn't going to break my grip. But he did manage to knock us off balance. The two of us fell practically into the shadow of the offer cap's umbrella—a very bad place to be.

Fast as a whip, the thing had its roots around our wrists and ankles. And now an evil-smelling mist began wafting down from its floppy cap. Most of the offers had disappeared, now that the plant was getting down its real business. Its central stalk tilted, maneuvering the mauve umbrella so that it might soon flop down upon us. I felt drowsy, and the spray was stinging my skin. As well as being a soporific, the mist was a digestive fluid.

Suddenly the purple umbrella shuddered—and slumped to one side. Ginnie had used her jiva tendrils to cut the stalk! The offer cap let out a telepathic scream that filled my mind with red and yellow jaggies. Ginnie was circling around, her tendrils lashing at the carnivorous plant.

Durkle had managed to free one of his wrists, and he'd snaked out a hand to catch hold of that short sword the plant had made as bait—this desirable item had remained on offer to the very end. It was indeed a real and solid blade. The boy slashed at the plant's roots, freeing our hands and ankles.

And then he crawled a few feet away from the plant and tugged me after him. Slowly the cap's frenzied alarm waves within my head died down—and the mist cleared away. I could think again. Belatedly joining the battle, Mijjy set the remains of the offer cap on fire.

"Got any more *good deals* for us?" I asked Durkle.

"This is an epic sword," protested the boy. The weapon was perhaps two feet long, with an embossed grip and an elegant handguard. "Those plant-things craft their kessence one particle at a time. This thing is flawless." Durkle sighted down the blade at me. "I rule."

"It's like nanotech telekinesis," I mused.

"You boys and your toys," said Ginnie. "Let's check out the Duke's castle."

Rather than starting up with a fresh cruiser couch, Ginnie and I decided that the three of us should teleport to a spot near the castle. This time Mijjy was able to help me figure it out.

Mijjy wove a basket of tendrils around me, and stretched more tendrils towards our target, a field near the Duke's castle. I could see via the tendrils, as if via cameras. I picked a comfortable-looking spot, and Mijjy prepared a second nest of tendrils there. Supposedly I'd land in it. In a certain sense Mijjy and I were sewing together two little balls of space. Ginnie and her jiva were making similar preparations.

"And you, Durkle?" I asked. "Do you want me to carry you?"

"I can teleport fine," insisted Durkle. "I merge into the one mind of Flimsy. Like a yuel does."

Meanwhile, Mijjy showed me a kind of head-trick whereby I viewed our target location as being the same spot as where we were standing. It was a little like crossing my eyes—but it didn't involved my eyes. It was more like flipping the two halves of my brain.

"Anticipation relocation dimension, Jim," Mijjy said.

"Go," I said.

It worked. Ginnie and I landed in a rolling meadow, thick with dark green grass and star-shaped flowers, everything lit by the Earthmost Jiva. Beyond the field rose—a giant geranium.

"The castle," said Durkle, who'd just appeared at our side as well.

"A plant?"

"Everything in Flimsy is organically grown kessence," said Durkle. "Even my sword." He was besotted with his little prize, country boy that he was.

The geranium was taller than the mightiest redwood tree, with thick bent branches, storms of pink flowers, and parking-lot-sized leaves ten meters thick. The stems and the dusty green leaves had windows and entryways. The plant had a big bulge on the lowest part of the stem, like a gall. Four or five flims were busy on the ground near there, digging in kessence, and squirting on that same silvery fertilizer that Monin had used.

Higher up in the plant, some people were gazing down at us, and others were buzzing from leaf to leaf. The leaves and flowers swayed in the breeze; the brightly garbed nobles jiggled like gnats. A shimmering tracery of tendrils kept the flying courtiers aloft. The tendrils were bumpy pale lines that emanated from the living castle itself.

"I like this," said Ginnie. "I could live in that castle for awhile. It's is the best thing I've seen in Flimsy."

"So let's go ahead and—" I began.

Foomp! Foomp! Foomp! Three large blue baboons appeared, seemingly from thin air, each nearly the size of a person, dropping to the ground in front of us.

"Yuels!" exclaimed Durkle, uneasily raising his sword.

"Let's bail," said Ginnie. Still more yuels were teleporting in, thick and fast.

"Let me talk to the yuels for a minute," I said, wanting to slow down the pace. I was tired of being stampeded from one crisis to the next. "You yourself said the yuels aren't so bad, Durkle. They gave you your body."

In a minute the flow of yuels had petered out. Sixty of them were mounded in front of us. They weren't acting at all aggressive.

"I want to be friends," I called. "I'm a visitor from Earth."

"Recruit," said one yuel. "Inform," said another. That sounded harmless enough, and at this point the yuels were still just lying there in a heap.

"They're melting," remarked Ginnie.

Indeed the yuel's bodies were beginning to droop and flow. In a minute, their hundred-and-twenty eyes were like raisins in a great mound of blue dough.

"Tell me what's really going on," I asked the slowly shifting form.

"Kidnap," teeped the yuel-mound conversationally. It was kneading itself into the shape of a fat creature with four sturdy legs. "Swap."

A head the size of car appeared along one end of the blue monster. A trumpet-like trunk grew from the head end, along with a fierce pair of tusks. The yuels were taking on the shape of a good-sized elephant.

"It's a group yuel," exclaimed Durkle. "I've heard of that. The yuels band together into these big elephants for fighting and for self-defense."

The eyes migrated to the head and pooled into two great orbs. A crack formed along the sides of the head and opened into a slackly grinning mouth. The trunk raised and—

"Time to hop!" yelled Ginnie.

But our jivas weren't responding. I could feel Mijjy inside me, waiting and watching. We'd been set up. The jivas wanted this scenario to proceed. Like some surreal street-musician, the elephant rose on his rear legs, put his two front legs together and crooned a song.

"*Weep no more, my Ginnie, oh, weep no more, today. We will sing this song for our Yuelsville home, for our Yuelsville home far away.*"

I stretched my arms forward, wanting to send out jiva tendrils—but still nothing happened. Deep within me, the recalcitrant Mijjy giggled.

Ginnie took off running, but in moments the blue elephant had dropped to his feet, darted forward, and grabbed her with his trunk. As if in a circus, the yuel elephant lifted Ginnie into the air, and seated her upon one of his thick tusks.

And now with the dainty grace of an opera singer, the elephant pivoted and galumphed across the meadow. As the monster ran, he broke into a herd of individual yuels that disappeared in puffs of light—they were teleporting away.

In the thick of the pack was Ginnie, perched atop a single yuel as if riding bareback. And then, with a final flash, she and her yuel were gone.

20: The Castle

oments later, Weena came flying down from the castle, riding on a little carpet of ethereal geranium tendrils, wriggly and pale yellow.

"Are you too shy to enter ?" inquired Weena in a friendly tone. Her astral body was perky and trim. "Is that why you're waiting out here, Jim? Fear not, everyone awaits your entrance. Where's Ginnie?"

"She's gone," I said curtly. "Kidnapped by the yuels."

"Just as well," said Weena, sounding pleased. "She was a little too low-class for you."

"Did you send those yuels?" I blurted out. "To get rid of her? Our jivas wouldn't save us. Did you set that up too?"

"I have no idea what you're talking about," said Weena airily.

Almost certainly she was lying. But I couldn't do much about it. Maybe later I'd see that Weena got what was coming to her. But for now—given that she could teep me—I had to be careful about my conscious thoughts.

"Can I come inside the castle too?" piped up Durkle.

"No," said Weena firmly. "I don't trust people without jivas. Go ahead and be a low-class flim in a yuel-built body—but don't expect equal rights. Would you go home now please?"

"You're a bitch," said Durkle. He paused for a moment, thinking. "So, okay, maybe I'll hop back to the monster pit. I'll ride it one more time. And visit Yuelsville. And then the Funger Gardens amusement park."

I wondered if Durkle might mess around with those offer cap plants again—or have a try at conjugating with Swoozie. But those would be his own decisions. He was a big boy.

"Be careful," was all I told him. There was no way to have a real conversation with Weena standing over us. "I hope to see you soon."

"I'll be fine," said Durkle, slashing at the air with his little sword. "Here's a tip. The yuels might help you if things don't work out with the jivas."

As he'd mentioned before, Durkle had his own way of teleporting. He didn't send out tendrils or anything like that. Instead he began to glow. He became a pure shape of light that contracted to a point and vanished.

"What a pest," said Weena shaking her head. And now she held out her arms for a hug. "Aren't you at all pleased to see me?"

I hung back, trying to control my speech and my thoughts. I was in some sense Weena's captive here. Even if I no longer believed that Weena would help me reunite with Val, I depended on her good will for my own survival.

"It's—I don't really feel the same about you anymore, Weena," I said carefully. "Not after seeing you kill Header with the axe."

"I already told you that it wasn't Header whom I axed," said Weena dismissively. "He'd become a dangerous zombie, a yuel inside a corpse. Really it was the Graf who killed Header, not me."

"And—and you know I'm upset about my wife," I added, wanting again to hear what she'd say.

"I swear to you, Jim, I played no part in that tragedy." Weena studied me, doing her best to reach deeper into my mind. "I have a theory about why you've been snubbing me," she said after bit. "For a few hours there, I appeared old and unattractive. And so you set your sights on that bohemian little surfer girl. That's how men are. And, Jim, I know that you conjugated with Ginnie last night. But I can conjugate with you too. I'm skilled at the techniques." She advanced on me and wrapped her arms around my waist. "Have you forgotten our merry dalliances in your cottage by the sea?"

"But you're always lying to me," I exclaimed, struggling to keep a lid on my feelings. "You're a heartless killer." Weena held me tighter, pressing her zickzack chest and belly against mine.

"We're a good fit," she said in a honeyed tone.

I regained control of my mind and feigned acquiescence. "Whatever you say."

"That's my boy. You can trust me."

I stepped onto Weena's carpet of geranium tendrils, and the wriggly little rug swept us into the air. We were gliding among the plant's enormous leaves. The leaves rocked in the gentle breeze, giving off faint bass notes like enormous drum skins. The air was filled with the pleasantly the acrid smell of geranium. Other flims were floating around on tendrils. Some seemed to be guards, others were elegantly clad nobles of the realm. Most of the flims smiled at Weena and bowed ingratiatingly, but one fellow shook his fist.

"Petty miser," said Weena, giving him the finger, a gesture she'd learned in Santa Cruz. "He maintains that my dear Charles has overspent. But his great work is worth any price. You'll understand, Jim. I know that you're a bit of a scientist yourself." Already she was taking my loyalty for granted again. Good.

We reached a leaf near the top of the geranium and floated in through a large hole. The leaf was all but hollow within, the size of a banquet hall, glowing with green-tinged light. The tendrils lowered us to the cushiony floor.

I'd expected to find a medieval scene in this so-called castle—oak tables, suits of armor, tapestries, blazing hearths—but it wasn't like that. Perhaps fifty flims were wandering around or lounging on turgid hassocks and couches that bulged from the floor. They were all ghosts with jivas, all of them in sumptuous clothes. The materials were shiny and richly hued, with intricate embossed patterns, a bit like brocade, or perhaps like animated bas-reliefs. The patterns were subtly changing as I watched.

"The nobles' clothes are all kessence," Weena murmured to me. "Much more elegant that mere zickzack."

Large plant nodules grew from the floor. These bulb-like shapes were displaying elaborate designs on their surfaces. Fairly often someone would issue a command, and a bulb would form a puckered slit, then spit out a kessence copy of the image that had been on display—a bit like an offer cap might do, but without any menacing intent. The Duke was a wealthy and generous host.

In the space of a minute, I saw several gifts appear. A guy started buzzing around the room on a soft motorcycle that seemed to be alive. Laughing shrilly and more loudly than seemed necessary, three women began bathing themselves in handfuls of jewels, pouring the vibrant gems over each other. Two couples started a badminton game, batting a blooming birdie back and forth. And a fat ghost set to work eating a newly made and golden-brown turkey. The nobles were living high on the hog.

Discarded items lay around the edges of the room—probably these were recent outputs of the special bulbs. Lesser ghosts—the Duke's guards—shuffled around, carrying the abandoned goodies to a slit in the plant where the leaf met its stem, feeding the kessence back into the great geranium.

"Recycling?" I asked Weena.

"Yes," she said. "It's a token gesture. The effort of making things uses considerable kessence, which is lost for good. The castle is horribly in debt. Wizard Charles's great experiment has proved costlier than any of us imagined."

A pair of things like lizards scampered across the floor in front of us. With a quick, graceful motion, Weena scooped them up. One of the creatures had two heads and six legs, the other was slightly different. Their colorful skins were bumpy all over, like broccoli, and somewhat translucent, with other colors lurking below.

"These lizards are pure kessence, and are designed by Charles himself," said Weena, popping one into her mouth. "Quite wonderful. Taste."

She handed me the remaining lizard. His outer layers were a milky blue, with orange channels beneath the surface. The channels were edged by curly swirls, and bore veins of deep purple in their centers. The veins demarcated the shape of his skeleton. As I considered eating the little beast, his three heads stared at me with beady eyes. And when I lifted the lizard toward my mouth, he hit me with a telepathic scream.

"Don't you hear that?" I asked Weena, nearly dropping the lizard. He was furiously twisting in my grip.

"Well, of course there's a human ghost within," said Weena, carelessly. "Ghosts give our lizards pep. You eat the lizard, and the resident soul shrinks to a sprinkle. It's no great affair." She picked at her teeth and flicked a sparkling fragment out into the air—the ghost from the creature she'd just eaten.

"I—I'm not hungry."

Weena shrugged, then took back my lizard and bit into it. A

crescendo of teeped anguish rolled over us—and came to an abrupt stop.

"I'll present you to the Duke now," said Weena, striding forward. "Come."

The Duke was sitting with his Duchess and some other nobles. He was a small man with a big jiva inside him. He wore a flowing purple robe embossed with tiny green dragon's heads that were animated so as to toss their snouts from side to side. His chest was swelled out, and his little legs dangled. The skin of his face was beef-pink, and a smeary white mustache perched above his droll, round mouth. I stepped forward and bowed.

"Welcome to the castle, Jim," said the Duke. "It's damn rare to see astral travelers make it in this far—aside from Weena and the Wizard. You came at a real good time." I'd been expecting a well-kippered British accent, but the Duke sounded like a random guy from a blue-collar bar back home.

"I've told Jim but few details, my Duke," said Weena. "He knows only that he made the tunnel, that he opened the door, and that when he revisits Earth he'll be delivering a package."

"Yes, and I'm wondering what that would—" I began.

"We're taxing Earth to pay my debts," said the Duke with a wheezing chuckle. "That's all there is to it. A pretty little birdie put the idea in my head." He smiled at the Duchess.

"Tax them how?" I asked.

"You're gonna carry ten thousand jiva eggs over there," said the Duke. "There'll be some bleeding-heart protesters, sure, but I'm betting that the regular folks are gonna be happy with their jivas. You don't have to sweat no details. The eggs'll know what to do."

"It's not like those debts are our fault," said the Duchess in a low tone. She had the same coarse style of speech as her husband. "Don't jump to conclusions. The debts are from our so-called Wizard, Charles Howard. Him and his Atum's Lotus scam. The Duke and I keep thinking the guy's shot his wad—and then Weena begs us for more time. These two con artists have been stringing us along for—shit, this is crazy—about a century. All we ever wanted was a simple tunnel back to Earth where our kessence and zickzack bodies can pass through. We're not interested in Charles' crazy bullshit about a ladder to God. Okay, it's been exciting to watch the Atum's Lotus grow, but by now..."

She trailed off and shook her head. Despite her diction, the

Duchess looked very much the part of a grande dame. Her body was outstandingly graceful. Wavy brunette hair framed her handsomely angular face, and she wore a teal and purple suit with subtly moving sequins on its surface.

"Charles Howard's put us on the map, hon," the Duke told her. "Everyone who matters wants to visit here to see our Atum's Lotus."

"I thought Charles Howard was an archaeologist?" I put it, hoping to figure out what they were talking about.

"My Charles has broadened his interests," said Weena. "He's always had an interest in Darwin's theory of evolution. He sees archaeology as a psychic zoology, if you will. Now—as the Duchess says, Charles and I were originally commissioned to build a tunnel back to Earth. The Duke and his associates wanted to be able to revisit Earth without being obliterated by Flimsy's central light. They wanted to be able to bring their kessence bodies and their personalities and their jivas through. And of course Charles and I wanted to go back as well."

"And now that you've set up that border snail, we've got our tunnel, Weena," said the Duchess. "So—face it—your and Charles's boondoggle is done."

"Charles's goals have moved beyond any mere tunnel," said Weena. "We've discussed this, Your Grace. The ladder, as you term it. A discreet and non-destructive pathway to the core of Flimsy. That's what the current iteration of Atum's Lotus is for."

"Look, if someone wants the goddess of Flimsy to clean their clock, all they gotta do is sink into the Dark Gulf and ride the current across the sky," said the Duchess. "Or just teleport there if they want a frikkin' V.I.P. route to the drain hole."

"It's not possible to teleport to the core," said Weena firmly. "The goddess and the jivas don't allow for that. At present, the only beings who see the goddess are the sprinkles and destitute ghosts who are swept there by the living waters. They rain onto the goddess, perhaps to be sluiced through her navel into the white hole of reincarnation."

"But you're offering something better?" said the Duchess.

"Charles feels those who reach the center via the chants of Atum's Lotus will have the ability to orbit the goddess," persisted Weena. "You might say that Charles and I are presenting a new touristic possibility for our upper-class flims. Our Atum's Lotus will bring yet more cachet unto the Ducal residence. I implore Your Grace to ponder this new benison."

"I'm not saying it's all crap," grunted the Duke, finally speaking up. "Look at the Duchess's brooch, Jim. A bud from Atum's Lotus."

He gave a little tap to the pin that the Duchess wore upon the lapel of her coat. At the moment, it resembled a gem-encrusted orchid—but the brooch's form was continually changing. The orchid lips opened and folded back, the pistils pushed out and grew tiny reflective spheres, and now these spheres blossomed into starbursts of spikes. A faint little song came from the thing, hauntingly sweet.

"Amazing," I dutifully said. "Lovely."

"An ever-renewing form," said Weena. "A satellite fragment of Atum's Lotus. Charles trained this bud to accompany the Duchess wherever she goes."

"I'm proud to have Charles working here," said the Duke to his wife. "It gives our castle a high tone." Studying the brooch, he sighed with pleasure. "This thing is amazing."

"Yeah, yeah," said the Duchess impatiently. "My point is that we've got the nice, solid Earth tunnel we were looking for in the first place. So we don't need these expensive flourishes anymore. I could ditch this brooch in a minute. What's amazing is that you let busy little Weena write up a contract for a loan from the sleazy frikkin' Bulbers. And now they're in a position to be making threats?"

"There were certain terms that the Bulbers sought," said Weena, smoothly. "I was merely a facilitator."

"Facilitating a fifteen percent commission for yourself," said the Duchess, stamping her foot. "You'd already be a gone goose, Weena, if you hadn't of found that snail tunnel. At least we can use your tunnel to bail us out. We'll pay off the debt and close down Atum's Lotus for good. Enough's enough."

"I humbly offer the thought that Wizard Charles's work has justi-fied any and all expenses, Your Grace," said Weena. "And I admire the ingenuity of your solution. It is well if the Earthlings pitch in! Though they know it not, Atum's Lotus is the shrouded peak of their civilization's creations, a flower of song that blooms from their history's mud."

"Oh, you just act all high-flown about that Lotus because you're screwing Charles," said the Duchess dismissively. "For a while there, you were talking the same way about the Graf." The Duchess studied Weena for a moment, as if thinking something over. "Too bad you didn't let that little Durkle boy come in here. You never do anything right. I could have jumped the kid and eaten his tasty little soul." The Duchess laughed harshly.

"I—I hadn't realized..." stuttered Weena. This was the first time I'd ever seen her on the defensive.

"Did I tell you we've got a woman with a yuel-built body coming for a little stay?" continued the Duchess. "A hot little tramp. She'll be here soon. It's gonna be wild, hooking into that pure kessence funk. The yuels are sending us this girl to repay us for giving them that ghost who'd glommed onto Jim." The Duchess regarded me coolly, waiting to see my reaction.

"Let's not unpack every goddamn bit of our dirty laundry," chided the Duke. "Let's tell Jim about his delivery job now."

"Uh, yes," I said, fighting to control my anger. I could hardly even hear or see. "About the—the eggs?" I temporized. "I'm still not sure if—"

"You'll be upping the quality of people's lives," said the Duchess, in a tone that brooked no contradiction. "Forget about it! Jivas are great. Tonight you sleep in Weena's room, and tomorrow we'll be ready with the eggs. End of story. And don't go thinking there's any way to skeeve out of this. The jiva inside you is keeping close watch. Right, Mijjy?"

"Indeed, Your Grace," said my voice, taking on a fruity, obsequious tone. Mijjy was making me play the courtier. "Your will is mine."

And that was the end of my briefing. I would have liked to say something else, but Mijjy clamped shut my throat. The Duke and Duchess turned away, distracted by a noble doing a handstand.

Within my innermost self where Mijjy couldn't see, I decided that, come what may, I wouldn't be carrying any jiva eggs for these bastards. Before I'd do that, I'd lose my Earthly flesh, let my soul shrivel to a sprinkle, and let the sprinkle itself be ground into dust.

"Come, Jim," said Weena. "Don't look so distraught. We'll tour the attractions of the castle. With a special visit to my room." She gave me a suggestive nudge.

I forced a smile and nudged back. If I was going to survive, I'd need to work every possible angle that I had.

21: Weena's Tale

The geranium slung a pair of tendrils around our waists and we sailed up through the hole on the leaf's top surface. I could see the mouth of the Earthmost Jiva's burrow nearby. She hung in the sky like a great flaming beet, colored like a child's top, festooned with dangling tendrils. She was excited by the thought of me bearing a load of ten thousand jiva eggs to Earth. Now that she'd overheard my mission directive, she regarded me with the mixture of lust and cruelty that a thug might feel towards the intended victim of a rape.

"There are no passageways through the stems," chirped Weena, cheerful at my side. "We fly from leaf to leaf, using the geranium's tendrils. Some of the leaves are halls, and others hold apartments, with ample windows and lovely light. It's a shame you're not likely to move in with me long-term. I'd enjoy having two lovers to draw upon. We're terribly open-minded here." She paused to giggle. "In fact, I'll show you the group encounter room. That heart-shaped leaf down low? Fly us there, oh great geranium! Softly and sweetly."

"You're not fooling me with the happy talk," I said, my voice harsh. "You and the Duchess sent Ginnie to a second death. And now I'm supposed to infect Earth with jivas?"

"The yuels merely took Ginnie to Yuelsville," said Weena. "The yuel settlement in the swamp? She may find it congenial there. It's more

172

her kind of place than any castle, I'd say. You don't that common little girl anyway. Not when you've still got me."

"But let's talk about the eggs," I continued, unable to stop myself. For now Mijjy wasn't blocking me. She didn't much care what I said to Weena. "I saw the jivas busting out of the Dad-fruits in Durkle's garden," I continued. "I saw what happened to Val. Hatching ten thousand jivas will tear me to bits. There won't be an atom of me left."

"Oh, poor Jim," cooed Weena. "Is that really what you think?"

"It's a suicide mission, Weena. That's why you want to send the eggs with me."

"The eggs will be dormant, Jim. They won't hatch into your flesh. You'll release them, and they'll home in on every living human on Earth. One egg per person."

"So I'll be killing everyone in the world at once. Great."

Sensing the intensity of our discussion, the geranium had thoughtfully paused our progress. We were hanging in mid-air among the plant's lovely green leaves. Guards and cheerful nobles were flitting past. And here Weena and I were, discussing death and the end of the world.

"You're behaving like a sulky child," Weena told me. "Although farmer Monin's kessence Dad-fruits fall apart when hatching jivas, it's doesn't have to be that way."

"So what happened to Val and to Dick Simly?" I yelled, by now of point of bursting into tears.

"Growing a jiva need do no harm to a living human. It's—it's a process that's still being fine-tuned. We lost Val, yes, but I understand that Dick Simly is doing very—"

"Sure, sure," I snarled. "And the point is to leech kessence from Earth?"

"You might frame it that way, yes. The Duke has to pay his debts rather soon. Otherwise we'll lose much more than planet Earth. The Bulbers threaten to annihilate all the spirits in the entire Earth-zone of Flimsy. And, given the terms of their ninety-day loan, this is within their rights."

"Why not just turn off Atum's Lotus?" I said, still groping for a way out.

"Do you never listen to anyone?" said Weena impatiently. "Yes, the Duchess wants to halt Atum's Lotus. But this does nothing for repaying the Duke's ninety-day loan. And the kessence that we borrowed is gone. The Duke needs to redeem his debt, Jim. We're depending on you and your eggs."

The geranium tendrils resumed lowering us closer to the ground, wobbling back and forth like drifting feathers. Working the dirt below us was the same crew of flims that I'd noticed before. They were grubbing trenches into the soil and shoveling in shiny goo from a mound of pure kessence. Most of the mound was gone.

And now, as I watched, a pair of very strange creatures appeared and began spewing more kessence onto the mound. These guys weren't like any of the flims I'd seen thus far. They were purple teardrop-shaped blimps, not overly large, and with eyespots all over them, red dots in yellow irises. Ammonia-smelling clouds of steam drifted our way as they pooted kessence from their pointed rear ends.

"Those are the ones you're borrowing from?" I asked Weena.

"Boss Blinks Bulber and his assistant," said Weena. "Our contract is with Boss Blinks—a stinky blimp. And now Blinks wants to foreclose."

"The Bulbers are ghosts of aliens?"

"Boss Blinks was an aeroform on Jupiter," said Weena.

"Another race in our own solar system!" I exclaimed. "And the Bulbers have their own little terrain in Flimsy? How come I never knew any of this?"

"What do ants know of airplanes?" said Weena. "Rhetorical question. Never mind the Bulbers for now. Here comes something pleasant to distract you!"

We dove into the heart-shaped leaf—and found a large orgy underway. Flexible bands connected pairs, triples and larger clusters of flims, some in the throes of intense conjugation, some languidly blissed out. The air was perfumed with a rich smell of ozone and decaying plants. Landscapes of light played along the leafy walls. The oversweet sounds of orchestral strings drooled through the air like fermented honey. A laughing male noble proffered Weena his crotch tube, with writhing feelers on its tip, a-drip with kessence. He even introduced himself to me. His name was Sandy.

Weena made as if to nestle Sandy's shaft between her legs, but then flipped it back to him, wrapping her arms around me and feigning besotted devotion. The man gave me a cheerful wave, then did a flip and let his organ merge into the band connecting a pair of moaning

female flims.

To many newly-arrived Earthlings, the scene might not have seemed erotic. But I confess that it turned me on. After last night's embraces with Ginnie, I understood what conjugation was all about.

"Ready for my room?" Weena breathed into my ear.

I was aroused. And remember that I'd almost been in love with Weena in Santa Cruz. Her astral body was impeccable, and I knew her to be inspired in bed. And for now, of course, it was in my best interests to play along.

"Of course I want to go to your room," I said, caressing her.

Weena's apartment was a pie-slice of a very large geranium leaf nearby. She had the place furnished with Victorian-inspired furniture that had been tweaked and amplified into more extreme colors and shapes. Her bed frame, for instance, was a dark mahogany ellipse, with fluted posts and a perpetually rippling canopy of star-patterned kessence-cloth.

Weena and I lay together and found a sensual pleasure as great as any I'd ever known. But it was all ashes to me. I knew Weena to be the enemy of all life on Earth. Once our flood of passion had receded I began to question her, hoping to find a way out.

"So you've known this Charles Howard for over a hundred years?"

"Since the early 1900s," said Weena reflectively. "I was Charles's lover in Berkeley, as I told you. I was a statistician, on the cusp of becoming an old maid. I was helping him with his historical analyses. Not that his losing his job was all my fault. He was always getting fired."

"I suppose he was married?"

"Yes. He felt terribly guilty about our affair, but he couldn't give me up. He'd visit my rooming house every day. We'd make love and talk about mathematics and the Egyptian gods. Charles said I have a spiritual mind. It was wonderful to study with such a master."

I pressed on. "How does your chant work? How did you and Charles learn how to leave your bodies?"

"After his teaching job, Charles had started work for Randolph Crocker, figuring out the story of Amenhotep's gold casket. The chant is all written out on the sarcophagus in hieroglyphs. But it took Charles's genius to decipher it."

"Why did you two want to leave your bodies in the first place?"

"Charles's wife had, over the years, learned of our affair. A sweet woman, a poet. Charles didn't want to hurt her, and, even more, he couldn't bear the thought of another scandal. He'd had woman trouble before, back in England." Weena gazed into the distance, remembering. "I formed the far-fetched plan of learning astral travel. I studied some books of my grandmother's, consulted a scoundrel of a guru, and mastered certain techniques. But it was Charles who understood how to make the process truly work—thanks to Amenhotep's chant."

"And then you two left?"

"Well, Charles made it appear as if he'd dropped dead of a cerebral hemorrhage, directly outside the annual banquet of the Society of Philanthropic Inquiry in San Francisco. I was at the banquet as well." Weena laughed fondly. "Charles had just delivered a toast to female philosophers, all the while smiling at me. Once outside he went into a trance and dropped to the sidewalk. I helped him escape from the hospital."

"You're good at hospitals," I said sourly.

"Only when men are involved." Weena smiled at me. "Charles and I hastened to Randolph Crocker's mansion and enshrined ourselves in Amenhotep's sarcophagus. We performed our chant and—we were off."

"Just like you and I did the other day."

"Not exactly," said Weena. "It was much harder that first time. Charles and I were mere sprinkles, with no kessence to our names—and no jivas to help us. As is the norm for purely conceptual entities, our sprinkles jumped immediately to the afterworld, that is, to the Dark Gulf of Flimsy. Fighting our way to the surface of Flimsy was a years-long struggle for us."

"You weren't tempted to give up and come home?"

Weena sat up now, gathering her clothes together. "We soon learned that it would be much harder than we'd imagined to return to Earth—all but impossible. Traditionally, the only way to get out of Flimsy is to go all the way to the center, pass through the goddess of Flimsy, and therewith be erased. But in this process, even the internal structure of your sprinkle is destroyed. Only the barest notion of a soul is recycled. But of course Charles and I wanted to return with our memories intact."

"Before you and I left, you told me it was going to be easy to come back."

"It *is* easy, now that we've set up Snaily with a tunnel. And that's all thanks to Charles figuring out that Flimsy is inside every electron on Earth. That's the esoteric secret that we hadn't realized before. The Kingdom of Heaven is like a grain of mustard seed!"

"Skeeves already told me that," I said. "And you've talked about it, too."

"Skeeves," said Weena thoughtfully. "Every time I'd teep back to Earth to see how our bodies were doing, I'd see that horrible man taking unseemly liberties with me. So I got into his head and made him my slave."

"And then you sicced him on me."

"Well, yes. Once I learned about the mustard seed, I had to teep around Santa Cruz for someone who might pop a hole in an actual electron—and that's what led me to you, Jim. And I told Skeeves to help you find an exceedingly sharp tip."

"Our big experiment killed my wife," I said. "A glowing spore came into our house. It was a jiva egg."

"Yes," said Weena quietly. "I suppose that's true."

My voice caught. "The pathetic thing is that I was looking at a strand of Val's DNA. We were planning to have a baby."

"Yes, yes, it was very sad for you two," said Weena, obviously not giving a shit. "But it's not the case that I was monitoring your every move. When I heard about your wife's death from Skeeves, I realized that you really had broken the wall of an electron. So for me, in a way, it was good news. I had Skeeves fetch your test sample. The electron had healed over, but its wall was thin. I had access to a spot where a hungry young border snail could tunnel through."

"Good news," I echoed bitterly, hating Weena more than ever. Within me Mijjy stirred, on the ready to stop me from going too far.

"About the tunnel," chattered Weena obliviously. "The ironic thing is that, now that we have it, Charles doesn't even want to return to Earth. He's only interested in studying the center of Flimsy. He wants to use his Atum's Lotus to go there. But meanwhile the Duke wants to use my new tunnel to invade Earth with jivas. And I might as well tell you that the Graf and his friends want to invade your Earth with yuels."

"I'm totally against all of that," I said. "And I still want to find Val.

Not that you care. Why don't you just carry the eggs through the tunnel yourself? Or toss them through?"   Sensing my rising fury, Mijjy had placed a loop of warning pressure around my throat.

"The tunnel's too long for tossing something through," said Weena, combing out her hair. "Snaily wouldn't allow it. And carrying the eggs myself is a risk I don't care to take." She paused to rest her cool gaze upon me.

"The eggs will kill me," I said.

"Possibly not," said Weena. "And, as I say, the jivas may not even hurt their many new hosts. The giant jivas of the Dark Gulf have been designing fresh protocols. The real problem is that, once enough jivas start draining Earth's kessence day after day—something dire could ensue. You're taking ten thousand of eggs to start with, but they'll multiply. If Earth become sufficiently infested, it may fall to pieces. And in that case, the very last batch of dead souls may not make it to Flimsy at all. I wouldn't care to be marooned in a sinking ship."

Mijjy had tightening her buried tendrils around my throat to the point where I could hardly get my next words out.

"But that's fine for me, huh?" I croaked. "I'm a tool. Expendable. You killed my wife while you were testing out your *protocols*, and now you're going to vaporize me and everything else on—" My lips moved soundlessly. I couldn't say another word.

"You say these things, not I." Weena leaned forward. "We all do what we can, Jim, we all play our roles." She patted my cheek. "Don't look so pitiful, you poor dumb dear. How about another treat? I'll take you to experience Atum's Lotus now."

I was quite unable to answer.

"And, yes, we'll find Charles there as well," continued Weena, heedless of my distress. "He lives inside the Lotus, you see. It lies within the great gall at the base of the geranium's stalk. "

In silence Weena and I cruised out through a door in her leaf. The tendrils swept us down the geranium's stalk to the looming bulge that held Atum's Lotus. A little hole near the gall's top allowed us entrance.

22: Atum's Lotus

Harmonious and complex music was drifting from the door. We passed through to a wondrously surreal landscape, alighting upon a ridge of woven furrows. From here we had a deep view of gorges, undulating hills and rangy mountains. The space within the gall was warped to enormous size—I could barely see to the opposite side.

A choir of voices surrounded us, like a hundred Tuvan monks throat-singing a chant, with each voice layered into three or four overtones. A steady tabla beat threaded beneath the chant, and wrapped around it were sweet filigreed lines of melody, as if from electric guitars. Atum's Lotus was both shape and sound.

Looking into the deep spaces around us, I saw peaks alternating with saddles, and a deep valley meandering to our right. Low, curved walls wove back and forth along the landscape's ridges. They were like waist-high stone fences, curved in elegant rhythms that I could hear as lines of music within the chants.

The steeper slopes were terraced as if by rice paddies, with a puckered crater within each level spots. These lace-edged craters held their own little worlds of shape, echoing the larger landscape, this intricate Atum's Lotus that filled the geranium's gall. Mimicking the visual effect, each of the notes within the walls of sound around us was itself an intricate harmony of tinier notes.

Atum's Lotus was spun from rubbery, high-grade kessence—translucent and delicately shaded, like the substance of those lizards that the nobles ate. Yellows shaded to greens and mauves, faint struts of ultramarine glowed within. I surmised that Atum's Lotus was in some sense a part of the geranium plant itself.

Every particle of the great construct was vibrating, and the sounds came and went—sometimes as gentle as birdsong wafted upon a summer breeze, sometimes as rich and all-encompassing as a jamband in concert, sometimes like a symphony orchestra, occasionally settling down to a trance-inducing drone.

The great Lotus encompassed incalculable layers of detail. The ridge we'd landed on was lush with plant-like shapes—ferns, sunflowers, broccoli, toadstools, ferns. A sort of prickly pear cactus slumped beside me. Instead of thorns, its soft pads bore waving little elephant trunks.

The walls of the nearby valley had steepened, and some of its looselipped craters had morphed into caverns. Every part of Atum's Lotus was in slow, continuous motion, ceaselessly groping for fresh forms. And everything had a musical voice. For a moment I felt peace.

But then my sense of crisis came welling up again. It was easy to believe that this intricate growth would consume large amounts of kessence. Yet—how could the debts have mounted to the point where the Duke wanted to drain Earth dry? Madness.

Weena turned her face up, as if sniffing the air, then led me down the valley's slope. We made our way to a trellised balcony within one of the caverns, and found a gently curved ledge with fresh doorways opening off it. Everything was shimmering with subtle layers of hue. Sweet arpeggios of chimes cascaded from the walls. And leaning on the porch's wavy railing was—Charles Howard.

"Jim Oster?" he said, regarding me with his dreamy eyes. He wore the form of a muscular, suit-dressed man with a poet's bearded face. He reached out his hand and we shook.

"Hello, Charles," I said cautiously. Mijjy was letting me talk again. "This is exquisite."

"Atum's Lotus," said Charles. "Perhaps I'm near the culmination. I've been hoping to find a path to the heart of heaven—just short of the goddess's face."

So—another maniac. "How are you making these shapes and sounds?" I asked, leaning against the reverberant railing beside him.

Weena stood to one side, watching and listening. With a low rumble, the cavern around us was opening wider. And a chuckling washboard of ripples had formed in the kessence beneath our feet.

"It's an abstract process of evolution," said Charles. "But I'll assume you don't want a lecture. Suffice it to say that, some years ago, I inveigled the Duke into letting his geranium inaugurate my own mutational theater. My original claim was that I'd build him a solid tunnel between Flimsy to Earth. A tunnel that doesn't erase your personality or your kessence body. Weena and I had plans to return to Earth, all along, and we didn't want to go through the mind-blanching light at Flimsy's core. And of course the Duke and Duchess wanted a tunnel so they could invade Earth with jivas."

"And now Weena *has* a tunnel," I said, not sure where this conversation was going.

"Thanks to me," said Charles. "I'm the one who told her that Flimsy lies within every electron on Earth. And thus she was able to use a border snail to accomplish this rather humdrum goal."

"I know all about it," I said. "I'm the one who nicked the electron for Weena—so she had a place to set up her snail. It was a horrible mistake. I lost my wife."

"Life is sad," said Charles, and changed the subject. "I suppose you've nicked Weena as well. She's a sportive lass. I've rather lost my zest for catering to her sensual appetites."

"Charles!" interjected Weena. "You're terrible."

"Never mind all that," I growled, impatient to learn something that might help Val. "Give me some real info. Tell me about the evolution of Atum's Lotus, Charles. Don't hold back. I'm a genomicist."

"Genomicist?" said Charles slowly. "Is that a new word? Genes, yes. My basic idea is that there's an underlying hieroglyph for every shape—and every shape in turn represents a sound. The hieroglyphs are seeds, if you will. For quite some time, I've been absorbed in seeds that encode values for an octave of characteristic qualities: lassitude, rectitude, passion, fecundity, savor, transparency, fluidity and stink. In my model, the abstract space of all possible seed hieroglyphs is eight-dimensional. And Atum's Lotus is showing me tactile and sensual cross-sections of this parameter space's meta-form." Charles hunched forward and wriggled his fingers in my face. "Floopy goopy. Beauty is sooth." Weena giggled.

Rather than trying to tease out the meanings of Charles's gnomic utterances, I posed a different question. "Why does Atum's Lotus use so much kessence?"

"It's not that any one three-dimensional view of the underlying Atum's Lotus is so difficult to create. It's the search for the *next* view that's the crusher. Searches ramify like river valleys, like branching trees, like life stories. Searching for the most exalted view of an eight-dimensional parameter space burns through the kessence like a blast furnace through cord wood. And the more finely I tune my simulations, the more expensive the search becomes."

"But why do you have to search at all?"

"I've tracing a gyre through a space of form and sound," said Charles. "At this moment, for instance, our image of Atum's Lotus is quite lovely, but suppose we were to add a mountain over there, or perhaps a gorge? Do we need the sound of trumpets? Should the crater-mouths resemble platypus beaks? What if our forms deliquesce into globs and our sounds become burbles? I'm mimicking evolution, and I'm close to finding a bidirectional highway to the core of Flimsy—and beyond that—who knows? Perhaps a passageway to a heaven beyond heaven."

"Evolution," I echoed, not really understanding Charles's line of thought. "You must know that evolution is slow. Life on Earth's been cooking for billions of years."

"But I've hewn to an accelerated pace," said Charles. "Many, many times per second, our cunning geranium creates previews of the nearby topographies, assesses them, displays the best, and thus nudges my view of Atum's Lotus a step closer to the magic mantra of a safe and solid ladder to heaven. I muse and contemplate as we wind our way up the celestial hill, making each step firm and level. And by now—as Weena may have told you and our patrons—we've all but reached our goal."

"I have some unfortunate tidings, Charles," interrupted Weena. "The Duchess fails to see the value of your ladder to heaven, and she's turned the Duke against us too. They wish to terminate your quest. They keep harping on our burdensome debt to the Bulbers."

"A debtor in life; a debtor in death," said Charles.

"Poor dear," chirped Weena. "We have partial solutions. The Duke will use Jim here as our inter-world mailman. He'll journey to Earth to deliver some jiva eggs. The jivas will drain off kessence and pump it back to the castle. And in this wise, we'll get the Bulbers off our necks."

"That would be agreeable," said Charles mildly. "The Bulbers are tiresomely importunate. Yesterday one of them poked his smelly snout in here—as if he were a landlord inspecting his flat."

"Boss Blinks," said Weena, shaking her head. "A true vulgarian. But, as I say, Jim's eggs will bring in the payment that Blinks awaits."

Lulled by Charles's jargon and the talk of plans, Mijjy had let her attention wander. I seized the opportunity to speak out against the eggs.

"Ten fucking thousand jivas!" I cried, shaking Charles by the shoulders, praying that he might help. "They'll destroy our planet! Earth is where the *real* evolution is happening. You guys are going to trash it for the sake of some meaningless mind-game."

And then Mijjy was at me again. That same strangling pain encircled my throat. A hot needle entered the teep region of my soul. I gagged and dropped to my knees.

Nobody said anything for a few minutes. Charles and Weena looked more embarrassed than sympathetic. The flims were accustomed to seeing jivas exert their control. As the seconds oozed past, our cavern turned inside out, so that now our balcony was a balustrade upon a rounded hill top.

When Mijjy had finally relented, I rose cautiously to my feet, crouching over like an aged, aged man. Charles patted me on the shoulder. In the background, a vast, slow concerto rose and fell.

"So you fear bringing an Apocalypse upon Earth?" said Charles, trying to smooth things over. "In certain moods, I might once have welcomed a final cataclysm. The human race runs universities like factories. They benumb themselves with fripperies. And rarely does an independent thinker attain a proper post." He smiled. "But I've overcome my old grudges. There's the children to think of, the young lovers, the men and women in the full vigor of life, the aged duffers gumming crusts of bread. Let the people live, I say. We shouldn't harm our dear Mother Earth."

"And we shan't, Charles," said Weena brightly. "You mustn't fret about it. Atum's Lotus is more important than mere bookkeeping. Jim's going to square things, and I'm sure the Earthlings will be fine. Did I tell you that I'm hoping to collect a commission on the Earth-based kessence flow? I can use my share to keep Atum's Lotus alive. But arranging this is touchy, as the Duke and Duchess have turned so cold towards me of late. To make things worse, the Earthmost Jiva still nurses a hope of eating Atum's Lotus."

Charles shrugged, not really listening to her. "At this point it wouldn't much matter if we *did* halt the evolution of Atum's Lotus," he murmured, idly fiddling with a row of puckers on the railing "As I'm telling you, it's all but done. In the morning we'll have the chant." He flicked a sucker-disk, provoking a surprised little honk.

"I wish I could visit the center of Flimsy, too," I said in a neutral tone, not wanting to rile Mijjy. "I think my wife Val is there. Unless she's already been wiped blank and reincarnated."

"The Atum's Lotus ladder-mantra should indeed be of use," said Charles. "I believe it leads to a perch wherefrom one sees the goddess face to face."

"I've been there before," I said, thinking this over. "Like—camping with Val at Four Mile Beach? Heaven and the goddess are everywhere, if only you look."

Charles laughed. "The heaven beyond heaven is Earth! Well said, wise fool. Tarry with me, and we can plan the next installments of our careers."

"I'd enjoy that," I said. I'd decided Charles was a good guy.

He glanced over at Weena. Was that a glint of cunning I saw in his deep eyes? "No need to stand guard over us, " he told her. "I know you have much to do. Leave Jim in my care. Nothing can happen. Our jivas oversee our every word."

"Very well," said Weena. "I'm planning to rise quite early tomorrow morning—I have another meeting with the Duke. I'm going to revisit the issue of me getting that commission. Truly, he owes me fifteen percent, don't you agree? After all, I'm the one who brought in our transcendental mailman." She chucked me under the chin. "You'll be content here in Atum's Lotus, Jim?"

"Happy as clam," I said. "Waiting for my eggs." My touch of sarcasm provoked a warning pulse of pain.

Accompanied by a rising arpeggio of saxophone sounds, Weena drifted out through the hole in the top of the gall. Charles and I were alone. With Mijjy so vigilant, I didn't feel like talking. Charles understood. He, too, had a resident jiva to contend with. He merely gestured that I take a seat beside him. We lounged in companionable silence on a ledge of Atum's Lotus, gazing out at the slow, solemn beauty, savoring the ever-changing sounds. I felt myself a part of this great system, as if I were a gargoyle carved into a cathedral's stones, gently vibrating to the sounds of a massed choir within.

After awhile, I found myself thinking about Charles's future, and about how to avoid delivering those eggs. Ever so slowly, I realized that Charles was in fact talking to me about these things. He was using a low-level vibrational channel, imperceptible to the jivas. His conversation came in scraps, as a series of disconnected, sleepy thoughts. It was quite unlike spoken words, and far more oblique than jiva-mediated teep.

I glanced over at the man, and he gazed back at me, poker-faced. And still the images came. I saw the border snail withdrawing from her hole. I saw Charles flying in a circle around the towering, misty goddess of Flimsy. I saw myself exploding the Earthmost Jiva with a bomb.

I refrained from fully engaging my conscious mind, lest our jivas pick up on our seditious fancies. I thought of Four Mile Beach north of Santa Cruz—I visualized the seabirds upon the sand, the happy chaos of the waves, the mounded knots of kelp, and the cliff-swallows in their mud-daubed nests. I thought that, compared to the living beach, Atum's Lotus was, after all, a bit dull.

Charles replied with a diagram of a higher-dimensional inversion map that could fit a universe inside an electron—complete with a ladder to its center. He thought of a woman with a sweet and sad smile that might take a lifetime to decipher. This was the wife he'd left behind.

I thought of the flower-filled meadows above Four Mile Beach, of a fern-green grotto there with a twinkling pool of minnows, and of Val's ashes buried in the sandy soil.

Charles and I were on the same wavelength.

He was done marking time—my arrival had jolted him loose. He was ready for the journey to the heart of Flimsy, eager to meet the goddess, and perhaps on the point of diving into her core. Early tomorrow morning, he'd let the new chant of Atum's Lotus propel him to the center of Flimsy—a trip beyond the powers of simple teleportation.

And me? How was I to save the Earth and seek out Val? Charles now seemed to be suggesting a technique for killing jivas via a kind of psychic bazooka. The plan had something to do with a baseball gun—and something to do with an epic Halloween rock concert where I'd painted myself black and had dusted myself with glitter to look like the night sky. A third element was needed as well, and Charles seemed to say I could get it from Ginnie if I saw her again.

Our conversation was in a very allusive and figurative form, far below the level of our conscious minds. And all the while, the artificial landscape around us was blooming in ever-mounting crescendos. Atum's Lotus was slowly approaching an apotheosis. Over and over, just when the process seemed complete, a new set of frills would develop, complete with a new thread of melody to divert the mounting chorus down a yet subtler path.

At some point I dropped off to sleep, pillowing my head on the soft flesh of this throbbing musical plant. I entered a looping dream wherein I reviewed my exchanges with Charles Howard, polishing and editing the memories—gradually honing them towards an explicit plan of action. I was at one with Atum's Lotus.

I awoke to Charles shaking my shoulder. The roof overhead had been torn away. Atum's Lotus was broadcasting a solemn mantra overlaid with shrilling strings. A flowing river of light was etched against the sky. It took me a moment to realize that this was a giant jiva feeler. It was the Earthmost Jiva, avidly probing into our hideaway.

"Here comes the bully beet," said Charles. "The long-expected surprise attack. I'm ready. And Atum's Lotus is done." He was standing beside me, glaring up at the cruel tendril. "You'll vanquish them, Jim. You'll save the world. You and the surfer girl."

"What about you?"

"I'll shuffle off my mortal coil and be reborn a squalling babe. As you say, the heaven beyond heaven is our original home."

The Earthmost Jiva's tendril slapped up against Charles. Atum's Lotus pulsed a massive drum-beat in sympathy. Charles's resident jiva popped out and scurried off like the cowardly parasite that she was. But the man himself stood firm in the face of his fate. The glowing tentacle forked and branched, sending roots into each part of my friend's hearty frame. Charles laughed, as if welcoming his physical annihilation.

In seconds, the Earthmost Jiva had drained Charles down to an idiosyncratic sprinkle which was the refined essence of the man's soul. I saw a hypnotically tumbling shape that was covered on every side with flickering, mutating hieroglyphs—perhaps spelling out the sequence of archetypes that had been Charles's life story.

The Earthmost Jiva would have liked to devour this darting sprinkle as well—but Charles invoked the perfected power of Atum's Lotus. The great shape pulsed out a rhythmic chant that was the sought-for ladder-mantra.

Seized by the wave of sound, Charles's sprinkle spun in the air for a moment, and then he shot upwards and disappeared, presumably on his way to the core of Flimsy. And perhaps from there he'd pass on to the heaven beyond heaven which is Earth.

Enraged by losing her prey, the Earthmost Jiva thrust her tendrils the deeper into Atum's Lotus. In her fury, she was strip-mining scars into the exquisitely articulated hills and vales. But still the great Lotus's supernal ladder-mantra could still be heard.

Spitefully the monster jiva's tendrils wrapped around me. Should I ride the mantra to Flimsy's core? But Mijjy was puppeteering me from within, holding me back. And now the Duchess came onto the scene. I glimpsed her outline against the blazing curve of the bulbous jiva.

"Go back to being a sun!" she yelled at the Earthmost Jiva. "Do it, you stupid, greedy beet! This Lotus is our personal stash, okay? It's fine that you killed Charles Howard, but Jim Oster is the guy who's gonna deliver your eggs! Leave him the fuck alone."

"Jim traitor secret plan jiva gun!" blustered the great jiva. But she released me nonetheless.

The Duchess looked into my mind, and quizzed Mijjy. Fortunately she had little to reveal. My conscious mind held only an inchoate wish to shoot a jiva with a bazooka.

"Acting all weird and sly won't get you off the hook, Jim," said the Duchess, landing at my side. "You're still making that delivery to clear our debt to the Bulbers. We'll have the eggs for you this afternoon."

Overhearing that, the Earthmost Jiva teeped something about the difficulty of making so many eggs on short order.

"That's what you're frikkin' *supposed* to be doing!" screamed the Duchess. "Instead of trashing our property. How would you like it if I invite a gang of yuels here to sing lullabies in your nest? I want those motherfucking eggs!" Her voice softened just a bit. "And maybe then we'll see about getting you some scraps of Atum's Lotus."

The Earthmost Jiva backed away. She really was a little afraid of the Duchess. Meanwhile the great wobbly blossom of Atum's Lotus was healing itself, all the while playing symphonic variations of Charles's ladder-mantra, endlessly elaborating her sounds and her forms. And the great gall on the side of the stem was sealing its roof back over.

"Come with me now, Jim," said the Duchess. Once again, a pale white mat of geranium vines formed beneath our feet. Bathed in the bright, hostile light of the Earthmost Jiva, the Duchess and I rose towards the geranium's uppermost leaf.

23: Lights Out

The top leaf contained the private Ducal residence—a somewhat smaller space than the great public hall I'd visited yesterday. The lounge was appointed with gilded sculptures of animals, a gently twitching shag rug, pastel murals of flowers, gilded antique furniture, and a pool of living water in the center of the room.

The fat little Duke was snacking on kessence lizards by the water's edge, with Weena and a very attractive ghost woman at his side. This new woman had flowing blonde hair and long, flexible limbs. Her puffy lips curved in a reckless grin. Somehow I felt like I'd seen her before.

"What's become of Charles?" keened Weena, running up to us. She must have seen the big jiva's attack. By now I was cynical enough to suppose that, whatever true grief she might feel, Weena was milking the tragedy. "Where has my lover gone?"

"He flew into the sky," I said shortly. "The Earthmost Jiva chewed him down to a sprinkle. You know that Charles was dreaming of a trip to the center of Flimsy. The new ladder-mantra works. So you might say that Atum's Lotus is done. But it's still evolving anyway. Even though the big jiva tried to eat it."

"You're an idiot," said Weena tearfully. "I hate you."

"I think this guy's totally hot," said the new woman from across the room. What was her story?

"This is Janie," said the Duchess, walking over to fondle the lissome form. "And, Janie, this is Jim. Janie teleported in from Yuelsville last night. The yuels sent her to repay us for letting them nab Ginnie. Ginnie had some piece of information that the yuels wanted. And, at our end, Weena didn't want Ginnie around. I think she was jealous."

"Oh, shut up!" yelled Weena. "Why is everyone against me?"

Janie laughed and looked pleased. "I thought it'd be interesting to see how you jiva-freaks live."

"Janie's a pistol," interjected the Duke. "I hope she stays with us for good. I'm ready for a new assistant."

"You big silly," said Janie, giving the Duke a playful slap. She rose to hug the Duchess, and favored Weena with a spiteful boo-hoo poor-you moue. In the midst of all this posing, Janie managed to give me a discreet wink as well. I didn't quite understand why.

"Doesn't anyone care about Charles?" wailed Weena. "How will I survive without him?"

"I care about paying Charles's debt," said the Duchess. "That's for sure. We've got a meeting with Boss Blinks in half an hour."

"Weena's been nagging me for a commission on the Earth tax," added the Duke, in an equally callous tone. "I guess that's what she means by survival."

"The question isn't whether you get a commission," the Duchess told Weena. "It's whether we kill you." Weena tried to say something back, but the Duchess cut her off with a menacing frown. "For now, you're to escort Jim to Monin's farm, okay?"

"I've told Janie to go along too," said the Duke in a studiously casual tone. "I told her I'd pay her extra."

"Yes," said the Duchess, giving the Duke a look. "Janie can take care of Weena."

"Have I lost your trust?" protested Weena. "Why burden me with this newcomer?"

"Why is everyone so uptight?" interrupted Janie. "That's *my* question. Why can't we all be friends?" She struck a cheesy, pouty pose. "*Good* friends."

"Not now, Janie," said the Duchess. "I want you meet Boss Blinks Bulber now—so you'll fully understand the Weena problem." She said this even though Weena was right there. Evidently Weena's feelings didn't matter anymore. "And, Jim, you come to the meeting too," added the Duchess. "It's time to start showing some goddamn team spirit."

"Blinks will be here any minute," said the Duke.

"Top-thecret wred alert," said Janie with a sarcastic lisp. She was acting as giddy as a high-school kid.

The Duke led us to a different lobe of the hollowed-out leaf—this was his so-called situation room. It had a straight wall along the inner side, and a rounded outer wall that followed the leaf's edge. Looking out through a long, low ribbon-window, I could see the monstrous, glaring Earthmost Jiva, the rolling meadows of Flimsy, and faraway glints from the Dark Gulf. For the thousandth time, I wondered if I'd find Val at the center.

The situation room was dominated by a pair of imposing thrones. The Duke and the Duchess ascended to their perches. Weena, Janie and I found seats on a rubbery sofa that ran along the rounded wall. I felt uneasy about Janie. She was a puzzle. I couldn't quite decipher the levels of betrayal going on.

In the center of the room, a transparent ball was suspended in the middle of a stalk that grew from floor to ceiling.

"See the model, Jim?" said Weena, pointing . Her voice was shaky; she was truly upset about Charles—and unnerved by the hostility of the Duke and Duchess. "You've inquired about Flimsy's geography," continued Weena, forcing a brave, bright tone. "Isn't this lovely?"

Grown by the geranium, the ball was a model of the afterworld. The upper hemisphere with filled with air, and the lower hemisphere with water—the Dark Gulf. A twinkling green ledge ran along the gulf's outer edge—the fields of Flimsy. Layered structures and hanging stalactites lurked beneath the fields—the underworld. The gloomy waters at the very bottom were a-jiggle with linked beets and radishes—the mega-jivas. A glowing haze drizzled from the domed sky's center into the heart of the Dark Gulf. The shifting column of mist represented the abode of the fabled goddess of Flimsy.

"Where are we right now?" asked Janie, for the first time sounding interested.

"I wonder if a stupid little tramp like you can grasp that this isn't drawn to scale," said Weena, glaring at her. "It's more along the lines of a cartoon. The band of green along the edge breaks into a septillion slots—so of course you can't see where we are."

As if to contradict Weena, the responsive display illuminated a hair-thin slice of the model's edge—and proceeded to zoom in on it.

The narrow slit of light expanded into a trapezoid that filled the ball, a toy landscape with hills and a swamp and even a little model of the giant geranium plant itself. Along the left edge of the trapezoid was a bluish zone with tiny blimps—some of our alien neighbors.

A sudden pooting noise distracted me—a snub-nosed Bulber was pushing in through an iris-like door in the situation room's outer wall.

"Hey there, Boss Blinks!" called the Duke from his throne. "We're getting our act together right now."

The Bulber circled the room, fouling the air with sulfur, then came to rest. He was about five meters long. He had at least twenty eyes on his pebbled mauve hide; the eyes were wobbly like fried eggs. Boss Blinks studied us for while, and then he made a blubbery sound that my teep transformed into colloquial speech. He sounded like a Chicago gangster.

"A deal's a deal," the Bulber was saying. "Me and the boys are gonna be stripping you clean tomorrow if you ain't paid up in full. You got a lotta nerve, thinking you can bullshit your way outta this, Duke. I notice that your jiva sun was trashing your Atum's Lotus, you dumb shit."

"We'll start paying you tomorrow!" shrilled the Duchess. "But it might take a little time until the full amount is—"

"Paid in full tomorrow," repeated Boss Blinks. "That's what the contract says. Weena wrote it up and you signed it. Once you're in default, we've got a legal right to loot the joint. Clause twenty-two."

"We'll pay you double what we owe," implored the Duke. "Just give us the chance to finish paying you."

"Maybe," said Boss Blinks after a pause. "I'll think it over. Depends on what kind of kessence we see coming in. And I mean starting early tomorrow."

"Our agent is leaving in a few minutes," said the Duchess, gesturing at me. "We're almost set."

"Heard that before," said the Bulber. He swam menacingly around the room once more, then wallowed out through the door he'd entered, leaving a smell of broccoli and ammonia.

"Way wack," said Janie in a subdued tone. She gave me a look that was almost sympathetic.

"Guards!" yelled the Duke right about then. Four sturdy ghosts trooped in from a side door and seized me by the legs and arms.

"The eggs are ready," explained the Duchess. "Take it like a man, Jim."

The room's leafy ceiling began to glow. Through a window I glimpsed a fiery tendril from the Earthmost Jiva, coming for me once again. The sky-beet was going to inoculate me with ten thousand jiva eggs—perhaps some of them had been passed up from the mega-monsters of the Dark Gulf.

With the guards grasping my limbs and Mijjy inside my body, I had no hope of fighting or running away.

The jiva-root poked through the same aperture that Blinks Bulber had used. Her tip swayed left and right, sniffing around. And then—gradually, gloatingly, gracefully—the glowing tendril encircled my neck. I wanted to thrash and kick, but Mijjy had me paralyzed.

"Hold him really still," the Duchess instructed her stooges.

"But what are you doing to him?" asked Janie, actually seeming upset.

Nobody answered aloud, but within me, Mijjy was singing joyful hymns of thanksgiving and praise.

My neck began to tingle as a zillion root hairs dug in, feeling for the deepest crannies of my soul. And now the transmission began. Pinpoints of energy caromed through my kessence. I was a pinball machine with ten thousand balls, a coal-chute funneling a city's worth of fuel. The eggs rattled through me, finding their way to their goal. I sensed a faint smell of musk and burning rubber. My neck was aflame with pain. It was like being choked and burnt and stabbed—all at once.

And now as the last few eggs straggled in, the sensation transcended pain and became a crazy kind of ecstasy. Mijjy within me was exceedingly agitated, and I felt an urgent sexual shudder from the Earthmost Jiva.

And then, quite suddenly, it was over. The now-limp tendril flickered, uncoiled and withdrew.

"Great," said the Duchess, leaning over me. "Just perfect. And, look, Duke. Jim's got a boner. He's into this—right, Jim?"

"Let him go," said the Duke to his guards.

My astral dick went limp. I raised my trembling hands to my neck, expecting to feel some rank, rubbery ruff. But my kessence skin was smooth, cool and bare.

"They shrank way down inside you, Jim," said Janie. "How nasty."

"Don't bum him out," said the Duchess sharply. "Remember that you're supposed to escort Jim to Monin's farm, too, Janie. Or we don't pay you at all."

"Fuck your threats," said Janie, unexpectedly flaring up. "I know you're welshers. Pay me up front or I'm going back to Yuelsville right now."

"Here," said the Duke impatiently extending a long tube from his body to pour a pile of kessence at Janie's feet. "Eat this. And then do as you've been told."

"More like it," said Janie, wading into the kessence mound, soaking the stuff up. Her statuesque body seemed to grow a size or two larger. She grunted with pleasure, flipped her blonde hair, and gave me a veiled, amused look, as if there were some joke I still wasn't getting. Once again she winked.

Finally it clicked. Janie was Ginnie in disguise. The yuels had given Ginnie a new body, and she'd come here as a double agent. Before I could consciously articulate this realization, I pushed it into my subconscious, lest Mijjy and the others see.

"Stay with them until Jim goes through the tunnel," the Duke was telling Janie. "And then you close the deal."

"Yeah baby," said Janie, her voice hard and tight.

"I still don't see why she has to—" began Weena.

"Get going now," said the Duchess coldly.

A mat of geranium tendrils swept the three of us to the field where I'd landed before, the field where the yuels had kidnapped Ginnie.

"Very well, then," said Weena, expecting to take control. We were standing in the grass, and the geranium tendrils were gone. "I can link us to Monin's farm. Your jiva will follow mine, Jim. You don't have to do a thing. And as for you, Janie, can you find a way to tag along?"

Very abruptly, Janie changed her form. Once again she was visibly Ginnie—with her warm brown eyes, her punky dark hair, and her lithe frame. She wanted Weena to understand exactly who she was.

Janie/Ginnie seized Weena by the shoulders and sang a yuel lullaby louder than I'd ever heard one before. Instantly Weena's jiva crawled out of her mouth. I felt a nasty wriggling in my throat as my own jiva left me as well.

Without a jiva in place, my zickzack skeleton collapsed. I was a wispy ghost, barely able to stand on my feet. Ginnie was still singing. My jiva and Weena's jiva went flying off, although I had a sense that those ten thousand eggs were still inside me. If anything, Ginnie's yuel lullaby made the eggs burrow the deeper.

Weena was fighting back, but feebly—she too had lost her skeleton, and she'd been taken by surprise. Ginnie gave Weena's body a vicious twist and—oh my god—tore off both her arms. She bit into one of the arms and threw the other to me.

"You eat too," said Ginnie. "You need the strength. It'll tide you over until we upgrade you to a primo yuel-built body." And now Ginnie continued tearing at Weena, gobbling down her kessence like a cannibal zombie.

I looked down at the limp arm I held. It's not as if Weena were really my friend. And without any zickzack skeleton I was flexible enough that my mouth could open really wide. I braced myself and wolfed down the arm. What a bizarre thing to do.

Ginnie fed me more. I needed it. My ghostly body took on solidity and form.

In a minute or two we'd reduced Weena's ghost to a sprinkle. Like an angry gnat, she buzzed around us, teeping maledictions.

"I'll punish you for this, Jim!" rasped Weena's voice within my head.

"Bitch," said Ginnie, flicking her fingers like frog-tongues. With a lucky grab, she managed to snag the sprinkle that was Weena's spark of soul. And now Ginnie bared her kessence-made teeth, raising her hand to her face.

"Are you sure that—" I began.

"It's thanks to Weena that a parasite came through the hole to kill your wife," said Ginnie, holding the trapped sprinkle tight. "Weena was the one who sent Skeeves to kill me with an axe. Weena lured you here to get infected with those jiva eggs. And now she's told Skeeves to trash your meat body back home. It's enough."

And with that, Ginnie bit into the shuddering mite that was Weena's soul. It cracked and melted against Ginnie's tongue. Weena was gone.

"Yes," I said. "Oh yes."

A great weight lifted from me with the knowledge that Weena was no more. I had some hope of charting my own course in Flimsy now. One way or another, I'd flout the jivas and find my way to Val.

"So now let's hop to Yuelsville," said Ginnie. "We'll regroup there and make a plan. I already met up with the Graf there."

"The Graf made it back to Flimsy?" I asked.

"Yeah. And I think he's basically on our side."

In the near distance, the Earthmost Jiva had flushed an angry shade of red. Her tendrils were lashing the air in fury.

"One thing before we go," I told Ginnie. "Teach me your yuel lullaby and I'll blast that frikkin' beet to bits."

Ginnie and I got a subliminal resonance thing happening, just like I'd done with Charles last night. This yuel-style form of telepathy worked pretty well, especially for something like a song.

Even though I'd heard yuel lullabies several times before now, I'd been unable to internalize any of them. But now, with my resident jiva gone, I was open to the information. In just a few moments Ginnie had taught me her tune. It felt like an anthem.

I pinched off a ball of kessence from my body. I set the yuel lullaby to vibrating within the ball like a standing wave—I thought of the glob as a yuelball now. Running solely on instinct, I widened my mouth and throat so much that my floppy body became an erect tube. I chucked the yuelball down my throat, cradling it in the bottom of my gut like a cannonball in a cannon. I tensed my throat, preparing for a rapid rush of contractions.

And now, as if on cue, the jiva swooped towards us, blazing with hate and menace. And, like a living bazooka, I hocked my yuelball into her fat flank.

I maintained a subliminal linkage to my yuelball, and I could feel how it expanded like a star within the Earthmost Jiva's form—sending the sweet, insufferable music of my yuel lullaby into her tiniest parts.

The monster jiva tried to flee in every direction at once—and exploded into a million gobbets of jiva-flesh, each fragment flaming and crackling with her stolen energies.

I'd been a rebel my whole life, but never with this kind of success.

"Hog roast with fireworks," said Ginnie, her elfin face lit in reds and yellows. She looked calmer and more powerful than when she'd been hosting a jiva. As the remnants of the Earthmost Jiva fizzled out, the world around us turned to night.

I'd killed the sun.

24: Yuelsville

"**K**ick *ass!*" said Ginnie in the dark.

The Duke's castle was lit from within, with a few of the nobles buzzing around, trying to figure out what had happened. Scraps of the Earthmost Jiva were burning on the ground.

"So let's go to Yuelsville now," continued Ginnie. "I bet the yuels can help you get rid of those eggs. They're nice, even if they talk funny."

"Nice? The yuels back on Earth were snarling and charging at us. And when we got to the castle here, they kidnapped you."

"I'm better off now," said Ginnie gently. "We had it backwards all along. The jivas are evil and the yuels are good. The yuels love me now. I helped them resurrect Rickben."

"Rickben the yuel?"

"Remember how I ate a little piece of him that was drooping across my foot? Back at the Whipped Vic?"

"I don't know. Maybe. I don't want to see Rickben again." I was feeling a little dizzy from my bazooka push.

"When I ate that noodle of Rickben's flesh, it put all his information inside me," said Ginnie. "His life, his shape, his memories—all hidden in my kessence. Somehow the yuels here could sense it. That's why they were so glad to abduct me for the Duke."

"Did the yuels tell you to kill Weena?"

"Weena wanted me out of the way. And the Duke and Duchess wanted the yuels to send a hit-woman to terminate Weena. It was a swap. But when the yuels mentioned the second part of the gig, I decided I should be the one. Double reverse! I was happy to take down that snotty Weena for once and for all. How could you have been that horrible woman's lover?"

"I was lonely. Who are you to talk? You were with Header, for God's sake."

"All Weena's fault," said Ginnie. "She got what she deserved."

I pointed across the fields to a spot where a light had begun to glow. "Look over there. That's the mouth of the burrow where the Earthmost Jiva lived. I bet a replacement's coming soon."

"I know how to hop without a jiva," said Ginnie, all amped up. "The trick is that you merge into the One Mind of Flimsy."

The leading bulge of a fat yellow jiva was already rising from the Earthmost Jiva's burrow. The root hairs of the new jiva's tendrils were reaching toward my mind, talking to me. The new Earthmost Jiva just so happened to be the former clerk of the platonic Sandwich shop in the underworld.

Apparently, there'd been a quick dog-eat-dog battle for succession. The ambitious clerk had eaten her rivals and claimed the prize. She knew exactly who I was and what I'd done. The only reason she wasn't killing me right away was because of the eggs buried in my body and soul.

"We're outta here," said Ginnie wrapping her arms around me. "I'll carry you."

Everything seemed to turn inside out and then—we were standing up to our knees in living water, with soggy mud underfoot.

"This is Yuelsville?" I asked.

"Well, I missed by a few hundred yards," said Ginnie. "I was rushing."

The sky was bright with the day's second dawn. We were amid odd trees, their reflections shaky in the swamp water.

"I don't want a showdown with that new jiva sun," I said. "I don't have the energy to be killing one after another."

"It's pretty safe in Yuelsville," said Ginnie. "We might as well to walk. We'll be there in a minute. It's on an island that rises up like a dome. Relax and enjoy the swamp."

The living water was green with sprinkles, as if verdant with algae and duckweed. We were amid trees like cypresses, bulbous at the bottom, and with roots that arched into knees. Ghosts were living in the trees, in flat nests and in huts wedged into the forks of the branches. The spaces within these nooks were oddly large. A little dome the size of a birdhouse might hold a whole extended family.

There must have been thousands of ghosts here, perhaps millions. They seemed to come from all over the Earth—India, Asia, Africa, Europe, Oceania and the Americas. None of them had jivas. Some had warped their bodies to resemble tree-sloths or parrots or jaguars. It was a haunted jungle here, with everyone companionably squawking and jabbering and singing out.

Lacking any zickzack, my body was quite floppy. Using my will-power to firm it up, I sloshed forward at Weena's side. Soon we spotted a fat blue elephant with long sharp tusks and a trumpet-shaped trunk. He was just like the creature that had kidnapped Ginnie near the castle. A group-yuel. Ginnie halted me with a cautioning gesture.

"He's on patrol," she whispered. "I don't think we should go near him."

So we circled around the elephant. But he heard us anyway. He raised his head and gave us a sour look, preparing to charge. Weena sang out a snatch of her yuel lullaby. The elephant went back to slurping water with his funneled trunk.

We splashed along, and soon the intersecting patterns of the trees had shifted to reveal a dramatic prospect onto the isle of Yuelsville. A shaft of the new jiva's light illuminated the curved slopes. It was like a Garden of Eden amid the teeming jungle.

I could make out a pair of yuels as large as men. They were shaped like bats with kangaroo tails. They flapped their ragged wings, and rubbed their toothed faces together. Each of them had a swelling bulb at the end of his tail. It was a courting ritual.

In their growing excitement, the mating yuels stumbled down the island's bank to wallow in the shallows of the living water. They splashed and roared with pleasure, brandishing their distended tails. I had a clear sense that the tail-pods were on the point of spewing out clouds of yuel spores.

But now the water churned and grew muddy. A great yellow root shot upwards, twining around the amorous pair. A jiva tendril!

One of the yuels screamed as the fierce tentacle raked away his kessence flesh. The other yuel managed to break free, and, beating his leathery wings, rose into the air, crying out for help. A herd of four or five trumpeting yuel elephants converged on the scene.

As Ginnie and I watched, the elephants tusked into the muck and unearthed a buried killer beet—perhaps she'd tunneled up from the underworld. After numbing the jiva with yuel lullabies, the elephants fastened their funnel-shaped trunks to the jiva and drained her substance away.

"See?" said Ginnie. "It's safe here."

"More or less," I said.

Ginnie tugged my hand, urging me onward. Angling past the elephants and the remains of the vanquished jiva, we made it ashore. To our left was a muddy village, to the right was—an amusement park?

"Funger Gardens," said Ginnie. "Even people with jivas can come there. The yuels run it as a business."

"How do you know so much?" I demanded. "You were only in Yuelsville for about ten minutes before you turned into a hottie and hopped back to hump the Duke and the Duchess."

"Jealous much?" said Ginnie with a light laugh. "I learned so fast because I used yuel telepathy. It's that subliminal thing that you and I did when I gave you that lullaby. And I can tell that you used yuel teep with Charles Howard, too. You'll be better at it after we get you a yuel-built body. Hey, how are those eggs?"

I shrugged. I felt no fresh signs of life within me. The eggs were waiting for Earth. Not that I was planning to take them there.

Smells of food drifted from Funger Gardens, along with tinkling carnival music and the throbbing rumble of the rides. Looking into the park, I saw merry ghosts riding on surreal devices crafted from marbled slabs and beams of kessence. Everyone was whooping it up.

Flims were feasting on pigpops, waffle cactuses, and hanks of spun kessence candy. An Iron Maiden ride impaled ghosts within chambers full of spikes—the clients screamed and thrashed, but once they exited, their bodies healed up. A roller coaster swept its riders to improbable heights, with the rails held in place by warped spatial geometries. And I even saw the upside-down ride that Weena had talked about. I felt a slight pang, remembering how friendly and relaxed she'd been on the Boardwalk beach a few days ago. And now she was beyond dead—her very soul had been annihilated.

Suddenly a little fortune-teller's tent appeared near us, popping up out of nowhere. The kessence fabric of the tent was displaying an image of drifting clouds. As I studied the apparition, the clouds grew darker. A virtual bolt of lightning raced jaggedly down one of the tent's walls, rending it in two. The halves rolled back like curtains and a curious little figure came hopping out.

She was something like a plump woman—but more abstract than that, more like a sculpture assembled from spheres: butt, belly, boobs, chin, eyes and topknot. Bouncing like a sack of rubber balls, she made a beeline for me.

"What is that thing?" murmured Ginnie. "Be careful."

This particular creature had a vibe unlike that of anything else I'd met in Flimsy thus far. She wasn't a jiva, nor a yuel, nor a ghost. She seemed austere, inevitable, elemental—like a boulder or a river or a molecule.

"Greetings, mailman Jim," said the figure in an amused, womanly voice. "You've made quite a mess. And it'll get worse."

"You're talking about the tunnel between the worlds?" I responded uncertainly.

"A tunnel like that can spell a planet's end," she said. "Once you've got an open channel like that, there's no keeping out the jivas and yuels. "

"Who are you?"

"I'm the goddess of Flimsy," she said. "I've appeared here to advise you. The tent is dramatic, no?" Her component balls jiggled. "And I love spheres. In order to preserve Earth, you'll need to close that tunnel by forcing the border snail back from your world. And before that, you'll need to drive out any invading jivas and yuels. I know that Weena left at least one jiva loose on Earth."

"But I'm full of jiva eggs. I shouldn't go to Earth at all."

"Yes, I see the eggs within you," said the lively balls. "Perhaps you can melt them before you go through. If not, you may have to call in an army of yuels to help fight the ten thousand jivas. But go to Earth you must. That's how the story-line runs."

"Why don't you just reach through the tunnel and get rid of that one jiva and then close the tunnel yourself? If you're really a goddess."

"My powers don't extend that far through my shell. Nobody but you can set Earth to rights, Jim. And nobody but you can close the tunnel. You're the one who made it."

"Alright, fine. I want to do all that. But—"

"But you also want to find the soul of your wife," said the bouncy balls. "I know this. You want to grow a flesh body for Val, and bring back her soul to live with you on Earth."

"That's—that's it exactly," I said. "Can you help with that part?"

"Yes," said the goddess of Flimsy. "But first secure Earth's safety. I love my jivas and my yuels. But my jivas and yuels are very greedy. They can destroy a planet. I've lost a number of my world-fruits this way."

"I'll do what I can," I said.

"You can," the little figure. She carried an aura of extreme super-natural power. "Be on your way and soon you'll reach your mission's end. You'll meet my truer form at Flimsy's core. Val is there with me. I helped protect her on the long ride across the sky. When we're all together, you'll carry out one last task—which is the true meaning of all these machinations. And then you and Val can go home."

"Thank you, goddess," I said.

Some elephant-yuels behind us let out a roar, and my focus on the goddess wavered. In that moment the little figure's orbs collapsed into a single ball. The ball darted back into the tent—and the tent disappeared. I felt a wave of exhilaration.

"Always talking about the dead wife," said Ginnie, but not in a critical way. She'd been quietly listening in.

"Yes, I'm still hung up on Val," I agreed. "I'm gonna get her back too!"

"I heard what the ball-woman promised," said Ginnie. "She claimed to be the goddess of Flimsy? I like that we never really know what's going on here. Flimsy is wilder than it seemed at first." She took me by the arm. "Good old Jim."

"Can you help me get back through that tunnel to Earth?" I asked. "Do you think you can teep Ira to open the door on the other side? Could—could you come with me?"

"We'll see," said Ginnie. "Dial back on the plans. Be here now."

We made our way through a line of yuel-elephants that protected the village. The trumpet-nosed group-yuels snuffled at us and, sensing no jiva vibes, they let us pass.

Awaiting us in a little clearing on the near side of the village was a yuel of a more familiar form: a blue baboon on all fours. He had snaggle teeth and hairless skin. His yellow eyes focused on me.

"Shit," I said. "Is that—"

"Am Rickbenning," confirmed the yuel, loping forward. "Thanking Ginnieing resurrecting." He studied me for a moment, his large yellow eyes warm. I picked up some faint yuel teep from him—an image of myself wielding a cruelly sparking jiva tendril.

"I'm, uh, sorry about—" I began.

"Forgiving tremble Jimming," said Rickben.

I bowed. "You're very kind."

"Lead, tour, introduce. Incinerate." The yuel teep that accompanied these words showed a termite mound, a cloaked man hunched over a keyboard, and a floppy mannequin blazing in a fireplace.

"What's he mean?" I asked uneasily.

"Remember that yuels don't use nouns," said Ginnie guardedly. "They make everything into a verb. Rickben is taking us to the Graf's house."

"To Jim is to seek," I said, hoping for the best. "To Jim is to dare."

Rickben showed his sharp teeth in a grin, and scampered ahead of us, holding high his blue tail, with the crimson pucker of his anus on display.

The buildings of Yuelsville resembled pointillist sand castles—irregular spires assembled from bright grains. The walls were a shimmering mixture of dun browns, lemon yellows, and pale reds. They were rough to the touch, with a drippy, poured quality, like cement.

The streets of Yuelsville were crowded with yuels and with ghosts in yuel-built bodies. They mingled freely, gathering in taverns to swill tankards of watered-down kessence.

A glowing orb on the street-corner showed an image of Flimsy like the one I'd seen in the Duke's situation room. And, to my surprise, a second orb was showing a map of Earth. A pack of several dozen yuels were staring at this display, jabbering about where on the green planet of the humans they'd like to live. Some of them were pointing at a red dot that marked the location of Santa Cruz. Probably they knew about my tunnel.

A few ghosts in curbside booths seemed to be working as prostitutes, that is, they were massaging the tails of yuels. I didn't see any of the tail tips actually popping, but I did see some yuel spores go drifting by.

Like the jiva egg that I'd seen at Monin's, the yuel spores resembled glowing balls with tiny, dark shapes at the center. But the yuel spores were blue instead of yellow, and they had a swooping style of motion that was quite dissimilar from the jittery hunting of the jiva eggs. Yet again I thought of the jiva egg that had floated into our bedroom on the night of the lightning strike—the jiva egg that had infected and killed Val. And now, somewhere deep inside me, I myself was carrying dormant jiva eggs. How horrible.

I tried to calm myself, remembering the goddess of Flimsy's suggestion that I might somehow melt the eggs. And then I was supposed to go to Earth, drive out any jivas or yuels that I found, close down the tunnel, return to Flimsy, and make my way to the core. How was all that going to work?

"Poor Jim," said Ginnie, seeing the tension on my face.

Gritting my teeth, I started walking again, following after Rickben. Turning down a side street, we passed a half-finished house. The air around it was alive with glinting, darting sprinkles. These well-fed sprinkles were like masons using millimeter-sized stones.

We passed a vast barn where the guardian elephants had broken apart into individual soldier yuels. They sat at a long table, feeding upon troughs of kessence. Indentured human ghosts brought the food, and sponged off the soldiers after their meals.

Rickben led us up a little slope, and we came to a stop before a yuel-built mansion with slitty windows and arched doors. Misshapen balconies adorned the sides, and a crooked tower had sprouted from the top, complete with a flying buttress. Rickben pounded on the house's crooked door. It swung open to reveal a pale, slender ghost with calculating eyes. He was swathed in a sumptuous and velvety cape of kessence.

"Hello, Graf," said Ginnie, not missing a beat. "This is my friend Jim."

"I'm glad you are returning, Ginnie," said the Graf in an old-world accent. "And of course we all know of Jim. The mailman who made the hole for Weena's tunnel between the worlds. You are creating interesting opportunities, Jim. Normally the border snails' tunnels are but fanciful rumors. Never in the human zone of Flimsy have we freely accessed such a tunnel before."

"I didn't mean to make it," I said. "I was just playing."

"Perhaps you don't know your own powers," said the Graf with a piercing gaze. "You opened the tunnel—and within you lies the power to close it. But please come in and take your ease. And then we are talking."

The Graf led us into his great hall. The windows held something like stained glass, although the images were alive and flowing, a little like the petals of the Atum's Lotus. A great bank of stalagmites grew along one wall, with a keyboard in front of them—it was like some old-school church organ. Ginnie skipped over and struck a few chords on the keys. The undulating rumble made Rickben the yuel howl with delight.

Ginnie, the Graf and I settled into leather armchairs before a roaring fire in a stone hearth. Some other musical instruments rested on the mantelpiece. Rickben stretched out on a thick rug, curving himself around so he could lick his butt.

"So you're glad to see Ginnie?" I asked the Graf.

"This girl and I have a bond," said the Graf. "We met death together. Weena was very furious that I had been going through the tunnel before her. But of course I was doing what seemed right. My long-term goal, you must understand, is to have no yuels or jivas on Earth at all, and to see your crazy tunnel being closed."

It surprised me to hear the Graf say this. Weena had always described him as a conniving villain. From the sound of it, he wanted more or less the same outcomes as me. Of course I could never be sure when a flim was lying.

"Your soul bounced right back here after Lover's Bluff?" I asked wanting to keep the conversation going. "Your kessence body was completely gone?"

"Not quite," said the Graf. "Weena's thugs burned most of my kessence, but some pieces were left over. A hand, I believe, and a leg. Perhaps I could have made myself a meager body from these scraps. But I left them for our dear Ginnie. And thus I became wholly insubstantial."

"So your sprinkle had to bail," said Ginnie.

"Quite so. As is natural in these cases, my denuded sprinkle jumped across to the Dark Gulf of Flimsy, just like the soul of an ordinary Joe Shmoe. And then I am fighting my way up through the underworld. A tedious and difficult journey."

"If you're really for saving Earth, I don't see why you wanted to import yuels," I put in.

"Yuels are the lesser of two evils," said the Graf with a shrug. "Knowing Weena so well, I was anticipating her scheme to flood Earth with jivas. So it seemed prudent to put some yuels in place to guard against a jiva invasion."

"And then what about the yuels?"

"Yuels are easier to handle than jivas. It's possible to enchant them with the powers of song." He sang a few notes and immediately Rickben looked up. "You see? Anyway, once Weena had told me how to find Monin's farm, I hid Rickben inside my body. I bribed Monin's wife to open the tunnel door on the Flimsy side. And I teeped Ginnie to open the tunnel door on the Earth side."

"How does Skeeves fit in?" I asked.

"Our executioner," said the Graf shaking his head. "Weena's catspaw. Is he still alive?"

"He's staying in the Whipped Vic," said Ginnie shortly. "The border snail's shell. I'd like to get even with him for what he did. But, just now, Graf, you gave me the chance to do something almost as good."

"You took care of Weena?" said the Graf. "Everything went well?"

"*Hell* yeah."

"Good girl. I am hoping you come to like it here in Yuelsville. You're welcome in my home for as long as you wish."

Rickben thumped his tail. It was getting a little thicker at the tip.

"See that, Ginnie?" said the Graf, with a puckish smile. "Rickben is stimulated by the sound of your voice. I knew this all along. The yuels are needing to be in the right mood to pop a pod of spores, you see. And I wanted Rickben to pop his tail and create a yuel army to defend against Weena's jivas. When you and I were romancing in that car, Rickben was almost at a climax. His pod was poking from my mouth like a tongue. But then came Skeeves and Header with the axe. Rickben failed to reach orgasm."

"Disappointments all around," said Ginnie dryly.

"But—why didn't Rickben ever get excited when Header was with Ginnie later on?" I said. "Rickben must have been watching from inside Header's skull. Why didn't he pop his spores then?"

Ginnie gave me a pitying look. "Header and I didn't have much of a sex life, Jim. I was dead, and Header was a stoned zombie."

"Rickben did manage to pinch off a Rickben Junior," said the Graf. "But Junior's antics with the sea lions led nowhere—he was too young to pop a pod."

"Just as well," I said. I sat there staring at the crackling fire with its flames licking into the heavy chimney.

"You are in turmoil," observed the Graf. "I think there is something you are wanting to tell me?"

"I have ten thousand jiva eggs inside me," I admitted. "I wonder if you can help me get rid of them?"

"I think this might be very easy," said the Graf. "Rickben!"

With a low grunt, Rickben seized me and—threw my whole body into the fire.

25: Down to Earth

I sizzled and burst into flame. Curiously, I felt little pain. Unlike a flesh body, a kessence body wasn't overzealous about sensory feedback. Clearly I knew I was burning to a crisp, and my body wasn't going to belabor the point. My hope was that the eggs were burning away too.

Quite soon I was nothing but a sprinkle, a crimson, seven-sided prism of a gem-like substance immune to flames. I floated up from the fire and ashes, borne on the hot currents of air.

As a sprinkle, I had very odd visual input. It was as if I were seeing through a wide-angle lens the size of a pinhead. The warped perspectives swept wildly as I moved.

Observing that I had some slight control over the direction I was drifting in, I steered myself away from the fireplace. Gaining confidence, I began buzzing around the perimeter of the Graf's den, tracing loopy, undulating curves.

The Graf peered up at me. He was weirdly foreshortened by my insect-like vision. He set to work opening a trunk or chest.

So far as I could tell, every bit of my personality was still here. It was kind of great to be so small and agile. Even so, I was feeling an urge to spiral down through the floor—down into the Dark Gulf. That was where we naked sprinkles belonged.

Ginnie whistled sharply to catch my attention. She was pointing at the limp body at a floppy mannequin on the floor—a human-shaped slug of kessence, vaguely pink. The Graf had taken the figure from his trunk. I understood that this was to be my new body. So be it.

I flew down and landed on the pinkish humanoid form. Instantly I bloomed into it, and the yuel-built body was mine. I felt powerful and nimble. The body was high-quality kessence, and the limbs had dense cores that took the place of zickzack bones.

"Looking good," said Ginnie, watching as I stood up and stretched.

"Are my eggs gone now?" I asked the Graf.

He held out his hands to his sides, palm up. "This is hard to be deciding," he said. "Those eggs had burrowed far down into you and were lying deeply dormant—who knows? Possibly they have been hiding in the naked sprinkle that is your soul. But we are hoping for best. We are moving on."

"Okay then," I said. "I'm going back through the tunnel to Earth. Weena left a jiva named Sukie there. I'll kill her, and then I'll figure out how to close the tunnel. The goddess of Flimsy says it has to be me."

"I am commending your grit," said the Graf. "But you are needing a Plan B. What if the result of your noble mission is to infest Santa Cruz with ten thousand jivas?"

"Maybe then I call in the yuels?" I suggested.

"Exactly," said the Graf. He handed me a kind of flute that had been lying on his mantelpiece. "Play this if you need for me to send Rickben and his mating partner. We will hear you."

The flute was only a foot long—more like a piccolo. It was of glistening, silvery kessence, and it had an intricate cluster of round keys. I blew across the mouthpiece and tootled a note. I knew how to play from my pre-skater days in junior-high marching band. This particular flute was a sweet little instrument with rich overtones and a buttery sound. I sounded a trill that I remembered from "Winter Wonderland." Rickben rolled on his back and clawed the air with delight.

"Get funky!" said Ginnie.

"The summoning signal goes like this," said the Graf, humming a simple tune like an advertising jingle, or like an arena-rock riff. I practiced for a few minutes and got it down. The Graf showed me how to open up a slit in the kessence flesh of my leg and stash the flute inside. It was convenient to be so doughy.

"I'll go now," I said, flexing my leg. "Are you willing to help me, Ginnie?"

"Well—I'll come as far as the tunnel," she said. "I haven't decided about the rest of it. Like I said, I'm starting to enjoy it here."

We bid the Graf farewell. "Remember Plan B," he admonished, wagging his finger.

Outside it had turned to late evening. In the distance glowed a faint curve of the new Earthmost Jiva. She'd nearly gone back into the underworld for the night. Could *she* tell whether or not I'd successfully destroyed my load of eggs? There was no way to know. In any case, she was leaving me alone.

"So let's hop to Monin's farm," I said to Ginnie. "Can you show me how that yuel-style teleportation thing works? I didn't quite get how you did it before."

"It's yogic," said Ginnie. "You merge your mind into the whole of Flimsy, and focus on the spot where you want to be. And then you go for it. That part feels like doing a back-flip off a diving board."

I stared at the sky and felt down into my new body. Flimsy was all around me. I could sense the goddess at the core. She was willing to help me. The spot where we wanted to go was—over there. I pushed towards it and had the same odd, tumbling feeling as before.

And then Ginnie and I were together in the rolling green fields near the vertical wall of living water that bounded the edge of Flimsy. I saw no sign of Monin's farm. Oh, right, the farm was hidden by the space-maze of the border snail.

It felt a little creepy, the two of us alone in these otherworldly meadows. With the night coming on, I could see the glowing of the sprinkles in the sky and in the huge wall of Flimsy. Looking down at the grass, I noticed a fat little black beetle near our feet. I didn't like his vibes. I took a step away.

Meanwhile Ginnie teeped for the mind of the border snail, just like she'd been doing back in Cruz. "Okay, the snail remembers me," she announced shortly. She started pacing back and forth across the empty-seeming green field. "This way, that way, this way," she said. I followed close behind.

Threading the invisible maze took longer than I'd expected, and while we walked, the night fully fell. Soon I couldn't see the sky anymore, for we were shrouded by the maze's space-warp fuzz. Finally we reached the ultimate turn and Monin's mauve domes came into view, with lights glowing in the windows.

The farmer and his family were in there having supper. I could see Durkle at the table as well, which made me glad. I'd been a little worried about him.

I would have liked to talk with the boy, but stealth seemed like the way to go. For sure I didn't want to tell Monin's family that I was planning to close down their tunnel and, more than likely, to chase their border snail away. My changes would upend the family's existence.

"Maybe I go back to Yuelsville now," whispered Ginnie. "I'm thinking I'll move in with the Graf. We might start making music."

"Don't leave yet," I murmured. "I need you. At least help me get the door at this end open. And—and someone has to teep down to Earth and tell Ira to open the door at his end."

"Can't you do those things yourself?" said Ginnie a little condescendingly.

I tried teeping to the border snail but for whatever reason the alien beast's tiny, suspicious mind was closed to me. I crept over to the hatch that led to the snail and laid my hand on it. Just as I'd feared, the door wouldn't open for me anymore. I gave Ginnie a pleading look.

Ginnie had only to touch the door—and it opened. The insides still smelled of violets and decay. The great snail's flexible eyestalks came poking out from within. Slowly, slowly she began pushing out her head.

I tried teeping to Earth to alert Ira—but I couldn't seem to bring anything into focus. Ginnie had no trouble with this either. She contacted Ira and told him to go into the back yard of the Whipped Vic and to open the snail door there. While she was at it, Ginnie teeped Snaily about the plan.

"Look," I begged Ginnie, "I'll never make it back from Earth without you. Please come."

"Mr. Cosmic Mailman," said Ginnie, gently mocking me. But I had the feeling she was proud that I needed her.

"We'll save the world!" I told her, my voice rising with enthusiasm. "And we'll bring Ira over here too."

"Oh, all right," said Ginnie. Her face turned a little grim. "I guess I've got a special errand too. I was almost thinking of dropping it and

212 ● Rudy Rucker

moving on." She was talking about settling her score with Skeeves.

By now the border snail's head was fully out of the hole, and she was starting to open her mouth. Almost time to go.

Just then Monin's main door opened and a figure came out—a youth carrying a sword. Durkle.

"Hey," I called to him a low tone. "It's Jim and Ginnie. We're about to go back through the snail."

Durkle softly closed the house's door and walked over. "I *thought* I heard something," he said, checking out our new bodies. "Ditched your jivas, huh? Way to go. I had big fun on my way back. I conjugated with Swoozie."

"Good boy! And we're about to save Earth."

"Can I come?" asked Durkle. "It's a drag being home. Mom and Dad treat me like a kid."

"Wait here for us to come back," I said quickly. "It won't take long. I just have to kill this one jiva named Sukie. We'll come back here and you can open the door for us. And then I'll bring you along for the next leg. I have all these different things I'm supposed to do."

"Busy guy," said Durkle, echoing Ginnie. "Mr. Mailman."

A sudden thought popped into my head. "Can you give me some of that silvery fertilizer you use in your garden? I forget what you call the stuff, it came from a tube?"

"Ultragrow," said Durkle. "Hold on." He made his way over to another of the domes, which served as a garden shed, and returned with a object the size and shape of a toothpaste tube, with a tight cap on the end.

"Beautiful," I said, and stashed the tube inside the flesh of one of my thighs, just like I'd done with the flute.

"So where's Weena?" asked Durkle.

"I killed her," said Ginnie.

"Good move," said the boy. "You two are such outlaws. Tell me more about—" Suddenly his voice broke into a cracked yell. "Behind you!"

A ragged beetle was scrabbling towards us—the same one I'd seen before, but now he was a foot long. The crooked insect rose from the grass with his wings a-buzz. Durkle slashed at him with his sword—and completely missed.

With two swift snaps of his mandibles, the shiny beetle snipped off Durkle's hand at the wrist. The boy howled with pain and surprise.

Monin and Yerba appeared at the house's main door, crying out in alarm. Durkle staggered over to them, carrying his severed hand.

The fierce beetle swept through an arc and closed in on Ginnie and me. The lights of the house reflected off his body in shades of amber and maroon. He was herding us towards the border snail. Not hesitating to think it over, Ginnie and I scrambled into the willing snail's large mouth. I let Ginnie go first.

The tunnel was quite different this time through. It was tight and slimy, as if we were being born. Lacking jivas, neither Ginnie nor I had the ability to reach out and widen the spatial width of the aperture. We wormed forward through the narrow passage as rapidly as we could. At this point I couldn't tell if the menacing beetle was following us or not.

Soon we came to the two-meter wall of living water that crossed the tunnel. With the tunnel so narrow, we became more tangled in the snail's feeder tendrils than before. I was afraid of mistakenly pushing through the snail's body wall and ending up in some savagely inconceivable limbo. Cautiously Ginnie and I wriggled onward, like spelunkers traversing an underground stream.

The sprinkles nibbled off a bit of our kessence—but my larger concern was that I felt something nipping at my heels.

I teeped to Ginnie, urging her to hurry. We struggled a little further until, quite suddenly, her thrashing form was gone. But then, thank heavens, I too slid from of the snail's Earth-side mouth. I was wet and slimy all over, lying in the back yard of the Whipped Vic. It was morning here, morning in July. The sky was hazy and bright.

My faithful dog Droog stood over me, licking my kessence face. Quickly I felt down into myself, fearing a rush of jiva eggs. But everything was calm. Burning my old body in the Graf's fireplace must have done the job.

"Surf zombie!" said Ira, staring down at me. "Up from the crypt!" He looked tattered and worn.

Already on her feet, Ginnie stretched her arms straight ahead and gamely mimed a few zombie steps. "Eat, eat, eat! Kill, kill, kill!" The wispy Ira chortled at her clowning. He was glad to have us back.

But now the fun stopped. The sinister beetle was crawling from the border snail's mouth.

"Look out!" I yelled.

Blessedly, the beetle was interested in something other than attacking us. Chittering softly, he scuttled across the body of the snail and in through the door to the basement.

"What the fuck was that thing?" said the wispy Ira. "New friend of yours?"

"He showed up at the last minute," I said. "He followed us through."

"Beetle..." said Ginnie, thoughtfully. "Scarab! Maybe he's an Egyptian ghost?"

"I'm the bull-goose E-gyptologist around here," came a voice from inside of the basement. The voice of Skeeves.

Ginnie's hands jerked up in alarm. And now she set herself, gathering her strength. Her pretty features tightened into a battle-mask. "All right," she said. "All frikkin' right." She took a first step towards the basement door.

"You're going after him?" said Ira, a catch in his voice. "He's really out of control. And I don't guess I love him anymore. But I wonder if—"

"He killed both of us," said Ginnie. "And never mind about any frikkin' voices in his head. It's time to settle the score."

"Okay," said Ira with a sigh. "If you can. If you're strong enough."

The snail was already withdrawing her head, and it was easy to get through the door into the basement. Ginnie led the way, with me behind her, and Ira in the rear with the dog. My senses were strained to the max. Initially I was more concerned about spotting the sarcophagus than with finding Skeeves. I was relieved to see the golden casket still in place, presumably with my flesh body safe within. As for the beetle—did I see some odd movement in the patterns of the sarcophagus's golden frieze?

At this point Skeeves took over my attention. He was at the far end of the basement, standing by a weird little staircase that I'd noticed last week. Presumably it led into the core of the house's shrunken, twisted passageways. Up where Skeeves lived.

Skeeves was naked and very stoned. He had Egyptian hieroglyphs painted all over his skin in ocher and red.

"I lost my spirit familiar," he muttered. "Sexy Weena. Her body turned to mush. That scuttlebug thing that crawled under the sarcophagus just now—is that Skeevey's new pet?"

"You're done now," said Ginnie, striding towards him. She'd grown accustomed to having a certain amount of power in Flimsy. She grabbed Skeeves by the throat. But she was, after all, only a kessence ghost. And with no jivas in us, we had very little material force.

"Do I feel a draft? said Skeeves with a bully's sarcasm. "Did you leak a reek?" He caught Ginnie's wrists in one hand, and threw her across his shoulders like a stole. Reveling in his dominance, he strode over to the gold sarcophagus and thumped a rhythm on the lid with his free hand. "*Ankh salaam Amenhotep,*" chanted Skeeves. "*Ruh nuh port mu hurra!*"

I definitely didn't like seeing him mess with the sarcophagus. And I was concerned about what he might do to Ginnie. It occurred to me that if I were to get back into my flesh body, I'd have a better ability to deal with Skeeves. But I didn't want to lose focus on all the other things that—

Suddenly my deliberations became moot. Moving faster than the eye could follow, the dark scarab darted out from patterns on the sarcophagus and pounced onto Skeeves's face. Skeeves screamed luridly. Ginnie twisted free of his grip and darted over to my side. The beetle was some kind of spirit. I had the feeling he was male—and that his powers were of a far higher order than mine.

The beetle was even larger than before—he covered Skeeves's face and neck entirely. I could hear a horrible, pulpy, chewing sound. Blood streamed down Skeeves's neck, pouring from his ruined tissues. His bare skull teeth were visible; his voice had become a husky croak.

"Do it," said Ginnie softly. And now she, Ira, and Droog backed away and left the basement.

I alone stayed rooted to the spot, unwilling to leave the scene. I had an intense personal interest in the sarcophagus and its contents, and I was loath to leave them with this nightmare scarab.

The beetle's insufferable munching continued—and in minutes, Skeeves's body was completely gone. I could see the tiny glowing spark of Skeeves's naked sprinkle. It flew in a dwindling gyre, as if preparing to drill down to the land of Flimsy that lies within each of our world's electrons.

But now, with a rapid twist, the hovering beetle caught and ate the sprinkle too. Skeeves, like Weena, had been fully annihilated.

The beetle executed a stuttering, folding motion that was too intricate to follow. It seemed as if it merged back into the cryptic symbols decorating Amenhotep's sarcophagus. But it was hard to be sure. I stood stock still for another full minute, waiting to see what came next.

"Are you okay?" called Ginnie through the door.

"I'm fine," I said. "And Skeeves is gone."

"Right on."

Moving slowly and cautiously, I walked over to the sarcophagus and tipped back the lid.

The golden interior glistened, alive with blank reflections. The sarcophagus was completely empty.

26: Missing Me

Out in the back yard, Ira was in tears. "You never knew Skeeves like he was back in the day," he was telling Ginnie. And now Ira turned to me. "You remember Skeeves out on Four Mile Beach, right, Jim? He was so hard, so outlaw, so gnarly."

"All of that," I said. In some respects I'd been in awe of Skeeves myself. But I was very glad that he was gone.

"What about that beetle?" asked Ginnie, peering into the basement past the snail.

"Fuck the beetle," I said. "My body's missing."

"I was meaning to tell you about that," said Ira, rubbing his insubstantial eyes. "Those other bodies in the casket with you—Weena and that dude with the beard? They turned to stinky mush all of a sudden. I guess that was yesterday. It was super foul, you could smell it all through the Whipped Vic. Skeeves was mad about it. He got me to help him carry the casket out of the maze and dump all the crap into the street. And then we hosed it off and brought it back inside."

"All the crap," I echoed. "And that included me?"

"Well—you know," said Ira. "Skeeves didn't really like you anymore. He said that when you were talking to him at the party, you called him an asshole."

"Oh, I didn't realize he was so sensitive. What happened to my body after you guys threw it into the street?"

217

"The pigs showed up," said Ira. "I think they took you to the Santa Cruz hospital. You were still breathing. I heard them talking about it through the maze. I figured you'd be fine."

"This is bad," I said, thinking it over. "That sarcophagus has a vibe on it, you know? I'm only out of my body because of some Egyptian magic spell that Weena knew. I bet my body's not doing very well on its own. And those doctors might start in with their so-called heroic measures. Shock treatment. Surgical interventions. We've gotta get my body back, dude. It was much safer in that sarcophagus."

"But what about the beetle?" reiterated Ginnie.

"He merged into those hammered golden patterns on the side of the casket, okay? I'll take my chances with that beetle over any frikkin' gang of doctors. Anyway, the beetle was only after Skeeves."

"He might turn on you next," said Ginnie. "In case you hadn't thought of that."

"Relax, would you?"

"I'm thinking the beetle is the angry soul of Amenhotep," said Ira. "Do you guys know the story about Skeeves burning Amenhotep's mummy in a fireplace? He said the mummy-smoke got him higher than he'd ever been."

"And he said the smoke killed Crocker—the guy he got the sarcophagus from," I added. "Skeeves said that made Crocker a lightweight."

"Skeeves was no lightweight," said Ira, smiling and shaking his head. The conversation came to a pause.

I could see the old van sitting in the Whipped Vic's driveway. "Do you have the keys for Skeeves's beater?" I asked Ira. "I want to move my body before it's too late."

"Okay, but you drive," said Ira, fluttering his insubstantial hands. "I'm too ghostly."

"Take some of this, poor Ira," said Ginnie, digging a handful of kessence out of her side and handing it to him. I gave him some of my substance as well.

"That's so kind of you," said Ira, his voice flooding with emotion. "I'm fading away here. There's not much reason for me to stay any longer, now that, now that—"

"World's smallest violin," said Ginnie, making that rubbing gesture with her thumb and finger once again. "Crack!"

"Keep it together, Ira," I said. "With any luck, we'll all be going to

Flimsy really soon. But first I'd like you to help Ginnie and me load the sarcophagus into the back of Skeeves's van."

"What for?" said Ira. "I don't want to touch it now."

"The Whipped Vic is gonna disappear," I said patiently. "When we go back through the tunnel to Flimsy, I'm pulling the snail and her shell after us. So I have to park the sarcophagus and my body somewhere else."

"Like where?" challenged Ira.

"We'll talk about that later. I've got a plan."

Ginnie, too, was reluctant to touch the sarcophagus, now that the scary beetle was hiding in its bas-reliefs. But I gave them a pep talk, and finally we three specters managed to lug the sarcophagus out to the van. I did most of the heavy lifting—my new yuel-built kessence body was pretty solid.

There was an odd kind of interface between my kessence body and the physical world. Although my body barely cast a shadow, if I focused on my hands or my feet, I could firm them up. And, if I paid close attention, I could move physical objects around.

In particular, I was able to manipulate the van's steering wheel and pedals well enough to drive. As I cruised towards the hospital with Droog and my two friends, I noticed a remarkably vivid balloon bobbing above a car dealership that lay a couple of blocks to one side of our route. I could see that the balloon was in the shape of a huge green beet, with a wriggly band of gold around its waist and a floppy purple cap on top—

"That's Sukie," I said softly. The sight of the big jiva made me feel agitated and quavery.

"I know," said Ira from the back seat. "She's been there all week. I guess it's, like, a kind of camouflage? Like in that mystery story where the guy tacks a stolen letter to his wall and nobody sees it?"

"Swing over there and nail her with a yuelball right now, Jim," said Ginnie. "I hate those frikkin' jivas."

"Let me focus on saving my body first," I insisted. I felt like too many things were happening too fast. And just then the guy behind us started honking and pointing at our van. Maybe he thought the van was empty and that it was randomly rolling along. I accelerated and ditched him. Frikkin' busybody.

I parked in the lot of the Santa Cruz Hospital. I left Droog in the van with a window half open. Ira and Ginnie came into the hospital with me. Although a few of the more zonked patients could see us, most of the employees couldn't, and it was pretty easy for us three to breeze past the checkpoints and through the corridors.

On a hunch, I led us to same floor where I'd gone with my brain attack. Just like before, nurse Alice was sitting behind the counter. Her short hair was blonde with black roots. She wore a trim white uniform with a wide skirt. Right now there weren't any other nurses around. Alice was busy with her computer.

"Hey," I said, leaning close to her.

She looked up and, blessedly, managed to see me. "Can I help you?" Her face was plain but, in its kindness, beautiful.

"I'm Jim Oster?"

Alice cocked her head, studying me. "I don't think so. Mr. Oster's in a coma. And you're—" She groped for the word.

"Not flesh," I said. "I'm Jim Oster's spirit in an astral body. And these are my ghost friends Ginnie and Ira. Most people can't see us. We want to move my body to a safer place."

"Delusions," said nurse Alice, as if speaking to herself. "Lack of sleep. Way, way too much coffee."

"You're sensitive and empathetic," I said. "A wonderful person. That's why you can see me. I'm a spirit, but I'm real."

"Go away," said Alice, making a shooing motion. "Begone. I don't need this." She leaned her face into her hands and stayed like that, as if taking a time out.

So, what the hell, we started down the hall, looking in the rooms. Soon I found my poor, abandoned bod, lying alone under a sheet—a melancholy and pathetic sight.

"Wait in the hall," I told Ginnie and Ira. "I want to do this alone." I went into the room.

My body was pale and somewhat emaciated. They'd shaved my chin and my head, and a few dozen wires were taped to my bare scalp. A feeding tube snaked into my forearm, and a catheter drain ran from my crotch. Next to the bed was a quietly beeping machine with a monitor drawing wiggly green graphs. Breath and pulse were regular, my brain waves were flat-lined. I was stupid to have left my dear flesh for this long.

"I'll unplug you from the heart-attack machine," I said softly. I began peeling the wires off my forlorn, bald head. It was terrible to see my face from this perspective; it was like looking into some mad, crooked mirror. My body twitched and fluttered, as if reacting to my spirit's presence.

I was seized by a sudden fear that I'd been in the hospital continuously for weeks, and that my elaborate recent adventures were the hallucinations of a dying man. I was tempted to dive down into my clammy, long-suffering flesh—and never mind my pipe-dreams of saving the Earth and resurrecting Val.

"You're absolutely right to move your body," said nurse Alice, cutting off my despairing thoughts. She was in the room's doorway with a wheelchair. Ginnie and Ira stood beside her. "The hospital's gotten court approval to remove your life support tomorrow. I've decided that I'll help you get your body out of here. I'll write up a release form later on. The admin will be glad to have you gone."

"How long have I been in here?" I asked.

"The police brought you in yesterday," said nurse Alice. "I recognized you right away. You're a nice man. That high-strung woman who picked you up before—she's gone?"

"Gone," said Ginnie, speaking up. "And now Jim's on a big quest to save Earth from these evil aliens called jivas."

"A jiva killed my wife," I told nurse Alice. "Do you still remember her? Val?"

"I do," said Alice, her voice low and thoughtful. "I saw what was inside her that day. And that's why I want to believe you now. It kind of fits that you showed up here now. It's as if everything's coming together. As if it's the end of the world."

"You never told me what you saw that day," I said tensely.

"It wasn't an embryo at all," said Alice, stepping into the room. "It was more like a kind of root, only rounded in the middle, and with nasty, slick colors. Orange and green. I still dream about it sometimes. And here's the crazy part. This week, on my way to work, I've been seeing a shape like that in the sky. Supposedly it's only a car lot's advertising balloon. But I'm scared."

"It's not a balloon," I said. "It's a jiva. And I'm going to kill it."

Nurse Alice laughed uneasily. "If only you can. I haven't been able to sleep this week at all." A ping sounded in the hall. "Hurry up and wrestle that body into this wheel chair," she said. "Your clothes are in the drawer. I'll find someone to watch the desk. I'll take you and your friends out through the staff elevator."

We got the hospital gown off my body and dragged my jeans, red

T-shirt and blue-checked flannel shirt onto it. Onto me. It was wildly unpleasant to be seeing myself this way.

With nurse Alice along, nobody paid much attention as we wheeled my body across the lot and lifted it into the van. Droog pranced around, getting in the way.

The moment I laid my body in the sarcophagus, it looked better. My cheeks regained some color. My whole form seemed to relax and fill out. It was like tucking someone onto their own comfortable bed—instead of leaving them on a padded bench in a death-row cell.

I had the feeling that Alice was still wondering if this was for real.

"You're wonderful," I told her. "And just wait, that jiva will be gone later today."

"Good luck," she said with a tight, anxious smile. And then she was on her way back inside.

Thinking ahead, I rooted in the van's accumulated mounds of grunge and found a jeans and T-shirt combo that could fit Val, should she return. I stuffed them into the casket with my clothed body.

Taking the wheel, I drove fast down some back roads and made it to a pull-out near Four Mile Beach. And then we had to maneuver the sarcophagus and my body across a meadow of summer-yellowed grass and Queen Anne's lace—tall stalks with intricate green leaves and big compound flowers like white doilies on top. Droog was sniffing everything. By now the morning fog had cleared away—it was a sunny July day. Butterflies drifted across the flowers; grasshoppers buzzed and leapt.

As I didn't want my body to be out in the sunlight where everyone could see it, we were pushing the closed sarcophagus across the meadow like a sled, with the plants tip-tapping the shiny sides. The ancient casket was gorgeous in the full sun, with its bands of hieroglyphs in gold, carnelian and lapis lazuli. Although the face of Amenhotep on the lid was serene it seemed in some sense watchful—with its large, embossed eyes. But there were no signs of that dark beetle who'd disappeared among the hammered ankhs and ibises along the base. Now and then the heavy box would fetch up against a tuft of grass and we'd have to redouble our efforts.

"This is ridiculous," complained the feeble Ira at one such pause. "It's way too hard."

"Jim and I are doing the real work, bitch," said Ginnie. "Why don't you just walk along behind us and straighten up the plants. We don't want to be leaving a big obvious skid track."

"But why the fuck are we doing this?" asked Ira.

"Because I buried my wife's ashes on the bluff here," I said. "Okay? I want to be next to her."

"How goth," said Ginnie.

And so the two of us pushed on, bending down nearly parallel to the ground, making our legs firm and fat. The intense physical effort was depleting my supply of kessence—but my astral body still had plenty to spare.

We reached the bluff with its sandy hollows. In the midday sun, the glassy ocean waves were a brilliant shade of ultramarine blue. Droog seemed to remember about Val. He made his way to the little pyramid-rock that I'd set in place as her gravestone. Waving off the dog, I knelt down and dug with both hands until I'd reached the first dry white flecks of my wife's cremated bones. I sat on the ground beside the little hole, collecting my thoughts. And then I drew the tube of Durkle's ultragrow from within my left thigh.

"A method to his madness," said Ginnie, understanding what was up.

"I'm hoping this will get Val's body to start growing here," I explained for Ira's sake as I squeezed silvery goo from the tube. "I want to get her body ready for when I bring her spirit back." I stirred the ultragrow into the sand, feeling a tingle in my hands. And then I covered the hole with a low mound of sand.

Ira and Ginnie watched, sitting on the ground and leaning against the sarcophagus. They seemed to have forgotten any worries about the beetle spirit.

"Now we get that thing out of sight," I said. "I don't want some gunjy freak to be stealing it. And I don't want my body to get cooked by the sun. Look, there's a long low spot right here. All we have to do is scrape it a foot or two deeper. Please?"

Ginnie, Ira and I got it done, with Droog joining in. The digging wasn't all that hard—the sand was loose. And Ginnie found that we could reshape our kessence hands into trowels. The sarcophagus fit readily into the trench, and we heaped the sand up along its sides.

At the last minute, I opened the sarcophagus lid for a final check. My body was looking much, much better than in the stroke ward.

"Good night, Jim," said Ginnie. I closed the lid and we scattered a thin layer of sand across the top. With any luck, I'd be back to reclaim my body quite soon.

We went across the meadow and got back in the van.

"Now for Sukie, and then it's back to the Whipped Vic," I said.

"Check this out," said Ginnie. She'd found a couple of filthy old towels on the floor. She draped one over her head and tossed one on me. "This way it won't look like the van's empty while we're driving around town."

"*Salaam*."

On the drive into town, Ginnie and I taught Ira how to sing the yuel lullaby. We found it pretty easy to teep with Ira, maybe because he'd absorbed kessence from both of us. The three of us were in synch.

I hadn't been exactly clear on which car lot Sukie was hovering over, so when I pulled up to it, I had a jolt of surprise. Sukie was above, of all places, Simly The Best—the car dealership owned by my landlord Dick Simly, the very guy that Weena had—

"Is Dick Simly dead or not?" I asked Ira.

"What?"

"The guy whose body Sukie and those other jivas hatched from?"

"I'm way outta the loop," said Ira, hunching down low in the back seat. "Don't bother me right now. I want to be sure I remember that yuel lullaby."

I threw off my towel and got out of the car, invisible to most of the people here. Sukie's long tapering tail trailed down to the ground where it was rooted in the asphalt of the lot. She was a sitting duck. And sure enough, there was sleek, earnest Dick Simly inside the dealership, showing an electric car to a granola yuppie woman with frizzy hair.

So far, neither Dick nor the jiva had noticed me. I set my yuel lullaby to vibrating within my mind and body. I scooped a glob of kessence from my belly and I molded it into a yuelball. I had a teep connection to the yuelball, and I was able to keep the yuel lullaby going inside it. I was about ready to—

Oh shit, here came Dick Simly, striding across the asphalt, wearing his full-gospel salesman's grin. A slender tendril from Sukie ran into the center of Dick's scalp—like a remote control cable.

"Haven't seen you around," boomed Dick. "Diane and I assumed you'd left town. Did you know that your eviction went through?

The papers are on the front door. The sheriff put your stuff in a warehouse. I hope you're okay with this." He stepped forward as if to lay his hand upon my shoulder.

I took a quick step back. I didn't have time to think about the eviction. "I know what happened to you with the jivas," I said. "I'm surprised you survived."

"I'm a latter-day jivaic saint," said Dick. His manic grin grew still wider and he pointed to the heavens—or to Sukie.

And now the big jiva took action. Like a smooth-moving snake, her tail wriggled free of the ground. She sent an odd, slide-whistle chirp in my direction, an unpleasant sound that cut through my yuel lullaby and dug deep into my head. And then the giant beet began rising into the sky, perhaps hoping to get out of range.

Quicker than it takes to tell it, I let my body go slack and opened my mouth wide. I merged my kessence legs into my butt, taking on the shape of a cannon. I shoved my singing yuelball into my mouth and swallowed it down.

Dick Simly guessed what was coming. He crouched as if to tackle me, but Ginnie and Droog were at my side to back me up. Droog sank his teeth into Simly's calf, and Ginnie began singing a yuel lullaby right into the man's face, driving Sukie's tendril from his head. Dick Simly gave a sharp yell—but then he looked relieved.

Not wasting any time, I pulsed an intense washboard of ridges along the length of my throat. My yuelball shot upwards at the speed of sound.

Sukie veered to one side. But my yuelball had a stubby pair of fins, and I used my teep to steer it directly for the jiva, no matter how she zigged and zagged.

The impact was good, even orgasmic. I could feel my yuelball blossoming into the crannies of Sukie's ungainly form. And now the stinky tinkle of my lullaby tore her into flaming chunks. The lumps of kessence rained like brimstone upon Simly's fuel-efficient cars.

Victory!

Dick Simly had run inside. Ginnie and Ira began scavenging among the fallen scraps of kessence, stamping out the flames and eating what they could. I returned to my humanoid shape and followed their example, bulking up for the rest of my mission.

But hold on—something was wrong. The slide-whistle sound that Sukie had made—it had started a change way down inside me.

Something was awakening within the sprinkle that lay at my core. The jiva eggs. They'd been hiding there in infinitesimal form.

My neck swelled into a spiky ruff. Jiva eggs flew from the ruff's tips like popcorn from an overheated pan, like sparks from a log, like glowing thistledown.

27: Pied Piper

Within seconds, I'd spawned ten thousand eggs.

They were lavender specks, tiny globules with thread-like tails. Each of them was haloed by a golden aura the size of a grape. They drifted with the air currents, jittering along their paths, guiding their progress with the motions of their hair-thin tails. Right now three them were circling my head as if wanting to settle back into me.

I began chanting my yuel lullaby, and the jiva eggs zigzagged away. So long as I kept the song going, I could carve a safe space for myself within the swarm of parasitic eggs. I was a clumsy fool to have carried them over here—but I didn't have to let any of them incubate and grow to maturity inside me as well. Ginnie and Ira stood beside me, both of them singing as well.

Droog had no understanding of the situation. When an egg drifted near his nose, he snapped at it. With a quick darting motion, the egg made its way inside the dog's mouth. Droog widened his eyes and sat back on his haunches, listening into himself.

All around us the eggs were dispersing past the cars and the smoldering remnants of Sukie. Although Dick Simly was safe inside his air-conditioned showroom, a few salesmen and customers had been infested. These men and women were standing quite still, with their hands resting on their bellies—like statues of the expectant Madonna.

Across the street, the jiva seeds drifted in through the open windows and swinging doors of shops, finding hosts. And thousands of their sisters were riding the sea-breeze across the roofs to the blocks beyond.

Still humming the yuel lullaby, I returned my attention to Droog. The egg within him was maturing very fast. His belly was swollen, as if he'd eaten a week's worth of garbage. His sides jiggled with motions of the quickening jiva within.

And now Droog heaved himself to his feet. He stretched out his neck, coughing deep in his throat. A strand of drool hung from his lower jaw. He retched, and a pale purple tendril appeared beside his tongue. He strained and gasped, forcing something up. The mauve tendril lengthened. And then a shape like a wriggling parsnip slid from Droog's toothy snout.

The dog shook his head hard, flapping his ears to demarcate the end of his ordeal. He seemed quite unharmed, although—I now noticed— an ethereal control-thread led from the new jiva to Droog's head. Using the kessence-forces in my fingers, I yanked the tendril from my dog's skull. He looked glad.

Meanwhile, across the lot, the infested salesmen and customers were bent forward, vomiting up jivas of their own. These eggs were incubating within their hosts' stomachs, and growing to adulthood in less than three minutes. Evidently the jivas now viewed us as a valuable resource, and they'd learned to parasitize humans in a non-destructive way. If only that first jiva egg had treated my Val so gently.

Droog's newly hatched jiva drifted across the car lot to join the others. The jivas clustered together as if conferring, bumping each other like party balloons. Rather than flying immediately into the sky, the little group dug their tendrils into the asphalt. Rapidly they plumped up, as if feeding upon the kessence inherent in ordinary matter.

Looking up and down the street, I could see hundreds of people puking up jivas. The jivas emerged as lean and pale as white radishes, but quickly they swelled and took on colors.

"I like those big jivas," said Ira. "They're as pretty as Easter eggs."

Each jiva had her own special look. Their beet-like bodies were shaded in pairs of harmonious tones, usually with an elegant row of contrasting spots. They'd grown themselves topknots like party hats—imagine domed miters, floppy tams, rubbery crowns, and striped stovepipes. And the jivas' long, writhing tendrils were bedizened with balls, donuts, and disks.

"You screwed the pooch on this one," said Ginnie, sardonically amused. "You came here to kill one single jiva and you made ten thousand more. See how the jivas have little kessence threads leading to their former hosts? Slaves of the puppetmasters, dude. We're exiles in zombietown."

I glared at her, humming my protective lullaby like some far-gone monk obsessing on a mantra. "We'll drive to the Whipped Vic for Plan B," I said finally.

I got Skeeves's van started and we drove off. Dick Simly was in his showroom, watching us. He shook his fist at me. That was my thanks for getting Sukie out of his head. An asshole all the way.

I drove very fast, slewing the car this way and that. A few of the jiva-controlled humans threw rocks or bottles at us as we passed. Seemed like we had a bad rep on zombie street. At least they weren't going all out to stop us. I figured the jivas didn't know about my Plan B. They didn't realize that, hopeless as things now looked, I was still planning to win.

Once we were off the main drag I felt safe enough to stop my chant. What with the van windows rolled up, we were protected from any laggard eggs that still hadn't found a host.

By now there were jivas growing from each stretch of pavement, and above every meager plot of grass. The jivas had sunk thick tendrils into the soil, and sometimes I had to steer around them. With the jivas bobbing on every side, Santa Cruz had an undersea feel, like a kelp forest. Away from the town center, the jiva-controlled humans were content to stare through the stalks—like wary fish.

I headed towards the general location of the Whipped Vic, expecting to get precise instructions from Ginnie in a minute, the usual odd-ball sequence of lefts, rights, and double reverses that that would lead in though the snail's protective maze of space warps.

"Do you notice how all the trees and bushes are wilting?" observed Ginnie for now. She was staring out of the van's window. "Much worse than this morning. Everything looks—wan."

For that matter, the pavement beneath the car's tires was less solid than an hour ago, more cracked and crumbly. I recalled Weena saying that the jivas could weaken the structure of ordinary matter by drawing off its vital forces. Their prime mission here was, after all, to pump kessence from Earth to the Duke's castle in Flimsy. And presumably the border snail was willing to serve as their conduit.

Glancing upwards, I saw that some of the bigger jivas had sprouted extra tendrils that ran out horizontally like bright-colored phone wires. Up ahead of us, the feeder tendrils converged like power lines leading to a transformer station. And the node's location was on Yucca Street, the home of the Whipped Vic.

"Turn right, then left, then back up," said Ginnie.

"We'll follow the flow," I said, pointing to the ever-denser bundle of jiva tendrils overhead. They gave off a low drone. Faint undulations moved along the colorful tubes—successive gulps of kessence. "Never mind giving me directions."

There were thousands of the low-hanging jivaic power lines. I swerved back and forth, tracking their turns. I approached the hazy zone around the Whipped Vic—and the pulsing cables led us though the maze.

We pulled into the driveway and hopped out of the van, once again singing our protective yuel lullabies. In the back yard the snail's door lay discarded on the ground, covered by a massive tangle of the humming pastel jiva tendrils. There was a smell like elephants and kerosene. The tendrils had twined themselves into a fat cable that led into the basement and through the border snail's mouth.

Presumably they led through the snail to Monin's farm, and thence to the Duke's castle in the land of Flimsy—which was hidden down inside one of the Whipped Vic basement's electrons.

Ira was kind of elated by the scene. "This feels like a sinister factory surrounded by chain-link fences with graphical images of trespassers knocked dead by implacable stylized sparks," he said. "An alien industrial site involving forces yet more weird than e-lectricity."

"It's dangerous for sure," said Ginnie. "Hurry up and get help, Jim."

I pulled the magic flute from my leg. Its chrome-like substance glinted with colored highlights from the jiva tendrils. Fitting my fingers to the little flute's elegant keys, I blew across the mouthpiece, playing the catchy jingle of the summoning call. Getting my rhythm, I began playing the tune over and over, each time a little louder, directing my toots towards the border snail's stuffed mouth.

Droog didn't like my noise or the tendrils; he was lying down flat on the ground. No yuels had appeared as yet, but the jivas were noticing the disturbance. Daughter-tendrils branched from the pipeline tubes, deceptively slender vines that felt their way towards me, surely hoping to do me in.

Ginnie and Ira redoubled their yuel lullabies. They'd found a way to vibrate their whole kessence bodies, pulsing out sound with the energy of a low-rider's thuddy bass units. The delicate attack-tendrils drew back a few feet. I played faster and more forcefully. Just then, *aha*, the wad of cables parted. Two yuels came wriggling through, both of them shaped like blue baboons.

Their great golden eyes locked upon mine. I could pick up their yuel teep—it was Rickben and his boyfriend Gaylord. They were singing yuel lullabies too. Agile as acrobats, the two yuels began a wild session of sex play, rolling on the ground at our feet. Droog went and hid under the back steps. He didn't like any of this.

The two yuels rubbed their flat-nosed faces against each other and raked each other's bellies with their claws. Each of them had a throbbing bulb at the end of his tail. The stiff tails twined around each other and then—thrilling climax!—the pods at the tips touched. Rickben and Gaylord howled like banshees. A thick cloud of yuel spores floated across the ragged lawn.

On the instant, baby yuels began popping up from the ground—like speeded-up mushrooms after a storm. Droog poked his snout from under the steps, sniffing at them. There were easily a thousand of the yuel-sprouts nourishing themselves on fecund Mother Earth's dirt. They looked like blue tubes with cup-shaped caps, and they were already singing yuel lullabies—it seemed to be a skill that they were born with.

The tangle of jiva tails faltered in their busy pumping. As the massed chorus of wee lullabies grew in force, the tendrils began to withdraw, first in ones and twos, then in clumps, and then all the rest of them at once. Pulling their tendrils all the way back from the Duke's castle didn't seem to take them much time at all.

And now, as if worn down by the intense traffic through her body's tube, the border snail abruptly stopped maintaining the space-maze that had hidden her from the outer world. Yuels blanketed the neighborhood lawns as far as I could see, thousands upon thousands of them. As they fattened up from the soil, they were rapidly popping loose and taking on the standard blue baboon form.

Some of the neighbors were wandering around, disconsolate and confused. I was glad to see that their jiva control-tendrils were gone. We were free agents on this strangely altered stretch of Yucca Street. And, at least for now, none of the locals wanted to mess with me.

Like some charismatic revival preacher, I reached out with my mind and linked my thoughts with the mob of fledgling blue baboons. I think there may have been twenty thousand of them. Working with rapid strings of images, I teeped the new yuels what I'd learned about killing jivas with yuelballs. And then I showed them the strategy that I wanted us to use. We were going to trap the jivas beneath a shrinking dome of sound.

The yuels understood. For the moment they suspended their songs, lest they drive the jivas further away. Flexing their protean bodies, all but a thousand of the yuels spouted membranous wings, flapping and grinning. They lifted off like a horde of demons, rising into the heavens to float above the highest-flying of the jivas. Meanwhile the baboon-shaped yuels took off for the far borders of Santa Cruz, traveling in high, elastic bounds. And once the jivas were surrounded on every side, the yuels began again to sing.

Like beaters herding game, the yuels drove the jivas across the town and down from the sky—condensing them into zone immediately above Yucca Street, directly in front of the Whipped Vic. The ten thousand beautiful beets were trapped in a mobile cage of hovering yuels. The disoriented jivas bounced awkwardly against each other, their tendrils spooled and twirled. The bat-shaped yuels thrashed their wings in tight circles, chorusing their numbing song; the blue baboons capered and gloated. It was awesome and terrifying, an apocalyptic scene.

And now the slaughter began. The yuels launched their first round of yuelballs, and the jivas began exploding into flaming shards, which the yuels guided away from the houses and towards the asphalt of the street. A few of the jivas survived the first fusillade, but a second brought them low as well. The rubble stretched perhaps a hundred yards along the street in a rick some fifty feet high and fifty feet across. The spectacular sheets of flame had an oddly geometric look to them, like stylized fins and triangles. And as the remains burned, they began dwindling away. For a time, none of us could speak.

"It's like the End Times," said Ira finally. He was covering his awe with a hillbilly accent. "We're saved, brother Jim."

"Except now Earth's infested with yuels," said Ginnie.

"You two lead them back," I said, gathering my wits. "You know how the yuels love music. You'll be pied pipers. Listen to this riff."

I tootled a tasty arpeggio, the trill from "Winter Wonderland" that I'd learned in my marching-band days. Ginnie and Ira began broadcasting massive music from their shimmering kessence forms, building a matrix of their own acoustical stylings around my staccato riffs. The yuels harkened and drew closer, gliding down from the air. We three began playing with true abandon, layering on a glutton's feast of notes. The yuels crowded tight around us, worshipping the joyful noise.

And now, stutter-stepping and jamming, Ginnie and Ira led the yuels into the wide open mouth of the border snail. I stood to one side, piping the yuels on their way. It felt as if my life had become an epic movie.

Quite soon all the yuels were gone, and the shell-shocked neighbors cheered. A rackety noise sounded from the sky. The police and the news teams were here—now that the show was nearly over.

I had only one more task to do here. I had to close the snail's tunnel. But first I sent Droog away.

"Go ocean," I told him. "Dig sand. Val bury. Jim sleep."

Uncertainly he sniffed at me. All this drama had disturbed him. And he didn't want to leave my side, even though I was but a ghost of his old master.

"Go on," I urged him again, taking hold of his body and pushing him towards the sea. "Jim come later." I was able to reinforce my message with some low-level teep.

Droog loped off. Goddess willing, I'd be with him soon.

Now for the snail. I put the flute back to my lips and began warbling a snake-charmer-style melody based on my memories of a certain Frank Zappa song, "It Must Be a Camel." I'd practiced this tune back in junior high. It was like the slow undulating tune that a circus orchestra plays while a glistening acrobat vaults to alight atop the pyramid formed by his fellows. I swayed my piccolo back and forth, getting into it. The snail's eyestalks perked up, she was fully focusing on me.

Moving very smoothly, I stepped into the snail's mouth. By now her throat was lax and roomy, and I could have marched straight through. But I paused to stick my head back out, playing the flute as cajolingly as I knew. First one, then another of the snail's eyestalks bent down and poked inside her own mouth to watch me.

Playing ever more sweetly, I backed deeper into the snail's gullet. Her entranced eyestalks followed me. Her snout came along too, and, bit by bit, the rest of her body, flowing into her mouth from every side, with the mouth moving along after me as well. It was as if someone were to swallow their own jaws, lips and face—beginning a process of turning inside out.

In other words—I'd lured the snail into crawling down her own throat! Yes, it was paradoxical, but it was happening. The border snail faltered for a moment when we reached the wall of living water within her—she was on the point of drawing back. Quickly I molded one of my legs into a fishnet and scooped a nice load of sprinkles from within the watery wall. Still playing my undulating snail-charmer music, I dangled the net of sprinkles near her eyestalks. She followed me right through the water wall, fully withdrawing from the Earth-bound snail-shell that had been the Whipped Vic.

But I still needed to do something more if I was to prevent the snail from returning to Santa Cruz later on. I thought back to the stroke of lightning that had started this mess last year. I'd felt a tingle in my spine that time, and when the lightning had hit, it had been like an echo of a process within my own nervous system.

At some level I'd called down the lightning that had made the hole. Perhaps my terrible power had come from those electric eel genes I'd been handling at Wiggler Labs. Be that as it may, if my thoughts had caused the lightning then I should have the ability to—play the lightning backwards.

Not quite knowing what I was doing, I groped down into my memories of that terrible night with Val. Once again I felt a kind of effervescence in my spinal cord, as if it were full of ginger-ale. This time, instead of letting the energy boil into my brain, I sent it into the tips of my fingers, and thence into my flute.

I played the sound of a backwards thunderclap, and the sound of a lightning bolt that congealed from the Earth and leapt into a cloudy sky.

A gong sounded, an unblemished, spherical gong.

I'd healed the single damaged electron that had opened the tunnel from Flimsy to Earth. The border snail would never be able to push through at this spot again.

28: The Goddess

I emerged through the snail's other mouth, entering the afterworld once again. Ginnie and Ira were standing there with Durkle and his family. It looked like mid-afternoon.

"We did it!" enthused Ginnie, unusually effervescent. "We saved Earth!"

"Glad you made it, Jim," said Durkle.

I stood there grinning; I felt elated and dazed.

The space-maze around Monin's farm was gone. I could see the yuels heading across the rolling, flower-dotted meadows, freed into the vast realm of Flimsy. A lot of them seemed to be headed for Yuelsville.

As I walked across the grass, the border snail kept on crawling after me, flowing through her Flimsy-side mouth, turning herself partly inside out. But now that I'd ceased my flute song, she seemed to think better of this. She bucked and squirmed, withdrawing her head and backing up through her body. Probably she hoped to crawl back through to Earth, but I'd eliminated the weak spot that she'd used. As she thrashed about righting herself, Snaily shattered her dome.

"Get away from there before you ruin our whole house!" cried Monin's wife Yerba. She was holding baby Nyoo against her shoulder. Stepping closer, Yerba sweetened her voice and called, "Here Snaily, here you go girl, come to Yerba for your treat!"

The border snail slimed forward into the yard again, right-side out and lacking a shell. Yerba tossed her a ball of kessence dusted with sprinkles. Seen bare, Snaily was but a ten-meter-long slug with eyestalks on either end, her body striped in shades of purple and yellow. She wasn't as large as I would have expected, but the size question was, to say the least, iffy. After all, how far *is* it from an empire inside an electron to a vacant lot in Santa Cruz?

The snail raised one of her heads, looking us over, and then she began stolidly to crawl past Monin's domes and towards the nearby wall of living water that sloped down from the sky.

"Don't leave!" Monin called to Snaily. "We need your space-maze, or the jivas will be pillaging my garden. They'll plant their eggs without bothering to pay me."

"Maybe you should start gardening something instead of host-bodies for jiva eggs," I told Monin. "Jivas suck."

"You're a troublemaker," Monin snapped. "Get out of here and don't come back."

"My plans exactly," I said.

"I'm going with Jim," said Durkle. "More adventure!" He ran into the house to fetch his little sword.

"Let's not be cross with each other," said Yerba. "You're upsetting the baby. If we have to move, Monin, we'll move. With Grandpa gone, it'll be easy." She turned to me. "One of those jivas ate Grandpa because he kept messing with their tubes. Just as well. I'd rather be in a village or a town than on a farm, Monin. Or maybe at court."

"Farming's all I know," grumbled Monin.

Durkle reappeared with his sword. Yerba insisted that we all have a snack before any of us set out. So we sat down in their kitchen for a chat and some kessence. I held baby Nyoo in my lap.

Yerba was heating up a lump of kessence in her angular zickzack oven, while Monin set the one-legged table with shell-like plates. Vines like honeysuckle ran along the edges of the ceiling, perfuming the room. A niche in the next room held a glowing model of the new Earthmost Jiva.

"This is so amazing!" exclaimed Ira, lounging in his elegant zickzack chair. "I always thought I'd end up in Hell with pitchfork devils, or singing hymns on boring clouds, or—likeliest of all—no place at all. Flimsy is good."

"Wait till you see the night sky," I told him. "Flimsy is like a giant organism. Living water flows through the sky like sap in a plant."

"Whatever you do, don't swallow a jiva," Ginnie told Ira. "We'll be safe from them in Yuelsville."

"Do people have sex here?" asked Ira.

"Sort of," said Ginnie. "We do it paramecium-style. Sharing kessence through bands of slime. It's sick, but it's hot. I'm sure you can find a cute guy to conjugate with. There's millions of them in the swamps around Yuelsville."

"Better all the time," said Ira.

"So where are you planning on going, Jim?" Yerba asked me, as she set a turkey-shaped lump of kessence on the table for us. "With my little boy tagging along."

"I'm going to the core of Flimsy," I said. "I'm hoping to find my wife's ghost."

"Durkle is *not* going to the core," said Yerba decisively. "Most of the flims and sprinkles who go there get their minds wiped out. The goddess sends their naked souls into the septillion worlds for reincarnation."

"I don't know how Jim even thinks he'll get to the core," said Monin sourly. "Nobody can teleport that far. The only way to go there is to ride the living water inside the wall, and you probably starve or get eaten by sprinkles before you—"

"Correction," I interrupted. "Ever heard of Atum's Lotus?"

"Of course," said Monin. "That's what those ten thousand jiva tails were for. Pumping kessence through our Snaily to the Duke's castle so he can repay his loan from the Bulbers. And now Snaily's sick of working with us. And Grandpa's gone. And this is all your doing? Thanks a lot, jerk."

"Is Atum's Lotus as beautiful as they say?" asked Yerba, lost in her own thoughts. "I'd love to see it, Monin. Maybe—maybe if we give up this farm we could go work for the Duke."

"No," said Monin curtly. "We'd go live with my brother. I'm thinking that Durkle and Flam could help me start farming pig pops."

"Pig *head*," said Yerba. "That's what you are. None of us wants to farm. We're not in Flanders."

"I'm trying to tell you that I'm teleporting to the Duke's castle right now," I said. "And then I'll use Atum's Lotus to catapult me to Flimsy's core. Durkle, you can come as far as the castle with me. But your mother's probably right about you not going to the core."

"Fine," said Durkle readily. "The core is annihilation, man. But, yeah, I'd like another look at castle. This time try harder to get me inside."

We finished off the food and downed a few shots of living water, which gave me a nice buzz. And then we went outside.

"*Adios*," said Ginnie, giving me a hug. "I hope you find her, Jim. And I hope she's worth it. You're a good guy."

"And you—I hope you have fun in Yuelsville," I said. I'd grown quite fond of Ginnie's street-wise looks and her quirky chatter. "I'll miss you."

"So come look me up."

"I'm going to Earth."

"Not forever," said Ginnie, drawing out the final word in a raised pitch, as if it were a question. California uptalk. She stepped back from me and turned to Ira, taking a gruffer tone. "Yo, I'm gonna show you how to teleport."

A minute later the two of them were gone. Meanwhile the border snail had inched a hundred feet up the wall of Flimsy. She seemed to have found a spot where she might settle down for bit. One of her ends was rooting into the wall, delving through its rubbery skin. The ten-meter Snaily had no hope of tunneling all the way through the hundred-meter wall, but nonetheless, she could seine for sprinkles.

I bid a brief farewell to Monin and Yerba.

"See if you can get us all invited to the castle," Yerba urged Durkle. "Never mind what your father says. I'm sure the Duke needs more retainers."

And then the boy and I teleported on our way. We found a substantial mound of jiva-delivered kessence slumped beside the Duke's giant geranium, quite near the gall on its stalk that held Atum's Lotus. The torn-off top of the gall had healed over, and there was still a little entrance hole near the top. That's where I needed to go.

Remembering the former Earthmost Jiva's attack on Atum's Lotus, I turned to study her replacement, who was glowing like a sun nearby. I could tell that she was watching me. Fortunately, she didn't seem inclined to attack. Maybe she was a little frightened. After all, I'd killed the previous Earthmost Jiva with a yuelball.

The thuggish alien mini-blimp, Boss Blinks Bulber, was hovering over the faintly glowing heap of kessence, annoyingly blocking my path to the hole in the gall. The kessence was like pale-blue gelatin;

it looked vaguely radioactive. Members of the Duke's court were doing their best to haul off bits of it for themselves, and the Bulber was brushing them back by shooting sparks from his rear.

The sparks didn't seem to be lethal, but they were definitely keeping the flims at bay. With his two dozen jiggly eyes, Boss Blinks didn't miss much. All the while, his sleazy Bulber pals kept teleporting in and out, making off with great scoops of the kessence.

"Hi, Jim," said a handsome flim man standing in the field near the geranium. "We met in the orgy room? I'm Sandy. I was flirting with Weena, but she wanted you."

"Jim's saucy," piped Durkle.

"Yeah, yeah," I said. I kind of recognized this Sandy guy, but I didn't want to get into a big talk about Weena. "What's up with the Bulbers?"

"The jivas pumped enough kessence to repay Boss Blinks, but he keeps saying we owe him even more. He says that he and the other Bulbers plan to eat our castle, too."

I didn't feel a great deal of loyalty to the Duke and Duchess—after all, they'd saddled me with that load of jiva eggs. But the Bulbers pissed me off. And Boss Blinks was in my way.

"What do you think?" I asked Durkle.

"Maybe I can pop that farty blimp," said Durkle, swiping at the air with his two-foot-long sword.

"He'll try and crisp you," said Sandy. "You'll want to thicken your hide."

"If you can distract Boss Blinks for just a minute, that'll be enough," I said, fixing my gaze on the gall. "You go after him, and I'll bail you out."

"Berserker time," said Durkle, puffing himself up. Swaggering a bit, the boy made his way to the other side of the kessence mound, with Boss Blinks watching him all the while. And then, with a shrill whoop, Durkle did a teleportation hop right onto the back of the five-meter blimp and began hacking at the gasbag with his sword. A nest of electrical sparks blossomed forth. Durkle hung tough and continued chopping.

I seized the moment to teleport myself to the hole in the gall and to dive inside before Boss Blinks could think to stop me. As before, I was surrounded by intricate sheets of sound. I'd landed on a wobbly trellis of nautilus-shells linked by richly embossed hawsers. As before,

I saw crevasses and spires on every side.

The Atum's Lotus seemed, in some sense, to recognize me. As if resuming an interrupted conversation, the thing's choral voices segued into a variation on the ladder-to-heaven chant that Charles had ridden towards to the core of Flimsy. This was exactly what I was after.

Although the subtleties of the tune had eluded me before, this time I was able to integrate it into my psyche. It was a somewhat strange and slippery sequence of sounds. So now to rescue Durkle!

I clambered up the mutating gnomic forms within the Lotus and poked my head from the hole in the gall. Boss Blinks was directly before me, with poor Durkle lying inert on the blimp's upper surface. Was I too late?

Giving it everything I had, I sang the supernal ladder-mantra. The Bulber spun like a top, casting Durkle's limp form onto the heap of kessence. I formed my face into a trumpet bell and sang the ladder song still louder. And now Boss Blinks went arcing through the air—towards the core of Flimsy.

A second Bulber was snout-down on the kessence mound, feeding. But now, noticing what I'd done to Boss Blinks, he fled. And no further aliens appeared.

I hopped down to where Durkle had landed on the baby blue pile of kessence. Vivified by the stuff's energies, he was already sitting up.

"We did it," I told him. "We saved the castle."

"Here," said Durkle, handing me his sword. "I want you to take this with you."

"You love this sword," I protested. "I can't—"

"I'll get a bigger one," said Durkle with his pinheaded, unquench-able, lovable optimism. "I'll go back to the swamp and trick one of those offer caps again."

"I actually believe you will," I said, smiling at him.

It was time to leave—if I waited much longer, I'd forget the lad-der-mantra. But now a voice called to me.

"Big thanks, big guy!" It was the Duchess, gliding down from the geranium-castle's upper leaves. She was as elegant as ever—and as coarse.

"I don't want to talk to you," I told her curtly.

"Oh, aren't *you* the important muckity-muck!" said the Duchess, dimpling her perfect cheek. "Carry a grudge much?"

"I'm leaving in ten seconds," I said flatly. "If you'd like to repay me for getting rid of Weena and Boss Blinks, why don't you take young Durkle into your castle for a tour. Or, better yet, let him move in. Those ten thousand jiva-tubes ruined his house. Let Durkle's parents come, too."

The Duchess drew herself up. "I don't particularly feature inviting trashy goobs with no jivas into my—"

"The parents have jivas, even though Durkle doesn't," I interrupted. "They're solid workers. Be good to them or I'll bring Boss Blinks back."

This last bit was a bluff, but the Duchess fell for it. "Well—maybe," she said. She regarded the handsome fourteen-year-old appraisingly. "Why don't I show you our orgy room for starters, hmm?"

Durkle waved a cheerful good-bye as the Duchess swept him into the geranium's leaves. He'd do fine.

I got my ladder-mantra going—it was kind of like an "*Om mane padme hum,*" only backwards and inside out and with ribbons on it. It got good to me. The vibrations percolated into my arms and legs. I spun thrice and I was gone, baby, gone.

The human-inhabited zone of Flimsy flashed beneath me, and then I was speeding across the Dark Gulf towards the core.

There was a sense in which all I was doing was flying to the center of an electron or, perhaps more accurately, to the center of the Platonic Electron that underlies each of our universe's instances of the form. So maybe the trip wasn't all that far.

But I was scaled to a tiny size, and the Electron felt vast to me. Perhaps I even got smaller as I moved along. For me the core seemed as far as—what can I say?—as far a red-shifted galaxy cluster half-way across our astronomical universe.

Not that I got bored on the way to Flimsy's core. The Atum's Lotus ladder-chant had quite taken me over, and time passed as in a dream. At some point I became aware of a bright, vertical column ahead of me. Sensing its importance, I broke the rhythm of my chant—and my trance was done. I tumbled heavily into a calm, turquoise sea.

The living water was warm against my naked body. Great green lily pads and their beautiful blooming flowers bedecked the sea's surface. Bright specks hung above the flowers like gnats. Up ahead, a steady rain was drizzling from the domed sky into the gulf—this was the column that I'd seen. The continual shower seemed to outline a hazy form. Surely I'd reached Flimsy's core.

Pausing to take in my immediate surroundings, I was glad to see no sign of the Bulber whom I'd sent this way. My only cause for worry was a substantial jiva tendril that hung in the clear waters like a sea snake. The orange, thickening tube descended into the Gulf's profound depths, and the narrow tip twitched restlessly on the surface. But the jiva was making no moves to seize me.

I hauled myself onto a lily pad. Studying its pale yellow flower, I saw tiny plump eggs along the stamen. The eggs were splitting open to release fresh sprinkles—newborn souls that lingered above the flower. Flimsy's core was a fountain of new life.

I returned my attention to the luminous form that stretched to the sky. As I gazed, she came into full focus—a misty, titanic woman, the goddess of Flimsy. She was a pattern in the rain of living water that drizzled from the sky, transient yet stable, an enduring part of Flimsy's flow.

"Hello," I said, knowing she would hear. "It's me."

The goddess's voice sounded in my ears like the whisper of a breeze. "Val awaits you. Look and see."

The air seemed to shimmer, and yes, there was Val's ghost, sitting on a lily pad not more than fifty feet from me. It was as if the goddess had been hiding her behind a wrinkle in space. I paddled over to my wife. She watched me, her face happy. Her peach-colored cloak was gone. She was nude, beautiful, the very image of her old self.

"You made it!" said smiling Val. "My hero with his sword. Am I still mad at you?" It was wonderful to see her beloved curves. And her voice was balm to my soul.

"I got rid of my jiva," I said. "I've been busy fixing things so you can come back."

"Rise from the dead?"

"I have a clone of your old body growing on the bluff by Four Mile Beach."

"I don't like science experiments," said Val, fluffing her shiny brown hair. "Don't you ever learn?"

"It won't be like that again," I said. "Nobody's gaming us now. Forgive me for making the hole to Flimsy. I had no idea. I love you, Val. Please let me bring you back."

"Okay," she said simply. I studied her intelligent eyes, olive-green with flecks of brown. She'd always been unpredictable. "Let's go," she added. "And stop staring like that."

"Drinking you in," I said, reaching out to touch the tingly substance of her face.

"I'm glad you came for me," said Val. "The goddess brought me here all at once."

"It's been a wild trip."

"Do me one favor now," said the murmurous voice of the air. "It's what all of this has been for."

"What?" I said.

"That jiva tendril in the water," said the goddess. "Chop off the tip. That's why you're here with your special sword. I can't cut the tip myself. That's an immutable rule."

"Won't the, uh, jiva be mad?" I temporized. "She's a big one."

"The biggest of them all," said the goddess. "The Core Jiva. She's hooked into all those bobbling bulbs in the Dark Gulf. The jivas pass sprinkles up the chain to her. Every now and then, I load myself up with sprinkles from the Core Jiva, so that I have a good supply for sowing the septillion worlds with souls. You beings keep multiplying. I get some new sprinkles from the lotus flowers, too. But not enough."

"And you recycle sprinkles from the sky's living water," I said. I wasn't eager to rile the incalculably large Core Jiva.

"I use many of those, yes," said the goddess. "And many of them drop back into the Dark Gulf and pass through another cycle. This is all as it should be. Maybe they get themselves kessence bodies, maybe they stay in the living water and coast back to me, maybe they get swallowed by jivas. But now and then I draw off the accumulation in the Core Jiva."

"How often?" I asked, still stalling.

"It takes me awhile to arrange a visit from a determined ghost with a special sword. The last one to open the Core Jiva's tail for me was a lizard-being—some three thousand years ago. I do have some control over your universe's flow, but the outcomes are far less direct than you might suppose. It took a very long chain of events indeed to bring you here to cut these few meters off the Core Jiva's tail."

Long chain of events—she was talking about Val's death, about Skeeves, about Weena and Charles, and even about Amenhotep! My mind boggled.

"So cut off the tail-tip," said Val, unfazed by the metaphysical baggage. "It's like we're stealing a dragon's hoard of gems."

The task was far easier than I'd expected. Val held the thin end of the tendril steady and I chopped it off with my sword. The tendril gave a heavy twitch as I cut through. My magical sword twisted out of my hand and sank—down and down into the clear, unfathomably deep water.

Val tossed aside the tail-tip I'd cut loose. Sprinkles were gushing from the main part of the tendril, filling the air with rainbow fog. Gracefully the goddess reached towards us, her arm growing to an unnatural length and reaching down to touch the sea. I felt the cool mist of living water on my face, and the gulf's surface riffled into chop. The goddess's arm was a waterspout.

The supple winds took hold of Val and me—and drew along the sprinkle-spraying jiva tendril as well. Twirling in the twinkling haze, we approached the goddess's body, zeroing in on the glowing navel at the center of her gently mounded belly. This was the door back to our world.

"Will our personalities be erased?" I asked.

"No, no," said the goddess. "You two amuse me. You're legends now. I'll give you a special spin."

The navel was almost upon us as, large as the Coliseum. We rode the vortex curves down into it, accompanied by the twinkling rain and the torrent of extra sprinkles from the Core Jiva's tail.

"All together now," said a breath in my ear.

Was it the goddess talking—or Val?

29: On the Bluff

Hand in hand, Val and I floated down from the foggy sky. We were spirits above the bluff overlooking Four Mile Beach. The odd perspective made it feel like a dream of flight. Directly below us was a dark-haired woman standing with her legs buried to the knees in the sand—Val's flesh body, full grown, her face blank and slack. Droog sat at her side. Sensing our ghostly presence, Droog looked up, his tongue lolling, his jaws open in a doggy smile.

"Go ahead," I urged Val. "You just slip in and you'll stick."

Moments later her new body was beautifully in motion, waving her arms, dancing with the surf, her breasts bouncing. Her feet still seemed rooted in the ground. Over the waters, the mid-morning July sun was breaking up the mist.

Droog and I scrabbled at the sand beside Val, uncovering the buried sarcophagus. I pried off the lid and slid into my waiting flesh. With a series of tingles, my soul locked into place. Once again I was alive in the usual sense of the word. It took some effort to rise to my feet. My joints were stiff and achey, my flesh clammy and cool. I was already wearing my jeans, red T-shirt and flannel over-shirt. I began waving my arms in a celebratory hula like Val, then tossed her the extra jeans and T-shirt that I'd stashed in the gold box.

"Come hug me," she called.

I stepped out of the casket, only to have a spiky, chitinous claw lash out from the sarcophagus's surface to trip me up. I staggered, regained my footing, and turned to face Amenhotep's six-legged beetle-spirit. He'd popped out from his virtual lair within the embossed golden designs on the side of the casket.

Growing to the size of a man, the scarab chewed the air with his mandibles, making a hideous twitter. His smooth back glistened in iridescent greens and lavenders; his belly was striped in elastic bands. Three of his claws held symbols of pharaonic majesty: a crook, a flail, and an ankh, gleaming as if with gold and lapis lazuli.

Droog was at my side, barking hard. The beetle moved towards us, with ghostly streamers of liquid kessence pouring from the hideous intricacies of his jaws. He was preparing to eat me whole.

"Not me!" I yelled, landing a kick to his belly. "I'm not Skeeves. And—dude—enough is enough."

"I can't get loose," cried Val behind me.

"I've got this," I assured her.

My long trip to the core of Flimsy had grooved the Atum's Lotus chant deeply into my mind, and now, almost automatically, I began singing the magic spell, directing it at the monstrous beetle. Although my body's unused voice was husky, it quickly grew in force.

The psychic forces of the ladder-mantra impacted Amenhotep with a powerful effect. He lost his balance and tumbled into the sarcophagus. He lay there rocking on his domed back, fretfully clawing the air with his skinny legs, chirping even more petulantly than before.

Drawing on the remnants of my occult powers, I warped my chant to compress the sarcophagus into a golden glowing ball—with the Egyptian beetle at its core. And then, with a final effort, I vaporized the orb, sending it over to Flimsy and towards the core—but without making a hole. The goddess could handle Amenhotep now.

"All right!" said Val. "Can we relax?" Droog shook his ears and wandered off to explore the meadow.

I helped Val pull free of the sand—it had released its hold on her. We hugged and kissed for awhile and then we paused, looking out to sea, taking it in. I felt the same deep, comforting union with her that I'd felt in the days before our troubles.

"It's good here," she said, drawing me closer. She smelled like spicy honey. We laid down and made love, fully our old selves. It was wonderful there atop the cliff, between the sky and the sea.

"The world is stranger than I'd ever dreamed," said Val when we were done. She was idly playing with my fingers.

"I feel like I can see things better than before," I said.

"But I don't want the same old life in Santa Cruz," said Val.

"The Simlys evicted me this week," I told her. "Our stuff is in a warehouse. I don't know about picking it up. I had this huge showdown here with the jivas and the yuels. Dick Simly and a few others know it was me. If the word spreads, people might sue me or arrest me or question me on TV."

"Let's leave and start over," said Val. "You'll wear a hat and grow a beard. We'll get fake IDs. As for that crap in the warehouse, what do I care? I'm back from the dead!"

"I did bring those clothes for you."

"Grunge beach," said Val, pulling on the crumpled jeans and T-shirt. "Val's mid-summer look. You know—while I was over in Flimsy I kept thinking I should have tried living in San Francisco. Or Portland. Or maybe Mexico."

"Anywhere," I said, getting my own clothes back on. The dog had rejoined us. "As long as we're together."

"Dear Jim."

We walked to Route 1 and hitched a ride.